There was a time when literature and religion were one. The writer consciously and sometimes too obviously reflected his and his society's preoccupation with the relationship between God and man. One need only think of Homer, Sophocles, Virgil, Dante, the author of *Beowulf*, and the great romances and morality plays of medieval literature. At some point, however, literature and religion appeared to go their separate ways. The literature of our own time especially seems to insist upon its secularity, perhaps even its anti-religious position. Yet the stories in this volume persuasively argue that the modern writer continues to use his art to explore man's religious instinct and, in a time when the idea of God seems so obscure, to suggest new ways for man to answer the old questions of faith, salvation, and transcendence.

JOHN O'BRIEN, presently an assistant professor of English at Aurora College, is the author of *Interviews with Black Writers* and has published in such journals as *American Scholar, Chicago Review,* and *Oyez!* RICHARD FINHOLT has taught English at the University of Illinois at Chicago Circle and College of DuPage. His articles on Mailer, Joyce, and Poe have appeared, among other places, in *Georgia Review* and *Modern Fiction Studies.*

No Signs from Heaven

Theological Tradition and the Modern Literary Imagination

Edited and with an Introduction by

John O'Brien
and Richard Finholt

A LAUREL ORIGINAL

Published by
Dell Publishing Co., Inc.
1 Dag Hammarskjold Plaza
New York, New York 10017

Copyright © 1975 by John O'Brien and Richard Finholt

ACKNOWLEDGMENTS

"Recollections of Father Zossima's Youth Before He Became a Monk" by Fyodor Dostoyevsky: From THE BROTHERS KARAMAZOV by Fyodor Dostoyevsky, translated by Constance Garnett. Published by Random House, Inc.

"Before the Law" and "An Imperial Message" by Franz Kafka: Reprinted by permission of Schocken Books Inc. from THE PENAL COLONY by Franz Kafka. Copyright © 1948 by Schocken Books Inc.

"Saint Emmanuel the Good, Martyr" by Miguel de Unamuno: From ABEL SANCHEZ AND OTHER STORIES, translated and with an Introduction by Anthony Kerrigan. Reprinted by permission of Henry Regnery Company.

"The Sisters" by James Joyce: From DUBLINERS by James Joyce. Copyright © 1967 by the Estate of James Joyce. All rights reserved. Reprinted by permission of The Viking Press, Inc.

"The Light of the World" by Ernest Hemingway: From WINNER TAKE NOTHING by Ernest Hemingway. Reprinted by permission of Charles Scribner's Sons. Copyright 1933 Charles Scribner's Sons; renewal copyright © 1961 Mary Hemingway.

"Parker's Back" by Flannery O'Connor: Reprinted with the permission of Farrar, Straus & Giroux, Inc. from EVERYTHING THAT RISES MUST CONVERGE by Flannery O'Connor, copyright © 1965 by The Estate of Mary Flannery O'Connor.

"Night-Sea Journey" by John Barth: Copyright © 1966 by John Barth. From the book LOST IN THE FUNHOUSE by John Barth. Reprinted by permission of Doubleday & Company, Inc. First published in Esquire.

"Lifeguard" by John Updike: copyright © 1961 by John Updike. Reprinted from PIGEON FEATHERS AND OTHER STORIES by John Updike, by permission of Alfred A. Knopf, Inc. First appeared in The New Yorker.

"Eli, the Fanatic" by Philip Roth: From GOODBYE, COLUMBUS by Philip Roth. Copyright © 1959 by Philip Roth. Reprinted by permission of Houghton Mifflin Company.

"Angel Levine" by Bernard Malamud: Reprinted with the permission of Farrar, Straus & Giroux, Inc., from THE MAGIC BARREL by Bernard Malamud, copyright © 1955, 1958 by Bernard Malamud.

From "The Blood of the Lamb" by Peter De Vries: Copyright © 1961 by Peter De Vries. From THE BLOOD OF THE LAMB by Peter De Vries by permission of Little, Brown and Co.

"Easter Sunday" by James R. Giles: Copyright © 1975 by James R. Giles. Used by permission of the author.

From "Jesus Christs" by A. J. Langguth: From pp. 12–14, 149, 170–171, 178–179, 193 (hardbound edition) in JESUS CHRISTS by A. J. Langguth. Copyright © 1968 by A. J. Langguth. By permission of Harper & Row, Publishers.

"Behold the Man" by Michael Moorcock: Reprinted by permission of the author and the author's agents, Scott Meredith Literary Agency, Inc., 580 Fifth Avenue, New York, New York 10036.
From "Love in the Ruins" by Walker Percy: Reprinted with the permission of Farrar, Straus & Giroux, Inc., from LOVE IN THE RUINS by Walker Percy, copyright © 1971 by Walker Percy.

Laurel ® TM 674623, Dell Publishing Co., Inc.
Printed in the United States of America
First printing—January 1975

We would like to give thanks to James Mellard for showing us *how* to read modern literature and to Arra Garab for showing us *what* it means. Jerome Klinkowitz contributed his enthusiasm and suggestions along the way. Mark Trumbo, Lloyd Richardson, and David Arthur of Aurora College provided the atmosphere in which the study of religion and literature is fostered. Pat and Mark Gordon and Mary and Tom Tyler lent aid of which they are unaware. Finally, special thanks to Mary Kay and Jeanne for thinking it a good idea.

"The Earth, sayest thou? The Human race?
By Me created? Sad its lot?
Nay: I have no remembrance of such place:
Such world I fashioned not."

—THOMAS HARDY
from "God-Forgotten"

Whither, O, whither art thou fled,
My Lord, my Love?
My searches are my daily bread;
Yet never prove.

—GEORGE HERBERT
from "The Search"

No signs from Heaven come today
To add to what the heart doth say.

—FYODOR DOSTOYEVSKY
from *The Brothers Karamazov*

Contents

Introduction

T. S. Eliot was the prophet of the modern age, the voice to warn us that modern man is spiritually hollow and the work of his hands a wasteland, because the Word (with God in the beginning, according to St. John) remains unheard and unspoken in our time. Perhaps because of Eliot's pronouncements, it is taken for granted that the literary artist in the modern era has chosen to turn his face away from God, toward the world, and that ours is a secular, arid literature, from which the image of God and the hope of salvation have been purposefully purged. However, the preponderance of theological, Judeo-Christian themes and symbols to be found among the works of many modern writers disputes the popular contention that the issues of God and salvation are no longer relevant to, or consistent with, modern humanistic aspirations. Literature reflects the mood of an age, and writers from Hawthorne and Dostoyevsky to Updike and Roth have consistently grappled with, and often anticipated, the great crises in modern theology. Atheism, the death of God, and an ever-widening schism between established religion and the peculiarly modern needs of its followers pose problems for the writer as well as the theologian. Our literature reflects the deeply felt need to sustain old values and ancient beliefs by adapting them to the mind-tearing tensions of the modern situation.

I

The world view of Western man, molded around the image of the Judeo-Christian God, persisted for almost two thousand years and thematically as well as formally shaped the literary perspective, but this vision has become clouded in the modern world because that central image seems to be vanishing. To the positivists, such as Auguste Comte, the question of God is irrelevant. Born into a world that no longer thought it needed a deity, Comte merely formalized a post-Christian philosophy that people were already practicing. Just as no modern theologian feels the need to disprove the existence of Apollo, positivists maintain that the refutation of the Christian God is equally unnecessary, and that the loss of God's image simply represents a necessary stage in the achievement of human freedom.

The early Christian had seen the coming of Christ as the ultimate sign of freedom, as Henri de Lubac describes in *The Drama of Atheistic Humanism*: "No more circle! No more blind hazard! No more *Fate*! Transcendent God, God the friend of man, revealed in Jesus, opened for all a way which nothing would ever bar again." As early as the Renaissance, however, man was becoming comfortable in a world whose link with God was weakening. Christ, whose birth had seemed to ensure man a purpose and a destiny, also represented the all-powerful deity now felt to be blocking the way to self-fulfillment and individualistic freedom. In such an intellectual climate, reaching its apex in the late nineteenth century, the death of God and the demythologizing of the life of Jesus became inevitable.

As though in fulfillment of Comte's early prophecies of the possibilities of human improvement, the discoveries of late-nineteenth-century science seemed to promise heavenly bliss on earth, and modern technology following the Industrial Revolution appeared to provide the means of achieving it. With the advent of modern psychology in the works of Freud and Jung, came the assertion that much that man had previously ascribed to God and the powers of the unseen are really *projections* emanating from his own unconscious. Furthermore, concurrent findings in the biological and physical sciences seemed to confirm that man could be self-sufficient beyond his dreams, with the potential to control and dominate nature. Even history, as redefined by Hegel and Marx, appeared to be yielding up its laws to the dialectical mind, so that man might no longer be slave to time and chance.

Philosophy was also dominated by an expansive confidence in man's innate possibility. According to Hegel's romantic idealism, the human mind possesses the ability to achieve the universal through dialectical thought, and the Neoplatonic immanentism of Swedenborg and Emerson held that mankind's connections to eternal verities are absolute and almost automatic, since God's essence is immanent in nature, history, and man himself.

By the turn of this century, everything seemed to be within man's reach. Political and social ideologies glimpsed the arrival of a utopian world on the horizon. Though they might not offer man the promise of eternal life, they might give him a share in a self-perpetuating and evolving state or society as it moved toward an apocalyptic future. The notion of human perfectibility, both the dream and the possibility of the modern age, beguiled even the leaders of the twentieth-century Church. It initiated the reform movement in Judaism and modernism in Christianity. In such movements a radical reinterpretation of doctrine was necessitated by new humanistic assumptions. As explained by Herbert Wallace Schneider, "The specifically Christian or Jewish elements in doctrine were regarded as liabilities of faith, as restrictions upon the more universal and rational worship of God."

However, the betrayal of traditional faith in God in favor of a secular faith in human possibilities was not without its price. For one thing, the new freedom gave man the terrifying responsibility for his own fate. In *The Dangling Man*, Saul Bellow reflects that,

> Six hundred years ago, a man was what he was born to be. Satan and the Church, representing God, did battle over him. He, by reason of his choice, partially decided the outcome. But whether, after life, he went to hell or to heaven, his place among other men was given. It could not be contested. But, since, the stage has been reset and human beings only walk on it, and, under this revision, we have, instead, history to answer to. We were important enough then for our souls to be fought over. Now, each of us is responsible for his own salvation, which is his greatness. And that, that greatness, is the rock our hearts are abraded on.

Dostoyevsky, for one, did not believe that modern man had the capacity to bring water forth from that rock. In the "Recollections of Father Zossima's youth . . ." the conscience-stricken Mihail calls the modern era "the period of isolation," and he explains that,

> . . . every one strives to keep his individuality as apart as possible, wishes to secure the greatest possible fullness of life for himself; but meantime all his efforts result not in attaining fullness of life but self-destruction, for instead of self-realization he ends by arriving at complete solitude.

For Mihail and Father Zossima, modern man can secure salvation only by recapturing the sense of joy in God's creation and the spirit of "brotherly love," which were left behind in the search for individual responsibility.

Freedom from religion led to another danger: It became a vacuum to be filled by new and more tyrannical gods, which threaten to undermine the newfound self-reliance of modern man. Auguste Comte had warned that, "once God has been shut out, his place must be taken by something else, if you do not want him to come back." Science, industrialism, and imperialism are that looked-for "something else," born out of man's supreme confidence that he possessed the seeds of his own deification. The irony of humanism has been that, after its initial idealistic thrust, instead of restoring man to a preeminent place in nature, it has paved the way for his ultimate dissolution. Science, which in the nineteenth century looked forward to the reestablishment of Eden, has delivered in this century the fire-bombed Dresden and the leveled Hiroshima. After the German concentration camps and two world wars, Eden no longer seemed the next logical stage. Science and the state, the new gods of humanism, failed to convert the vision of human possibility into constructive action, and humanists of this century, with their absolute confidence in both, have been led down a garden path only to find that it is littered with corpses and has a cataclysmic vision at its end. Even psychology, begun as the most humanistic of the sciences, has revealed not so much the wonder of the self but a self shackled by the deterministic laws of biology, environment, and experience. Modern man finds himself a dispossessed tenant in the house he conceived and built.

This disillusionment with secular gods has led to the

modern crisis of confidence and the contemporary existential view that human experience may be meaningless. And this view is reflected in our literature. In John Barth's fantasy "Night-Sea Journey," the reader is treated to the philosophical speculations of a human sperm, the humorous inadequacy of which become frightening when the reader realizes that they are the analogical equivalents of the reader's own philosophy. Most of the sperm population speculate, not altogether inaccurately, that swimming the dark sea is an "heroic enterprise" and that "Love it is that drives and sustains us!" The narrator replies, "I translate: we don't know *what* drives and sustains us, only that we are most miserably driven and, imperfectly, sustained. *Love* is how we call our ignorance of what whips us." Franz Kafka's parable "Before the Law," excerpted from *The Trial*, teaches a similar moral about the human perspective: it is pitiable in its grotesque limitations. The young hero of Peter De Vries's novel *The Blood of the Lamb*, Don Wanderhope, bearing a symbolic name and bitter over his inability "to cage this dance of atoms in a single definition," driven by a hopeless love to the point of vulnerability, achieves, finally, a limited perspective, "composed," as he says, "of delicately balanced contradictions." He is no closer to the truth of human existence or to the identity of the "force" that drives us, but he has learned "the vanity (if not outrage)" of his attempt to discover the pattern of the universe. Human faith, whether placed in the new gods or in the old God, operates from an absurdly limited perspective. Because of this, De Vries implies, modern man should take very little pride in, rest very little hope in, what he chooses to believe. As Dr. Simpson tells Wanderhope, " 'You believe what you must in order to stave off the conviction that it's all a tale told by an idiot.' "

If God is dead, as Nietzsche proclaimed a century ago, the Church has killed him. The Church's function was to have been to act as an outpost of eternity, to resist man's ever-present inclination to forget his God and construct golden calves in his place. However, the Church in modern times, under the influence of modernism's willingness to sacrifice eternal truths for relevance, has not only failed in this mission but may have acquiesced in the building of a golden calf called humanism. Once the Church began to question the absolute truth of its doctrine, then all it had left, as James Giles's story "Easter Sunday" suggests, was to continue to supply man with an outlet for his psychological need for ritual; it becomes a form empty of content, an empty vessel ready to be filled for any secular purpose. In Robert Heinlein's *Stranger in a Strange Land*, for example, liturgical rituals have been adopted by the commerical religion of Fosterism. There is a bar and a quick-lunch stand in the church, and along the walls are slot machines that, for the right price, issue religious slogans: "GOD-WATCHES-YOU" pays three-to-one, and "FOSTER-LOVES-YOU" hits the jackpot. Cleansed of one's sins and money, the churchgoer can advance to the bar for drinks. Heinlein is writing futuristic satire, but Nathan Scott in his book *The Broken Circle* has observed a similar attempt by some contemporary theologians to make a union of the sacred and the profane. Theologians like Thomas J. J. Altizer, who call themselves Christian atheists or Christian positivists, and who triumphantly declare traditional doctrine and the hope of salvation to be irrelevant, seem to create a Christianity that is indistinguishable from the desacralized world that it would supposedly transform. Both as an intellectual system and as a moral force in its society, organized religion, both Christian and Jewish, appears to have fallen into disrepute, perhaps having lived up to Marx's accusation that religion is nothing but the opiate of the people.

II

It would appear, then, that we live in a humanistic age, one having hubris enough to pronounce God dead and go on from there, one so fiercely individualistic that the venerable authority of the Church has been all but swept away. But, at the same time, the irony implicit in the failure of positivism, bearing the seeds of existential despair, has been steadily undermining the faith of nineteenth-century romanticism in man's capacity to save himself. Ours is an age of "delicately balanced contradictions," an age accepting no easy answers from either the Church or the State, from either the theologians or the humanistic philosophers. And this is recorded in our literature. We are, wrote T. S. Eliot, the "children at the

gate/Who will not go away and cannot pray"; we are
"Those who walk in darkness, who chose thee and/oppose
thee."

The stories collected here exist as artifact, as evidence
that the rewards of materialism and the naiveté of humanism never have been a match for the strength of what the
Death of God theologian Gabriel Vahanian has called
"the religious instinct." These writers reflect a counter-
trend to secularism. They do not simply play with old
myths, but deal quite earnestly and sometimes urgently
(though often ironically) with Judeo-Christian themes and
symbols. The Word may remain unheard in our generation,
but this, if we believe the testimony of these writers, is
not necessarily because modern man is not listening.
Echoes of George Herbert's cry of devotional despair
resound in our literature today as loudly as in the seven-
teenth century:

> Whither, O, whither art thou fled,
>   My Lord, my Love?
> My searches are my daily bread;
>   Yet never prove.

As Dostoyevsky's famous couplet from *The Brothers
Karamazov* suggests, modern man feels less that he has
turned his face from God than that God has betrayed
man's faith:

> No signs from Heaven come today
> To add to what the heart doth say.

The heart still says what it has always said, it still yearns
as it has always yearned, but the mind of modern man
now begins to perceive the irony behind the old rituals,
the irony of his yearning: The heart of man can only go
halfway in its quest for revelation, for signs from God, and
then it must wait faithfully and courageously for God to
meet it there. This is the theme of Samuel Beckett's
important play *Waiting for Godot*, in which Vladimer and
Estragon find themselves waiting in vain for the God-
figure Godot. At one point in Act Two Vladimer states,
with a pride in their courage to face the despair of their
existential situation, "We are not saints, but we have kept
our appointment."

In his desperation to keep his appointment, modern man may stray down humanistic byways, losing sight of the divine image of his quest, but this may be because, in the absence of word from God, he is forced to follow his questing heart to its heretical limits. Jesus said that "The Kingdom of God is within you," and modern man takes him at his word, challenging God to speak to us through the heart if He cares to be heard because that is the only authority we bow to anymore. This is a way of stating a central tenet of the Christian brand of existentialism that has grown out of the thought of the nineteenth-century philosopher Sören Kierkegaard, modified in this century by theologians like Reinhold Niebuhr, Karl Barth, and Rudolf Bultmann. Kierkegaard followed Kant and Hegel in emphasizing the gulf between subjective and objective, but, unlike Hegel, he held out little hope that the gulf could be bridged by human powers alone. Since God is infinitely subjective and man and his environment finitely objective, God can never be immanent in nature or history or man, and consequently, no amount of scientific observation or dialectical thinking will reveal God's ways to man, unless God chooses to reveal Himself *subjectively* through man's innermost recesses of faith. God chooses to reveal Himself to Abraham in Kierkegaard's *Fear and Trembling* only after Abraham has surrendered his human concepts of rationality and morality and accepted the necessity to sacrifice his son Isaac to God's imponderable will. Kierkegaard saw clearly that faith like that of Abraham involves an act of individual courage, what Paul Tillich would later call the "Existential courage to be as oneself," and he characterized it as a "leap of faith." John Updike's smug and somewhat effete divinity student in "Lifeguard" sees the "savage and senseless rages" of the dark sea as the metaphor for the spiritual void into which modern man must blindly leap:

We enter the sea with a shock; our skin and blood shout in protest. But, that instant, that leap, past, what do we find? Ecstasy and buoyance. Swimming offers a parable. We struggle and thrash, and drown; we succumb, even in despair, and float, and are saved.

Updike leaves it for the reader to decide whether the "ecstasy and buoyance" of his student's metaphysical speculations represent such a leap of faith or whether they are "brimful" of nothing but humanistic self-deception.

Following Kierkegaard's lead, Niebuhr and Barth rejected the romantic assumption of human self-reliance (Emerson's phrase), the assumption that man can reach divine truth through his own rational or spiritual powers. They reemphasized the orthodox doctrine of the necessity of divine transcendence in the process of revelation, of the need for God to reach out and catch the individual courageous enough to leap out to be caught. But they also warned not to look for this revelation in nature or history but in the vagaries of personal experience. In other words, the reliance of existential man, as it was for the man of the romantic age, must still rest on individual perception and emotion; only now, God's role in the process of human salvation, once almost forgotten, has been once more exalted. The man of the modern age, like James Joyce's Father Flynn in "The Sisters," has felt the awful distance separating his impotence from God's majesty, and, if it does not leave him paralyzed like Father Flynn, it has burned all the prideful self-sufficiency out of him. Modern man bases his quest for salvation on inner verification rather than objective corroboration, because Kierkegaard has taught him that God cannot be found through an individual's *own* powers of observation or reason, that God, if He can be found, can only be found by the light of that inner voice that one hopes to be God's voice. A whole generation of Hemingway disciples have maintained that, "If it *feels* right, it is right." And existential man, ever faithful to his inner voice and sometimes grown impatient with heaven's silence, either angrily denies God or, as Updike's lifeguard says of Kierkegaard, Berdyaev, and Barth, he defiantly attempts "to scourge God into being" and "surmount the void."

This modern attitude has evolved quite naturally out of the generative ideas of Christian thought, which, according to Suzanne K. Langer in *Philosophy in a New Key*, postulated above all else the "great ideal of personal experience." In fact, the scientific age seems to have reinforced this concept in our time, because, according to Professor Langer, "Genuine empiricism is above all a reflection on the ways our concepts and beliefs are built up out of the fleeting and disconnected reports our eyes and ears make to the mind." The scientist prefers to ignore the philosophical implications of this problem, but the existentialist broods over it, finally despairing of the capacity of human observation and reason to ever validate the tenets of human existence. The existentialist thinker, according to Gabriel Vahanian, must then seek "the mythical possibilities of an unmythical, scientifically oriented self-consciousness." In the end he is left with the subjective data emanating from his *uniquely* personal experience, and the religiously oriented existentialist, therefore, will follow doctrinal precepts only as long as they receive inner sanction. But he knows that his leap of faith, if he chooses to make it, will be blind and perhaps risk blasphemy, because nothing, neither sense-data nor science nor history, can ever corroborate the dictates of his religious instinct.

Certain of the stories collected in this volume portray a hero who has set out on a religious quest, and it seems a peculiarity of the modern experience that in each case the protagonist has only the vaguest idea of what or who he is seeking; in each case, that is, the quest is predicated more on feeling than on thought; in each case the hero leaps blindly for salvation.

Manischevitz, in Bernard Malamud's "Angel Levine," must make just such a leap of faith if he is to save the life of his dying wife. Like Abraham, he is being asked to believe the unbelievable; in his case, that a black man from Harlem is not only Jewish but a "bona fide angel of God" come to help him. His "choice" to believe seems to be the cause of his wife's recovery, but beyond this it saves Manischevitz from the hardness of heart that kept him from seeing that "there are Jews everywhere," in every race and creed, bound together by the stubborn faith that overcomes fear and anguish.

Eli Peck, in Philip Roth's "Eli, the Fanatic," *chooses* to be crazy, chooses to alienate himself from the unreflective but peaceful cocktail coexistence of his suburban life, in order to pursue the psychological and possibly spiritual implications of a *feeling* aroused in him by a strange apparition of Jewish suffering long since, so reason tells him, anachronistic:

His right fist was beating his chest. And then Eli
heard a sound rising with each knock on the chest.
What a moan! It could raise hair, stop hearts, water
eyes. And it did all three to Eli, plus more. Some
feeling crept into him for whose deepness he could
find no word.

The feeling probes for the meaning of the Jewish ethnic
experience, and Eli discovers that in order to pursue this
feeling to its source, in order to heal the break between
himself and the God of his ethnic tradition, he must
literally sell all he possesses—his friends, his wife, his child.
The feeling dictates a clean break, and Eli cheerfully
assumes the blindness of the quest.

Parker, in Flannery O'Connor's "Parker's Back," is
driven by despair and an increasingly painful bewilderment to seek the symbolic fulfillment of the aesthetically
right tattoo to fill the void on his back and in his soul. He
does not know what the tattoo should be, but his quest is
guided by the feeling that he will know what it is when
he finds it. He wants a picture of "God" to please his
"saved" wife, but none of the contemporary pictures of
Christ in the tattooist's book move him, but as he flips
through the book the images proceed backward in time:

Parker's heart began to beat faster and faster until it
appeared to be roaring inside him like a generator.
He flipped the pages quickly, feeling that when he
reached the one ordained, a sign would come . . . On
one of the pages a pair of eyes glanced at him
swiftly. Parker sped on, then stopped. His heart too
appeared to cut off; there was absolute silence. It
said as plainly as if silence were a language itself,
GO BACK.

Parker returned to the picture—the haloed head
of a flat stern Byzantine Christ with all-demanding
eyes. He sat there trembling; his heart began slowly
to beat again as if it were being brought to life by a
subtle power.

Because the biblical age of objective corroboration has
long since passed, Parker can never know for sure
whether God has in fact reached across the void to whisper

silence into his heart or whether his questing heart has merely seized on the psychologically right *image* of peace. In either case, however, his experience, whether religious or psychological, demonstrates the abiding relevance of St. Augustine's declaration: "My heart is restless until it rests in thee."

The fact that the object of Parker's quest is a symbol illustrates another point that Professor Langer makes about the modern intellectual perspective. Even for the modern scientist, for whom seeing is still believing, symbols have become the only possible verifications for most laboratory propositions; the scientist cannot observe the results of his experiments directly with his senses but must rely on needles and graphs and that most abstract of all symbolic systems, mathematics. Professor Langer observes that we live in an age of "symbolic transformation," in which we need the "use of symbols to attain, as well as to organize belief."

It should not be surprising to discover, then, that though Judeo-Christian doctrines have lost their vitality and authority in our time, their shared system of symbols remains as strong as ever, if not stronger. The heart of man still cries out for a Messiah as it did in Jesus' time, and in modern literature we witness the Messiah story and the Christ story told and retold with mesmerizing intensity. Fyodor Dostoyevsky's "The Grand Inquisitor" from *The Brothers Karamazov* (which was thought to be too often anthologized to need collection here) tells the story of a Jesus returned to earth during the Spanish Inquisition after fifteen centuries without signs from Heaven to find a Church that has forsaken the true gospel in favor of the "miracle, mystery, and authority" that Jesus renounced when he resisted the temptation of Satan on the mountaintop, to find a Church that has freely chosen to give its weak and miserable followers peace on earth as the fair exchange for eternal damnation. The Grand Inquisitor by implication is accusing Jesus of having been an elitist, of having placed salvation beyond the grasp of the common man when he rejected Satan's plan for winning them, of having known all along that Christianity, by its very beauty, morality, and subtlety, is beyond the capabilities of the mass of ugly, immoral, and desperately unsubtle men that Christ came to save. Dostoyevsky's Jesus, like his

Father in Heaven, remains silent and goes away without offering modern man any guidance.

The various retellings of the Christ story in modern literature seem to be attempts to bridge the gap of two millenniums, a gap as wide as time is irreversible, between the religious instinct of modern man and its image of the Messiah, the object of its desire. In a humanistic age, one begins by identifying most strongly with the human dimension of the Jesus story. The Old and New Testaments told the story from God's point of view, and now it is retold from the human point of view. A. J. Langguth's vision of Jesus, for example, portrays a neurotic truth-seeker barely distinguishable from those he would save; a man, in short, for our time:

> It's God, Jesus. Listen to me.
> It's not God. It's one of my own voices.
> Believe me.
> It's a voice I've heard coming from my own heart.
> Please.
> You've fooled me too often.

And Karl Glogauer, the hero with a Messiah complex in Michael Moorcock's "Behold the Man," actually bridges the two-thousand-year gap in a time machine, driven by his "weakness and fear" to confront the reality of the Christian message once and for all, only to be met with the irony that he himself has been the historical Jesus all along: modern man apotheosized as his own savior with none of his questions answered, the blind ordained to lead the blind.

While this may prove a crushing irony to modern man, the remaking of the Messiah after our own image is a necessary step in the salvation of modern man, according to the nineteenth-century American transcendentalist Theodore Parker; for, as he states in his famous "A Discourse on the Transient and Permanent in Christianity," "it is not so much by the Christ who lived so blameless and beautiful eighteen centuries ago that we are saved directly, but by the Christ we form in our hearts and live out in our daily life that we save ourselves, God working with us both to will and to do." To make this image or symbol come alive in our hearts, Parker suggests, we must recognize a historical Jesus of human passions and fears and needs, like ourselves, with whom we can *identify*. "But if," Parker warns,

> as some Christians began to do, you take a heathen view, and make him [Jesus] a God, the Son of God in a peculiar and exclusive sense, much of the significance of his character is gone. His virtue has no merit, his love no feeling, his cross no burthen, his agony no pain. His death is an illusion, his resurrection but a show. For if he were not a man, but a god, what are all these things? . . . It is all nothing. . . . Then his resignation is no lesson, his life no model, his death no triumph to you or me, who are not gods, but mortal men. . . .

The modern literary imagination, then, begins by recognizing the heart's need for a symbol, like the Jesus story, that is infused with the dramatic elements and conflicts long since denied by orthodox doctrine. Thus, Jesus becomes a heroic figure, more like Prometheus than Zeus; he becomes a tragic figure, more like Oedipus than Teiresias; he becomes, if necessary, an almost ridiculous figure. As Walker Percy's hero and Christ-figure, Thomas More, says of himself in *Love in the Ruins*:

> It is the new Christ, the spotted Christ, the maculate Christ, the sinful Christ. The old Christ died for our sins and it didn't work, we were not reconciled. The new Christ shall reconcile man with his sins. The new Christ lies drunk in a ditch.

But amidst all these considerations about the image of the Messiah and what it symbolizes, it must be emphasized that the modern writer uses his particular conception of a Messiah or Christ-figure as a means of organizing belief rather than as an object in which to believe, because, in an age lacking signs from Heaven, the problem becomes less *what* to believe in and more *how* to believe. The peroxide blond whore in Ernest Hemingway's "The Light of the World" is a bad believer. She has created an image in her mind of one-time middleweight boxing champion Stanley Ketchel that makes him "like a God . . . So white and clean and beautiful . . ." He is a kind of Christ-figure to her in that he is the object of her belief; "I loved him like you love God," she says, "My soul belongs to Steve Ketchel." But the real Ketchel, shot by his father for attempting to rape his stepmother, was the inverse of all that could be considered Christlike. By this irony, Hemingway implies that there must be something seriously wrong with Peroxide's powers of belief if she can love a man with such a misguided love, if she can believe in a man so utterly undeserving of belief. On the other hand, the 350-pound whore Alice, whose memories of Ketchel are less sublime but more moving because more real, demonstrates the kind of hardheaded refusal to be self-deceived that would seem necessary if modern man is ever to learn *how* to believe in whatever he must believe in. Alice's strength of character represents for Hemingway a real "Light of the World," and she becomes Christlike in her ability to distill essence from appearance, to separate the Faithful from the Pharisees. And the proof of her right-mindedness, as with Jesus, is the beauty that shines through her plain appearance.

Religious faith in our time has become an act of courage, the courage to strip oneself bare of illusion, to "wait without idols" in W. H. Auden's phrase, and the courage, as Dostoyevsky put it, to love life and its Creator "with one's inside, with one's stomach . . . regardless of logic." It is recorded in our literature.

III

Detached, then, from doctrine and illumined only by his own perceptions, the artist seeks to reestablish the sacral dimension to man's experience. Some of the authors here represented have been able only to define the theological dilemmas awaiting modern man. Nathaniel Hawthorne in "Young Goodman Brown" focused on the predicament man would face when, without recourse to faith and unable to deal with the overwhelming evil of the world by himself, he is confronted with evidence of the perversity of the human heart. Goodman Brown discovers that, robbed of his certitude in the existence of a beneficent God, he is unable to love his fellow human beings. Franz Kafka foresaw the enormous despair of modern man when he awoke to the fact that he no longer understood God's announced plan for humanity, that he had dutifully labored in a faith that increasingly appeared to be at odds with the world of experience. In fact, as his parable "An Imperial Message," excerpted from *The Great Wall of China*, suggests, the distance between God and man is now so great that not even God can transcend it anymore, though man continues to dream that it is so.

Other writers have heard these cries of desperation and have answered. As if in response to Kafka's description of the crisis of faith, Miguel de Unamuno counsels in "Saint Emmanuel the Good, Martyr" that, even without the certainty of a still transcendent God, man must continue to act as though faith were still possible. Father Emmanuel follows Jesus' commandment to love despite his own inability to believe in a God who ordains such love. And Edgar Allan Poe in "A Descent into the Maelström" tells the tale of two men who literally descend to the depths of fear and abject despair; one man to die because he selfishly seeks to save his life, and the other to live because his vision of God through the blinding mists of terror teaches him " 'how magnificent a thing it was to die in such a manner, and how foolish it was in me to think of so paltry a consideration as my own individual life, in view of so wonderful a manifestation of God's power.' " The salvation of Poe's sailor is a question of mind over matter, of rationality conquering irrational terror. And the fact that the sailor is able to reason his way out of inevitable destruction symbolizes, like the rainbow at the depths of the Maelström, that Creation is somehow more rational than capricious, and that, at the depths of our minds, God has provided us with a "pathway between Time and Eternity."

The theological perspectives of these stories are varied, and, at times, conflicting. For example, Flannery O'Connor's insistence upon the recovery of faith, often relegating love to an insignificant role, seems to oppose Unamuno's feeling that, since faith is denied modern man, love must fill the void. But the differences in approach are not significant. What *is* significant is that such theological preoccupations have engaged some of the most important writers of our time. They have engaged those writers long denounced from the pulpit as prophets of doom who have betrayed their responsibility to reaffirm the truth and beauty of man's relationship to his God.

What is remarkable about these writers is not that their work often reflects our lives as nightmarish and dark but that, without the reinforcements of an ordered culture, they have been able to go on insisting that man is not yet lost. Without the benefit of an intact theological tradition, they have reaffirmed in a common spirit beliefs about the spiritual condition and future of mankind that traditional religion once spoke of with such persuasive conviction. This literature admits that modern man is experiencing the darkest hour of his dark night of the soul. But it also contains the prophecy that he will profit by the rigors of his experience, that he will be made whole by the suffering of doubt and hopeful by the realization that he has, after all, survived. The stories in this volume, then, are parables for our time, stories of modern man in search of an elusive God. They are stories of the sometimes heroic attempt of modern man to move beyond alienation and disbelief, to keep the appointment so long promised but not yet granted.

Nathaniel Hawthorne

YOUNG GOODMAN BROWN

Young Goodman Brown came forth at sunset into the street at Salem village; but put his head back, after crossing the threshold, to exchange a parting kiss with his young wife. And Faith, as the wife was aptly named, thrust her own pretty head into the street, letting the wind play with the pink ribbons of her cap while she called to Goodman Brown.

"Dearest heart," whispered she, softly and rather sadly, when her lips were close to his ear, "prithee put off your journey until sunrise and sleep in your own bed tonight. A lone woman is troubled with such dreams and such thoughts that she's afeard of herself sometimes. Pray tarry with me this night, dear husband, of all nights in the year."

"My love and my Faith," replied young Goodman Brown, "of all nights in the year, this one night must I tarry away from thee. My journey, as thou callest it, forth and back again, must needs be done 'twixt now and sunrise. What, my sweet, pretty wife, dost thou doubt me already, and we but three months married?"

"Then God bless you!" said Faith, with the pink ribbons; "and may you find all well when you come back."

"Amen!" cried Goodman Brown. "Say thy prayers, dear Faith, and go to bed at dusk, and no harm will come to thee."

So they parted; and the young man pursued his way until, being about to turn the corner by the meetinghouse, he looked back and saw the head of Faith still peeping after him with a melancholy air, in spite of her pink ribbons.

"Poor little Faith!" thought he, for his heart smote him. "What a wretch am I to leave her on such an errand! She talks of dreams, too. Methought as she spoke there was trouble in her face, as if a dream had warned her what work is to be done tonight. But no, no; 'twould kill her to think it. Well, she's a blessed angel on earth; and after this one night I'll cling to her skirts and follow her to heaven."

With this excellent resolve for the future, Goodman Brown felt himself justified in making more haste on his present evil purpose. He had taken a dreary road, darkened by all the gloomiest trees of the forest, which barely stood aside to let the narrow path creep through, and closed immediately behind. It was all as lonely as could be; and there is this peculiarity in such a solitude, that the traveler knows not who may be concealed by the innumerable trunks and the thick boughs overhead; so that with lonely footsteps he may yet be passing through an unseen multitude.

"There may be a devilish Indian behind every tree," said Goodman Brown to himself; and he glanced fearfully behind him as he added, "What if the devil himself should be at my very elbow!"

His head being turned back, he passed a crook of the road, and, looking forward again, beheld the figure of a man, in grave and decent attire, seated at the foot of an old tree. He arose at Goodman Brown's approach and walked onward side by side with him.

"You are late, Goodman Brown," said he. "The clock of the Old South was striking as I came through Boston, and that is full fifteen minutes agone."

"Faith kept me back awhile," replied the young man, with a tremor in his voice caused by the sudden appearance of his companion, though not wholly unexpected.

It was now deep dusk in the forest, and deepest in that part of it where these two were journeying. As nearly as could be discerned, the second traveler was about fifty years old, apparently in the same rank of life as Goodman Brown, and bearing a considerable resemblance to him, though perhaps more in expression than features. Still they might have been taken for father and son. And yet, though the elder person was as simply clad as the younger, and as simple in manner too, he had an indescribable air of one who knew the world and who would not have felt abashed at the governor's dinner table or in King William's court, were it possible that his affairs should call him thither. But the only thing about him that could be fixed upon as remarkable was his staff, which bore the likeness of a great black snake, so curiously wrought that it might almost be seen to twist and wriggle itself like a living serpent. This, of course, must have been an ocular deception, assisted by the uncertain light.

"Come, Goodman Brown," cried his fellow traveler, "this is a dull pace for the beginning of a journey. Take my staff, if you are so soon weary."

"Friend," said the other, exchanging his slow pace for a full stop, "having kept covenant by meeting thee here, it is my purpose now to return whence I came. I have scruples touching the matter thou wot'st of."

"Sayest thou so?" replied he of the serpent, smiling apart. "Let us walk on, nevertheless, reasoning as we go; and if I convince thee not thou shalt turn back. We are but a little way in the forest yet."

"Too far! too far!" exclaimed the goodman, unconsciously resuming his walk. "My father never went into the woods on such an errand, nor his father before him. We have been a race of honest men and good Christians since the days of the martyrs; and shall I be the first of the name of Brown that ever took this path and kept—"

"Such company, thou wouldst say," observed the elder person, interpreting his pause. "Well said, Goodman Brown! I have been as well acquainted with your family as with ever a one among the Puritans; and that's no trifle to say. I helped your grandfather, the constable, when he lashed the Quaker woman so smartly through the streets of Salem; and it was I that brought your father a pitch-pine knot, kindled at my own hearth, to set fire to an Indian village, in King Philip's War. They were my good friends, both; and many a pleasant walk have we had along this path, and returned merrily after midnight. I would fain be friends with you for their sake."

"If it be as thou sayest," replied Goodman Brown, "I marvel they never spoke of these matters; or, verily, I marvel not, seeing that the least rumor of the sort would have driven them from New England. We are a people of prayer, and good works to boot, and abide no such wickedness."

"Wickedness or not," said the traveler with the twisted staff, "I have a very general acquaintance here in New

England. The deacons of many a church have drunk the communion wine with me; the selectmen of divers towns make me their chairman; and a majority of the Great and General Court are firm supporters of my interest. The governor and I, too— But these are state secrets."

"Can this be so?" cried Goodman Brown, with a stare of amazement at his undisturbed companion. "Howbeit, I have nothing to do with the governor and council; they have their own ways, and are no rule for a simple husbandman like me. But, were I to go on with thee, how should I meet the eye of that good old man, our minister at Salem village? Oh, his voice would make me tremble both Sabbath day and lecture day."

Thus far the elder traveler had listened with due gravity, but now burst into a fit of irrepressible mirth, shaking himself so violently that his snakelike staff actually seemed to wriggle in sympathy.

"Ha! ha! ha!" shouted he again and again; then composing himself. "Well, go on, Goodman Brown, go on; but, prithee, don't kill me with laughing."

"Well, then, to end the matter at once," said Goodman Brown, considerably nettled, "there is my wife, Faith. It would break her dear little heart; and I'd rather break my own."

"Nay, if that be the case," answered the other, "e'en go thy ways, Goodman Brown. I would not for twenty old women like the one hobbling before us that Faith should come to any harm."

As he spoke he pointed his staff at a female figure on the path, in whom Goodman Brown recognized a very pious and exemplary dame, who had taught him his catechism in youth, and was still his moral and spiritual adviser, jointly with the minister and Deacon Gookin.

"A marvel, truly, that Goody Cloyse should be so far in the wilderness at nightfall," said he. "But with your leave, friend, I shall take a cut through the woods until we have left this Christian woman behind. Being a stranger to you, she might ask whom I was consorting with and whither I was going."

"Be it so," said his fellow-traveler. "Betake you the woods, and let me keep the path."

Accordingly the young man turned aside, but took care to watch his companion, who advanced softly along the road until he had come within a staff's length of the old dame. She, meanwhile, was making the best of her way, with singular speed for so aged a woman, and mumbling some indistinct words—a prayer, doubtless—as she went. The traveler put forth his staff and touched her withered neck with what seemed the serpent's tail.

"The devil!" screamed the pious old lady.

"Then Goody Cloyse knows her old friend?" observed the traveler, confronting her and leaning on his writhing stick.

"Ah, forsooth, and is it your worship indeed?" cried the good dame. "Yea, truly is it, and in the very image of my old gossip, Goodman Brown, the grandfather of the silly fellow that now is. But—would your worship believe it?— my broomstick hath strangely disappeared, stolen, as I suspect, by that unhanged witch Goody Cory, and that, too, when I was all anointed with the juice of smallage, and cinquefoil, and wolf's bane—"

"Mingled with fine wheat and the fat of a new-born babe," said the shape of old Goodman Brown.

"Ah, your worship knows the recipe," cried the old lady, cackling aloud. "So, as I was saying, being all ready for the meeting, and no horse to ride on, I made up my mind to foot it; for they tell me there is a nice young man to be taken into communion tonight. But now your good worship will lend me your arm, and we shall be there in a twinkling."

"That can hardly be," answered her friend. "I may not spare you my arm, Goody Cloyse; but here is my staff, if you will."

So saying, he threw it down at her feet, where, perhaps, it assumed life, being one of the rods which its owner had formerly lent to the Egyptian magi. Of this fact, however, Goodman Brown could not take cognizance. He had cast up his eyes in astonishment, and, looking down again, beheld neither Goody Cloyse nor the serpentine staff, but his fellow-traveler alone, who waited for him as calmly as if nothing had happened.

"That old woman taught me my catechism," said the young man; and there was a world of meaning in this simple comment.

They continued to walk onward, while the elder traveler exhorted his companion to make good speed and persevere in the path, discoursing so aptly that his arguments seemed rather to spring up in the bosom of his auditor than to be suggested by himself. As they went, he plucked a branch of maple to serve for a walking stick, and began to strip it of the twigs and little boughs, which were wet with evening dew. The moment his fingers touched them they became strangely withered and dried up as with a week's sunshine. Thus the pair proceeded, at a good free pace, until suddenly, in a gloomy hollow of the road, Goodman Brown sat himself down on the stump of a tree and refused to go any farther.

"Friend," said he stubbornly, "my mind is made up. Not another step will I budge on this errand. What if a wretched old woman do choose to go to the devil when I thought she was going to Heaven: is that any reason why I should quit my dear Faith and go after her?"

"You will think better of this by and by," said his acquaintance composedly. "Sit here and rest yourself awhile; and when you feel like moving again, there is my staff to help you along."

Without more words, he threw his companion the maple stick, and was as speedily out of sight as if he had vanished into the deepening gloom. The young man sat a few moments by the roadside, applauding himself greatly, and thinking with how clear a conscience he should meet the minister in his morning walk, nor shrink from the eye of good old Deacon Gookin. And what calm sleep would be his that very night, which was to have been spent so wickedly, but so purely and sweetly now, in the arms of Faith! Amidst these pleasant and praiseworthy meditations, Goodman Brown heard the tramp of horses along the road, and deemed it advisable to conceal himself within the verge of the forest, conscious of the guilty purpose that had brought him thither, though now so happily turned from it.

On came the hoof tramps and the voices of the riders, two grave old voices, conversing soberly as they drew near. These mingled sounds appeared to pass along the road, within a few yards of the young man's hiding place; but, owing doubtless to the depth of the gloom at that particular spot, neither the travelers nor their steeds were visible. Though their figures brushed the small boughs by the wayside, it could not be seen that they intercepted, even for a moment, the faint gleam from the strip of bright sky athwart which they must have passed. Goodman Brown alternately crouched and stood on tiptoe, pulling aside the branches and thrusting forth his head as far as he durst without discerning so much as a shadow. It vexed him the more, because he could have sworn, were such a thing possible, that he recognized the voices of the minister and Deacon Gookin, jogging along quietly, as they were wont to do, when bound to some ordination or ecclesiastical council. While yet within hearing, one of the riders stopped to pluck a switch.

"Of the two, reverend sir," said the voice like the deacon's, "I had rather miss an ordination dinner than tonight's meeting. They tell me that some of our community are to be here from Falmouth and beyond, and others from Connecticut and Rhode Island, besides several of the Indian powwows, who, after their fashion, know almost as much deviltry as the best of us. Moreover, there is a goodly young woman to be taken into communion."

"Mighty well, Deacon Gookin!" replied the solemn old tones of the minister. "Spur up, or we shall be late. Nothing can be done, you know, until I get on the ground."

The hoofs clattered again; and the voices, talking so strangely in the empty air, passed on through the forest, where no church had ever been gathered or solitary Christian prayed. Whither, then, could these holy men be journeying so deep into the heathen wilderness? Young Goodman Brown caught hold of a tree for support, being ready to sink down on the ground, faint and overburdened with the heavy sickness of his heart. He looked up to the sky, doubting whether there really was a heaven above him. Yet there was the blue arch, and the stars brightening in it.

"With heaven above and Faith below, I will yet stand firm against the devil!" cried Goodman Brown.

While he still gazed upward into the deep arch of the firmament and had lifted his hands to pray, a cloud, though no wind was stirring, hurried across the zenith and hid the brightening stars. The blue sky was still visible, except directly overhead, where this black mass of cloud was sweeping swiftly northward. Aloft in the air, as if from the depths of the cloud, came a confused and doubtful sound of voices. Once the listener fancied that he could distinguish the accents of townspeople of his own, men and women, both pious and ungodly, many of whom he had met at the communion table, and had seen others rioting at the tavern. The next moment, so indistinct were the sounds, he doubted whether he had heard aught but the murmur of the old forest, whispering without a wind. Then came a stronger swell of those familiar tones, heard daily in the sunshine at Salem village, but never until now from a cloud of night. There was one voice, of a young woman, uttering lamentations, yet with an uncertain sorrow, and entreating for some favor, which, perhaps, it would grieve her to obtain; and all the unseen multitude, both saints and sinners, seemed to encourage her onward.

"Faith!" shouted Goodman Brown, in a voice of agony and desperation; and the echoes of the forest mocked him, crying, "Faith! Faith!" as if bewildered wretches were seeking her all through the wilderness.

The cry of grief, rage, and terror was yet piercing the night when the unhappy husband held his breath for a response. There was a scream, drowned immediately in a louder murmur of voices, fading into far-off laughter, as the dark cloud swept away, leaving the clear and silent sky above Goodman Brown. But something fluttered lightly down through the air and caught on the branch of a tree. The young man seized it, and beheld a pink ribbon.

"My Faith is gone!" cried he, after one stupefied moment. "There is no good on earth; and sin is but a name. Come, devil; for to thee is this world given."

And, maddened with despair, so that he laughed loud and long, did Goodman Brown grasp his staff and set forth again, at such a rate that he seemed to fly along the forest path rather than to walk or run. The road grew wilder and drearier and more faintly traced, and vanished at length, leaving him in the heart of the dark wilderness, still rushing onward with the instinct that guides mortal man to evil. The whole forest was peopled with frightful sounds—the creaking of the trees, the howling of wild beasts, and the yell of Indians; while sometimes the wind tolled like a distant church bell, and sometimes gave a broad roar around the traveler, as if all Nature were laughing him to scorn. But he was himself the chief horror of the scene, and shrank not from its other horrors.

"Ha! ha! ha!" roared Goodman Brown when the wind laughed at him. "Let us hear which will laugh loudest. Think not to frighten me with your deviltry. Come witch, come wizard, come Indian powwow, come devil himself, and here comes Goodman Brown. You may as well fear him as he fear you."

In truth, all through the haunted forest there could be nothing more frightful than the figure of Goodman Brown. On he flew among the black pines, brandishing his staff with frenzied gestures, now giving vent to an inspiration of horrid blasphemy, and now shouting forth such laughter as set all the echoes of the forest laughing like demons around him. The fiend in his own shape is less hideous than when he rages in the breast of man. Thus sped the demoniac on his course, until, quivering among the trees, he saw a red light before him, as when the felled trunks and branches of a clearing have been set on fire and throw up their lurid blaze against the sky at the hour of midnight. He paused, in a lull of the tempest that had driven him onward, and heard the swell of what seemed a hymn, rolling solemnly from a distance with the weight of many voices. He knew the tune; it was a familiar one in the choir of the village meetinghouse. The verse died heavily away, and was lengthened by a chorus, not of human voices, but of all the sounds of the benighted wilderness pealing in awful harmony together. Goodman Brown cried out, and his cry was lost to his own ear by its unison with the cry of the desert.

In the interval of silence he stole forward until the light glared full upon his eyes. At one extremity of an open space, hemmed in by the dark wall of the forest, arose a rock, bearing some rude, natural resemblance either to an altar or a pulpit, and surrounded by four blazing pines, their tops aflame, their stems untouched, like candles at an evening meeting. The mass of foliage that had overgrown the summit of the rock was all on fire, blazing high into the night and fitfully illuminating the whole field. Each pendent twig and leafy festoon was in a blaze. As the red light arose and fell, a numerous congregation alternately shone forth, then disappeared in shadow, and again grew, as it were, out of the darkness, peopling the heart of the solitary woods at once.

"A grave and dark-clad company," quoth Goodman Brown.

In truth they were such. Among them, quivering to and fro between gloom and splendor, appeared faces that would be seen next day at the council board of the province, and others which, Sabbath after Sabbath, looked devoutly Heavenward, and benignantly over the crowded pews, from the holiest pulpits in the land. Some affirm that the lady of the governor was there. At least there were high dames well known to her, and wives of honored husbands, and widows, a great multitude, and ancient maidens, all of excellent repute, and fair young girls, who trembled lest their mothers should espy them. Either the sudden gleams of light flashing over the obscure field bedazzled Goodman Brown, or he recognized a score of the church members of Salem village famous for their especial sanctity. Good old Deacon Gookin had arrived, and waited at the skirts of that venerable saint, his revered pastor. But, irreverently consorting with these grave, reputable, and pious people, these elders of the church, these chaste dames and dewy virgins, there were men of dissolute lives and women of spotted fame, wretches given over to all mean and filthy vice, and suspected even of horrid crimes. It was strange to see that the good shrank not from the wicked, nor were the sinners abashed by the saints. Scattered also among their pale-faced enemies were the Indian priests, or powwows, who had often scared their native forest with more hideous incantations than any known to English witchcraft.

"But where is Faith?" thought Goodman Brown; and, as hope came into his heart, he trembled.

Another verse of the hymn arose, a slow and mournful strain, such as the pious love, but joined to words which expressed all that our nature can conceive of sin, and darkly hinted at far more. Unfathomable to mere mortals is the lore of fiends. Verse after verse was sung; and still the chorus of the desert swelled between like the deepest tone of a mighty organ; and with the final peal of that dreadful anthem there came a sound, as if the roaring wind, the rushing streams, the howling beasts, and every other voice of the unconcerted wilderness were mingling and according with the voice of guilty man in homage to the prince of all. The four blazing pines threw up a loftier flame, and obscurely discovered shapes and visages of horror on the smoke wreaths above the impious assembly. At the same moment the fire on the rock shot redly forth and formed a glowing arch above its base, where now appeared a figure. With reverence be it spoken, the figure bore no slight similitude, both in garb and manner, to some grave divine of the New England churches.

"Bring forth the converts!" cried a voice that echoed through the field and rolled into the forest.

At the word, Goodman Brown stepped forth from the shadow of the trees and approached the congregation, with whom he felt a loathful brotherhood by the sympathy of all that was wicked in his heart. He could have wellnigh sworn that the shape of his own dead father beckoned him to advance, looking downward from a smoke wreath, while a woman, with dim features of despair, threw out her hand to warn him back. Was it his mother? But he had no power to retreat one step, nor to resist, even in thought, when the minister and good old Deacon Gookin seized his arms and led him to the blazing rock. Thither came also the slender form of a veiled female, led between Goody Cloyse, that pious teacher of the catechism, and Martha Carrier, who had received the devil's promise to be queen of hell. A rampant hag was she. And there stood the proselytes beneath the canopy of fire.

"Welcome, my children," said the dark figure, "to the communion of your race. Ye have found thus young your nature and your destiny. My children, look behind you!"

They turned; and flashing forth, as it were, in a sheet of flame, the fiend worshipers were seen; the smile of welcome gleamed darkly on every visage.

"There," resumed the sable form, "are all whom ye have reverenced from youth. Ye deemed them holier than yourselves, and shrank from your own sin, contrasting it with their lives of righteousness and prayerful aspirations heavenward. Yet here are they all in my worshiping assembly. This night it shall be granted you to know their secret deeds: how hoary-bearded elders of the church have whispered wanton words to the young maids of their households; how many a woman, eager for widow's weeds, has given her husband a drink at bedtime and let him sleep his last sleep in her bosom; how beardless youths have made haste to inherit their fathers' wealth; and how fair damsels—blush not, sweet ones—have dug little graves in the garden, and bidden me, the sole guest, to an infant's funeral. By the sympathy of your human hearts for sin ye shall scent out all the places—whether in church, bed-chamber, street, field, or forest—where crime has been committed, and shall exult to behold the whole earth one stain of guilt, one mighty blood spot. Far more than this. It shall be yours to penetrate, in every bosom, the deep mystery of sin, the fountain of all wicked arts, and which inexhaustibly supplies more evil impulses than human power—than my power at its utmost—can make manifest in deeds. And now, my children, look upon each other."

They did so; and, by the blaze of the hell-kindled torches, the wretched man beheld his Faith, and the wife her husband, trembling before that unhallowed altar.

"Lo, there ye stand, my children," said the figure, in a deep and solemn tone, almost sad with its despairing awful-ness, as if his once angelic nature could yet mourn for our miserable race. "Depending upon one another's hearts, ye had still hoped that virtue were not all a dream. Now are ye undeceived. Evil is the nature of mankind. Evil must be your only happiness. Welcome again, my children, to the communion of your race."

"Welcome," repeated the fiend worshipers, in one cry of despair and triumph.

And there they stood, the only pair, as it seemed, who were yet hesitating on the verge of wickedness in this dark world. A basin was hollowed, naturally, in the rock. Did it contain water, reddened by the lurid light? or was it blood? or, perchance, a liquid flame? Herein did the shape of evil dip his hand and prepare to lay the mark of baptism upon their foreheads, that they might be partakers of the mys-tery of sin, more conscious of the secret guilt of others, both in deed and thought, than they could now be of their own. The husband cast one look at his pale wife, and Faith at him. What polluted wretches would the next glance show them to each other, shuddering alike at what they disclosed and what they saw!

"Faith! Faith!" cried the husband, "look up to Heaven, and resist the wicked one."

Whether Faith obeyed he knew not. Hardly had he spoken when he found himself amid calm night and soli-tude, listening to a roar of the wind which died heavily away through the forest. He staggered against the rock, and felt it chill and damp; while a hanging twig, that had been all on fire, besprinkled his cheek with the coldest dew.

The next morning young Goodman Brown came slowly into the street of Salem village, staring around him like a bewildered man. The good old minister was taking a walk along the graveyard to get an appetite for breakfast and meditate his sermon, and bestowed a blessing, as he passed, on Goodman Brown. He shrank from the venerable saint as if to avoid an anathema. Old Deacon Gookin was at domestic worship, and the holy words of his prayer were heard through the open window. "What God doth the wizard pray to?" quoth Goodman Brown. Goody Cloyse, that excellent old Christian, stood in the early sunshine at her own lattice, catechizing a little girl who had brought her a pint of morning's milk. Goodman Brown snatched away the child as from the grasp of the fiend himself. Turning the corner by the meetinghouse, he spied the head of Faith, with the pink ribbons, gazing anxiously forth, and bursting into such joy at sight of him that she skipped along the street and almost kissed her husband before the whole village. But Goodman Brown looked sternly and sadly into her face, and passed on without a greeting.

Had Goodman Brown fallen asleep in the forest and only dreamed a wild dream of a witch meeting?

Be it so if you will: but, alas! it was a dream of evil omen for young Goodman Brown. A stern, a sad, a darkly meditative, a distrustful, if not a desperate man did he become from the night of that fearful dream. On the Sabbath day, when the congregation were singing a holy psalm, he could not listen because an anthem of sin rushed loudly upon his ear and drowned all the blessed strain. When the minister spoke from the pulpit with power and fervid eloquence, and, with his hand on the open Bible, of the sacred truths of our religion, and of saintlike lives and triumphant deaths, and of future bliss or misery unutterable, then did Goodman Brown turn pale, dreading lest the roof should thunder down upon the gray blasphemer and his hearers. Often, awaking suddenly at midnight, he shrank from the bosom of Faith; and at morning or eventide, when the family knelt down at prayer, he scowled and muttered to himself, and gazed sternly at his wife, and turned away. And when he had lived long, and was borne to his grave a hoary corpse, followed by Faith, an aged woman, and children and grandchildren, a goodly procession, besides neighbors not a few, they carved no hopeful verse upon his tombstone, for his dying hour was gloom.

Edgar Allan Poe

A DESCENT INTO THE MAELSTRÖM*

The ways of God in Nature, as in Providence, are not as *our*
ways; nor are the models that we frame any way commensurate
to the vastness, profundity, and unsearchableness of His works,
which have a depth in them greater than the well of Democritus.
                                        Joseph Glanville

We had now reached the summit of the loftiest crag. For
some minutes the old man seemed too much exhausted to
speak.

"Not long ago," said he at length, "and I could have
guided you on this route as well as the youngest of my
sons; but, about three years past, there happened to me an
event such as never happened before to mortal man—or
at least such as no man ever survived to tell of—and the
six hours of deadly terror which I then endured have
broken me up body and soul. You suppose me a *very* old
man—but I am not. It took less than a single day to
change these hairs from a jetty black to white, to weaken
my limbs, and to unstring my nerves, so that I tremble at
the least exertion, and am frightened at a shadow. Do you
know I can scarcely look over this little cliff without getting giddy?"

The "little cliff," upon whose edge he had so carelessly
thrown himself down to rest that the weightier portion of
his body hung over it, while he was only kept from falling
by the tenure of his elbow on its extreme and slippery
edge—this "little cliff" arose, a sheer unobstructed preci-
pice of black shining rock, some fifteen or sixteen hundred feet from the world of crags beneath us. Nothing
would have tempted me to be within half a dozen yards

* *Graham's Magazine,* May 1841; 1845.—Text corrected by J. L.
Graham copy.

of its brink. In truth so deeply was I excited by the peril-
ous position of my companion, that I fell at full length
upon the ground, clung to the shrubs around me, and
dared not even glance upward at the sky—while I struggled in vain to divest myself of the idea that the very
foundations of the mountain were in danger from the fury
of the winds. It was long before I could reason myself
into sufficient courage to sit up and look out into the distance.

"You must get over these fancies," said the guide, "for
I have brought you here that you might have the best
possible view of the scene of that event I mentioned—and
to tell you the whole story with the spot just under your
eye."

"We are now," he continued, in that particularizing
manner which distinguished him—"we are now close upon
the Norwegian coast—in the sixty-eighth degree of latitude
—in the great province of Nordland—and in the dreary
district of Lofoden. The mountain upon whose top we sit
is Helseggen, the Cloudy. Now raise yourself up a little
higher—hold on to the grass if you feel giddy—so—and
look out, beyond the belt of vapor beneath us, into the
sea."

I looked dizzily, and beheld a wide expanse of ocean,
whose waters wore so inky a hue as to bring at once to
my mind the Nubian geographer's account of the *Mare
Tenebrarum*. A panorama more deplorably desolate no
human imagination can conceive. To the right and left, as
far as the eye could reach, there lay outstretched, like
ramparts of the world, lines of horridly black and beetling
cliff, whose character of gloom was but the more forcibly
illustrated by the surf which reared high up against it its
white and ghastly crest, howling and shrieking for ever.
Just opposite the promontory upon whose apex we were
placed, and at a distance of some five or six miles out at
sea, there was visible a small, bleak-looking island; or,
more properly, its position was discernible through the
wilderness of surge in which it was enveloped. About two
miles nearer the land, arose another of smaller size, hide-
ously craggy and barren, and encompassed at various
intervals by a cluster of dark rocks.

The appearance of the ocean, in the space between the
more distant island and the shore, had something very

unusual about it. Although, at the time, so strong a gale was blowing landward that a brig in the remote offing lay to under a double-reefed trysail, and constantly plunged her whole hull out of sight, still there was here nothing like a regular swell, but only a short, quick, angry cross dashing of water in every direction—as well in the teeth of the wind as otherwise. Of foam there was little except in the immediate vicinity of the rocks.

"The island in the distance," resumed the old man, "is called by the Norwegians Vurrgh. The one midway is Moskoe. That a mile to the northward is Ambaaren. Yonder are Iflesen, Hoeyholm, Keildholm, Suarven, and Buckholm. Further off—between Moskoe and Vurrgh—are Otterholm, Flimen, Sandflesen, and Skarholm. These are the true names of the places—but why it has been thought necessary to name them at all, is more than either you or I can understand. Do you hear any thing? Do you see any change in the water?"

We had now been about ten minutes upon the top of Helseggen, to which we had ascended from the interior of Lofoden, so that we had caught no glimpse of the sea until it had burst upon us from the summit. As the old man spoke, I became aware of a loud and gradually increasing sound, like the moaning of a vast herd of buffaloes upon an American prairie; and at the same moment I perceived that what seamen term the *chopping* character of the ocean beneath us, was rapidly changing into a current which set to the eastward. Even while I gazed, this current acquired a monstrous velocity. Each moment added to its speed—to its headlong impetuosity. In five minutes the whole sea, as far as Vurrgh, was lashed into ungovernable fury; but it was between Moskoe and the coast that the main uproar held its sway. Here the vast bed of the waters, seamed and scarred into a thousand conflicting channels, burst suddenly into phrensied convulsion—heaving, boiling, hissing—gyrating in gigantic and innumerable vortices, and all whirling and plunging on to the eastward with a rapidity which water never elsewhere assumes, except in precipitous descents.

In a few minutes more, there came over the scene another radical alteration. The general surface grew somewhat more smooth, and the whirlpools, one by one, disappeared, while prodigious streaks of foam became apparent where none had been seen before. These streaks, at length, spreading out to a great distance, and entering into combination, took unto themselves the gyratory motion of the subsided vortices, and seemed to form the germ of another more vast. Suddenly—very suddenly—this assumed a distinct and definite existence, in a circle of more than half a mile in diameter. The edge of the whirl was represented by a broad belt of gleaming spray; but no particle of this slipped into the mouth of the terrific funnel, whose interior, as far as the eye could fathom it, was a smooth, shining, and jet-black wall of water, inclined to the horizon at an angle of some forty-five degrees, speeding dizzily round and round with a swaying and sweltering motion, and sending forth to the winds an appalling voice, half shriek, half roar, such as not even the mighty cataract of Niagara ever lifts up in its agony to Heaven.

The mountain trembled to its very base, and the rock rocked. I threw myself upon my face, and clung to the scant herbage in an excess of nervous agitation.

"This," said I at length, to the old man—"this *can* be nothing else than the great whirlpool of the Maelström."

"So it is sometimes termed," said he. "We Norwegians call it the Moskoe-ström, from the island of Moskoe in the midway."

The ordinary account of this vortex had by no means prepared me for what I saw. That of Jonas Ramus, which is perhaps the most circumstantial of any, cannot impart the faintest conception either of the magnificence, or of the horror of the scene—or of the wild bewildering sense of *the novel* which confounds the beholder. I am not sure from what point of view the writer in question surveyed it, nor at what time; but it could neither have been from the summit of Helseggen, nor during a storm. There are some passages of his description, nevertheless, which may be quoted for their details, although their effect is exceedingly feeble in conveying an impression of the spectacle.

"Between Lofoden and Moskoe," he says, "the depth of the water is between thirty-six and forty fathoms; but on the other side, toward Ver (Vurrgh) this depth decreases so as not to afford a convenient passage for a vessel, without the risk of splitting on the rocks, which happens even in the calmest weather. When it is flood, the stream runs up the country between Lofoden and Moskoe with a boisterous rapidity; but the roar of its impetuous ebb to the sea is scarce equalled by the loudest and most dreadful cata- racts; the noise being heard several leagues off, and the vortices or pits are of such an extent and depth, that if a ship comes within its attraction, it is inevitably absorbed and carried down to the bottom, and there beat to pieces against the rocks; and when the water relaxes, the frag- ments thereof are thrown up again. But these intervals of tranquillity are only at the turn of the ebb and flood, and in calm weather, and last but a quarter of an hour, its violence gradually returning. When the stream is most boisterous, and its fury heightened by a storm, it is dan- gerous to come within a Norway mile of it. Boats, yachts, and ships have been carried away by not guarding against it before they were within its reach. It likewise happens frequently, that whales come too near the stream, and are overpowered by its violence; and then it is impossible to describe their howlings and bellowings in their fruitless struggles to disengage themselves. A bear once, attempting to swim from Lofoden to Moskoe, was caught by the stream and borne down, while he roared terribly, so as to be heard on shore. Large stocks of firs and pine trees, after being absorbed by the current, rise again broken and torn to such a degree as if bristles grew upon them. This plainly shows the bottom to consist of craggy rocks, among which they are whirled to and fro. This stream is regulated by the flux and reflux of the sea—it being constantly high and low water every six hours. In the year 1645, early in the morning of Sexagesima Sunday, it raged with such noise and impetuosity that the very stones of the houses on the coast fell to the ground."

In regard to the depth of the water, I could not see how this could have been ascertained at all in the immediate vicinity of the vortex. The "forty fathoms" must have ref- erence only to portions of the channel close upon the shore either of Moskoe or Lofoden. The depth in the centre of the Moskoe-ström must be unmeasurably greater; and no better proof of this fact is necessary than can be obtained from even the sidelong glance into the abyss of the whirl which may be had from the highest crag of Helseggen. Looking down from this pinnacle upon the howling Phleg- ethon below, I could not help smiling at the simplicity with which the honest Jonas Ramus records, as a matter difficult of belief, the anecdotes of the whales and the bears, for it appeared to me, in fact, a self-evident thing, that the largest ships of the line in existence, coming within the influence of that deadly attraction, could resist it as little as a feather the hurricane, and must disappear bodily and at once.

The attempts to account for the phenomenon—some of which, I remember, seemed to me sufficiently plausible in perusal—now wore a very different and unsatisfactory aspect. The idea generally received is that this, as well as three smaller vortices among the Feroe islands, "have no other cause than the collision of waves rising and falling, at flux and reflux, against a ridge of rocks and shelves, which confines the water so that it precipitates itself like a cataract; and thus the higher the flood rises, the deeper must the fall be, and the natural result of all is a whirlpool or vortex, the prodigious suction of which is sufficiently known by lesser experiments."—These are the words of the Encyclopædia Britannica. Kircher and others imagine that in the centre of the channel of the maelström is an abyss penetrating the globe, and issuing in some very remote part—the Gulf of Bothnia being somewhat decidedly named in one instance. This opinion, idle in itself, was the one to which, as I gazed, my imagination most readily assented; and, mentioning it to the guide, I was rather surprised to hear him say that, although it was the view almost universally entertained of the subject by the Norwegians, it nevertheless was not his own. As to the former notion he confessed his inability to comprehend it; and here I agreed with him—for, however conclusive on paper, it becomes altogether unintelligible, and even absurd, amid the thunder of the abyss.

"You have had a good look at the whirl now," said the old man, "and if you will creep round this crag, so as to get in its lee, and deaden the roar of the water, I will tell you a story that will convince you I ought to know something of the Moskoe-ström."

I placed myself as desired, and he proceeded.

"Myself and my two brothers once owned a schooner-rigged smack of about seventy tons burthen, with which we were in the habit of fishing among the islands beyond Moskoe, nearly to Vurrgh. In all violent eddies at sea there is good fishing, at proper opportunities, if one has only the courage to attempt it; but among the whole of the Lofoden coastmen, we three were the only ones who made a regular business of going out to the islands, as I tell you. The usual grounds are a great way lower down to the southward. There fish can be got at all hours, without much risk, and therefore these places are preferred. The choice spots over here among the rocks, however, not only yield the finest variety, but in far greater abundance; so that we often got in a single day, what the more timid of the craft could not scrape together in a week. In fact, we made it a matter of desperate speculation—the risk of life standing instead of labor, and courage answering for capital.

"We kept the smack in a cove about five miles higher up the coast than this; and it was our practice, in fine weather, to take advantage of the fifteen minutes' slack to push across the main channel of the Moskoe-ström, far above the pool, and then drop down upon anchorage somewhere near Otterholm, or Sandflesen, where the eddies are not so violent as elsewhere. Here we used to remain until nearly time for slack-water again, when we weighed and made for home. We never set out upon this expedition without a steady side wind for going and coming—one that we felt sure would not fail us before our return—and we seldom made a miscalculation upon this point. Twice, during six years, we were forced to stay all night at anchor on account of a dead calm, which is a rare thing indeed just about here; and once we had to remain on the grounds nearly a week, starving to death, owing to a gale which blew up shortly after our arrival, and made the channel too boisterous to be thought of. Upon this occasion we should have been driven out to sea in spite of everything, (for the whirlpools threw us round and round so violently, that, at length, we fouled our anchor and dragged it) if it had not been that we drifted into one of the innumerable cross currents—here to-day and gone to-morrow—which drove us under the lee of Flimen, where, by good luck, we brought up.

"I could not tell you the twentieth part of the difficulties we encountered 'on the ground'—it is a bad spot to be in, even in good weather—but we make shift always to run the gauntlet of the Moskoe-ström itself without accident; although at times my heart has been in my mouth when we happened to be a minute or so behind or before the slack. The wind sometimes was not as strong as we thought it at starting, and then we made rather less way than we could wish, while the current rendered the smack unmanageable. My eldest brother had a son eighteen years old, and I had two stout boys of my own. These would have been of great assistance at such times, in using the sweeps, as well as afterward in fishing—but, somehow, although we ran the risk ourselves, we had not the heart to let the young ones get into the danger—for, after all said and done, it *was* a horrible danger, and that is the truth.

"It is now within a few days of three years since what I am going to tell you occurred. It was on the tenth of July, 18—, a day which the people of this part of the world will never forget— for it was one in which blew the most terrible hurricane that ever came out of the heavens. And yet all the morning, and indeed until late in the afternoon, there was a gentle and steady breeze from the southwest, while the sun shone brightly, so that the oldest seaman among us could not have foreseen what was to follow.

"The three of us—my two brothers and myself—had crossed over to the islands about two o'clock P.M., and soon nearly loaded the smack with fine fish, which, we all remarked, were more plenty that day than we had ever known them. It was just seven, *by my watch*, when we weighed and started for home, so as to make the worst of the Ström at slack-water, which we knew would be at eight.

"We set out with a fresh wind on our starboard quarter, and for some time spanked along at a great rate, never dreaming of danger, for indeed we saw not the slightest reason to apprehend it. All at once we were taken aback by a breeze from over Helseggen. This was most unusual—something that had never happened to us before—and I began to feel a little uneasy, without exactly knowing why. We put the boat on the wind, but could make no headway at all for the eddies, and I was upon the point of proposing to return to the anchorage, when, looking astern, we saw the whole horizon covered with a singular copper-colored cloud that rose with the most amazing velocity.

"In the meantime the breeze that had headed us off fell away and we were dead becalmed, drifting about in every direction. This state of things, however, did not last long enough to give us time to think about it. In less than a minute the storm was upon us—in less than two the sky was entirely overcast—and what with this and the driving spray, it became suddenly so dark that we could not see each other in the smack.

"Such a hurricane as then blew it is folly to attempt describing. The oldest seaman in Norway never experienced any thing like it. We had let our sails go by the run before it cleverly took us; but, at the first puff, both our masts went by the board as if they had been sawed off—the mainmast taking with it my youngest brother, who had lashed himself to it for safety.

"Our boat was the lightest feather of a thing that ever sat upon water. It had a complete flush deck, with only a small hatch near the bow, and this hatch it had always been our custom to batten down when about to cross the Ström, by way of precaution against the chopping seas. But for this circumstance we should have foundered at once —for we lay entirely buried for some moments. How my elder brother escaped destruction I cannot say, for I never had an opportunity of ascertaining. For my part, as soon as I had let the foresail run, I threw myself flat on deck, with my feet against the narrow gunwale of the bow, and with my hands grasping a ring-bolt near the foot of the fore-mast. It was mere instinct that prompted me to do this—which was undoubtedly the very best thing I could have done—for I was too much flurried to think.

"For some moments we were completely deluged, as I say, and all this time I held my breath, and clung to the bolt. When I could stand it no longer I raised myself upon my knees, still keeping hold with my hands, and thus got my head clear. Presently our little boat gave herself a shake, just as a dog does in coming out of the water, and thus rid herself, in some measure, of the seas. I was now trying to get the better of the stupor that had come over me, and to collect my senses so as to see what was to be done, when I felt somebody grasp my arm. It was my elder brother, and my heart leaped for joy, for I had made sure that he was overboard—but the next moment all this joy was turned into horror—for he put his mouth close to my ear, and screamed out the word '*Moskoe-ström!*'

"No one ever will know what my feelings were at that moment. I shook from head to foot as if I had had the most violent fit of the ague. I knew what he meant by that one word well enough—I knew what he wished to make me understand. With the wind that now drove us on, we were bound for the whirl of the Ström, and nothing could save us!

"You perceive that in crossing the Ström *channel*, we always went a long way up above the whirl, even in the calmest weather, and then had to wait and watch carefully for the slack——but now we were driving right upon the pool itself, and in such a hurricane as this! 'To be sure,' I thought, 'we shall get there just about the slack—there is some little hope in that'—but in the next moment I cursed myself for being so great a fool as to dream of hope at all. I knew very well that we were doomed, had we been ten times a ninety-gun ship.

"By this time the first fury of the tempest had spent itself, or perhaps we did not feel it so much, as we scudded before it, but at all events the seas, which at first had been kept down by the wind, and lay flat and frothing, now got up into absolute mountains. A singular change, too, had come over the heavens. Around in every direction it was still as black as pitch, but nearly overhead there burst out, all at once, a circular rift of clear sky—as clear as I ever saw—and of a deep bright blue—and through it there blazed forth the full moon with a lustre that I never before knew her to wear. She lit up every thing about us with the greatest distinctness—but, oh God, what a scene it was to light up!

"I now made one or two attempts to speak to my brother —but in some manner which I could not understand, the din had so increased that I could not make him hear a single word, although I screamed at the top of my voice in his ear. Presently he shook his head, looking as pale as death, and held up one of his fingers, as if to say *'listen!'*

"At first I could not make out what he meant—but soon a hideous thought flashed upon me. I dragged my watch from its fob. It was not going. I glanced at its face by the moonlight, and then burst into tears as I flung it far away into the ocean. *It had run down at seven o'clock! We were behind the time of the slack, and the whirl of the Ström was in full fury!*

"When a boat is well built, properly trimmed, and not deep laden, the waves in a strong gale, when she is going large, seem always to slip from beneath her—which appears strange to a landsman—and this is what is called *riding*, in sea phrase.

"Well, so far we had ridden the swells very cleverly; but presently a gigantic sea happened to take us right under the counter, and bore us with it as it rose—up—up—as if into the sky. I would not have believed that any wave could rise so high. And then down we came with a sweep, a slide, and a plunge that made me feel sick and dizzy, as if I was falling from some lofty mountain-top in a dream. But while we were up I had thrown a quick glance around—and that one glance was all sufficient. I saw our exact position in an instant. The Moskoe-ström whirlpool was about a quarter of a mile dead ahead—but no more like the every-day Moskoe-ström than the whirl, as you now see it, is like a mill-race. If I had not known where we were, and what we had to expect, I should not have recognised the place at all. As it was, I involuntarily closed my eyes in horror. The lids clenched themselves together as if in a spasm.

"It could not have been more than two minutes afterwards until we suddenly felt the waves subside, and were enveloped in foam. The boat made a sharp half turn to larboard, and then shot off in its new direction like a thunderbolt. At the same moment the roaring noise of the water was completely drowned in a kind of shrill shriek—such a sound as you might imagine given out by the water-pipes of many thousand steam-vessels letting off their steam all together. We were now in the belt of surf that always surrounds the whirl; and I thought, of course, that another moment would plunge us into the abyss—down which we could only see indistinctly on account of the amazing velocity with which we were borne along. The boat did not seem to sink into the water at all, but to skim like an air-bubble upon the surface of the surge. Her starboard side was next the whirl, and on the larboard arose the world of ocean we had left. It stood like a huge writhing wall between us and the horizon.

"It may appear strange, but now, when we were in the very jaws of the gulf, I felt more composed than when we were only approaching it. Having made up my mind to hope no more, I got rid of a great deal of that terror which unmanned me at first. I supposed it was despair that strung my nerves.

"It may look like boasting—but what I tell you is truth —I began to reflect how magnificent a thing it was to die in such a manner, and how foolish it was in me to think of so paltry a consideration as my own individual life, in view of so wonderful a manifestation of God's power. I do believe that I blushed with shame when this idea crossed my mind. After a little while I became possessed with the keenest curiosity about the whirl itself. I positively felt a *wish* to explore its depths, even at the sacrifice I was going to make; and my principal grief was that I should never be able to tell my old companions on shore about the mysteries I should see. These, no doubt, were singular fancies to occupy a man's mind in such extremity—and I have often thought since, that the revolutions of the boat around the pool might have rendered me a little light-headed.

"There was another circumstance which tended to restore my self-possession; and this was the cessation of the wind, which could not reach us in our present situation— for, as you saw for yourself, the belt of the surf is considerably lower than the general bed of the ocean, and this latter now towered above us, a high, black, mountainous ridge. If you have never been at sea in a heavy gale, you can form no idea of the confusion of mind occasioned by the wind and spray together. They blind, deafen, and strangle you, and take away all power of action or reflection. But we were now, in a great measure, rid of these annoyances—just as death-condemned felons in prison are allowed petty indulgences, forbidden them while their doom is yet uncertain.

"How often we made the circuit of the belt it is impossible to say. We careered round and round for perhaps an hour, flying rather than floating, getting gradually more and more into the middle of the surge, and then nearer and nearer to its horrible inner edge. All this time I had never let go of the ring-bolt. My brother was at the stern, holding on to a large empty water-cask which had been securely lashed under the coop of the counter, and was the only thing on deck that had not been swept overboard when the gale first took us. As we approached the brink of the pit he let go his hold upon this, and made for the ring, from which, in the agony of his terror, he endeavored to force my hands, as it was not large enough to afford us both a

secure grasp. I never felt deeper grief than when I saw
him attempt this act—although I knew he was a madman
when he did it—a raving maniac through sheer fright. I
did not care, however, to contest the point with him. I
knew it could make no difference whether either of us held
on at all; so I let him have the bolt, and went astern to
the cask. This there was no great difficulty in doing; for
the smack flew round steadily enough, and upon an even
keel—only swaying to and fro with the immense sweeps
and swelters of the whirl. Scarcely had I secured myself
in my new position, when we gave a wild lurch to starboard, and rushed headlong into the abyss. I muttered a
hurried prayer to God, and thought all was over.

"As I felt the sickening sweep of the descent, I had instinctively tightened my hold upon the barrel, and closed
my eyes. For some seconds I dared not open them—while
I expected instant destruction, and wondered that I was
not already in my death-struggles with the water. But
moment after moment elapsed. I still lived. The sense of
falling had ceased; and the motion of the vessel seemed
much as it had been before while in the belt of foam, with
the exception that she now lay more along. I took courage
and looked once again upon the scene.

"Never shall I forget the sensation of awe, horror, and
admiration with which I gazed about me. The boat
appeared to be hanging, as if by magic, midway down,
upon the interior surface of a funnel vast in circumfer-
ence, prodigious in depth, and whose perfectly smooth
sides might have been mistaken for ebony, but for the
bewildering rapidity with which they spun around, and for
the gleaming and ghastly radiance they shot forth, as the
rays of the full moon, from that circular rift amid the
clouds which I have already described, streamed in a flood
of golden glory along the black walls, and far away down
into the inmost recesses of the abyss.

"At first I was too much confused to observe any thing
accurately. The general burst of terrific grandeur was all
that I beheld. When I recovered myself a little, however,
my gaze fell instinctively downward. In this direction I
was able to obtain an unobstructed view, from the manner
in which the smack hung on the inclined surface of the
pool. She was quite upon an even keel—that is to say, her
deck lay in a plane parallel with that of the water—but

this latter sloped at an angle of more than forty-five degrees, so that we seemed to be lying upon our beam-ends. I could not help observing, nevertheless, that I had scarcely more difficulty in maintaining my hold and footing in this situation, than if we had been upon a dead level; and this, I suppose, was owing to the speed at which we revolved.

"The rays of the moon seemed to search the very bottom of the profound gulf; but still I could make out nothing distinctly, on account of a thick mist in which every thing there was enveloped, and over which there hung a magnificent rainbow, like that narrow and tottering bridge which Musselmen say is the only pathway between Time and Eternity. This mist, or spray, was no doubt occasioned by the clashing of the great walls of the funnel, as they all met together at the bottom—but the yell that went up to the Heavens from out of that mist I dare not attempt to describe.

"Our first slide into the abyss itself, from the belt of foam above, had carried us to a great distance down the slope; but our farther descent was by no means proportionate. Round and round we swept—not with any uniform movement—but in dizzying swings and jerks, that sent us sometimes only a few hundred feet—sometimes nearly the complete circuit of the whirl. Our progress downward, at each revolution, was slow, but very perceptible.

"Looking about me upon the wide waste of liquid ebony on which we were thus borne, I perceived that our boat was not the only object in the embrace of the whirl. Both above and below us were visible fragments of vessels, large masses of building timber and trunks of trees, with many smaller articles, such as pieces of house furniture, broken boxes, barrels and staves. I have already described the unnatural curiosity which had taken the place of my original terrors. It appeared to grow upon me as I drew nearer and nearer to my dreadful doom. I now began to watch, with a strange interest, the numerous things that floated in our company. I *must* have been delirious—for I even sought *amusement* in speculating upon the relative velocities of their several descents toward the foam below. 'This fir tree,' I found myself at one time saying, 'will certainly be the next thing that takes the awful plunge and disappears,'—and then I was disappointed to find that the wreck of a Dutch merchant ship overtook it and went down before. At length, after making several guesses of this nature, and being deceived in all—this fact—the fact of my invariable miscalculation, set me upon a train of reflection that made my limbs again tremble, and my heart beat heavily once more.

"It was not a new terror that thus affected me, but the dawn of a more exciting *hope*. This hope arose partly from memory, and partly from present observation. I called to mind the great variety of buoyant matter that strewed the coast of Lofoden, having been absorbed and then thrown forth by the Moskoe-ström. By far the greater number of the articles were shattered in the most extraordinary way —so chafed and roughened as to have the appearance of being stuck full of splinters—but then I distinctly recollected that there were *some* of them which were not disfigured at all. Now I could not account for this difference except by supposing that the roughened fragments were the only ones which had been *completely absorbed*—that the others had entered the whirl at so late a period of the tide, or, from some reason, had descended so slowly after entering, that they did not reach the bottom before the turn of the flood came, or of the ebb, as the case might be. I conceived it possible, in either instance, that they might thus be whirled up again to the level of the ocean, without undergoing the fate of those which had been drawn in more early or absorbed more rapidly. I made, also, three important observations. The first was, that as a general rule, the larger the bodies were, the more rapid their descent;—the second, that, between two masses of equal extent, the one spherical, and the other *of any other shape,* the superiority in speed of descent was with the sphere;— the third, that, between two masses of equal size, the one cylindrical, and the other of any other shape, the cylinder was absorbed the more slowly. Since my escape, I have had several conversations on this subject with an old school-master of the district; and it was from him that I learned the use of the words 'cylinder' and 'sphere.' He explained to me—although I have forgotten the explanation—how what I observed was, in fact, the natural consequence of the forms of the floating fragments—and showed me how it happened that a cylinder, swimming in a vortex, offered more resistance to its suction, and was drawn in with greater difficulty than an equally bulky body, of any form whatever.*

"There was one startling circumstance which went a great way in enforcing these observations, and rendering me anxious to turn them to account, and this was that, at every revolution, we passed something like a barrel, or else the broken yard or the mast of a vessel, while many of these things, which had been on our level when I first opened my eyes upon the wonders of the whirlpool, were now high up above us, and seemed to have moved but little from their original station.

"I no longer hesitated what to do. I resolved to lash myself securely to the water-cask upon which I now held, to cut it loose from the counter, and to throw myself with it into the water. I attracted my brother's attention by signs, pointed to the floating barrels that came near us, and did every thing in my power to make him understand what I was about to do. I thought at length that he comprehended my design—but, whether this was the case or not, he shook his head despairingly, and refused to move from his station by the ring-bolt. It was impossible to force him; the emergency admitted of no delay; and so, with a bitter struggle, I resigned him to his fate, fastened myself to the cask by means of the lashings which secured it to the counter, and precipitated myself with it into the sea, without another moment's hesitation.

"The result was precisely what I had hoped it might be. As it is myself who now tell you this tale—as you see that I *did* escape—and as you are already in possession of the mode in which this escape was effected, and must therefore anticipate all that I have farther to say—I will bring my story quickly to conclusion. It might have been an hour, or thereabout, after my quitting the smack, when, having descended to a vast distance beneath me, it made three or four wild gyrations in rapid succession, and, bearing my loved brother with it, plunged headlong, at once and forever, into the chaos of foam below. The barrel to which I was attached sunk very little farther than half the distance between the bottom of the gulf and the spot at which I leaped overboard, before a great change took place

* See Archimedes, *De Incidentibus in Fluido,* lib. 2.

in the character of the whirlpool. The slope of the sides of the vast funnel became momently less and less steep. The gyrations of the whirl grew, gradually, less and less violent. By degrees, the froth and the rainbow disappeared, and the bottom of the gulf seemed slowly to uprise. The sky was clear, the winds had gone down, and the full moon was setting radiantly in the west, when I found myself on the surface of the ocean, in full view of the shores of Lofoden, and above the spot where the pool of the Moskoe-ström *had been*. It was the hour of the slack—but the sea still heaved in mountainous waves from the effects of the hurricane. I was borne violently into the channel of the Ström, and in a few minutes, was hurried down the coast into the 'grounds' of the fishermen. A boat picked me up—exhausted from fatigue—and (now that the danger was removed) speechless from the memory of its horror. Those who drew me on board were my old mates and daily companions—but they knew me no more than they would have known a traveller from the spirit-land. My hair, which had been raven black the day before, was as white as you see it now. They say too that the whole expression of my countenance had changed. I told them my story—they did not believe it. I now tell it to *you*—and I can scarcely expect you to put more faith in it than did the merry fishermen of Lofoden."

Fyodor Dostoyevsky

From *The Brothers Karamazov*

Recollections of Father Zossima's youth before he became a monk. The duel

I spent a long time, almost eight years, in the military cadet school at Petersburg, and in the novelty of my surroundings there, many of my childish impressions grew dimmer, though I forgot nothing. I picked up so many new habits and opinions that I was transformed into a cruel, absurd, almost savage creature. A surface polish of courtesy and society manners I did acquire together with the French language.

But we all, myself included, looked upon the soldiers in our service as cattle. I was perhaps worse than the rest in that respect, for I was so much more impressionable than my companions. By the time we left the school as officers, we were ready to lay down our lives for the honour of the regiment, but no one of us had any knowledge of the real meaning of honour, and if any one had known it, he would have been the first to ridicule it. Drunkenness, debauchery and devilry were what we almost prided ourselves on. I don't say that we were bad by nature, all these young men were good fellows, but they behaved badly, and I worst of all. What made it worse for me was that I had come into my own money, and so I flung myself into a life of pleasure, and plunged headlong into all the recklessness of youth.

I was fond of reading, yet strange to say, the Bible was the one book I never opened at that time, though I always carried it about with me, and I was never separated from it; in very truth I was keeping that book "for the day and the hour, for the month and the year," though I knew it not.

After four years of this life, I chanced to be in the town

of K. where our regiment was stationed at the time. We
found the people of the town hospitable, rich and fond of
entertainments. I met with a cordial reception everywhere,
as I was of a lively temperament and was known to be well
off, which always goes a long way in the world. And then a
circumstance happened which was the beginning of it all.

I formed an attachment to a beautiful and intelligent
young girl of noble and lofty character, the daughter of
people much respected. They were well-to-do people of influence and position. They always gave me a cordial and
friendly reception. I fancied that the young lady looked on
me with favour and my heart was aflame at such an idea.
Later on I saw and fully realised that I perhaps was not
so passionately in love with her at all, but only recognised
the elevation of her mind and character, which I could not
indeed have helped doing. I was prevented, however, from
making her an offer at the time by my selfishness, I was
loth to part with the allurements of my free and licentious
bachelor life in the heyday of my youth, and with my
pockets full of money. I did drop some hint as to my feelings, however, though I put off taking any decisive step for
a time. Then, all of a sudden, we were ordered off for two
months to another district.

On my return two months later, I found the young lady
already married to a rich neighbouring landowner, a very
amiable man, still young though older than I was, connected with the best Petersburg society, which I was not,
and of excellent education, which I also was not. I was so
overwhelmed at this unexpected circumstance that my
mind was positively clouded. The worst of it all was that, as
I learned then, the young landowner had been a long while
betrothed to her, and I had met him indeed many times
in her house, but blinded by my conceit I had noticed
nothing. And this particularly mortified me; almost everybody had known all about it, while I knew nothing. I was
filled with sudden irrepressible fury. With flushed face I
began recalling how often I had been on the point of de-
claring my love to her, and as she had not attempted to
stop me or to warn me, she must, I concluded, have been
laughing at me all the time. Later on, of course, I reflected
and remembered that she had been very far from laughing
at me; on the contrary, she used to turn off any lovemaking on my part with a jest and begin talking of other

subjects; but at that moment I was incapable of reflecting and was all eagerness for revenge. I am surprised to remember that my wrath and revengeful feelings were extremely repugnant to my own nature, for being of an easy temper, I found it difficult to be angry with any one for long, and so I had to work myself up artificially and became at last revolting and absurd.

I waited for an opportunity and succeeded in insulting my "rival" in the presence of a large company. I insulted him on a perfectly extraneous pretext, jeering at his opinion upon an important public event—it was in the year 1826*—and my jeer was, so people said, clever and effective. Then I forced him to ask for an explanation, and behaved so rudely that he accepted my challenge in spite of the vast inequality between us, as I was younger, a person of no consequence, and of inferior rank. I learned afterwards for a fact that it was from a jealous feeling on his side also that my challenge was accepted; he had been rather jealous of me on his wife's account before their marriage; he fancied now that if he submitted to be insulted by me and refused to accept any challenge, and if she heard of it, she might begin to despise him and waver in her love for him. I soon found a second in a comrade, an ensign of our regiment. In those days though duels were severely punished, yet duelling was a kind of fashion among the officers—so strong and deeply rooted will a brutal prejudice sometimes be.

It was the end of June, and our meeting was to take place at seven o'clock the next day on the outskirts of the town—and then something happened that in very truth was the turning-point of my life. In the evening, returning home in a savage and brutal humour, I flew into a rage with my orderly Afanasy, and gave him two blows in the face with all my might, so that it was covered with blood. He had not long been in my service and I had struck him before, but never with such ferocious cruelty. And, believe me, though it's forty years ago, I recall it now with shame and pain. I went to bed and slept for about three hours; when I waked up the day was breaking. I got up—I did not want to sleep any more—I went to the window—

* Probably the public event was the Decembrist plot against the Tsar, of December 1825, in which the most distinguished men in Russia were concerned.—TRANSLATOR'S NOTE.

opened it, it looked out upon the garden; I saw the sun rising; it was warm and beautiful, the birds were singing.

What's the meaning of it, I thought, I feel in my heart as it were something vile and shameful? Is it because I am going to shed blood? No, I thought, I feel it's not that. Can it be that I am afraid of death, afraid of being killed? No, that's not it, that's not it at all. . . . And all at once I knew what it was; it was because I had beaten Afanasy the evening before! It all rose before my mind, it all was as it were repeated over again; he stood before me and I was beating him straight on the face and he was holding his arms stiffly down, his head erect, his eyes fixed upon me as though on parade. He staggered at every blow and did not even dare to raise his hands to protect himself. That is what a man has been brought to, and that was a man beating a fellow creature! What a crime! It was as though a sharp dagger had pierced me right through. I stood as if I were struck dumb, while the sun was shining, the leaves were rejoicing and the birds were trilling the praise of God. . . . I hid my face in my hands, fell on my bed and broke into a storm of tears. And then I remembered my brother Markel and what he said on his deathbed to his servants: "My dear ones, why do you wait on me, why do you love me, am I worth your waiting on me?"

Yes, am I worth it? flashed through my mind. After all what am I worth, that another man, a fellow creature, made in the likeness and image of God, should serve me? For the first time in my life this question forced itself upon me. He had said, "Mother, my little heart, in truth we are each responsible to all for all, it's only that men don't know this. If they knew it, the world would be a paradise at once."

"God, can that too be false?" I thought as I wept. "In truth, perhaps, I am more than all others responsible for all, a greater sinner than all men in the world." And all at once the whole truth in its full light appeared to me: what was I going to do? I was going to kill a good, clever, noble man, who had done me no wrong, and by depriving his wife of happiness for the rest of her life, I should be torturing and killing her too. I lay thus in my bed with my face in the pillow, heedless how the time was passing. Suddenly my second, the ensign, came in with the pistols to fetch me.

"Ah," said he, "it's a good thing you are up already, it's time we were off, come along!"

I did not know what to do and hurried to and fro undecided; we went out to the carriage, however.

"Wait here a minute," I said to him. "I'll be back directly, I have forgotten my purse."

And I ran back alone, straight to Afanasy's little room.

"Afanasy," I said, "I gave you two blows on the face yesterday, forgive me," I said.

He started as though he were frightened, and looked at me; and I saw that it was not enough, and on the spot, in my full officer's uniform, I dropped at his feet and bowed my head to the ground.

"Forgive me," I said.

Then he was completely aghast.

"Your honour . . . sir, what are you doing? Am I worth it?"

And he burst out crying as I had done before, hid his face in his hands, turned to the window and shook all over with his sobs. I flew out to my comrade and jumped into the carriage.

"Ready," I cried. "Have you ever seen a conqueror?" I asked him. "Here is one before you."

I was in ecstasy, laughing and talking all the way, I don't remember what about.

He looked at me. "Well, brother, you are a plucky fellow, you'll keep up the honour of the uniform, I can see."

So we reached the place and found them there, waiting us. We were placed twelve paces apart; he had the first shot. I stood gaily, looking him full in the face; I did not twitch an eyelash, I looked lovingly at him, for I knew what I would do. His shot just grazed my cheek and ear.

"Thank God," I cried, "no man has been killed," and I seized my pistol, turned back and flung it far away into the wood.

"That's the place for you," I cried.

I turned to my adversary.

"Forgive me, young fool that I am, sir," I said, "for my unprovoked insult to you and for forcing you to fire at me. I am ten times worse than you and more, maybe. Tell that to the person whom you hold dearest in the world."

I had no sooner said this than they all three shouted at me.

"Upon my word," cried my adversary, annoyed, "if you did not want to fight, why did not you let me alone?"

"Yesterday I was a fool, to-day I know better," I answered him gaily.

"As to yesterday, I believe you, but as for to-day, it is difficult to agree with your opinion," said he.

"Bravo," I cried, clapping my hands. "I agree with you there too, I have deserved it!"

"Will you shoot, sir, or not?"

"No, I won't," I said, "if you like, fire at me again, but it would be better for you not to fire."

The seconds, especially mine, were shouting too: "Can you disgrace the regiment like this, facing your antagonist and begging his forgiveness! If I'd only known this!"

I stood facing them all, not laughing now.

"Gentlemen," I said, "is it really so wonderful in these days to find a man who can repent of his stupidity and publicly confess his wrongdoing?"

"But not in a duel," cried my second again.

"That's what's so strange," I said. "For I ought to have owned my fault as soon as I got here, before he had fired a shot, before leading him into a great and deadly sin; but we have made our life so grotesque, that to act in that way would have been almost impossible, for only after I have faced his shot at the distance of twelve paces could my words have any significance for him, and if I had spoken before, he would have said 'he is a coward, the sight of the pistols had frightened him, no use to listen to him.' Gentlemen," I cried suddenly, speaking straight from my heart, "look around you at the gifts of God, the clear sky, the pure air, the tender grass, the birds; nature is beautiful and sinless, and we, only we, are sinful and foolish, and we don't understand that life is heaven, for we have only to understand that and it will at once be fulfilled in all its beauty, we shall embrace each other and weep."

I would have said more but I could not; my voice broke with the sweetness and youthful gladness of it, and there was such bliss in my heart as I had never known before in my life.

"All this is rational and edifying," said my antagonist, "and in any case you are an original person."

"You may laugh," I said to him, laughing too, "but afterwards you will approve of me."

"Oh, I am ready to approve of you now," said he; "will you shake hands, for I believe you are genuinely sincere."

"No," I said, "not now, later on when I have grown worthier and deserve your esteem, then shake hands and you will do well."

We went home, my second upbraiding me all the way, while I kissed him. All my comrades heard of the affair at once and gathered together to pass judgment on me the same day.

"He has disgraced the uniform," they said; "let him resign his commission."

Some stood up for me: "He faced the shot," they said.

"Yes, but he was afraid of his other shot and begged for forgiveness."

"If he had been afraid of being shot, he would have shot his own pistol first before asking forgiveness, while he flung it loaded into the forest. No, there's something else in this, something original."

I enjoyed listening and looking at them. "My dear friends and comrades," said I, "don't worry about my resigning my commission, for I have done so already. I have sent in my papers this morning and as soon as I get my discharge I shall go into a monastery—it's with that object I am leaving the regiment."

When I had said this every one of them burst out laughing.

"You should have told us of that first, that explains everything, we can't judge a monk."

They laughed and could not stop themselves, and not scornfully, but kindly and merrily. They all felt friendly to me at once, even those who had been sternest in their censure, and all the following month, before my discharge came, they could not make enough of me. "Ah, you monk," they would say. And every one said something kind to me, they began trying to dissuade me, even to pity me: "What are you doing to yourself?"

"No," they would say, "he is a brave fellow, he faced fire and could have fired his own pistol too, but he had a dream the night before that he should become a monk, that's why he did it."

It was the same thing with the society of the town. Till then I had been kindly received, but had not been the object of special attention, and now all came to know me at once and invited me; they laughed at me, but they loved me. I may mention that although everybody talked openly of our duel, the authorities took no notice of it because my antagonist was a near relation of our general, and as there had been no bloodshed and no serious consequences, and as I resigned my commission, they took it as a joke. And I began then to speak aloud and fearlessly, regardless of their laughter, for it was always kindly and not spiteful laughter. These conversations mostly took place in the evenings, in the company of ladies; women particularly liked listening to me then and they made the men listen.

"But how can I possibly be responsible for all?" every one would laugh in my face. "Can I, for instance, be responsible for you?"

"You may well not know it," I would answer, "since the whole world has long been going on a different line, since we consider the veriest lies as truth and demand the same lies from others. Here I have for once in my life acted sincerely and, well, you all look upon me as a madman. Though you are friendly to me, yet, you see, you all laugh at me."

"But how can we help being friendly to you?" said my hostess, laughing. The room was full of people. All of a sudden the young lady rose, on whose account the duel had been fought and whom only lately I had intended to be my future wife. I had not noticed her coming into the room. She got up, came to me and held out her hand.

"Let me tell you," she said, "that I am the first not to laugh at you, but on the contrary I thank you with tears and express my respect for you and for your action then."

Her husband too came up and then they all approached me and almost kissed me. My heart was filled with joy, but my attention was especially caught by a middle-aged man who came up to me with the others. I knew him by name already, but had never made his acquaintance nor exchanged a word with him till that evening.

THE MYSTERIOUS VISITOR

He had long been an official in the town; he was in a prominent position, respected by all, rich and had a reputation for benevolence. He subscribed considerable sums to the almshouse and the orphan asylum; he was very charitable, too, in secret, a fact which only became known after his death. He was a man of about fifty, almost stern in appearance and not much given to conversation. He had been married about ten years and his wife, who was still young, had borne him three children. Well, I was sitting alone in my room the following evening, when my door suddenly opened and this gentleman walked in.

I must mention, by the way, that I was no longer living in my former quarters. As soon as I resigned my commission, I took rooms with an old lady, the widow of a government clerk. My landlady's servant waited upon me, for I had moved into her rooms simply because on my return from the duel I had sent Afanasy back to the regiment, as I felt ashamed to look him in the face after my last interview with him. So prone is the man of the world to be ashamed of any righteous action.

"I have," said my visitor, "with great interest listened to you speaking in different houses the last few days and I wanted at last to make your personal acquaintance, so as to talk to you more intimately. Can you, dear sir, grant me this favour?"

"I can, with the greatest pleasure and I shall look upon it as an honour." I said this, though I felt almost dismayed, so greatly was I impressed from the first moment by the appearance of this man. For though other people had listened to me with interest and attention, no one had come to me before with such a serious, stern and concentrated expression. And now he had come to see me in my rooms. He sat down.

"You are, I see, a man of great strength of character," he said; "as you have dared to serve the truth, even when by doing so you risked incurring the contempt of all."

"Your praise is, perhaps, excessive," I replied.

"No, it's not excessive," he answered; "believe me, such a course of action is far more difficult than you think. It is that which has impressed me, and it is only on that account that I have come to you," he continued. "Tell me, please, that is if you are not annoyed by my perhaps unseemly curiosity, what were your exact sensations, if you can recall them, at the moment when you made up your mind to ask forgiveness at the duel? Do not think my question frivolous; on the contrary, I have in asking the question a secret motive of my own, which I will perhaps explain to you later on, if it is God's will that we should become more intimately acquainted."

All the while he was speaking, I was looking at him straight into the face and I felt all at once a complete trust in him and great curiosity on my side also, for I felt that there was some strange secret in his soul.

"You ask what were my exact sensations at the moment when I asked my opponent's forgiveness," I answered; "but I had better tell you from the beginning what I have not yet told any one else." And I described all that had passed between Afanasy and me, and how I had bowed down to the ground at his feet. "From that you can see for yourself," I concluded, "that at the time of the duel it was easier for me, for I had made a beginning already at home, and when once I had started on the road, to go further along it was far from being difficult, but became a source of joy and happiness."

I liked the way he looked at me as he listened. "All that," he said, "is exceedingly interesting. I will come to see you again and again."

And from that time forth he came to see me nearly every evening. And we should have become greater friends, if only he had ever talked of himself. But about himself he scarcely ever said a word, yet continually asked me about myself. In spite of that I became very fond of him and spoke with perfect frankness to him about all my feelings; for, thought I, what need have I to know his secrets, since I can see without that that he is a good man. Moreover, though he is such a serious man and my senior, he comes to see a youngster like me and treats me as his equal. And I learned a great deal that was profitable from him, for he was a man of lofty mind.

"That life is heaven," he said to me suddenly, "that I have long been thinking about"; and all at once he added, "I think of nothing else indeed." He looked at me and smiled. "I am more convinced of it than you are, I will tell you later why."

I listened to him and thought that he evidently wanted to tell me something.

"Heaven," he went on, "lies hidden within all of us— here it lies hidden in me now, and if I will it, it will be revealed to me to-morrow and for all time."

I looked at him; he was speaking with great emotion and gazing mysteriously at me, as if he were questioning me.

"And that we are all responsible to all for all, apart from our own sins, you were quite right in thinking that, and it is wonderful how you could comprehend it in all its significance at once. And in very truth, so soon as men understand that, the Kingdom of Heaven will be for them not a dream, but a living reality."

"And when," I cried out to him bitterly, "when will that come to pass? and will it ever come to pass? Is not it simply a dream of ours?"

"What then, you don't believe it," he said. "You preach it and don't believe it yourself. Believe me, this dream, as you call it, will come to pass without doubt; it will come, but not now, for every process has its law. It's a spiritual, psychological process. To transform the world, to recreate it afresh, men must turn into another path psychologically. Until you have become really, in actual fact, a brother to every one, brotherhood will not come to pass. No sort of scientific teaching, no kind of common interest, will ever teach men to share property and privileges with equal consideration for all. Every one will think his share too small and they will be always envying, complaining and attacking one another. You ask when it will come to pass; it will come to pass, but first we have to go through the period of isolation."

"What do you mean by isolation?" I asked him.

"Why, the isolation that prevails everywhere, above all in our age—it has not fully developed, it has not reached its limit yet. For every one strives to keep his individuality as apart as possible, wishes to secure the greatest possible fullness of life for himself; but meantime all his efforts result not in attaining fullness of life but self-destruction, for instead of self-realisation he ends by arriving at complete solitude. All mankind in our age have split up into units, they all keep apart, each in his own groove; each one holds aloof, hides himself and hides what he has, from the rest, and he ends by being repelled by others and repelling them. He heaps up riches by himself and thinks, 'how strong I am now and how secure,' and in his madness he does not understand that the more he heaps up, the more he sinks into self-destructive impotence. For he is accustomed to rely upon himself alone and to cut himself off from the whole; he has trained himself not to believe in the help of others, in men and in humanity, and only trembles for fear he should lose his money and the privileges that he has won for himself. Everywhere in these days men have, in their mockery, ceased to understand that the true security is to be found in social solidarity rather than in isolated individual effort. But this terrible individualism must inevitably have an end, and all will suddenly understand how unnaturally they are separated from one another. It will be the spirit of the time, and people will marvel that they have sat so long in darkness without seeing the light. And then the sign of the Son of Man will be seen in the heavens. . . . But, until then, we must keep the banner flying. Sometimes even if he has to do it alone, and his conduct seems to be crazy, a man must set an example, and so draw men's souls out of their solitude, and spur them to some act of brotherly love, that the great idea may not die."

Our evenings, one after another, were spent in such stirring and fervent talk. I gave up society and visited my neighbours much less frequently. Besides, my vogue was somewhat over. I say this, not as blame, for they still loved me and treated me good-humouredly, but there's no denying that fashion is a great power in society. I began to regard my mysterious visitor with admiration, for besides enjoying his intelligence, I began to perceive that he was brooding over some plan in his heart, and was preparing himself perhaps for a great deed. Perhaps he liked my not showing curiosity about his secret, not seeking to discover it by direct question nor by insinuation. But I noticed at last, that he seemed to show signs of wanting to tell me something. This had become quite evident, indeed, about a month after he first began to visit me.

"Do you know," he said to me once, "that people are very inquisitive about us in the town and wonder why I come to see you so often. But let them wonder, for *soon all will be explained*."

Sometimes an extraordinary agitation would come over him, and almost always on such occasions he would get up and go away. Sometimes he would fix a long piercing look upon me, and I thought "he will say something directly now." But he would suddenly begin talking of something ordinary and familiar. He often complained of headache too.

One day, quite unexpectedly indeed, after he had been talking with great fervour a long time, I saw him suddenly turn pale, and his face worked convulsively, while he stared persistently at me.

"What's the matter?" I said; "do you feel ill?"—he had just been complaining of headache.

"I . . . do you know . . . I murdered some one."

He said this and smiled with a face as white as chalk. "Why is it he is smiling?" The thought flashed through my mind before I realised anything else. I too turned pale.

"What are you saying?" I cried.

"You see," he said, with a pale smile, "how much it has cost me to say the first word. Now I have said it, I feel I've taken the first step and shall go on."

For a long while I could not believe him, and I did not believe him at that time, but only after he had been to see me three days running and told me all about it. I thought he was mad, but ended by being convinced, to my great grief and amazement. His crime was a great and terrible one.

Fourteen years before, he had murdered the widow of a landowner, a wealthy and handsome young woman who had a house in our town. He fell passionately in love with her, declared his feeling and tried to persuade her to marry him. But she had already given her heart to another man, an officer of noble birth and high rank in the service, who was at that time away at the front, though she was expecting him soon to return. She refused his offer and begged him not to come and see her. After he had ceased to visit her, he took advantage of his knowledge of the house to enter at night through the garden by the roof, at great risk of discovery. But as often happens, a crime committed with extraordinary audacity is more successful than others.

Entering the garret through the skylight, he went down the ladder, knowing that the door at the bottom of it was sometimes, through the negligence of the servants, left unlocked. He hoped to find it so, and so it was. He made his way in the dark to her bedroom, where a light was burning. As though on purpose, both her maids had gone off to a birthday-party in the same street, without asking leave. The other servants slept in the servants' quarters or in the kitchen on the ground-floor. His passion flamed up at the sight of her asleep, and then vindictive, jealous anger took possession of his heart, and like a drunken man, beside himself, he thrust a knife into her heart, so that she did not even cry out. Then with devilish and criminal cunning he contrived that suspicion should fall on the servants. He was so base as to take her purse, to open her chest with keys from under her pillow, and to take some things from it, doing it all as it might have been done by an ignorant servant, leaving valuable papers and taking only money. He took some of the larger gold things, but left smaller articles that were ten times as valuable. He took with him, too, some things for himself as remembrances, but of that later. Having done this awful deed, he returned by the way he had come.

Neither the next day, when the alarm was raised, nor at any time after in his life, did any one dream of suspecting that he was the criminal. No one indeed knew of his love for her, for he was always reserved and silent and had no friend to whom he would have opened his heart. He was looked upon simply as an acquaintance, and not a very intimate one, of the murdered woman, as for the previous fortnight he had not even visited her. A serf of hers called Pyotr was at once suspected, and every circumstance confirmed the suspicion. The man knew—indeed his mistress did not conceal the fact—that having to send one of her serfs as a recruit she had decided to send him, as he had no relations and his conduct was unsatisfactory. People had heard him angrily threatening to murder her when he was drunk in a tavern. Two days before her death, he had run away, staying no one knew where in the town. The day after the murder, he was found on the road leading out of the town, dead drunk, with a knife in his pocket and his right hand happened to be stained with blood. He declared that his nose had been bleeding, but no one believed him. The maids confessed that they had gone to a party and that the street-door had been left open till they returned. And a number of similar details came to light, throwing suspicion on the innocent servant.

They arrested him, and he was tried for the murder; but a week after the arrest, the prisoner fell sick of a fever and died unconscious in the hospital. There the matter ended and the judges and the authorities and every one in the town remained convinced that the crime had been committed by no one but the servant who had died in the hospital. And after that the punishment began.

My mysterious visitor, now my friend, told me that at first he was not in the least troubled by pangs of conscience. He was miserable a long time, but not for that reason; only from regret that he had killed the woman he loved, that she was no more, that in killing her he had killed his love, while the fire of passion was still in his veins. But of the innocent blood he had shed, of the murder of a fellow creature, he scarcely thought. The thought that his victim might have become the wife of another man was insupportable to him, and so, for a long time, he was convinced in his conscience that he could not have acted otherwise.

At first he was worried at the arrest of the servant, but his illness and death soon set his mind at rest, for the man's death was apparently (so he reflected at the time) not owing to his arrest or his fright, but a chill he had taken on the day he ran away, when he had lain all night dead drunk on the damp ground. The theft of the money and other things troubled him little, for he argued that the theft had not been committed for gain but to avert suspicion. The sum stolen was small, and he shortly afterwards subscribed the whole of it, and much more, towards the funds for maintaining an almshouse in the town. He did this on purpose to set his conscience at rest about the theft, and it's a remarkable fact that for a long time he really was at peace—he told me this himself. He entered then upon a career of great activity in the service, volunteered for a difficult and laborious duty, which occupied him two years, and being a man of strong will almost forgot the past. Whenever he recalled it, he tried not to think of it at all. He became active in philanthropy too, founded and helped to maintain many institutions in the town, did a good deal in the two capitals, and in both Moscow and Petersburg was elected a member of philanthropic societies.

At last, however, he began brooding over the past, and the strain of it was too much for him. Then he was attracted by a fine and intelligent girl and soon after married her, hoping that marriage would dispel his lonely depression, and that by entering on a new life and scrupulously doing his duty to his wife and children, he would escape from old memories altogether. But the very opposite of what he expected happened. He began, even in the first month of his marriage, to be continually fretted by the thought, "My wife loves me—but what if she knew?" When she first told him that she would soon bear him a child, he was troubled. "I am giving life, but I have taken life." Children came. "How dare I love them, teach and educate them, how can I talk to them of virtue? I have shed blood." They were splendid children, he longed to caress them; "and I can't look at their innocent candid faces, I am unworthy."

At last he began to be bitterly and ominously haunted by the blood of his murdered victim, by the young life he had destroyed, by the blood that cried out for vengeance. He had begun to have awful dreams. But, being a man of fortitude, he bore his suffering a long time, thinking: "I shall expiate everything by this secret agony." But that hope, too, was vain; the longer it went on, the more intense was his suffering.

He was respected in society for his active benevolence, though every one was overawed by his stern and gloomy character. But the more he was respected, the more intolerable it was for him. He confessed to me that he had thoughts of killing himself. But he began to be haunted by another idea—an idea which he had at first regarded as impossible and unthinkable, though at last it got such a hold on his heart that he could not shake it off. He dreamed of rising up, going out and confessing in the face of all men that he had committed murder. For three years this dream had pursued him, haunting him in different forms. At last he believed with his whole heart that if he confessed his crime, he would heal his soul and would be at peace for ever. But this belief filled his heart with terror, for how could he carry it out? And then came what happened at my duel.

"Looking at you, I have made up my mind."

I looked at him.

"Is it possible," I cried, clasping my hands, "that such a trivial incident could give rise to such a resolution in you?"

"My resolution has been growing for the last three years," he answered, "and your story only gave the last touch to it. Looking at you, I reproached myself and envied you," he said this to me almost sullenly.

"But you won't be believed," I observed; "it's fourteen years ago."

"I have proofs, great proofs. I shall show them."

Then I cried and kissed him.

"Tell me one thing, one thing," he said (as though it all depended upon me), "my wife, my children! My wife may die of grief, and though my children won't lose their rank and property, they'll be a convict's children and for ever! And what a memory, what a memory of me I shall leave in their hearts!"

I said nothing.

"And to part from them, to leave them for ever? It's for ever, you know, for ever!"

I sat still and repeated a silent prayer. I got up at last, I felt afraid.

"Well?" He looked at me.

"Go!" said I, "confess. Everything passes, only the truth remains. Your children will understand, when they grow up, the nobility of your resolution."

He left me that time as though he had made up his mind. Yet for more than a fortnight afterwards, he came to me every evening, still preparing himself, still unable to bring himself to the point. He made my heart ache. One day he would come determined and say fervently:

"I know it will be heaven for me, heaven, the moment I confess. Fourteen years I've been in hell. I want to suffer. I will take my punishment and begin to live. You can pass through the world doing wrong, but there's no turning back. Now I dare not love my neighbour nor even my own children. Good God, my children will understand, perhaps, what my punishment has cost me and will not condemn me! God is not in strength but in truth."

"All will understand your sacrifice," I said to him, "if not at once, they will understand later; for you have served truth, the higher truth, not of the earth."

And he would go away seeming comforted, but next day he would come again, bitter, pale, sarcastic.

"Every time I come to you, you look at me so inquisitively as though to say, 'he has still not confessed!' Wait a bit, don't despise me too much. It's not such an easy thing to do, as you would think. Perhaps I shall not do it at all. You won't go and inform against me then, will you?"

And far from looking at him with indiscreet curiosity, I was afraid to look at him at all. I was quite ill from anxiety, and my heart was full of tears. I could not sleep at night.

"I have just come from my wife," he went on. "Do you understand what the word 'wife' means? When I went out, the children called to me, 'Good-bye, father, make haste back to read "The Children's Magazine" with us.' No, you don't understand that! No one is wise from another man's woe."

His eyes were glittering, his lips were twitching. Suddenly he struck the table with his fist so that everything on it danced—it was the first time he had done such a thing, he was such a mild man.

"But need I?" he exclaimed, "must I? No one has been condemned, no one has been sent to Siberia in my place, the man died of fever. And I've been punished by my sufferings for the blood I shed. And I shan't be believed, they won't believe my proofs. Need I confess, need I? I am ready to go on suffering all my life for the blood I have shed, if only my wife and children may be spared. Will it be just to ruin them with me? Aren't we making a mistake? What is right in this case? And will people recognise it, will they appreciate it, will they respect it?"

"Good Lord!" I thought to myself, "he is thinking of other people's respect at such a moment!" And I felt so sorry for him then, that I believe I would have shared his fate if it could have comforted him. I saw he was beside himself. I was aghast, realising with my heart as well as my mind what such a resolution meant.

"Decide my fate!" he exclaimed again.

"Go and confess," I whispered to him. My voice failed me, but I whispered it firmly. I took up the New Testament from the table, the Russian translation, and showed him the Gospel of St. John, ch. xii, verse 24:

"Verily, verily, I say unto you, except a corn of wheat fall into the ground and die, it abideth alone: but if it die, it bringeth forth much fruit."

I had just been reading that verse when he came in. He read it.

"That's true," he said, but he smiled bitterly. "It's terrible the things you find in those books," he said, after a pause. "It's easy enough to thrust them upon one. And who wrote them? Can they have been written by men?"

"The Holy Spirit wrote them," said I.

"It's easy for you to prate," he smiled again, this time almost with hatred.

I took the book again, opened it in another place and showed him the Epistle to the Hebrews, ch. x, verse 31. He read:

"It is a fearful thing to fall into the hands of the living God."

He read it and simply flung down the book. He was trembling all over.

"An awful text," he said. "There's no denying you've picked out fitting ones." He rose from the chair. "Well!" he said, "Good-bye, perhaps I shan't come again . . . we shall meet in heaven. So I have been for fourteen years 'in the hands of the living God,' that's how one must think of those fourteen years. To-morrow I will beseech those hands to let me go."

I wanted to take him in my arms and kiss him, but I did not dare—his face was contorted and sombre. He went away.

"Good God," I thought, "what has he gone to face!" I fell on my knees before the ikon and wept for him before the Holy Mother of God, our swift defender and helper. I was half an hour praying in tears, and it was late, about midnight. Suddenly I saw the door open and he came in again. I was surprised.

"Where have you been?" I asked him.

"I think," he said, "I've forgotten something . . . my handkerchief, I think. . . . Well, even if I've not forgotten anything, let me stay a little."

He sat down. I stood over him.

I sat down. We sat still for two minutes; he looked intently at me and suddenly smiled—I remember that— then he got up, embraced me warmly and kissed me.

"Remember," he said, "how I came to you a second time. Do you hear, remember it!"

And he went out.

"To-morrow," I thought.

And so it was. I did not know that evening that the next

day was his birthday. I had not been out for the last few days so I had no chance of hearing it from any one. On that day he always had a great gathering, every one in the town went to it. It was the same this time. After dinner he walked into the middle of the room, with a paper in his hand—a formal declaration to the chief of his department who was present. This declaration he read aloud to the whole assembly. It contained a full account of the crime, in every detail.

"I cut myself off from men as a monster. God has visited me," he said in conclusion. "I want to suffer for my sin!"

Then he brought out and laid on the table all the things he had been keeping for fourteen years, that he thought would prove his crime, the jewels belonging to the murdered woman which he had stolen to divert suspicion, a cross and a locket taken from her neck with a portrait of her betrothed in the locket, her notebook and two letters; one from her betrothed, telling her that he would soon be with her, and her unfinished answer left on the table to be sent off next day. He carried off these two letters—what for? Why had he kept them for fourteen years afterwards instead of destroying them as evidence against him?

And this is what happened: every one was amazed and horrified, every one refused to believe it and thought that he was deranged, though all listened with intense curiosity. A few days later it was fully decided and agreed in every house that the unhappy man was mad. The legal authorities could not refuse to take the case up, but they too dropped it. Though the trinkets and letters made them ponder, they decided that even if they did turn out to be authentic, no charge could be based on those alone. Besides, she might have given him those things as a friend, or asked him to take care of them for her. I heard afterwards, however, that the genuineness of the things was proved by the friends and relations of the murdered woman, and that there was no doubt about them. Yet nothing was destined to come of it, after all.

Five days later, all had heard that he was ill and that his life was in danger. The nature of his illness I can't explain, they said it was an affection of the heart. But it became known that the doctors had been induced by his wife to investigate his mental condition also, and had come to the conclusion that it was a case of insanity. I betrayed nothing, though people ran to question me. But when I wanted to visit him, I was for a long while forbidden to do so, above all by his wife.

"It's you who have caused his illness," she said to me; "he was always gloomy, but for the last year people noticed that he was peculiarly excited and did strange things, and now you have been the ruin of him. Your preaching has brought him to this; for the last month he was always with you."

Indeed, not only his wife but the whole town were down upon me and blamed me. "It's all your doing," they said. I was silent and indeed rejoiced at heart, for I saw plainly God's mercy to the man who had turned against himself and punished himself. I could not believe in his insanity.

They let me see him at last, he insisted upon saying good-bye to me. I went in to him and saw at once, that not only his days, but his hours were numbered. He was weak, yellow, his hands trembled, he gasped for breath, but his face was full of tender and happy feeling.

"It is done!" he said. "I've long been yearning to see you, why didn't you come?"

I did not tell him that they would not let me see him.

"God has had pity on me and is calling me to Himself. I know I am dying, but I feel joy and peace for the first time after so many years. There was heaven in my heart from the moment I had done what I had to do. Now I dare to love my children and to kiss them. Neither my wife nor the judges, nor anyone has believed it. My children will never believe it either. I see in that God's mercy to them. I shall die, and my name will be without a stain for them. And now I feel God near, my heart rejoices as in Heaven. . . . I have done my duty."

He could not speak, he gasped for breath, he pressed my hand warmly, looking fervently at me. We did not talk for long, his wife kept peeping in at us. But he had time to whisper to me:

"Do you remember how I came back to you that second time, at midnight? I told you to remember it. You know what I came back for? I came to kill you!"

I started.

"I went out from you then into the darkness, I wandered about the streets, struggling with myself. And suddenly I hated you so that I could hardly bear it. Now, I thought, he is all that binds me, and he is my judge. I can't refuse to face my punishment to-morrow, for he knows all. It was not that I was afraid you would betray me (I never even thought of that) but I thought, 'How can I look him in the face if I don't confess?' And if you had been at the other end of the earth, but alive, it would have been all the same, the thought was unendurable that you were alive knowing everything and condemning me. I hated you as though you were the cause, as though you were to blame for everything. I came back to you then, remembering that you had a dagger lying on your table. I sat down and asked you to sit down, and for a whole minute I pondered. If I had killed you, I should have been ruined by that murder even if I had not confessed the other. But I didn't think about that at all, and I didn't want to think of it at that moment. I only hated you and longed to revenge myself on you for everything. The Lord vanquished the devil in my heart. But let me tell you, you were never nearer death."

A week later he died. The whole town followed him to the grave. The chief priest made a speech full of feeling. All lamented the terrible illness that had cut short his days. But all the town was up in arms against me after the funeral, and people even refused to see me. Some, at first a few and afterwards more, began indeed to believe in the truth of his story, and they visited me and questioned me with great interest and eagerness, for man loves to see the downfall and disgrace of the righteous. But I held my tongue, and very shortly after, I left the town, and five months later by God's grace I entered upon the safe and blessed path, praising the unseen finger which had guided me so clearly to it. But I remember in my prayer to this day, the servant of God, Mihail, who suffered so greatly.

Franz Kafka

BEFORE THE LAW

Before the Law stands a doorkeeper. To this doorkeeper there comes a man from the country and prays for admittance to the Law. But the doorkeeper says that he cannot grant admittance at the moment. The man thinks it over and then asks if he will be allowed in later. "It is possible," says the doorkeeper, "but not at the moment." Since the gate stands open, as usual, and the doorkeeper steps to one side, the man stoops to peer through the gateway into the interior. Observing that, the doorkeeper laughs and says: "If you are so drawn to it, just try to go in despite my veto. But take note: I am powerful. And I am only the least of the doorkeepers. From hall to hall there is one doorkeeper after another, each more powerful than the last. The third doorkeeper is already so terrible that even I cannot bear to look at him." These are difficulties the man from the country has not expected; the Law, he thinks, should surely be accessible at all times and to everyone, but as he now takes a closer look at the doorkeeper in his fur coat, with his big sharp nose and long, thin, black Tartar beard, he decides that it is better to wait until he gets permission to enter. The doorkeeper gives him a stool and lets him sit down at one side of the door. There he sits for days and years. He makes many attempts to be admitted, and wearies the doorkeeper by his importunity. The doorkeeper frequently has little interviews with him, asking him questions about his home and many other things, but the questions are put indifferently, as great lords put them, and always finish with the statement that he cannot be let in yet. The man, who has furnished himself with many things for his journey, sacrifices all he has, however valuable, to bribe the doorkeeper. The doorkeeper accepts everything, but always with the remark: "I am only taking it to keep you from thinking you have

omitted anything." During these many years the man fixes
his attention almost continuously on the doorkeeper. He
forgets the other doorkeepers, and this first one seems to
him the sole obstacle preventing access to the Law. He
curses his bad luck, in his early years boldly and loudly;
later, as he grows old, he only grumbles to himself. He
becomes childish, and since in his yearlong contemplation
of the doorkeeper he has come to know even the fleas in
his fur collar, he begs the fleas as well to help him and to
change the doorkeeper's mind. At length his eyesight begins
to fail, and he does not know whether the world is really
darker or whether his eyes are only deceiving him. Yet in
his darkness he is now aware of a radiance that streams
inextinguishably from the gateway of the Law. Now he
has not very long to live. Before he dies, all his experiences in these long years gather themselves in his head to
one point, a question he has not yet asked the doorkeeper.
He waves him nearer, since he can no longer raise his
stiffening body. The doorkeeper has to bend low toward
him, for the difference in height between them has altered
much to the man's disadvantage. "What do you want to
know now?" asks the doorkeeper; "you are insatiable."
"Everyone strives to reach the Law," says the man, "so
how does it happen that for all these many years no one
but myself has ever begged for admittance?" The doorkeeper recognzies that the man has reached his end, and,
to let his failing senses catch the words, roars in his ear:
"No one else could ever be admitted here, since this gate
was made only for you. I am now going to shut it."

Translated by Willa and Edwin Muir

Franz Kafka

AN IMPERIAL MESSAGE

The emperor, so a parable runs, has sent a message to you, the humble subject, the insignificant shadow cowering in the remotest distance before the imperial sun; the Emperor from his deathbed has sent a message to you alone. He has commanded the messenger to kneel down by the bed, and has whispered the message to him; so much store did he lay on it that he ordered the messenger to whisper it back into his ear again. Then by a nod of the head he has confirmed that it is right. Yes, before the assembled spectators of his death—all the obstructing walls have been broken down, and on the spacious and loftily mounting open staircases stand in a ring the great princes of the Empire—before all these he has delivered his message. The messenger immediately sets out on his journey; a powerful, an indefatigable man; now pushing with his right arm, now with his left, he cleaves a way for himself through the throng; if he encounters resistance he points to his breast, where the symbol of the sun glitters; the way is made easier for him than it would be for any other man. But the multitudes are so vast; their numbers have no end. If he could reach the open fields how fast he would fly, and soon doubtless you would hear the welcome hammering of his fists on your door. But instead how vainly does he wear out his strength; still he is only making his way through the chambers of the innermost palace; never will he get to the end of them; and if he succeeded in that nothing would be gained; he must next fight his way down the stairs; and if he succeeded in that nothing would be gained; the courts would still have to be crossed; and after the courts the second outer palace; and once more stairs and courts; and once more another palace; and so on for thousands of years; and if at last he should burst through the outermost gate—but never, never can that happen—the imperial capital would lie before him, the center of the world, crammed to bursting with its own sediment. Nobody could fight his way through here even with a message from a dead man. But you sit at your window when evening falls and dream it to yourself.

Translated by Willa and Edwin Muir

Miguel de Unamuno

SAINT EMMANUEL THE GOOD, MARTYR

If with this life only in view we have had hope in Christ, we are of all men the most to be pitied.   Saint Paul: 1 COR. 15:19.

Now that the bishop of the diocese of Renada, to which this my beloved village of Valverde de Lucerna belongs, is seeking (according to rumor), to initiate the process of beatification of our Don Manuel, or more correctly, Saint Emmanuel the Good, who was parish priest here, I want to state in writing, by way of confession (although to what end only God, and not I can say), all that I can vouch for and remember of that matriarchal man who pervaded the most secret life of my soul, who was my true spiritual father, the father of my spirit, the spirit of myself, Angela Carballino.

The other, my flesh-and-blood temporal father, I scarcely knew, for he died when I was still a very young girl. I know that he came to Valverde de Lucerna from the outside world—that he was a stranger—and that he settled here when he married my mother. He had brought a number of books with him: *Don Quixote*, some plays from the classic theatre, some novels, a few histories, the *Bertoldo*, everything all mixed together. From these books (practically the only ones in the entire village), I nurtured dreams as a young girl, dreams which in turn devoured me. My good mother gave me very little account either of the words or the deeds of my father. For the words and deeds of Don Manuel, whom she worshipped, of whom she was enamored, in common with all the rest of the village —in an exquisitely chaste manner, of course—had obliterated the memory of the words and deeds of her husband; him she commended to God, with full fervor, as she said her daily rosary.

Don Emmanuel I remember as if it were yesterday,

from the time when I was a girl of ten, just before I was taken to the convent school in the cathedral city of Renada. At that time Don Emmanuel, our saint, must have been about thirty-seven years old. He was tall, slender, erect; he carried himself the way our Buitre Peak carries its crest, and his eyes had all the blue depth of our lake. As he walked he commanded all eyes, and not only the eyes but the hearts of all; gazing round at us he seemed to look through our flesh as through glass and penetrate our hearts. We all of us loved him, especially the children. And the things he said to us! Not words, things! The villagers could scent the odor of sanctity, they were intoxicated with it.

It was at this time that my brother Lazarus, who was in America, from where he regularly sent us money with which we lived in decent leisure, had my mother send me to the convent school, so that my education might be completed outside the village; he suggested this move despite the fact that he had no special fondness for the nuns. "But since, as far as I know," he wrote us, "there are no lay schools there,—especially not for young ladies—we will have to make use of the ones that do exist. The important thing is for Angelita to receive some polish and not be forced to continue among village girls." And so I entered the convent school. At one point I even thought I would become a teacher; but pedagogy soon palled upon me.

At school I met girls from the city and I made friends with some of them. But I still kept in touch with people in our village, and I received frequent reports and sometimes a visit.

And the fame of the parish priest reached as far as the school, for he was beginning to be talked of in the cathedral city. The nuns never tired of asking me about him.

Ever since early youth I had been endowed, I don't very well know from where, with a large degree of curiosity and restlessness, due at least in part to that jumble of books which my father had collected, and these qualities were stimulated at school, especially in the course of a relationship which I developed with a girl friend, who grew excessively attached to me. At times she proposed that we enter the same convent together, swearing to an everlast-

ing "sisterhood"—and even that we seal the oath in blood.
At other times she talked to me, with eyes half closed, of
sweethearts and marriage adventures. Strangely enough, I
have never heard of her since, or of what became of her,
despite the fact that whenever our Don Manuel was
spoken of, or when my mother wrote me something about
him in her letters—which happened in almost every letter
—and I read it to her, this girl would exclaim, as if in
rapture: "What luck, my dear, to be able to live near a
saint like that, a live saint, of flesh and blood, and to be
able to kiss his hand; when you go back to your village
write me everything, everything, and tell me about him."

Five years passed at school, five years which now have
evanesced in memory like a dream at dawn, and when I
became fifteen I returned to my own Valverde de Lucerna.
By now everything revolved around Don Emmanuel: Don
Emmanuel, the lake and the mountain. I arrived home
anxious to know him, to place myself under his protection,
and hopeful he would set me on my path in life.

It was rumored that he had entered the seminary to
become a priest so that he might thus look after the sons
of a sister recently widowed and provide for them in place
of their father; that in the seminary his keen mind and his
talents had distinguished him and that he had subsequently
turned down opportunities for a brilliant career in the
church because he wanted to remain exclusively a part of
his Valverde de Lucerna, of his remote village which lay
like a brooch between the lake and the mountain reflected
in it.

How he did love his people! His life consisted in sal-
vaging wrecked marriages, in forcing unruly sons to submit
to their parents, or reconciling parents to their sons, and,
above all, of consoling the embittered and the weary in
spirit; meanwhile he helped everyone to die well.

I recall, among other incidents, the occasion when the
unfortunate daughter of old aunt Rabona returned to our
town. She had been in the city and lost her virtue there;
now she returned unmarried and castoff, and she brought
back a little son. Don Emmanuel did not rest until he had
persuaded an old sweetheart, Perote by name, to marry
the poor girl and, moreover, to legitimize the little creature
with his own name. Don Emmanuel told Perote:

"Come now, give this poor waif a father, for he hasn't got one except in heaven."

"But, Don Emmanuel, it's not my fault . . . !"

"Who knows, my son, who knows . . . ! And besides, it's not a question of guilt."

And today, poor Perote, inspired on that occasion to saintliness by Don Emmanuel, and now a paralytic and invalid, has for staff and consolation of his life the son he accepted as his own when the boy was not his at all.

On Midsummer's Night, the shortest night of the year, it was a local custom here (and still is) for all the old crones, and a few old men, who thought they were possessed or bewitched (hysterics they were, for the most part, or in some cases epileptics) to flock to the lake. Don Emmanuel undertook to fulfill the same function as the lake, to serve as a pool of healing, to treat his charges and even, if possible, to cure them. And such was the effect of his presence, of his gaze, and above all of his voice—the miracle of his voice!—and the infinitely sweet authority of his words, that he actually did achieve some remarkable cures. Whereupon his fame increased, drawing all the sick of the environs to our lake and our priest. And yet once when a mother came to ask for a miracle in behalf of her son, he answered her with a sad smile:

"Ah, but I don't have my bishop's permission to perform miracles."

He was particularly interested in seeing that all the villagers kept themselves clean. If he chanced upon someone with a torn garment he would send him to the church: "Go and see the sacristan, and let him mend that tear." The sacristan was a tailor, and when, on the first day of the year, everyone went to congratulate him on his saint's day—his holy patron was Our Lord Jesus Himself—it was by Don Emmanuel's wish that everyone appeared in a new shirt, and those that had none received the present of a new one from Don Emmanuel himself.

He treated everyone with the greatest kindness; if he favored anyone, it was the most unfortunate, and especially those who rebelled. There was a congenital idiot in the village, the fool Blasillo, and it was toward him that Don Emmanuel chose to show the greatest love and concern; as a consequence he succeeded in miraculously teaching him things which had appeared beyond the idiot's comprehension. The fact was that the embers of understanding feebly glowing in the idiot were kindled whenever, like a pitiable monkey, he imitated his Don Emmanuel.

The marvel of the man was his voice; a divine voice which brought one close to weeping. Whenever he officiated at Solemn High Mass and intoned the prelude, a tremor ran through the congregation and all within sound of his voice were moved to the depths of their being. The sound of his chanting, overflowing the church, went on to float over the lake and settle at the foot of the mountain. And when on Good Friday he intoned "My God, my God, my God, why hast Thou forsaken me?" a profound shudder swept through the multitude, like the lash of a northeaster across the waters of the lake. It was as if these people heard the Lord Jesus Christ himself, as if the voice sprang from the ancient crucifix, at the foot of which generations of mothers had offered up their sorrows. And it happened that on one occasion his mother heard him and was unable to contain herself, and cried out to him right in the church, "My son!," calling her child. And the entire congregation was visibly affected. It was as if the mother's cry had issued from the half-open lips of the Mater Dolorosa—her heart transfixed by seven swords—which stood in one of the chapels of the nave. Afterwards, the fool Blasillo went about piteously repeating, as if he were an echo, "My God, my God, my God, why hast Thou forsaken me?" with such effect that everyone who heard him was moved to tears, to the great satisfaction of the fool, who prided himself on this triumph of imitation.

The priest's effect on people was such that no one ever dared to tell him a lie, and everyone confessed themselves to him without need of a confessional. So true was this that on one occasion, when a revolting crime had been committed in a neighboring village, the judge—a dull fellow who badly misunderstood Don Emmanuel—called on the priest and said:

"Let us see, Don Manuel, if you can get this bandit to admit the truth."

"So that afterwards you may punish him?" asked the saintly man. "No, Judge, no; I will not extract from any man a truth which could be the death of him. That is a matter between him and his God. . . . Human justice is none of my affair. 'Judge not that ye be not judged,' said our Lord."

"But the fact is, Father, that I, a judge . . ."

"I understand. You, Judge, must render unto Caesar that which is Caesar's, while I shall render unto God that which is God's."

And, as Don Emmanuel departed, he gazed at the suspected criminal and said:

"Make sure, only, that God forgives you, for that is all that matters."

Everyone went to Mass in the village, even if it were only to hear him and see him at the altar, where he appeared to be transfigured, his countenance lit from within. He introduced one holy practice to the popular cult; it consisted in assembling the whole town inside the church, men and women, ancients and youths, some thousand persons; there we recited the Creed, in unison, so that it sounded like a single voice: "I believe in God, the Almighty Father, Creator of heaven and earth . . ." and all the rest. It was not a chorus, but a single voice, a simple united voice, all the voices based on one on which they formed a kind of mountain, whose peak, lost at times in the clouds, was Don Emmanuel. As we reached the section "I believe in the resurrection of the flesh and life everlasting," the voice of Don Emmanuel was submerged, drowned in the voice of the populace as in a lake. In truth, he was silent. And I could hear the bells of that city which is said hereabouts to be at the bottom of the lake—bells which are also said to be audible on Midsummer's Night—the bells of the city which is submerged in the spiritual lake of our populace; I was hearing the voice of our dead, resurrected in us by the communion of saints. Later, when I had learned the secret of our saint, I understood that it was as if a caravan crossing the desert lost its leader as they approached the goal of their trek, whereupon his people lifted him on their shoulders to bring his lifeless body into the promised land.

When it came to dying themselves, most of the villagers refused to die unless they were holding on to Don Emmanuel's hand, as if to an anchor chain.

In his sermons he never inveighed against unbelievers, Masons, liberals or heretics. What for, when there were none in the village? Nor did it occur to him to speak against the wickedness of the press. On the other hand, one of his most frequent themes was gossip, against which he lashed out.

"Envy," he liked to repeat, "envy is nurtured by those who prefer to think they are envied, and most persecutions are the result of a persecution complex rather than of an impulse to persecute."

"But Don Emmanuel, just listen to what that fellow was trying to tell me . . ."

"We should concern ourselves less with what people are trying to tell us than with what they tell us without trying . . ."

His life was active rather than contemplative, and he constantly fled from idleness, even from leisure. Whenever he heard it said that idleness was the mother of all the vices, he added: "And also of the greatest vice of them all, which is to think idly." Once I asked him what he meant and he answered: "Thinking idly is thinking as a substitute for doing, or thinking too much about what is already done instead of about what must be done. What's done is done and over with, and one must go on to something else, for there is nothing worse than remorse without possible relief." Action! Action! Even in those early days I have already begun to realize that Don Emmanuel fled from being left to think in solitude, and I guessed that some obsession haunted him.

And so it was that he was always occupied, sometimes even occupied in searching for occupations. He wrote very little on his own, so that he scarcely left us anything in writing, even notes; on the other hand, he acted as scrivener for everyone else, especially mothers, for whom he composed letters to their absent sons.

He also worked with his hands, pitching in to help with some of the village tasks. At threshing time he reported to the threshing floor to flail and winnow, meanwhile teaching and entertaining the workers by turn. Sometimes he took the place of a worker who had fallen sick. One day in the dead of winter he came upon a child, shivering with the bitter cold. The child's father had sent him into the woods to bring back a strayed calf.

"Listen," he said to the child, "you go home and get warm, and tell your father that I am bringing back the calf." On the way back with the animal he ran into the

father, who had come out to meet him, thoroughly
ashamed of himself.

In winter he chopped wood for the poor. When a certain magnificent walnut tree died—"that matriarchal walnut," he called it, a tree under whose shade he had played
as a boy and whose fruit he had eaten for so many years
—he asked for the trunk, carried it to his house and, after
he had cut six planks from it, which he put away at the
foot of his bed, he made firewood of the rest to warm the
poor. He also was in the habit of making handballs for
the boys and a goodly number of toys for the younger
children.

Often he used to accompany the doctor on his rounds,
adding his presence and prestige to the doctor's prescrip-
tions. Most of all he was interested in maternity cases and
the care of children; it was his opinion that the old wives'
sayings "from the cradle to heaven" and the other one
about "little angels belong in heaven" were nothing short
of blasphemy.[1] The death of a child moved him deeply.

"A child stillborn," I once heard him say, "or one who
dies soon after birth, is the most terrible of mysteries to
me. It's as if it were a suicide. Or as if the child were
crucified."

And once, when a man had taken his own life and the
father of the suicide, an outsider, asked Don Emmanuel if
his son could be buried in consecrated ground, the priest
answered:

"Most certainly, for at the last moment, in the very last
throes, he must certainly have repented. There is no doubt
of it whatsoever in my mind."

From time to time he would visit the local school to
help the teacher, to teach alongside him—and not only the
catechism. The simple truth was that he fled relentlessly
from idleness and from solitude. He went so far in this
desire of his to mingle with the villagers, especially the
youth and the children, that he even attended the village
dances. And more than once he played the drum to keep
time for the young men and women dancing; this kind of
activity, which in another priest would have seemed like a
grotesque mockery of his calling, in him somehow took on
the appearance of a holy and religious exercise. When the

---

[1] "Teta y gloria" and "angelitos al cielo."

Angelus would ring out, he would put down the drum and sticks, take off his hat (all the others doing the same) and pray: "The angel of the Lord declared unto Mary: Hail Mary . . ." And afterwards: "Now, let us rest until tomorrow."

"First of all," he would say, "the village must be happy; everyone must be happy to be alive. To be satisfied with life is of first importance. No one should want to die until it is God's will."

"I want to die now," a recently widowed woman once told him, "I want to be with my husband . . ."

"And why now?" he asked. "Stay here and pray God for his soul."

One of his well-loved remarks was made at a wedding: "Ah, if I could only change all the water in our lake into wine, into a dear little wine which, no matter how much of it one drank, would always make one joyful without intoxicating . . . or, if intoxicating, would make one joyfully drunk."

Once upon a time a band of poor acrobats came through the village. The leader—who arrived on the scene with a gravely ill and pregnant wife and three sons to help him—played the clown. While he was in the village square making all the children, and even some of the adults, laugh with glee, his wife suddenly fell desperately ill and had to leave; she went off accompanied by a look of anguish from the clown and a howl of laughter from the children. Don Emmanuel hurried after, and, a little later, in a corner of the inn's stable, he helped her give up her soul in a state of grace. When the performance was over and the villagers and the clown learned of the tragedy, they came to the inn, and there the poor bereaved clown, in a voice choked with tears, told Don Emmanuel, as he took his hand and kissed it: "They are quite right, Father, when they say you are a saint." Don Emmanuel took the clown's hand in his and replied before everyone:

"It's you who are the saint, good clown. I watched you at your work and understood that you do it not only to provide bread for your children, but also to give joy to the children of others. And I tell you now that your wife, the mother of your children, whom I sent to God while you worked to give joy, is at rest in the Lord, and that you will join her there, and that the angels, whom you will make laugh with happiness in heaven, will reward you with their laughter."

And everyone present wept, children and elders alike, as much from sorrow as from a mysterious joy in which all sorrow was drowned. Later, recalling that solemn hour, I have come to realize that the imperturbable joyousness of Don Emmanuel was merely the temporal, earthly form of an infinite, eternal sadness which the priest concealed from the eyes and ears of the world with heroic saintliness.

His constant activity, his ceaseless intervention in the tasks and diversions of everyone, had the appearance, in short, of a flight from himself, of a flight from solitude. He confirmed this suspicion: "I have a fear of solitude," he would say. And still, from time to time he would go off by himself, along the shores of the lake, to the ruins of the abbey where the souls of pious Cistercians seem still to repose, although history has long since buried them in oblivion. There, the cell of the so-called Father-Captain can still be found, and it is said that the drops of blood spattered on the walls as he flagellated himself can still be seen. What thoughts occupied our Don Emmanuel as he walked there? I remember a conversation we held once in which I asked him, as he was speaking of the abbey, why it had never occurred to him to enter a monastery, and he answered me:

"It is not at all because of the fact that my sister is a widow and I have her children and herself to support—for God looks after the poor—but rather because I simply was not born to be a hermit, an anchorite; the solitude would crush my soul; and, as far as a monastery is concerned, my monastery is Valverde de Lucerna. I was not meant to live alone, or die alone. I was meant to live for my village, and die for it too. How should I save my soul if I were not to save the soul of my village as well?"

"But there have been saints who were hermits, solitaries . . ." I said.

"Yes, the Lord gave them the grace of solitude which He has denied me, and I must resign myself. I must not throw away my village to win my soul. God made me that way. I would not be able to resist the temptations of the desert. I would not be able, alone, to carry the cross of birth . . ."

I have summoned up all these recollections, from which
my faith was fed, in order to portray our Don Emmanuel
as he was when I, a young girl of sixteen, returned from
the convent of Renada to our "monastery of Valverde de
Lucerna," once more to kneel at the feet of our "abbot."

"Well, here is the daughter of Simona," he said as soon
as he saw me, "made into a young woman, and knowing
French, and how to play the piano, and embroider, and
heaven knows what else besides! Now you must get ready
to give us a family. And your brother Lazarus; when does
he return? Is he still in the New World?"

"Yes, Father, he is still in the New World."

"The New World! And we in the Old. Well then, when
you write him, tell him for me, on behalf of the parish
priest, that I should like to know when he is returning
from the New World to the Old, to bring us the latest
from over there. And tell him that he will find the lake
and the mountain as he left them."

When I first went to him for confession, I became so
confused that I could not enunciate a word. I recited the
"Forgive me, Father, for I have sinned," in a stammer,
almost a sob. And he, observing this, said:

"Good heavens, my dear, what are you afraid of, or of
whom are you afraid? Certainly you're not trembling now
under the weight of your sins, nor in fear of God. No,
you're trembling because of me, isn't that so?"

At this point I burst into tears.

"What have they been telling you about me? What fairy
tales? Was it your mother, perhaps? Come, come, please
be calm; you must imagine you are talking to your
brother . . ."

At this I plucked up courage and began to tell him of
my anxieties, doubts and sorrows.

"Bah! Where did you read all this, Miss Intellectual. All
this is literary nonsense. Don't succumb to everything you
read just yet, not even to Saint Theresa. If you need to
amuse yourself, read the *Bertoldo*, as your father before
you did."

I came away from my first confession to that holy man
deeply consoled. The initial fear—simple fright more than
respect—with which I had approached him, turned into a
profound pity. I was at that time a very young woman,
almost a girl still; and yet, I was beginning to be a woman,

in my innermost being I felt the juice and stirrings of maternity, and when I found myself in the confessional at the side of the saintly priest, I sensed a kind of unspoken confession on his part in the soft murmur of his voice. And I remembered how when he had intoned in the church the words of Jesus Christ: "My God, my God, why hast Thou forsaken me?" his own mother had cried out in the congregation: "My son!"; and I could hear the cry that had rent the silence of the temple. And I went to him again for confession—and to comfort him.

Another time in the confessional I told him of a doubt which assailed me, and he responded:

"As to that, you know what the catechism says. Don't question me about it, for I am ignorant; in Holy Mother Church there are learned doctors of theology who will know how to answer you."

"But you are the learned doctor here."

"Me? A learned doctor? Not even in thought! I, my little doctress, am only a poor country priest. And those questions, . . . do you know who whispers them into your ear? Well . . . the Devil does!"

Then, making bold, I asked him point-blank:

"And suppose he were to whisper these questions to you?"

"Who? To me? The Devil? No, we don't even know each other, my daughter, we haven't met at all."

"But if he did whisper them? . . ."

"I wouldn't pay any attention. And that's enough of that; let's get on, for there are some people, really sick people, waiting for me."

I went away thinking, I don't know why, that our Don Emmanuel, so famous for curing the bedeviled, didn't really even believe in the Devil. As I started home, I ran into the fool Blasillo, who had probably been hovering around outside; as soon as he saw me, and by way of treating me to a display of his virtuosity, he began the business of repeating—and in what a manner!—"My God, my God, why hast Thou forsaken me?" I arrived home utterly saddened and locked myself in my room to cry, until finally my mother arrived.

"With all these confessions, Angelita, you will end by going off to a nunnery."

"Don't worry, Mother," I answered her. "I have plenty to do here, in the village, and it will be my only convent."

"Until you marry."

"I don't intend to," I rejoined.

The next time I saw Don Emmanuel I asked him, looking straight into his eyes:

"Is there really a Hell, Don Emmanuel?"

And he, without altering his expression, answered:

"For you, my daughter, no."

"For others, then?"

"Does it matter to you, if you are not to go there?"

"It matters for the others, in any case. Is there a Hell?"

"Believe in Heaven, the Heaven we can see. Look at it there"—and he pointed to the heavens above the mountain, and then down into the lake, to the reflection.

"But we are supposed to believe in Hell as well as in Heaven," I said.

"That's true. We must believe everything believed and taught by our Holy Mother Church, Catholic, Apostolic, and Roman. And now, that will do!"

I thought I read a deep unknown sadness in his eyes, eyes which were as blue as the waters of the lake.

Those years passed as if in a dream. Within me, a reflected image of Don Emmanuel was unconsciously taking form. He was an ordinary enough man in many ways, of such daily use as the daily bread we asked for in our Paternoster. I helped him whenever I could with his tasks, visiting the sick, his sick, the girls at school, and helping, too, with the church linen and the vestments; I served in the role, as he said, of his deaconess. Once I was invited to the city for a few days by a school friend, but I had to hurry home, for the city stifled me—something was missing, I was thirsty for a sight of the waters of the lake, hungry for a sight of the peaks of the mountain; and even more, I missed my Don Emmanuel, as if his absence called to me, as if he were endangered by my being so far away, as if he were in need of me. I began to feel a kind of maternal affection for my spiritual father; I longed to help him bear the cross of birth.

My twenty-fourth birthday was approaching when my brother Lazarus came back from America with the small fortune he had saved up. He came back to Valverde de

Lucerna with the intention of taking me and my mother to live in a city, perhaps even Madrid.

"In the country," he said, "in these villages, a person becomes stupefied, brutalized and spiritually impoverished." And he added: "Civilization is the very opposite of everything countryfied. The idiocy of village life! No, that's not for us; I didn't have you sent away to school so that later you might spoil here, among these ignorant peasants."

I said nothing, though I was disposed to resist emigration. But our mother, already past sixty, took a firm stand from the start: "Change pastures at my age?" she demanded at once. A little later she made it quite clear that she could not live out of sight of her lake, her mountain, and, above all, of her Don Emmanuel.

"The two of you are like those cats that get attached to houses," my brother muttered.

When he realized the complete sway exercised over the entire village—especially over my mother and myself—by the saintly priest, my brother began to resent him. He saw in this situation an example of the obscurantist theocracy which, according to him, smothered Spain. And he commenced to spout the old anti-clerical commonplaces, to which he added anti-religious and "progressive" propaganda brought back from the New World.

"In the Spain of sloth and flabby useless men, the priests manipulate the women, and the women manipulate the men. Not to mention the idiocy of the country, and this feudal backwater!"

"Feudal," to him, meant something frightful. "Feudal" and "medieval" were the epithets he employed to condemn something completely.

The failure of his diatribes to move us and their total lack of effect upon the village—where they were listened to with respectful indifference—disconcerted him no end. "The man does not exist who could move these clods." But, he soon began to understand—for he was an intelligent man, and therefore a good one—the kind of influence exercised over the village by Don Emmanuel, and he came to appreciate the effect of the priest's work in the village.

"This priest is not like the others," he announced. "He is, in fact, a saint."

"How do you know what the others are like," I asked.
To which he answered:

"I can imagine."

In any case, he did not set foot inside the church nor
did he miss an opportunity to parade his incredulity—
though he always exempted Don Emmanuel from his
scorning accusations. In the village, an unconscious expect-
ancy began to build up, the anticipation of a kind of duel
between my brother Lazarus and Don Emmanuel—in
short, it was expected that Don Emmanuel would convert
my brother. No one doubted but that in the end the priest
would bring him into the fold. On his side, Lazarus was
eager (he told me so himself, later) to go and hear Don
Emmanuel, to see and hear him in the church, to get to
know him and to talk with him, so that he might learn
the secret of his spiritual hold over our souls. And he let
himself be coaxed to this end, so that finally—"out of
curiosity," as he said—he went to hear the preacher.

"Now, this is something else again," he told me as soon
as he came from hearing Don Emmanuel for the first time.
"He's not like the others; still, he doesn't fool me, he's too
intelligent to believe everything he must teach."

"You mean you think he's a hypocrite?"

"A hypocrite . . . no! But he has a job by which he must
live."

As for me, my brother undertook to see that I read the
books he brought me, and others which he urged me to
buy.

"So your brother Lazarus wants you to read," Don
Emmanuel queried. "Well, read, my daughter, read and
make him happy by doing so. I know you will read only
worthy books. Read even if only novels; they are as good
as the books which deal with so-called 'reality.' You are
better off reading than concerning yourself with village
gossip and old wives' tales. Above all, though, you will do
well to read devotional books which will bring you contentment in life, a quiet, gentle contentment, and peace."

And he, did he enjoy such contentment?

It was about this time that our mother fell mortally
sick and died. In her last days her one wish was that Don
Emmanuel should convert Lazarus, whom she expected to
see again in heaven, in some little corner among the stars

from where they could see the lake and the mountain of Valverde de Lucerna. She felt she was going there now, to see God.

"You are not going anywhere," Don Emmanuel would tell her; "you are staying right here. Your body will remain here, in this land, and your soul also, in this house, watching and listening to your children though they do not see or hear you."

"But, Father," she said, "I am going to see God."

"God, my daughter, is all around us, and you will see Him from here, right from here. And all of us in Him, and He in all of us."

"God bless you," I whispered to him.

"The peace in which your mother dies will be her eternal life," he told me.

And, turning to my brother Lazarus: "Her heaven is to go on seeing you, and it is at this moment that she must be saved. Tell her you will pray for her."

"But—"

"But what? . . . Tell her you will pray for her, to whom you owe your life. And I know that once you promise her, you *will* pray, and I know that once you pray . . ."

My brother, his eyes filled with tears, drew near our dying mother and gave her his solemn promise to pray for her.

"And I, in heaven, will pray for you, for all of you," my mother responded. And then, kissing the crucifix and fixing her eyes on Don Emmanuel, she gave up her soul to God.

"Into Thy hands I commend my spirit," prayed the priest.

My brother and I stayed on in the house alone. What had happened at the time of my mother's death had established a bond between Lazarus and Don Emmanuel. The latter seemed even to neglect some of his charges, his patients and his other needy to look after my brother. In the afternoons, they would go for a stroll together, walking along the lake or toward the ruins, overgrown with ivy, of the old Cistercian abbey.

"He's an extraordinary man," Lazarus told me. "You know the story they tell of how there is a city at the bottom of the lake, submerged beneath the water, and that on

Midsummer's Night at midnight the sound of its church
bells can be heard . . ."

"Yes, a city 'feudal and medieval' . . ."

"And I believe," he went on, "that at the bottom of Don
Emmanuel's soul there is a city, submerged and inun-
dated, and that sometimes the sound of its bells can be
heard . . ."

"Yes . . . And this city submerged in Don Emmanuel's
soul, and perhaps—why not?—in yours as well, is certainly the cemetery of the souls of our ancestors, the
ancestors of our Valverde de Lucerna . . . 'feudal and
medieval'!"

In the end, my brother began going to Mass. He went
regularly to hear Don Emmanuel. When it became known
that he was prepared to comply with his annual duty of
receiving Communion, that he would receive when the
others received, an intimate joy ran through the town,
which felt that by this act he was restored to his people.
The rejoicing was of such nature, moreover, so open-
handed and honest, that Lazarus never did feel that he
had been "vanquished" or "overcome."

The day of his Communion arrived; of Communion
before the entire village, with the entire village. When it
came time for my brother's turn, I saw Don Emmanuel—
white as January snow on the mountain, and moving like
the surface of the lake when it is stirred by the northeast
wind—come up to him with the holy wafer in his hand,
which trembled violently as it reached out to Lazarus's
mouth; at that moment the priest had an instant of faint-
ness and the wafer dropped to the ground. My brother
himself recovered it and placed it in his mouth. The people
saw the tears on Don Emmanuel's face, and everyone
wept, saying: "What great love he bears!" And then, because it was dawn, a cock crowed.

On returning home I locked myself in with my brother;
alone with him I put my arms around his neck and kissed
him.

"Lazarus, Lazarus, what joy you have given us all today;
the entire village, the living and the dead, and especially
our mother. Did you see how Don Emmanuel wept for
joy? What joy you have given us all!"

"It was for that reason that I did what I did," he answered me.

"For what? To give us pleasure? Surely you did it for your own sake, first of all; because of your conversion."

And then Lazarus, my brother, grown as pale and tremulous as Don Emmanuel when he was giving Communion, bade me sit down, in the very chair where our mother used to sit. He took a deep breath, and, in the intimate tone of a familiar and domestic confession, he told me:

"Angelita, the time has come when I must tell you the truth, the absolute truth, and I shall tell you because I must, because I cannot, I ought not, conceal it from you, and because, sooner or later, you are bound to intuit it anyway, if only halfway—which would be worse."

Thereupon, serenely and tranquilly, in a subdued voice, he recounted a tale that drowned me in a lake of sorrow. He told how Don Emmanuel had appealed to him, particularly during the walks to the ruins of the old Cistercian abbey, to set a good example, to avoid scandalizing the townspeople, to take part in the religious life of the community, to feign belief even if he did not feel any, to conceal his own ideas—all this without attempting in any way to catechize him, to instruct him in religion, or to effect a true conversion.

"But it is possible?" I asked in consternation.

"Possible and true. When I said to him: 'Is this you, the priest, who suggests I dissimulate?' he replied, hesitatingly: 'Dissimulate? Not at all! That is not dissimulation. "Dip your fingers in holy water, and you will end by believing," as someone said.' And I, gazing into his eyes, asked him: 'And you, celebrating the Mass, have you ended by believing?' He looked away and stared out at the lake, until his eyes filled with tears. And it was in this way that I came to understand his secret."

"Lazarus!" I cried out, incapable of another word.

At that moment the fool Blasillo came along our street, crying out his: "My God, my God, why hast Thou forsaken me?" And Lazarus shuddered, as if he had heard the voice of Don Emmanuel, or of Christ.

"It was then," my brother at length continued, "that I really understood his motives and his saintliness; for a saint he is, Sister, a true saint. In trying to convert me to his holy cause—for it is a holy cause, a most holy cause —he was not attempting to score a triumph, but rather was doing it to protect the peace, the happiness, the illusions, perhaps, of his charges. I understood that if he thus deceives them—if it *is* deceit—it is not for his own advantage. I submitted to his logic,—and that was my conversion.

"I shall never forget the day on which I said to him: 'But, Don Emmanuel, the truth, the truth, above all!'; and he, all a-tremble, whispered in my ear—though we were all alone in the middle of the countryside—'The truth? The truth, Lazarus, is perhaps something so unbearable, so terrible, something so deadly, that simple people could not live with it!'

" 'And why do you show me a glimpse of it now, here, as if we were in the confessional?' I asked. And he said: 'Because if I did not, I would be so tormented by it, so tormented, that I would finally shout it in the middle of the plaza, which I must never, never, never do . . . I am put here to give life to the souls of my charges, to make them happy, to make them dream they are immortal—and not to destroy them. The important thing is that they live sanely, in concord with each other,—and with the truth, with my truth, they could not live at all. Let them live. That is what the Church does, it lets them live. As for true religion, all religions are true as long as they give spiritual life to the people who profess them, as long as they console them for having been born only to die. And for each people the truest religion is their own, the religion that made them . . . And mine? Mine consists in consoling myself by consoling others, even though the consolation I give them is not ever mine.' I shall never forget his words."

"But then this Communion of yours has been a sacrilege," I dared interrupt, regretting my words as soon as I said them.

"Sacrilege? What about the priest who gave it to me? And his Masses?"

"What martyrdom!" I exclaimed.

"And now," said my brother, "there is one more person to console the people."

"To deceive them, you mean?" I said.

"Not at all," he replied, "but rather to confirm them in their faith."

"And they, the people, do they really believe, do you think?"

"About that, I know nothing! . . . They probably believe without trying, from force of habit, tradition. The important thing is not to stir them up. To let them live from their thin sentiments, without acquiring the torments of luxury. Blessed are the poor in spirit!"

"That then is the sentiment you have learned from Don Emmanuel. . . . And tell me, do you feel you have carried out your promise to our mother on her deathbed, when you promised to pray for her?"

"Do you think I *could* fail her? What do you take me for, sister? Do you think I would go back on my word, my solemn promise made at the hour of death to a mother?"

"I don't know. . . . You might have wanted to deceive her so she could die in peace."

"The fact is, though, that if I had not lived up to my promise, I would be totally miserable."

"And . . ."

"I carried out my promise and I have not neglected for a single day to pray for her."

"Only for her?"

"Well, now, for whom else?"

"For yourself! And now, for Don Emmanuel."

We parted and went to our separate rooms, I to weep through the night, praying for the conversion of my brother and of Don Emmanuel. And Lazarus, to what purpose, I know not.

From that day on I was fearful of finding myself alone with Don Emmanuel, whom I continued to aid in his pious works. And he seemed to sense my inner state and to guess at its cause. When at last I came to him in the confessional's penitential tribunal (who was the judge, and who the offender?) the two of us, he and I, bowed our heads in silence and began to cry. It was he, finally, Don Emmanuel, who broke the terrible silence, with a voice which seemed to issue from the tomb:

"Angelita, you have the same faith you had when you were ten, don't you? You believe, don't you?"

"I believe, Father."

"Then go on believing. And if doubts come to torment you, suppress them utterly, even to yourself. The main thing is to live . . ."

I summoned up courage, and dared to ask, trembling:

"But, Father, do you believe?"

For a brief moment he hesitated, and then, mastering himself, he said:

"I believe!"

"In what, Father, in what? Do you believe in the after life? Do you believe that in dying we do not die in every way, completely? Do you believe that we will see each other again, that we will love each other in a world to come? Do you believe in another life?"

The poor saint was sobbing.

"My child, leave off, leave off!"

Now, when I come to write this memoir, I ask myself: Why did he not deceive me? Why did he not deceive me as he deceived the others? Why did he afflict himself? Why could he not deceive himself, or why could he not deceive me? And I want to believe that he was afflicted because he could not deceive himself into deceiving me.

"And now," he said, "pray for me, for your brother, and for yourself—for all of us. We must go on living. And giving life."

And, after a pause:

"Angelita, why don't you marry?"

"You know why I do not."

"No, no; you must marry. Lazarus and I will find you a suitor. For it would be good for you to marry, and rid yourself of these obsessions."

"Obsessions, Don Emmanuel?"

"I know well enough what I am saying. You should not torment yourself for the sake of others, for each of us has more than enough to do answering for himself."

"That it should be you, Don Emmanuel, who says this! That you should advise me to marry and answer for myself alone and not suffer over others! That it should be you!"

"Yes, you are right, Angelita. I am no longer sure of what I say. I am no longer sure of what I say since I began to confess to you. Only, one must go on living. Yes! One must live!"

And when I rose to leave the church, he asked me:

"Now, Angelita, in the name of the people, do you absolve me?"

I felt pierced by a mysterious and priestly prompting and said:

"In the name of the Father, the Son and the Holy Ghost, I absolve you, Father."

We quitted the church, and as I went out I felt the quickening of maternity within me.

My brother, now totally devoted to the work of Don Emmanuel, had become his closest and most zealous collaborator and companion. They were bound together, moreover, by their common secret. Lazarus accompanied the priest on his visits to the sick, and to schools, and he placed his resources at the disposition of the saintly man. A little more zeal, and he would have learned to help celebrate Mass. All the while he was sounding deeper in the unfathomable soul of the priest.

"What manliness!" he exclaimed to me once. "Yesterday, as we walked along the lake he said: 'There lies my direst temptation.' When I interrogated him with my eyes, he went on: 'My poor father, who was close to ninety when he died, was tormented all his life, as he confessed to me himself, by a temptation to suicide, by an instinct to self-destruction which had come to him from a time before memory—from birth, from his *nation*, as he said—and was forced to fight against it always. And this fight grew to be his life. So as not to succumb to this temptation he was forced to take precautions, to guard his life. He told me of terrible episodes. His urge was a form of madness, —and I have inherited it. How that water beckons me in its deep quiet! . . . an apparent quietude reflecting the sky like a mirror—and beneath it the hidden current! My life, Lazarus, is a kind of continual suicide, or a struggle against suicide, which is the same thing. . . . Just so long as our people go on living!' And then he added: 'Here the river eddies to form a lake, so that later, flowing down the plateau, it may form into cascades, waterfalls, and torrents, hurling itself through gorges and chasms. Thus does life eddy in the village; and the temptation to suicide is the greater beside the still waters which at night reflect the stars, than it is beside the crashing falls which drive one back in fear. Listen, Lazarus, I have helped poor villagers to die well, ignorant, illiterate villagers, who had scarcely ever been out of their village, and I have learned from their own lips, or divined it when they were silent, the real cause of their sickness unto death, and there at the head of their deathbed I have been able to see into the black abyss of their life-weariness. A weariness a thousand times worse than hunger! For our part, Lazarus, let us go on with our kind of suicide of working for the people, and let them dream their life as the lake dreams the heavens.'

"Another time," said my brother, "as we were coming back, we spied a country girl, a goatherd, standing erect on a height of the mountain slope overlooking the lake and she was singing in a voice fresher than its waters. Don Emmanuel took hold of me, and pointing to her said: 'Look, it's as though time had stopped, as though this country girl had always been there just as she is, singing in the way she is, and as though she would always be there, as she was before my consciousness began, as she will be when it is past. That girl is a part of nature—not of history—along with the rocks, the clouds, the trees, and the waters.' He has such a subtle feeling for nature, he infuses it with spirit!

"I shall not forget the day when snow was falling and he asked me: 'Have you ever seen a greater mystery, Lazarus, than the snow falling, and dying, in the lake, while a hood is laid upon the mountain?' "

Don Emmanuel had to moderate and temper my brother's zeal and his neophyte's rawness. As soon as he heard that Lazarus was going about inveighing against some of the popular superstitions he told him forcefully:

"Leave them alone! It's difficult enough making them understand where orthodox belief leaves off and where superstition begins. It's hard enough, especially for us. Leave them alone, then, as long as they get some comfort. . . . It's better for them to believe everything, even things that contradict one another, than to believe nothing. The idea that someone who believes too much ends by not believing in anything is a Protestant notion. Let us not protest! Protestation destroys contentment and peace."

My brother told me, too, about one moonlit night when they were returning to town along the lake (whose surface a mountain breeze was stirring, so that the moonbeams topped the whitecaps), Don Emmanuel turned to him and said:

"Look, the water is reciting the litany and saying: *ianua caeli, ora pro nobis;* gate of heaven, pray for us."

Two evanescent tears fell from his lashes to the grass, where the light of the full moon shone upon them like dew.

And time went hurrying by, and my brother and I began to notice that Don Emmanuel's spirits were failing, that he could no longer control completely the deep rooted sadness which consumed him; perhaps some treacherous illness was undermining his body and soul. In an effort to rouse his interest, Lazarus spoke to him of the good effect the organization of a type of Catholic agrarian syndicate would have.

"A syndicate?" Don Emmanuel repeated sadly. "A syndicate? And what is that? The Church is the only syndicate I know. And you have certainly heard 'My kingdom is not of this world.' Our kingdom, Lazarus, is not of this world . . ."

"And of the other?"

Don Emmanuel bowed his head:

"The other is here. Two kingdoms exist in this world. Or rather, the other world. . . . Ah, I don't really know what I'm saying. But as for the syndicate, that's a vestige from your days of 'progressivism.' No, Lazarus, no; religion does not exist to resolve the economic or political conflicts of this world, which God handed over to men for their disputes. Let men think and act as they will, let them console themselves for having been born, let them live as happily as possible in the illusion that all this has a purpose. I don't propose to advise the poor to submit to the rich, nor to suggest to the rich that they subordinate themselves to the poor; but rather to preach resignation in everyone, and charity toward everyone. For even the rich man must resign himself—to his riches, and to life; and the poor man must show charity—even to the rich. The Social Question? Ignore it, for it is none of our business. So, a new society is on the way, in which there will be neither rich nor poor, in which wealth will be justly divided, in which everything will belong to everyone—and so, what then? Won't this general well-being and comfort lead to even greater tedium and weariness of life? I know well enough that one of those chiefs of what they call the Social Revolution has already said that religion is the opium of the people. Opium . . . Opium . . . Yes, opium it is. We should give them opium, and help them sleep, and dream. I, myself, with my mad activity, give myself opium. And still I don't manage to sleep well, let alone dream well. . . . What a fearful nightmare! . . . I, too, can say, with the Divine Master: 'My soul is weary unto death.' No, Lazarus, no; no syndicates for us. If *they* organize them, well and good—they would be distracting themselves in that way. Let them play at syndicates, if that makes them happy."

The entire village began to realize that Don Emmanuel's spirit was weakening, that his strength was waning. His very voice—that miracle of a voice—acquired a kind of quaking. Tears came into his eyes for any reason whatever—or for no reason. Whenever he spoke to people about the other world, about the other life, he was compelled to pause at frequent intervals, and he would close his eyes. "It is a vision," people would say, "he has a vision of what lies ahead." At such moments the fool Blasillo was the first to break into tears. He wept copiously these days, crying now more than he laughed, and even his laughter had the sound of tears.

The last Easter Week which Don Emmanuel was to celebrate among us, in this world, in this village of ours, arrived, and all the village sensed the impending end of tragedy. And how the words did strike home when for the last time Don Emmanuel cried out before us: "My God, my God, why hast Thou forsaken me?"! And when he repeated the words of the Lord to the Good Thief ("All thieves are good," Don Emmanuel used to tell us): "Tomorrow shalt thou be with me in Paradise." . . . ! And then, the last general Communion which our saint was to give! When he came to my brother to give him the Host—his hand steady this time—, just after the liturgical ". . . *in vitam aeternam*," he bent down and whispered to him: "There is no other life but this, no life more eternal . . . let them dream it eternal . . . let it be eternal for a few years . . ."

And when he came to me he said: "Pray, my child, pray for us all." And then, something so extraordinary happened that I carry it now in my heart as the greatest of mysteries: he bent over and said, in a voice which seemed to belong to the other world: ". . . and pray, too, for our Lord Jesus Christ."

I stood up, going weak as I did so, like a somnambulist. Everything around me seemed dream-like. And I thought: "Am I to pray, too, for the lake and the mountain?" And next: "Am I bewitched, then?" Home at last, I took up the crucifix my mother had held in her hands when she had given up her soul to God, and, gazing at it through my tears and recalling the "My God, my God, why hast Thou forsaken me?" of our two Christs, the one of this earth and the other of this village, I prayed: "Thy will be done on earth as it is in heaven," and then, "And lead us not into temptation. Amen." After this I turned to the statue of the Mater Dolorosa—her heart transfixed by seven swords— which had been my poor mother's most sorrowful comfort, and I prayed again: "Holy Mary, Mother of God, pray for us sinners, now and in the hour of our death. Amen." I had scarcely finished the prayer, when I asked myself: "Sinners? Sinners are we? And what is our sin, what is it?" And all day I brooded over the question.

The next day I presented myself before Don Emmanuel —Don Emmanuel now in the full sunset of his magnificent religiosity—and I said to him:

"Do you remember, my Father, years ago when I asked you a certain question you answered: 'That question you must not ask me; for I am ignorant; there are learned doctors of the Holy Mother Church who will know how to answer you'?"

"Do I remember? . . . Of course. And I remember I told you those were questions put to you by the Devil."

"Well, then, Father, I have come again, bedeviled, to ask you another question put to me by my Guardian Devil."

"Ask it."

"Yesterday, when you gave me Communion, you asked me to pray for all of us, and even for . . ."

"That's enough! . . . Go on."

"I arrived home and began to pray; when I came to the part 'Pray for us sinners, now and at the hour of our death,' a voice in me asked: 'Sinners? Sinners are we? And what is our sin?' What is our sin, Father?"

"Our sin?" he replied. "A great doctor of the Spanish Catholic Apostolic Church has already explained it; the great doctor of *Life Is a Dream* has written 'The greatest sin of man is to have been born.' That, my child, is our sin; to have been born."

"Can it be atoned, Father?"

"Go and pray again. Pray once more for us sinners, now and at the hour of our death. . . . Yes, at length the dream is atoned . . . at length life is atoned . . . at length the cross of birth is expiated and atoned, and the drama comes to an end. . . . And as Calderón said, to have done good, to have feigned good, even in dreams, is something which is not lost."

The hour of his death arrived at last. The entire village saw it come. And he made it his finest lesson. For he would not die alone or at rest. He died preaching to his people in the church. But first, before being carried to the church (his paralysis made it impossible for him to move), he summoned Lazarus and me to his bedside. Alone there, the three of us together, he said:

"Listen to me: watch over these poor sheep; find some comfort for them in living, and let them believe what I could not. And Lazarus, when your hour comes, die as I die, as Angela will die, in the arms of the Holy Mother Church, Catholic, Apostolic, and Roman; that is to say, of the Holy Mother Church of Valverde de Lucerna. And now, farewell; until we never meet again, for this dream of life is coming to an end . . ."

"Father, Father," I cried out.

"Do not grieve, Angela, only go on praying for all sinners, for all who have been born. Let them dream, let them dream . . . O, what a longing I have to sleep, to sleep, sleep without end, sleep for all eternity, and never dream! Forgetting this dream! . . . When they go to bury me, let it be in a box made from the six planks I cut from the old walnut tree—poor old tree!—in whose shade I played as a child, when I began the dream. . . . In those days, I did really believe in life everlasting. That is to say, it seems to me now that I believed. For a child, to believe is the same as to dream. And for a people, too. . . . You'll find those six planks I cut at the foot of the bed."

He was seized by a sudden fit of choking, and then, composing himself once more, he went on:

"You will recall that when we prayed together, animated by a common sentiment, a community of spirit, and we came to the final verse of the Creed, you will remember that I would fall silent. . . . When the Israelites were coming to the end of their wandering in the desert, the Lord told Aaron and Moses that because they had not believed in Him they would not set foot in the Promised Land with their people; and he bade them climb the heights of Mount Hor, where Moses ordered Aaron stripped of his garments, so that Aaron died there, and then Moses went up from the plains of Moab to Mount Nebo, to the top of Pisgah, looking into Jericho, and the Lord showed him all of the land promised to His people, but said to him: 'You will not go there.' And there Moses died, and no one knew his grave. And he left Joshua to be chief in his place. You, Lazarus, must be my Joshua, and if you can make the sun stand still, make it stop, and never mind progress. Like Moses, I have seen the face of God—our supreme dream—face to face, and as you already know, and as the Scripture says, he who sees God's face, he who sees the eyes of the dream, the eyes with which He looks at us, will die inexorably and forever. And therefore, do not let our people, so long as they live, look into the face of God. Once dead, it will no longer matter, for then they will see nothing . . ."

"Father, Father, Father," I cried again.

And he said:

"Angela, you must pray always, so that all sinners may go on dreaming, until they die, of the resurrection of the flesh and the life everlasting . . ."

I was expecting "and who knows it might be . . ." But instead, Don Emmanuel had another attack of coughing.

"And now," he finally went on, "and now, in the hour of my death, it is high time to have me brought, in this very chair, to the church, so that I may take leave there of my people, who await me."

He was carried to the church and brought, in his armchair, into the chancel, to the foot of the altar. In his hands he held a crucifix. My brother and I stood close to him, but the fool Blasillo wanted to stand even closer. He wanted to grasp Don Emmanuel by the hand, so that he could kiss it. When some of the people nearby tried to stop him, Don Emmanuel rebuked them and said:

"Let him come closer. . . . Come, Blasillo, give me your hand."

The fool cried for joy. And then Don Emmanuel spoke:

"I have very few words left, my children; I scarcely feel I have strength enough left to die. And then, I have nothing new to tell you, either. I have already said everything I have to say. Live with each other in peace and contentment, in the hope that we will all see each other again some day, in that other Valverde de Lucerna up there among the nighttime stars, the stars which the lake reflects over the image of the reflected mountain. And pray, pray to the Most Blessed Mary, and to our Lord. Be good . . . that is enough. Forgive me whatever wrong I may have done you inadvertently or unknowingly. After I give you my blessing, let us pray together, let us say the Paternoster, the Ave Maria, the Salve, and the Creed."

Then he gave his blessing to the whole village, with the crucifix held in his hand, while the women and children cried and even some of the men wept softly. Almost at once the prayers were begun. Don Emmanuel listened to them in silence, his hand in the hand of Blasillo the fool, who began to fall asleep to the sound of the praying. First the Paternoster, with its "Thy will be done on earth as it is in heaven"; then the Ave Maria, with its "Pray for us sinners, now and in the hour of our death"; followed by the Salve, with its "mourning and weeping in this vale of tears"; and finally, the Creed. On reaching "The resurrection of the flesh and life everlasting" the people sensed that their saint had yielded up his soul to God. It was not necessary to close his eyes even, for he died with them closed. When an attempt was made to wake Blasillo, it was found that he, too, had fallen asleep in the Lord forever. So that later there were two bodies to be buried.

The village immediately repaired en masse to the house of the saint to carry away holy relics, to divide up pieces of his garments among themselves, to carry off whatever they could find as a memento of the blessed martyr. My brother preserved his breviary, between the pages of which he discovered a carnation, dried as in a herbarium and mounted on a piece of paper, and upon the paper a cross and a certain date.

* * *

No one in the village seemed able to believe that Don Emmanuel was dead; everyone expected to see him—perhaps some of them did—taking his daily walk along the side of the lake, his figure mirrored in the water, or silhouetted against the background of the mountain. They continued to hear his voice, and they all visited his grave, around which a veritable cult sprang up, old women "possessed by devils" came to touch the cross of walnut, made with his own hands from the tree which had yielded the six planks of his casket.

The ones who least of all believed in his death were my brother and I. Lazarus carried on the tradition of the saint, and he began to compile a record of the priest's words. Some of the conversations in this account of mine were made possible by his notes.

"It was he," said my brother, "who made me into a new man. I was a true Lazarus whom he raised from the dead. He gave me faith."

"Ah, faith . . ."

"Yes, faith, faith in the charity of life, in life's joy. It was he who cured me of my delusion of 'progress,' of my belief in its political implications. For there are, Angela, two types of dangerous and harmful men: those who, convinced of life beyond the grave, of the resurrection of the flesh, torment other people—like the inquisitors they are—so that they will despise this life as a transitory thing and work for the other life; and then, there are those who, believing only in this life . . ."

"Like you, perhaps . . ."

"Yes, and like Don Emmanuel. Believing only in this world, this second group looks forward to some vague future society and exerts every effort to prevent the populace finding consoling joy from belief in another world . . ."

"And so . . ."

"The people should be allowed to live with their illusion."

The poor priest who came to the parish to replace Don Emmanuel found himself overwhelmed in Valverde de Lucerna by the memory of the saint, and he put himself in the hands of my brother and myself for guidance. He wanted only to follow in the footsteps of the saint. And my brother told him: "Very little theology, Father, very little theology. Religion, religion, religion." Listening to him, I smiled to myself, wondering if this was not a kind of theology, too.

I had by now begun to fear for my poor brother. From the time Don Emmanuel died it could scarcely be said that he lived. Daily he went to the priest's tomb; for hours on end he stood gazing into the lake. He was filled with nostalgia for deep, abiding peace.

"Don't stare into the lake so much," I begged him.

"Don't worry. It's not this lake which draws me, nor the mountain. Only, I cannot live without his help."

"And the joy of living, Lazarus, what about the joy of living?"

"That's for others. Not for those of us who have seen God's face, those of us on whom the Dream of Life has gazed with His eyes."

"What; are you preparing to go and see Don Emmanuel?"

"No, sister, no. Here at home now, between the two of us, the whole truth—bitter as it may be, bitter as the sea into which the sweet waters of our lake flow—the whole truth for you, who are so set against it . . ."

"No, no, Lazarus. You are wrong. Your truth is not the truth."

"It's my truth."

"Yours, perhaps, but surely not . . ."

"His, too."

"No, Lazarus. Not now, it isn't. Now, he must believe otherwise; now he must believe . . ."

"Listen, Angela, once Don Emmanuel told me that there are truths which, though one reveals them to oneself, must be kept from others; and I told him that telling me was the same as telling himself. And then he said, he confessed to me, that he thought that more than one of the great saints, perhaps the very greatest himself, had died without believing in the other life."

"Is it possible?"

"All too possible! And now, sister, you must be careful that here, among the people, no one even suspects our secret . . ."

"Suspect it?" I cried in amazement. "Why even if I were to try, in a fit of madness, to explain it to them, they wouldn't understand it. The people do not understand your words, they understand your actions much better. To try and explain all this to them would be like reading some pages from Saint Thomas Aquinas to eight-year-old children, in Latin."

"All the better. In any case, when I am gone, pray for me and for him and for all of us."

At length, his own time came. A sickness which had been eating away at his robust nature seemed to flare with the death of Don Emmanuel.

"I don't so much mind dying," he said to me in his last days, "as the fact that with me another piece of Don Emmanuel dies too. The remainder of him must live on with you. Until, one day, even we dead will die forever."

When he lay in the throes of death, the people of the village came in to bid him farewell (as is customary in our towns) and they commended his soul to the care of Don Emmanuel the Good, Martyr. My brother said nothing to them; he had nothing more to say. He had already said everything there was to say. He had become a link between the two Valverde de Lucernas—the one at the bottom of the lake and the one reflected in its surface. He was already one more of us who had died of life, and, in his way, one more of our saints.

I was desolate, more than desolate; but I was, at least, among my own people, in my own village. Now, having lost my Saint Emmanuel, the father of my soul, and my own Lazarus, my more than carnal brother, my spiritual brother, now it is I realize that I have aged. But, have I really lost them then? Have I grown old? Is my death approaching?

I must live! And he taught me to live, he taught us to live, to feel life, to feel the meaning of life, to merge with the soul of the mountain, with the soul of the lake, with the soul of the village, to lose ourselves in them so as to remain in them forever. He taught me by his life to lose myself in the life of the people of my village, and I no longer felt the passing of the hours, and the days, and the years, any more than I felt the passage of the water in the lake. It began to seem that my life would always be thus. I no longer felt myself growing old. I no longer lived in myself, but in my people, and my people lived in me. I tried to speak as they spoke, as they spoke without

trying. I went into the street—it was the one highway—
and, since I knew everyone, I lived in them and forgot
myself (while, on the other hand, in Madrid, where I went
once with my brother, I had felt a terrible loneliness,
since I knew no one, and had been tortured by the sight
of so many unknown people).

Now, as I write this memoir, this confession of my
experience with saintliness, with a saint, I am of the opinion that Don Emmanuel the Good, my Don Emmanuel,
and my brother, too, died believing they did not believe,
but that, without believing in their belief, they actually
believed, with resignation and in desolation.

But why, I have asked myself repeatedly, did not Don
Emmanuel attempt to convert my brother deceitfully, with
a lie, pretending to be a believer himself without being
one? And I have finally come to think that Don Emmanuel realized he would not be able to delude him, that with
him a fraud would not do, that only through the truth,
with his truth, would he be able to convert him; that he
knew he would accomplish nothing if he attempted to
enact the comedy—the tragedy, rather—which he played
out for the benefit of the people. And thus did he win him
over, in effect, to his pious fraud; thus did he win him
over to the cause of life with the truth of death. And thus
did he win me, who never permitted anyone to see
through his divine, his most saintly, game. For I believed
then, and I believe now, that God—as part of I know not
what sacred and inscrutable purpose—caused them to
believe they were unbelievers. And that at the moment of
their passing, perhaps, the blindfold was removed.

And I, do I believe?

As I write this—here in my mother's old house, and I
past my fiftieth year and my memories growing as dim
and blanched as my hair—outside it is snowing, snowing
upon the lake, snowing upon the mountain, upon the
memory of my father, the stranger, upon the memory of
my mother, my brother Lazarus, my people, upon the
memory of my Saint Emmanuel, and even on the memory
of the poor fool Blasillo, my Saint Blasillo—and may he
help me in heaven! The snow effaces corners and blots out
shadows, for even in the night it shines and illuminates.
Truly, I do not know what is true and what is false, nor

what I saw and what I merely dreamt—or rather, what I dreamt and what I merely saw—, nor what I really knew or what I merely believed true. Neither do I know whether or not I am transferring to this paper, white as the snow outside, my consciousness, for it to remain in writing, leaving me without it. But why, any longer, cling to it?

Do I really understand any of it? Do I really believe in any of it? Did what I am writing about here actually take place, and did it take place in just the way I tell it? Is it possible for such things to happen? Is it possible that all this is more than a dream dreamed within another dream? Can it be that I, Angela Carballino, a woman in her fifties, am the only one in this village to be assailed by far-fetched thoughts, thoughts unknown to everyone else? And the others, those around me, do they believe? And what does it mean, to believe? At least they go on living. And now they believe in Saint Emmanuel the Good, Martyr, who, with no hope of immortality for himself, preserved their hope in it.

It appears that our most illustrious bishop, who set in motion the process for beatifying our saint from Valverde de Lucerna, is intent on writing an account of Don Emmanuel's life, something which would serve as a guide for the perfect parish priest, and with this end in mind he is gathering information of every sort. He has repeatedly solicited information from me; more than once he has come to see me; and I have supplied him with all sorts of facts. But I have never revealed the tragic secret of Don Emmanuel and my brother. And it is curious that he has never suspected. I trust that what I have set down here will never come to his knowledge. For, all temporal authorities are to be avoided; I fear all authorities on this earth—even when they are church authorities.

But this is an end to it. Let its fate be what it will . . .

How, you ask, did this document, this memoir of Angela Carballino fall into my hands? That, reader, is something I must keep secret. I have transcribed it for you just as it is written, just as it came to me, with only a few, a very few editorial emendations. It recalls to you other things I have written? This fact does not gainsay its objectivity, its originality. Moreover, for all I know, perhaps I created real, actual beings, independent of me, beyond my control, characters with immortal souls. For all I know, Augusto Perez in my novel *Mist*[2] was right when he claimed to be more real, more objective than I myself, who had thought to have invented him. As for the reality of this Saint Emmanuel the Good, Martyr—as he is revealed to me by his disciple and spiritual daughter Angela Carballino—of his reality it has not occurred to me to doubt. I believe in it more than the saint himself did. I believe in it more than I do in my own reality.

And now, before I bring this epilogue to a close, I wish to recall to your mind, patient reader, the ninth verse of the Epistle of the forgotten Apostle, Saint Judas—what power in a name!—where we are told how my heavenly patron, St. Michael Archangel (Michael means "Who such as God?" and archangel means archmessenger) disputed with the Devil (Devil means accuser, prosecutor) over the body of Moses, and would not allow him to carry it off as a prize, to damnation. Instead, he told the Devil: "May the Lord rebuke thee." And may he who wishes to understand, understand!

I would like also, since Angela Carballino injected her own feelings into her narrative—I don't know how it could have been otherwise—to comment on her statement to the effect that if Don Emmanuel and his disciple Lazarus had confessed their convictions to the people, they, the people, would not have understood. Nor, I should like to add, would they have believed the pair. They would have believed in their works and not their words. And works stand by themselves, and need no words to back them up. In a village like Valverde de Lucerna one makes one's confession by one's conduct.

And as for faith, the people scarce know what it is, and care less.

I am well aware of the fact that no action takes place in this narrative, this *novelistic* narrative, if you will—the novel is, after all, the most intimate, the truest history, so that I scarcely understand why some people are outraged

---

[2] In the denouement of *Mist,* the protagonist Augusto Perez turns on Unamuno, and tells him that he, a creation of human thought and genius, is more real than his author, a product of blind animality.

to have the Bible called a novel, when such a designation actually sets it above some mere chronicle or other. In short, nothing happens. But I hope that this is because everything that takes place happens, and, instead of coming to pass, and passing away, remains forever, like the lakes and the mountains and the blessed simple souls fixed firmly beyond faith and despair, the blessed souls who, in the lakes and the mountains, outside history, in their divine novel, take refuge.

Salamanca, 1930

James Joyce

THE SISTERS

There was no hope for him this time: it was the third
stroke. Night after night I had passed the house (it was
vacation time) and studied the lighted square of window:
and night after night I had found it lighted in the same
way, faintly and evenly. If he was dead, I thought, I
would see the reflection of candles on the darkened blind
for I knew that two candles must be set at the head of a
corpse. He had often said to me: *I am not long for this
world*, and I had thought his words idle. Now I knew they
were true. Every night as I gazed up at the window I said
softly to myself the word *paralysis*. It had always sounded
strangely in my ears, like the word *gnomon* in the Euclid
and the word *simony* in the Catechism. But now it sounded
to me like the name of some maleficent and sinful being.
It filled me with fear, and yet I longed to be nearer to it
and to look upon its deadly work.

Old Cotter was sitting at the fire, smoking, when I
came downstairs to supper. While my aunt was ladling out
my stirabout he said, as if returning to some former
remark of his:

—No, I wouldn't say he was exactly . . . but there was
something queer . . . there was something uncanny about
him. I'll tell you my opinion. . . .

He began to puff at his pipe, no doubt arranging his
opinion in his mind. Tiresome old fool! When we knew
him first he used to be rather interesting, talking of faints
and worms; but I soon grew tired of him and his endless
stories about the distillery.

—I have my own theory about it, he said. I think it was
one of those . . . peculiar cases. . . . . But it's hard to
say. . . .

He began to puff again at his pipe without giving us his
theory. My uncle saw me staring and said to me:

—Well, so your old friend is gone, you'll be sorry to hear.

—Who? said I.

—Father Flynn.

—Is he dead?

—Mr Cotter here has just told us. He was passing by the house.

I knew that I was under observation so I continued eating as if the news had not interested me. My uncle explained to old Cotter.

—The youngster and he were great friends. The old chap taught him a great deal, mind you; and they say he had a great wish for him.

—God have mercy on his soul, said my aunt piously.

Old Cotter looked at me for a while. I felt that his little beady black eyes were examining me but I would not satisfy him by looking up from my plate. He returned to his pipe and finally spat rudely into the grate.

—I wouldn't like children of mine, he said, to have too much to say to a man like that.

—How do you mean, Mr Cotter? asked my aunt.

—What I mean is, said old Cotter, it's bad for children. My idea is: let a young lad run about and play with young lads of his own age and not be . . . Am I right, Jack?

—That's my principle, too, said my uncle. Let him learn to box his corner. That's what I'm always saying to that Rosicrucian there: take exercise. Why, when I was a nipper every morning of my life I had a cold bath, winter and summer. And that's what stands to me now. Education is all very fine and large. . . . Mr Cotter might take a pick of that leg of mutton, he added to my aunt.

—No, no, not for me, said old Cotter.

My aunt brought the dish from the safe and laid it on the table.

—But why do you think it's not good for children, Mr Cotter? she asked.

—It's bad for children, said old Cotter, because their minds are so impressionable. When children see things like that, you know, it has an effect. . . .

I crammed my mouth with stirabout for fear I might give utterance to my anger. Tiresome old red-nosed imbecile!

It was late when I fell asleep. Though I was angry with

old Cotter for alluding to me as a child I puzzled my head
to extract meaning from his unfinished sentences. In the
dark of my room I imagined that I saw again the heavy
grey face of the paralytic. I drew the blankets over my
head and tried to think of Christmas. But the grey face
still followed me. It murmured; and I understood that it
desired to confess something. I felt my soul receding into
some pleasant and vicious region; and there again I found
it waiting for me. It began to confess to me in a murmur-
ing voice and I wondered why it smiled continually and
why the lips were so moist with spittle. But then I remembered that it had died of paralysis and I felt that I too was
smiling feebly as if to absolve the simoniac of his sin.

The next morning after breakfast I went down to look
at the little house in Great Britain Street. It was an unas-
suming shop, registered under the vague name of *Drapery*.
The drapery consisted mainly of children's bootees and
umbrellas; and on ordinary days a notice used to hang in
the window, saying: *Umbrellas Re-covered*. No notice was
visible now for the shutters were up. A crape bouquet was
tied to the door-knocker with ribbon. Two poor women
and a telegram boy were reading the card pinned on the
crape. I also approached and read:

July 1st, 1895

The Rev. James Flynn
(formerly of S. Catherine's Church,
Meath Street), aged sixty-five years.
R.I.P.

The reading of the card persuaded me that he was dead
and I was disturbed to find myself at check. Had he not
been dead I would have gone into the little dark room
behind the shop to find him sitting in his arm-chair by the
fire, nearly smothered in his great-coat. Perhaps my aunt
would have given me a packet of High Toast for him and
this present would have roused him from his stupefied
doze. It was always I who emptied the packet into his
black snuff-box for his hands trembled too much to allow
him to do this without spilling half the snuff about the
floor. Even as he raised his large trembling hand to his
nose little clouds of smoke dribbled through his fingers

over the front of his coat. It may have been these constant
showers of snuff which gave his ancient priestly garments
their green faded look for the red handkerchief, blackened, as it always was, with the snuff-stains of a week,
with which he tried to brush away the fallen grains, was
quite inefficacious.

I wished to go in and look at him but I had not the
courage to knock. I walked away slowly along the sunny
side of the street, reading all the theatrical advertisements
in the shop-windows as I went. I found it strange that
neither I nor the day seemed in a mourning mood and I
felt even annoyed at discovering in myself a sensation of
freedom as if I had been freed from something by his
death. I wondered at this for, as my uncle had said the
night before, he had taught me a great deal. He had
studied in the Irish college in Rome and he had taught me
to pronounce Latin properly. He had told me stories about
the catacombs and about Napoleon Bonaparte, and he had
explained to me the meaning of the different ceremonies
of the Mass and of the different vestments worn by the
priest. Sometimes he had amused himself by putting difficult questions to me, asking me what one should do in certain circumstances or whether such and such sins were
mortal or venial or only imperfections. His questions
showed me how complex and mysterious were certain
institutions of the Church which I had always regarded as
the simplest acts. The duties of the priest towards the
Eucharist and towards the secrecy of the confessional
seemed so grave to me that I wondered how anybody had
ever found in himself the courage to undertake them; and
I was not surprised when he told me that the fathers of
the Church had written books as thick as the *Post Office
Directory* and as closely printed as the law notices in
the newspaper, elucidating all these intricate questions.
Often when I thought of this I could make no answer or
only a very foolish and halting one upon which he used to
smile and nod his head twice or thrice. Sometimes he
used to put me through the responses of the Mass which
he had made me learn by heart; and, as I pattered, he
used to smile pensively and nod his head, now and then
pushing huge pinches of snuff up each nostril alternately.
When he smiled he used to uncover his big discoloured

teeth and let his tongue lie upon his lower lip—a habit
which had made me feel uneasy in the beginning of our
acquaintance before I knew him well.

As I walked along in the sun I remembered old Cotter's
words and tried to remember what had happened afterwards in the dream. I remembered that I had noticed long
velvet curtains and a swinging lamp of antique fashion. I
felt that I had been very far away, in some land where
the customs were strange—in Persia, I thought. . . . But I
could not remember the end of the dream.

In the evening my aunt took me with her to visit the
house of mourning. It was after sunset; but the windowpanes of the houses that looked to the west reflected the
tawny gold of a great bank of clouds. Nannie received us
in the hall; and, as it would have been unseemly to have
shouted at her, my aunt shook hands with her for all. The
old woman pointed upwards interrogatively and, on my
aunt's nodding, proceeded to toil up the narrow staircase
before us, her bowed head being scarcely above the level
of the banister-rail. At the first landing she stopped and
beckoned us forward encouragingly towards the open door
of the dead-room. My aunt went in and the old woman,
seeing that I hesitated to enter, began to beckon to me
again repeatedly with her hand.

I went in on tiptoe. The room through the lace end of
the blind was suffused with dusky golden light amid which
the candles looked like pale thin flames. He had been
coffined. Nannie gave the lead and we three knelt down at
the foot of the bed. I pretended to pray but I could not
gather my thoughts because the old woman's mutterings
distracted me. I noticed how clumsily her skirt was hooked
at the back and how the heels of her cloth boots were
trodden down all to one side. The fancy came to me that
the old priest was smiling as he lay there in his coffin.

But no. When we rose and went up to the head of the
bed I saw that he was not smiling. There he lay, solemn
and copious, vested as for the altar, his large hands loosely
retaining a chalice. His face was very truculent, grey and
massive, with black cavernous nostrils and circled by a
scanty white fur. There was a heavy odour in the room—
the flowers.

We blessed ourselves and came away. In the little room
downstairs we found Eliza seated in his arm-chair in state.

I groped my way towards my usual chair in the corner
while Nannie went to the sideboard and brought out a
decanter of sherry and some wine-glasses. She set these on
the table and invited us to take a little glass of wine. Then,
at her sister's bidding, she poured out the sherry into the
glasses and passed them to us. She pressed me to take some
cream crackers also but I declined because I thought I
would make too much noise eating them. She seemed to
be somewhat disappointed at my refusal and went over
quietly to the sofa where she sat down behind her sister.
No one spoke: we all gazed at the empty fire-place.

My aunt waited until Eliza sighed and then said:

—Ah, well, he's gone to a better world.

Eliza sighed again and bowed her head in assent. My
aunt fingered the stem of her wine-glass before sipping a
little.

—Did he . . . peacefully? she asked.

—O, quite peacefully, ma'am, said Eliza. You couldn't
tell when the breath went out of him. He had a beautiful
death, God be praised.

—And everything . . . ?

—Father O'Rourke was in with him a Tuesday and
anointed him and prepared him and all.

—He knew then?

—He was quite resigned.

—He looks quite resigned, said my aunt.

—That's what the woman we had in to wash him said.
She said he just looked as if he was asleep, he looked
that peaceful and resigned. No one would think he'd make
such a beautiful corpse.

—Yes, indeed, said my aunt.

She sipped a little more from her glass and said:

—Well, Miss Flynn, at any rate it must be a great comfort for you to know that you did all you could for him.
You were both very kind to him, I must say.

Eliza smoothed her dress over her knees.

—Ah, poor James! she said. God knows we done all
we could, as poor as we are—we wouldn't see him want
anything while he was in it.

Nannie had leaned her head against the sofa-pillow and
seemed about to fall asleep.

—There's poor Nannie, said Eliza, looking at her, she's
wore out. All the work we had, she and me, getting in the

woman to wash him and then laying him out and then the coffin and then arranging about the Mass in the chapel. Only for Father O'Rourke I don't know what we'd have done at all. It was him brought us all them flowers and them two candlesticks out of the chapel and wrote out the notice for the *Freeman's General* and took charge of all the papers for the cemetery and poor James's insurance.

—Wasn't that good of him? said my aunt.

Eliza closed her eyes and shook her head slowly.

—Ah, there's no friends like the old friends, she said, when all is said and done, no friends that a body can trust.

—Indeed, that's true, said my aunt. And I'm sure now that he's gone to his eternal reward he won't forget you and all your kindness to him.

—Ah, poor James! said Eliza. He was no great trouble to us. You wouldn't hear him in the house any more than now. Still, I know he's gone and all to that. . . .

—It's when it's all over that you'll miss him, said my aunt.

—I know that, said Eliza. I won't be bringing him in his cup of beef-tea any more, nor you, ma'am, sending him his snuff. Ah, poor James!

She stopped, as if she were communing with the past and then said shrewdly:

—Mind you, I noticed there was something queer coming over him latterly. Whenever I'd bring in his soup to him I'd find him with his breviary fallen to the floor, lying back in the chair and his mouth open.

She laid a finger against her nose and frowned: then she continued:

—But still and all he kept on saying that before the summer was over he'd go out for a drive one fine day just to see the old house again where we were all born down in Irishtown and take me and Nannie with him. If we could only get one of them new-fangled carriages that makes no noise that Father O'Rourke told him about—them with the rheumatic wheels—for the day cheap, he said, at Johnny Rush's over the way there and drive out the three of us together of a Sunday evening. He had his mind set on that. . . . Poor James!

—The Lord have mercy on his soul! said my aunt.

Eliza took out her handkerchief and wiped her eyes with

it. Then she put it back again in her pocket and gazed into the empty grate for some time without speaking.

—He was too scrupulous always, she said. The duties of the priesthood was too much for him. And then his life was, you might say, crossed.

—Yes, said my aunt. He was a disappointed man. You could see that.

A silence took possession of the little room and, under cover of it, I approached the table and tasted my sherry and then returned quietly to my chair in the corner. Eliza seemed to have fallen into a deep revery. We waited respectfully for her to break the silence: and after a long pause she said slowly:

—It was that chalice he broke. . . . That was the beginning of it. Of course, they say it was all right, that it contained nothing, I mean. But still. . . . They say it was the boy's fault. But poor James was so nervous, God be merciful to him!

—And was that it? said my aunt. I heard something. . . . Eliza nodded.

—That affected his mind, she said. After that he began to mope by himself, talking to no one and wandering about by himself. So one night he was wanted for to go on a call and they couldn't find him anywhere. They looked high up and low down; and still they couldn't see a sight of him anywhere. So then the clerk suggested to try the chapel. So then they got the keys and opened the chapel and the clerk and Father O'Rourke and another priest that was there brought in a light for to look for him. . . . And what do you think but there he was, sitting up by himself in the dark in his confession-box, wide-awake and laughing-like softly to himself?

She stopped suddenly as if to listen. I too listened; but there was no sound in the house: and I knew that the old priest was lying still in his coffin as we had seen him, solemn and truculent in death, an idle chalice on his breast.

Eliza resumed:

—Wide-awake and laughing-like to himself. . . . So then, of course, when they saw that, that made them think that there was something gone wrong with him. . . .

Ernest Hemingway

THE LIGHT OF THE WORLD

When he saw us come in the door the bartender looked up and then reached over and put the glass covers on the two free-lunch bowls.

"Give me a beer," I said. He drew it, cut the top off with the spatula and then held the glass in his hand. I put the nickel on the wood and he slid the beer toward me.

"What's yours?" he said to Tom.

"Beer."

He drew that beer and cut it off and when he saw the money he pushed the beer across to Tom.

"What's the matter?" Tom asked.

The bartender didn't answer him. He just looked over our heads and said, "What's yours?" to a man who'd come in.

"Rye," the man said. The bartender put out the bottle and glass and a glass of water.

Tom reached over and took the glass off the free-lunch bowl. It was a bowl of pickled pig's feet and there was a wooden thing that worked like a scissors, with two wooden forks at the end to pick them up with.

"No," said the bartender and put the glass cover back on the bowl. Tom held the wooden scissors fork in his hand. "Put it back," said the bartender.

"You know where," said Tom.

The bartender reached a hand forward under the bar, watching us both. I put fifty cents on the wood and he straightened up.

"What was yours?" he said.

"Beer," I said, and before he drew the beer he uncovered both the bowls.

"Your goddam pig's feet stink," Tom said, and spit what he had in his mouth on the floor. The bartender didn't say anything. The man who had drunk the rye paid and went out without looking back.

"You stink yourself," the bartender said. "All you punks stink."

"He says we're punks," Tommy said to me.

"Listen," I said. "Let's get out."

"You punks clear the hell out of here," the bartender said.

"I said we were going out," I said. "It wasn't your idea."

"We'll be back," Tommy said.

"No you won't," the bartender told him.

"Tell him how wrong he is," Tom turned to me.

"Come on," I said.

Outside it was good and dark.

"What the hell kind of place is this?" Tommy said.

"I don't know," I said. "Let's go down to the station."

We'd come in that town at one end and we were going out the other. It smelled of hides and tan bark and the big piles of sawdust. It was getting dark as we came in, and now that it was dark it was cold and the puddles of water in the road were freezing at the edges.

Down at the station there were five whores waiting for the train to come in, and six white men and four Indians. It was crowded and hot from the stove and full of stale smoke. As we came in nobody was talking and the ticket window was down.

"Shut the door, can't you?" somebody said.

I looked to see who said it. It was one of the white men. He wore stagged trousers and lumbermen's rubbers and a mackinaw shirt like the others, but he had no cap and his face was white and his hands were white and thin.

"Aren't you going to shut it?"

"Sure," I said, and shut it.

"Thank you," he said. One of the other men snickered.

"Ever interfere with a cook?" he said to me.

"No."

"You interfere with this one," he looked at the cook. "He likes it."

The cook looked away from him holding his lips tight together.

"He puts lemon juice on his hands," the man said. "He

wouldn't get them in dishwater for anything. Look how white they are."

One of the whores laughed out loud. She was the biggest whore I ever saw in my life and the biggest woman. And she had on one of those silk dresses that change colors. There were two other whores that were nearly as big but the big one must have weighed three hundred and fifty pounds. You couldn't believe she was real when you looked at her. All three had those changeable silk dresses. They sat side by side on the bench. They were huge. The other two were just ordinary looking whores, peroxide blondes.

"Look at his hands," the man said and nodded his head at the cook. The whore laughed again and shook all over.

The cook turned and said to her quickly, "You big disgusting mountain of flesh."

She just kept on laughing and shaking.

"Oh, my Christ," she said. She had a nice voice. "Oh, my sweet Christ."

The two other whores, the big ones, acted very quiet and placid as though they didn't have much sense, but they were big, nearly as big as the biggest one. They'd have both gone well over two hundred and fifty pounds. The other two were dignified.

Of the men, besides the cook and the one who talked, there were two other lumberjacks, one that listened, interested but bashful, and the other that seemed getting ready to say something, and two Swedes. Two Indians were sitting down at the end of the bench and one standing up against the wall.

The man who was getting ready to say something spoke to me very low, "Must be like getting on top of a hay mow."

I laughed and said it to Tommy.

"I swear to Christ I've never been anywhere like this," he said. "Look at the three of them." Then the cook spoke up.

"How old are you boys?"

"I'm ninety-six and he's sixty-nine," Tommy said.

"Ho! Ho! Ho!" the big whore shook with laughing. She had a really pretty voice. The other whores didn't smile.

"Oh, can't you be decent?" the cook said. "I asked just to be friendly."

"We're seventeen and nineteen," I said.

"What's the matter with you?" Tommy turned to me.

"That's all right."

"You can call me Alice," the big whore said and then she began to shake again.

"Is that your name?" Tommy asked.

"Sure," she said. "Alice. Isn't it?" she turned to the man who sat by the cook.

"Alice. That's right."

"That's the sort of name you'd have," the cook said.

"It's my real name," Alice said.

"What's the other girls' names?" Tom asked.

"Hazel and Ethel," Alice said. Hazel and Ethel smiled. They weren't very bright.

"What's your name?" I said to one of the blondes.

"Frances," she said.

"Frances what?"

"Frances Wilson. What's it to you?"

"What's yours?" I asked the other one.

"Oh, don't be fresh," she said.

"He just wants us all to be friends," the man who talked said. "Don't you want to be friends?"

"No," the peroxide one said. "Not with you."

"She's just a spitfire," the man said. "A regular little spitfire."

The one blonde looked at the other and shook her head.

"Goddamned mossbacks," she said.

Alice commenced to laugh again and to shake all over.

"There's nothing funny," the cook said. "You all laugh but there's nothing funny. You two young lads; where are you bound for?"

"Where are you going yourself?" Tom asked him.

"I want to go to Cadillac," the cook said. "Have you ever been there? My sister lives there."

"He's a sister himself," the man in the stagged trousers said.

"Can't you stop that sort of thing?" the cook asked. "Can't we speak decently?"

"Cadillac is where Steve Ketchel came from and where Ad Wolgast is from," the shy man said.

"Steve Ketchel," one of the blondes said in a high voice as though the name had pulled a trigger in her. "His own father shot and killed him. Yes, by Christ, his own father. There aren't any more men like Steve Ketchel."

"Wasn't his name Stanley Ketchel?" asked the cook.

"Oh, shut up," said the blonde. "What do you know about Steve? Stanley. He was no Stanley. Steve Ketchel was the finest and most beautiful man that ever lived. I never saw a man as clean and as white and as beautiful as Steve Ketchel. There never was a man like that. He moved just like a tiger and he was the finest, free-est, spender that ever lived."

"Did you know him?" one of the men asked.

"Did I know him? Did I know him? Did I love him? You ask me that? I knew him like you know nobody in the world and I loved him like you love God. He was the greatest, finest, whitest, most beautiful man that ever lived, Steve Ketchel, and his own father shot him down like a dog."

"Were you out on the coast with him?"

"No. I knew him before that. He was the only man I ever loved."

Every one was very respectful to the peroxide blonde, who said all this in a high stagey way, but Alice was beginning to shake again. I felt it sitting by her.

"You should have married him," the cook said.

"I wouldn't hurt his career," the peroxide blonde said. "I wouldn't be a drawback to him. A wife wasn't what he needed. Oh, my God, what a man he was."

"That was a fine way to look at it," the cook said. "Didn't Jack Johnson knock him out though?"

"It was a trick," Peroxide said. "That big dinge took him by surprise. He'd just knocked Jack Johnson down, the big black bastard. That nigger beat him by a fluke."

The ticket window went up and the three Indians went over to it.

"Steve knocked him down," Peroxide said. "He turned to smile at me."

"I thought you said you weren't on the coast," some one said.

"I went out just for that fight. Steve turned to smile at me and that black son of a bitch from hell jumped up and hit him by surprise. Steve could lick a hundred like that black bastard."

"He was a great fighter," the lumberjack said.

"I hope to God he was," Peroxide said. "I hope to God they don't have fighters like that now. He was like a god, he was. So white and clean and beautiful and smooth and fast and like a tiger or like lightning."

"I saw him in the moving pictures of the fight," Tom said. We were all very moved. Alice was shaking all over and I looked and saw she was crying. The Indians had gone outside on the platform.

"He was more than any husband could ever be," Peroxide said. "We were married in the eyes of God and I belong to him right now and always will and all of me is his. I don't care about my body. They can take my body. My soul belongs to Steve Ketchel. By God, he was a man."

Everybody felt terribly. It was sad and embarrassing. Then Alice, who was still shaking, spoke. "You're a dirty liar," she said in that low voice. "You never layed Steve Ketchel in your life and you know it."

"How can you say that?" Peroxide said proudly.

"I say it because it's true," Alice said. "I'm the only one here that ever knew Steve Ketchel and I come from Mancelona and I knew him there and it's true and you know it's true and God can strike me dead if it isn't true."

"He can strike me too," Peroxide said.

"This is true, true, true, and you know it. Not just made up and I know exactly what he said to me."

"What did he say?" Peroxide asked complacently.

Alice was crying so she could hardly speak from shaking so.

"He said 'You're a lovely piece, Alice.' That's exactly what he said."

"It's a lie," Peroxide said.

"It's true," Alice said. "That's truly what he said."

"It's a lie," Peroxide said proudly.

"No, it's true, true, true, to Jesus and Mary true."

"Steve couldn't have said that. It wasn't the way he talked," Peroxide said happily.

"It's true," Alice said in her nice voice. "And it doesn't make any difference to me whether you believe it or not." She wasn't crying any more and she was calm.

"It would be impossible for Steve to have said that," Peroxide declared.

"He said it," Alice said and smiled. "And I remember when he said it and I *was* a lovely piece then exactly as he said, and right now I'm a better piece than you, you dried up old hot-water bottle."

"You can't insult me," said Peroxide. "You big mountain of pus. I have my memories."

"No," Alice said in that sweet lovely voice, "you haven't got any real memories except having your tubes out and when you started C. and M. Everything else you just read in the papers. I'm clean and you know it and men like me, even though I'm big, and you know it, and I never lie and you know it."

"Leave me with my memories," Peroxide said. "With my true, wonderful memories."

Alice looked at her and then at us and her face lost that hurt look and she smiled and she had about the prettiest face I ever saw. She had a pretty face and a nice smooth skin and a lovely voice and she was nice all right and really friendly. But my God she was big. She was as big as three women. Tom saw me looking at her and he said, "Come on. Let's go."

"Good-bye," said Alice. She certainly had a nice voice.

"Good-bye," I said.

"Which way are you boys going?" asked the cook.

"The other way from you," Tom told him.

Flannery O'Connor

PARKER'S BACK

Parker's wife was sitting on the front porch floor, snapping beans. Parker was sitting on the step, some distance away, watching her sullenly. She was plain, plain. The skin on her face was thin and drawn as tight as the skin on an onion and her eyes were grey and sharp like the points of two icepicks. Parker understood why he had married her—he couldn't have got her any other way—but he couldn't understand why he stayed with her now. She was pregnant and pregnant women were not his favorite kind. Nevertheless, he stayed as if she had him conjured. He was puzzled and ashamed of himself.

The house they rented sat alone save for a single tall pecan tree on a high embankment overlooking a highway. At intervals a car would shoot past below and his wife's eyes would swerve suspiciously after the sound of it and then come back to rest on the newspaper full of beans in her lap. One of the things she did not approve of was automobiles. In addition to her other bad qualities, she was forever sniffing up sin. She did not smoke or dip, drink whiskey, use bad language or paint her face, and God knew some paint would have improved it, Parker thought. Her being against color, it was the more remarkable she had married him. Sometimes he supposed that she had married him because she meant to save him. At other times he had a suspicion that she actually liked everything she said she didn't. He could account for her one way or another; it was himself he could not understand.

She turned her head in his direction and said, "It's no reason you can't work for a man. It don't have to be a woman."

"Aw shut your mouth for a change," Parker muttered.

If he had been certain she was jealous of the woman he worked for he would have been pleased but more likely she was concerned with the sin that would result if he and the woman took a liking to each other. He had told her that the woman was a hefty young blonde; in fact she was nearly seventy years old and too dried up to have an interest in anything except getting as much work out of him as she could. Not that an old woman didn't sometimes get an interest in a young man, particularly if he was as attractive as Parker felt he was, but this old woman looked at him the same way she looked at her old tractor —as if she had to put up with it because it was all she had. The tractor had broken down the second day Parker was on it and she had set him at once to cutting bushes, saying out of the side of her mouth to the nigger, "Everything he touches, he breaks." She also asked him to wear his shirt when he worked; Parker had removed it even though the day was not sultry; he put it back on reluctantly.

This ugly woman Parker married was his first wife. He had had other women but he had planned never to get himself tied up legally. He had first seen her one morning when his truck broke down on the highway. He had managed to pull it off the road into a neatly swept yard on which sat a peeling two-room house. He got out and opened the hood of the truck and began to study the motor. Parker had an extra sense that told him when there was a woman nearby watching him. After he had leaned over the motor a few minutes, his neck began to prickle. He cast his eye over the empty yard and porch of the house. A woman he could not see was either nearby beyond a clump of honeysuckle or in the house, watching him out the window.

Suddenly Parker began to jump up and down and fling his hand about as if he had mashed it in the machinery. He doubled over and held his hand close to his chest. "God dammit!" he hollered, "Jesus Christ in hell! Jesus God Almighty damm! God dammit to hell!" he went on, flinging out the same few oaths over and over as loud as he could.

Without warning a terrible bristly claw slammed the side of his face and he fell backwards on the hood of the truck. "You don't talk no filth here!" a voice close to him shrilled.

Parker's vision was so blurred that for an instant he

thought he had been attacked by some creature from above, a giant hawk-eyed angel wielding a hoary weapon. As his sight cleared, he saw before him a tall raw-boned girl with a broom.

"I hurt my hand," he said. "I HURT my hand." He was so incensed that he forgot that he hadn't hurt his hand. "My hand may be broke," he growled although his voice was still unsteady.

"Lemme see it," the girl demanded.

Parker stuck out his hand and she came closer and looked at it. There was no mark on the palm and she took the hand and turned it over. Her own hand was dry and hot and rough and Parker felt himself jolted back to life by her touch. He looked more closely at her. I don't want nothing to do with this one, he thought.

The girl's sharp eyes peered at the back of the stubby reddish hand she held. There emblazoned in red and blue was a tattooed eagle perched on a cannon. Parker's sleeve was rolled to the elbow. Above the eagle a serpent was coiled about a shield and in the spaces between the eagle and the serpent there were hearts, some with arrows through them. Above the serpent there was a spread hand of cards. Every space on the skin of Parker's arm, from wrist to elbow, was covered in some loud design. The girl gazed at this with an almost stupefied smile of shock, as if she had accidentally grasped a poisonous snake; she dropped the hand.

"I got most of my other ones in foreign parts," Parker said. "These here I mostly got in the United States. I got my first one when I was only fifteen year old."

"Don't tell me," the girl said, "I don't like it. I ain't got any use for it."

"You ought to see the ones you can't see," Parker said and winked.

Two circles of red appeared like apples on the girl's cheeks and softened her appearance. Parker was intrigued. He did not for a minute think that she didn't like the tattoos. He had never yet met a woman who was not attracted to them.

Parker was fourteen when he saw a man in a fair, tattooed from head to foot. Except for his loins which were girded with a panther hide, the man's skin was patterned in what seemed from Parker's distance—he was near the back of the tent, standing on a bench—a single intricate design of brilliant color. The man, who was small and sturdy, moved about on the platform, flexing his muscles so that the arabesque of men and beasts and flowers on his skin appeared to have a subtle motion of its own. Parker was filled with emotion, lifted up as some people are when the flag passes. He was a boy whose mouth habitually hung open. He was heavy and earnest, as ordinary as a loaf of bread. When the show was over, he had remained standing on the bench, staring where the tattooed man had been, until the tent was almost empty.

Parker had never before felt the least motion of wonder in himself. Until he saw the man at the fair, it did not enter his head that there was anything out of the ordinary about the fact that he existed. Even then it did not enter his head, but a peculiar unease settled in him. It was as if a blind boy had been turned so gently in a different direction that he did not know his destination had been changed.

He had his first tattoo some time after—the eagle perched on the cannon. It was done by a local artist. It hurt very little, just enough to make it appear to Parker to be worth doing. This was peculiar too for before he had thought that only what did not hurt was worth doing. The next year he quit school because he was sixteen and could. He went to the trade school for a while, then he quit the trade school and worked for six months in a garage. The only reason he worked at all was to pay for more tattoos. His mother worked in a laundry and could support him, but she would not pay for any tattoo except her name on a heart, which he had put on, grumbling. However, her name was Betty Jean and nobody had to know it was his mother. He found out that the tattoos were attractive to the kind of girls he liked but who had never liked him before. He began to drink beer and get in fights. His mother wept over what was becoming of him. One night she dragged him off to a revival with her, not telling him where they were going. When he saw the big lighted church, he jerked out of her grasp and ran. The next day he lied about his age and joined the navy.

Parker was large for the tight sailor's pants but the silly white cap, sitting low on his forehead, made his face by contrast look thoughtful and almost intense. After a month or two in the navy, his mouth ceased to hang open. His features hardened into the features of a man. He stayed in the navy five years and seemed a natural part of the grey mechanical ship, except for his eyes, which were the same pale slate-color as the ocean and reflected the immense spaces around him as if they were a microcosm of the mysterious sea. In port Parker wandered about comparing the run-down places he was in to Birmingham, Alabama. Everywhere he went he picked up more tattoos.

He had stopped having lifeless ones like anchors and crossed rifles. He had a tiger and a panther on each shoulder, a cobra coiled about a torch on his chest, hawks on his thighs, Elizabeth II and Philip over where his stomach and liver were respectively. He did not care much what the subject was so long as it was colorful; on his abdomen he had a few obscenities but only because that seemed the proper place for them. Parker would be satisfied with each tattoo about a month, then something about it that had attracted him would wear off. Whenever a decent-sized mirror was available, he would get in front of it and study his overall look. The effect was not of one intricate arabesque of colors but of something haphazard and botched. A huge dissatisfaction would come over him and he would go off and find another tattooist and have another space filled up. The front of Parker was almost completely covered but there were no tattoos on his back. He had no desire for one anywhere he could not readily see it himself. As the space on the front of him for tattoos decreased, his dissatisfaction grew and became general.

After one of his furloughs, he didn't go back to the navy but remained away without official leave, drunk, in a rooming house in a city he did not know. His dissatisfaction, from being chronic and latent, had suddenly become acute and raged in him. It was as if the panther and the lion and the serpents and the eagles and the hawks had penetrated his skin and lived inside him in a raging warfare. The navy caught up with him, put him in the brig for nine months and then gave him a dishonorable discharge.

After that Parker decided that country air was the only kind fit to breathe. He rented the shack on the embankment and bought the old truck and took various jobs which he kept as long as it suited him. At the time he met his

future wife, he was buying apples by the bushel and selling them for the same price by the pound to isolated
homesteaders on back country roads.

"All that there," the woman said, pointing to his arm, "is
no better than what a fool Indian would do. It's a heap of
vanity." She seemed to have found the word she wanted.
"Vanity of vanities," she said.

Well what the hell do I care what she thinks of it?
Parker asked himself, but he was plainly bewildered. "I
reckon you like one of these better than another anyway,"
he said, dallying until he thought of something that would
impress her. He thrust the arm back at her. "Which you
like best?"

"None of them," she said, "but the chicken is not as bad
as the rest."

"What chicken?" Parker almost yelled.

She pointed to the eagle.

"That's an eagle," Parker said. "What fool would waste
their time having a chicken put on themself?"

"What fool would have any of it?" the girl said and
turned away. She went slowly back to the house and left
him there to get going. Parker remained for almost five
minutes, looking agape at the dark door she had entered.

The next day he returned with a bushel of apples. He
was not one to be outdone by anything that looked like
her. He liked women with meat on them, so you didn't
feel their muscles, much less their old bones. When he
arrived, she was sitting on the top step and the yard was
full of children, all as thin and poor as herself; Parker
remembered it was Saturday. He hated to be making up to
a woman when there were children around, but it was
fortunate he had brought the bushel of apples off the
truck. As the children approached him to see what he
carried, he gave each child an apple and told it to get lost;
in that way he cleared out the whole crowd.

The girl did nothing to acknowledge his presence. He
might have been a stray pig or goat that had wandered
into the yard and she too tired to take up the broom and
send it off. He set the bushel of apples down next to her on
the step. He sat down on a lower step.

"Hep yourself," he said, nodding at the basket; then he
lapsed into silence.

She took an apple quickly as if the basket might disappear if she didn't make haste. Hungry people made Parker nervous. He had always had plenty to eat himself. He grew very uncomfortable. He reasoned he had nothing to say so why should he say it? He could not think now why he had come or why he didn't go before he wasted another bushel of apples on the crowd of children. He supposed they were her brothers and sisters.

She chewed the apple slowly but with a kind of relish of concentration, bent slightly but looking out ahead. The view from the porch stretched off across a long incline studded with iron weed and across the highway to a vast vista of hills and one small mountain. Long views depressed Parker. You look out into space like that and you begin to feel as if someone were after you, the navy or the government or religion.

"Who them children belong to, you?" he said at length.

"I ain't married yet," she said. "They belong to momma." She said it as if it were only a matter of time before she would be married.

Who in God's name would marry her? Parker thought.

A large barefooted woman with a wide gap-toothed face appeared in the door behind Parker. She had apparently been there for several minutes.

"Good evening," Parker said.

The woman crossed the porch and picked up what was left of the bushel of applies. "We thank you," she said and returned with it into the house.

"That your old woman?" Parker muttered.

The girl nodded. Parker knew a lot of sharp things he could have said like "You got my sympathy," but he was gloomily silent. He just sat there, looking at the view. He thought he must be coming down with something.

"If I pick up some peaches tomorrow I'll bring you some," he said.

"I'll be much obliged to you," the girl said.

Parker had no intention of taking any basket of peaches back there but the next day he found himself doing it. He and the girl had almost nothing to say to each other. One thing he did say was, "I ain't got any tattoo on my back."

"What you got on it?" the girl said.

"My shirt," Parker said. "Haw."

"Haw, haw," the girl said politely.

Parker thought he was losing his mind. He could not

believe for a minute that he was attracted to a woman like this. She showed not the least interest in anything but what he brought until he appeared the third time with two cantaloupes. "What's your name?" she asked.

"O. E. Parker," he said.

"What does the O.E. stand for?"

"You can just call me O.E.," Parker said. "Or Parker. Don't nobody call me by my name."

"What's it stand for?" she persisted.

"Never mind," Parker said. "What's yours?"

"I'll tell you when you tell me what them letters are the short of," she said. There was just a hint of flirtatiousness in her tone and it went rapidly to Parker's head. He had never revealed the name to any man or woman, only to the files of the navy and the government, and it was on his baptismal record which he got at the age of a month; his mother was a Methodist. When the name leaked out of the navy files, Parker narrowly missed killing the man who used it.

"You'll go blab it around," he said.

"I'll swear I'll never tell nobody," she said. "On God's holy word I swear it."

Parker sat for a few minutes in silence. Then he reached for the girl's neck, drew her ear close to his mouth and revealed the name in a low voice.

"Obadiah," she whispered. Her face slowly brightened as if the name came as a sign to her. "Obadiah," she said.

The name still stank in Parker's estimation.

"Obadiah Elihue," she said in a reverent voice.

"If you call me that aloud, I'll bust your head open," Parker said. "What's yours?"

"Sarah Ruth Cates," she said.

"Glad to meet you, Sarah Ruth," Parker said.

Sarah Ruth's father was a Straight Gospel preacher but he was away, spreading it in Florida. Her mother did not seem to mind his attention to the girl so long as he brought a basket of something with him when he came. As for Sarah Ruth herself, it was plain to Parker after he had visited three times that she was crazy about him. She liked him even though she insisted that pictures on the skin were vanity of vanities and even after hearing him curse, and even after she had asked him if he was saved and he had replied that he didn't see it was anything in particular to save him from. After that, inspired, Parker had said, "I'd be saved enough if you was to kiss me."

She scowled. "That ain't being saved," she said.

Not long after that she agreed to take a ride in his truck. Parker parked it on a deserted road and suggested to her that they lie down together in the back of it.

"Not until after we're married," she said—just like that.

"Oh that ain't necessary," Parker said and as he reached for her, she thrust him away with such force that the door of the truck came off and he found himself flat on his back on the ground. He made up his mind then and there to have nothing further to do with her.

They were married in the County Ordinary's office because Sarah Ruth thought churches were idolatrous. Parker had no opinion about that one way or the other. The Ordinary's office was lined with cardboard file boxes and record books with dusty yellow slips of paper hanging on out of them. The Ordinary was an old woman with red hair who had held office for forty years and looked as dusty as her books. She married them from behind the iron-grill of a stand-up desk and when she finished, she said with a flourish, "Three dollars and fifty cents and till death do you part!" and yanked some forms out of a machine.

Marriage did not change Sarah Ruth a jot and it made Parker gloomier than ever. Every morning he decided he had had enough and would not return that night; every night he returned. Whenever Parker couldn't stand the way he felt, he would have another tattoo, but the only surface left on him now was his back. To see a tattoo on his own back he would have to get two mirrors and stand between them in just the correct position and this seemed to Parker a good way to make an idiot of himself. Sarah Ruth who, if she had had better sense, could have enjoyed a tattoo on his back, would not even look at the ones he had elsewhere. When he attempted to point out especial details of them, she would shut her eyes tight and turn her back as well. Except in total darkness, she preferred Parker dressed and with his sleeves rolled down.

"At the judgement seat of God, Jesus is going to say to you, 'What you been doing all your life besides have pictures drawn all over you?' " she said.

"You don't fool me none," Parker said, "you're just afraid that hefty girl I work for'll like me so much she'll say, 'Come on, Mr. Parker, let's you and me . . .'"

"You're tempting sin," she said, "and at the judgement seat of God you'll have to answer for that too. You ought to go back to selling the fruits of the earth."

Parker did nothing much when he was at home but listen to what the judgement seat of God would be like for him if he didn't change his ways. When he could, he broke in with tales of the hefty girl he worked for. "'Mr. Parker,'" he said she said, "'I hired you for your brains.'" (She had added, "So why don't you use them?")

"And you should have seen her face the first time she saw me without my shirt," he said. "'Mr. Parker,' she said, 'you're a walking panner-rammer!'" This had, in fact, been her remark but it had been delivered out of one side of her mouth.

Dissatisfaction began to grow so great in Parker that there was no containing it outside of a tattoo. It had to be his back. There was no help for it. A dim half-formed inspiration began to work in his mind. He visualized having a tattoo put there that Sarah Ruth would not be able to resist—a religious subject. He thought of an open book with HOLY BIBLE tattooed under it and an actual verse printed on the page. This seemed just the thing for a while; then he began to hear her say, "Ain't I already got a real Bible? What you think I want to read the same verse over and over for when I can read it all?" He needed something better even than the Bible! He thought about it so much that he began to lose sleep. He was already losing flesh—Sarah Ruth just threw food in the pot and let it boil. Not knowing for certain why he continued to stay with a woman who was both ugly and pregnant and no cook made him generally nervous and irritable, and he developed a little tic in the side of his face.

Once or twice he found himself turning around abruptly as if someone were trailing him. He had had a granddaddy who had ended in the state mental hospital, although not until he was seventy-five, but as urgent as it might be for him to get a tattoo, it was just as urgent that he get exactly the right one to bring Sarah Ruth to heel. As he continued to worry over it, his eyes took on a hollow preoccupied expression. The old woman he worked for told him that if he couldn't keep his mind on what he was doing, she knew where she could find a fourteen-year-old colored boy who could. Parker was too preoccupied even to be offended. At any time previous, he would have left her then and there, saying drily, "Well, you go ahead on and get him then."

Two or three mornings later he was baling hay with the old woman's sorry baler and her broken down tractor in a large field, cleared save for one enormous old tree standing in the middle of it. The old woman was the kind who would not cut down a large old tree because it was a large old tree. She had pointed it out to Parker as if he didn't have eyes and told him to be careful not to hit it as the machine picked up hay near it. Parker began at the outside of the field and made circles inward toward it. He had to get off the tractor every now and then and untangle the baling cord or kick a rock out of the way. The old woman had told him to carry the rocks to the edge of the field, which he did when she was there watching. When he thought he could make it, he ran over them. As he circled the field his mind was on a suitable design for his back. The sun, the size of a golf ball, began to switch regularly from in front to behind him, but he appeared to see it both places as if he had eyes in the back of his head. All at once he saw the tree reaching out to grasp him. A ferocious thud propelled him into the air, and he heard himself yelling in an unbelievably loud voice, "GOD ABOVE!"

He landed on his back while the tractor crashed upside-down into the tree and burst into flame. The first thing Parker saw were his shoes, quickly being eaten by the fire; one was caught under the tractor, the other was some distance away, burning by itself. He was not in them. He could feel the hot breath of the burning tree on his face. He scrambled backwards, still sitting, his eyes cavernous, and if he had known how to cross himself he would have done it.

His truck was on a dirt road at the edge of the field. He moved toward it, still sitting, still backwards, but faster and faster; halfway to it he got up and began a kind of forward-bent run from which he collapsed on his knees twice. His legs felt like two old rusted rain gutters. He reached the truck finally and took off in it, zigzagging up the road. He drove past his house on the embankment and straight for the city, fifty miles distant.

Parker did not allow himself to think on the way to the city. He only knew that there had been a great change in his life, a leap forward into a worse unknown, and that there was nothing he could do about it. It was for all intents accomplished.

The artist had two large cluttered rooms over a chiropodist's office on a back street. Parker, still barefooted, burst silently in on him at a little after three in the afternoon. The artist, who was about Parker's own age—twenty-eight—but thin and bald, was behind a small drawing table, tracing a design in green ink. He looked up with an annoyed glance and did not seem to recognize Parker in the hollow-eyed creature before him.

"Let me see the book you got with all the pictures of God in it," Parker said breathlessly. "The religious one."

The artist continued to look at him with his intellectual, superior stare. "I don't put tattoos on drunks," he said.

"You know me!" Parker cried indignantly. "I'm O. E. Parker! You done work for me before and I always paid!"

The artist looked at him another moment as if he were not altogether sure. "You've fallen off some," he said. "You must have been in jail."

"Married," Parker said.

"Oh," said the artist. With the aid of mirrors the artist had tattooed on the top of his head a miniature owl, perfect in every detail. It was about the size of a half-dollar and served him as a show piece. There were cheaper artists in town but Parker had never wanted anything but the best. The artist went over to a cabinet at the back of the room and began to look over some art books. "Who are you interested in?" he said, "saints, angels, Christs or what?"

"God," Parker said.

"Father, Son or Spirit?"

"Just God," Parker said impatiently. "Christ. I don't care. Just so it's God."

The artist returned with a book. He moved some papers off another table and put the book down on it and told Parker to sit down and see what he liked. "The up-to-date ones are in the back," he said.

Parker sat down with the book and wet his thumb. He began to go through it, beginning at the back where the

up-to-date pictures were. Some of them he recognized—
The Good Shepherd, Forbid Them Not, The Smiling Jesus,
Jesus the Physician's Friend, but he kept turning rapidly
backwards and the pictures became less and less reassur-
ing. One showed a gaunt green dead face streaked with
blood. One was yellow with sagging purple eyes. Parker's
heart began to beat faster and faster until it appeared to
be roaring inside him like a great generator. He flipped the
pages quickly, feeling that when he reached the one ordained, a sign would come. He continued to flip through
until he had almost reached the front of the book. On one
of the pages a pair of eyes glanced at him swiftly. Parker
sped on, then stopped. His heart too appeared to cut off;
there was absolute silence. It said as plainly as if silence
were a language itself, GO BACK.

Parker returned to the picture—the haloed head of a flat
stern Byzantine Christ with all-demanding eyes. He sat
there trembling; his heart began slowly to beat again as if
it were being brought to life by a subtle power.

"You found what you want?" the artist asked.

Parker's throat was too dry to speak. He got up and
thrust the book at the artist, opened at the picture.

"That'll cost you plenty," the artist said. "You don't want
all those little blocks though, just the outline and some
better features."

"Just like it is," Parker said, "just like it is or nothing."

"It's your funeral," the artist said, "but I don't do that
kind of work for nothing."

"How much?" Parker asked.

"It'll take maybe two days work."

"How much?" Parker said.

"On time or cash?" the artist asked. Parker's other jobs
had been on time, but he had paid.

"Ten down and ten for every day it takes," the artist
said.

Parker drew ten dollar bills out of his wallet; he had
three left in.

"You come back in the morning," the artist said, putting
the money in his own pocket. "First I'll have to trace that
out of the book."

"No no!" Parker said. "Trace it now or gimme my money
back," and his eyes blared as if he were ready for a fight.

The artist agreed. Any one stupid enough to want a

Christ on his back, he reasoned, would be just as likely as not to change his mind the next minute, but once the work was begun he could hardly do so.

While he worked on the tracing, he told Parker to go wash his back at the sink with the special soap he used there. Parker did it and returned to pace back and forth across the room, nervously flexing his shoulders. He wanted to go look at the picture again but at the same time he did not want to. The artist got up finally and had Parker lie down on the table. He swabbed his back with ethyl chloride and then began to outline the head on it with his iodine pencil. Another hour passed before he took up his electric instrument. Parker felt no particular pain. In Japan he had had a tattoo of the Buddha done on his upper arm with ivory needles; in Burma, a little brown root of a man had made a peacock on each of his knees using thin pointed sticks, two feet long; amateurs had worked on him with pins and soot. Parker was usually so relaxed and easy under the hand of the artist that he often went to sleep, but this time he remained awake, every muscle taut.

At midnight the artist said he was ready to quit. He propped one mirror, four feet square, on a table by the wall and took a smaller mirror off the lavatory wall and put it in Parker's hands. Parker stood with his back to the one on the table and moved the other until he saw a flashing burst of color reflected from his back. It was almost completely covered with little red and blue and ivory and saffron squares; from them he made out the lineaments of the face—a mouth, the beginning of heavy brows, a straight nose, but the face was empty; the eyes had not yet been put in. The impression for the moment was almost as if the artist had tricked him and done the Physician's Friend.

"It don't have eyes," Parker cried out.

"That'll come," the artist said, "in due time. We have another day to go on it yet."

Parker spent the night on a cot at the Haven of Light Christian Mission. He found these the best places to stay in the city because they were free and included a meal of sorts. He got the last available cot and because he was still barefooted, he accepted a pair of second-hand shoes which, in his confusion, he put on to go to bed; he was still shocked from all that had happened to him. All night he lay awake in the long dormitory of cots with lumpy figures on them. The only light was from a phosphorescent cross glowing at the end of the room. The tree reached out to grasp him again, then burst into flame; the shoe burned quietly by itself; the eyes in the book said to him distinctly GO BACK and at the same time did not utter a sound. He wished that he were not in this city, not in this Haven of Light Mission, not in a bed by himself. He longed miserably for Sarah Ruth. Her sharp tongue and icepick eyes were the only comfort he could bring to mind. He decided he was losing it. Her eyes appeared soft and dilatory compared with the eyes in the book, for even though he could not summon up the exact look of those eyes, he could still feel their penetration. He felt as though, under their gaze, he was as transparent as the wing of a fly.

The tattooist had told him not to come until ten in the morning, but when he arrived at that hour, Parker was sitting in the dark hallway on the floor, waiting for him. He had decided upon getting up that, once the tattoo was on him, he would not look at it, that all his sensations of the day and night before were those of a crazy man and that he would return to doing things according to his own sound judgement.

The artist began where he left off. "One thing I want to know," he said presently as he worked over Parker's back, "why do you want this on you? Have you gone and got religion? Are you saved?" he asked in a mocking voice.

Parker's throat felt salty and dry. "Naw," he said, "I ain't got no use for none of that. A man can't save his self from whatever it is he don't deserve none of my sympathy." These words seemed to leave his mouth like wraiths and to evaporate at once as if he had never uttered them.

"Then why . . ."

"I married this woman that's saved," Parker said. "I never should have done it. I ought to leave her. She's done gone and got pregnant."

"That's too bad," the artist said. "Then it's her making you have this tattoo."

"Naw," Parker said, "she don't know nothing about it. It's a surprise for her."

"You think she'll like it and lay off you a while?"

"She can't hep herself," Parker said. "She can't say she don't like the looks of God." He decided he had told the artist enough of his business. Artists were all right in their place but he didn't like them poking their noses into the affairs of regular people. "I didn't get no sleep last night," he said. "I think I'll get some now."

That closed the mouth of the artist but it did not bring him any sleep. He lay there, imagining how Sarah Ruth would be struck speechless by the face on his back and every now and then this would be interrupted by a vision of the tree of fire and his empty shoe burning beneath it.

The artist worked steadily until nearly four o'clock, not stopping to have lunch, hardly pausing with the electric instrument except to wipe the dripping dye off Parker's back as he went along. Finally he finished. "You can get up and look at it now," he said.

Parker sat up but he remained on the edge of the table.

The artist was pleased with his work and wanted Parker to look at it at once. Instead Parker continued to sit on the edge of the table, bent forward slightly but with a vacant look. "What ails you?" the artist said. "Go look at it."

"Ain't nothing ail me," Parker said in a sudden belligerent voice. "That tattoo ain't going nowhere. It'll be there when I get there." He reached for his shirt and began gingerly to put it on.

The artist took him roughly by the arm and propelled him between the two mirrors. "Now *look*," he said, angry at having his work ignored.

Parker looked, turned white and moved away. The eyes in the reflected face continued to look at him—still, straight, all-demanding, enclosed in silence.

"It was your idea, remember," the artist said. "I would have advised something else."

Parker said nothing. He put on his shirt and went out the door while the artist shouted, "I'll expect all of my money!"

Parker headed toward a package shop on the corner. He bought a pint of whiskey and took it into a nearby alley and drank it all in five minutes. Then he moved on to a pool hall nearby which he frequented when he came to the city. It was a well-lighted barn-like place with a bar up one side and gambling machines on the other and pool tables in the back. As soon as Parker entered, a large man in a red and black checkered shirt hailed him by slapping him on the back and yelling, "Yeyyyyyy boy! O. E. Parker!"

Parker was not yet ready to be struck on the back. "Lay off," he said, "I got a fresh tattoo there."

"What you got this time?" the man asked and then yelled to a few at the machines. "O.E.'s got him another tattoo."

"Nothing special this time," Parker said and slunk over to a machine that was not being used.

"Come on," the big man said, "let's have a look at O.E.'s tattoo," and while Parker squirmed in their hands, they pulled up his shirt. Parker felt all the hands drop away instantly and his shirt fell again like a veil over the face. There was a silence in the pool room which seemed to Parker to grow from the circle around him until it extended to the foundations under the building and upward through the beams in the roof.

Finally some one said, "Christ!" Then they all broke into noise at once. Parker turned around, an uncertain grin on his face.

"Leave it to O.E.!" the man in the checkered shirt said. "That boy's a real card!"

"Maybe he's gone and got religion," some one yelled.

"Not on your life," Parker said.

"O.E.'s got religion and is witnessing for Jesus, ain't you, O.E.?" a little man with a piece of cigar in his mouth said wryly. "An o-riginal way to do it if I ever saw one."

"Leave it to Parker to think of a new one!" the fat man said.

"Yyeeeeeeyyyyyyy boy!" someone yelled and they all began to whistle and curse in compliment until Parker said, "Aaa shut up."

"What'd you do it for?" somebody asked.

"For laughs," Parker said. "What's it to you?"

"Why ain't you laughing then?" somebody yelled. Parker lunged into the midst of them and like a whirlwind on a summer's day there began a fight that raged amid over-turned tables and swinging fists until two of them grabbed him and ran to the door with him and threw him out. Then a calm descended on the pool hall as nerve shatter-ing as if the long barn-like room were the ship from which Jonah had been cast into the sea.

Parker sat for a long time on the ground in the alley behind the pool hall, examining his soul. He saw it as a spider web of facts and lies that was not at all important to him but which appeared to be necessary in spite of his opinion. The eyes that were now forever on his back were eyes to be obeyed. He was as certain of it as he had ever been of anything. Throughout his life, grumbling and sometimes cursing, often afraid, once in rapture, Parker had obeyed whatever instinct of this kind had come to him —in rapture when his spirit had lifted at the sight of the tattooed man at the fair, afraid when he had joined the navy, grumbling when he had married Sarah Ruth.

The thought of her brought him slowly to his feet. She would know what he had to do. She would clear up the rest of it, and she would at least be pleased. It seemed to him that, all along, that was what he wanted, to please her. His truck was still parked in front of the building where the artist had his place, but it was not far away. He got in it and drove out of the city and into the country night. His head was almost clear of liquor and he observed that his dissatisfaction was gone, but he felt not quite like himself. It was as if he were himself but a stranger to himself, driving into a new country though everything he saw was familiar to him, even at night.

He arrived finally at the house on the embankment, pulled the truck under the pecan tree and got out. He made as much noise as possible to assert that he was still in charge here, that his leaving her for a night without word meant nothing except it was the way he did things. He slammed the car door, stamped up the two steps and across the porch and rattled the door knob. It did not respond to his touch. "Sarah Ruth!" he yelled, "let me in."

There was no lock on the door and she had evidently placed the back of a chair against the knob. He began to beat on the door and rattle the knob at the same time.

He heard the bed springs screak and bent down and put his head to the keyhole, but it was stopped up with paper. "Let me in!" he hollered, bamming on the door again. "What you got me locked out for?"

A sharp voice close to the door said, "Who's there?"

"Me," Parker said, "O.E."

He waited a moment.

"Me," he said impatiently, "O.E."

Still no sound from inside.

He tried once more. "O.E.," he said, bamming the door two or three more times. "O. E. Parker. You know me."

There was a silence. Then the voice said slowly, "I don't know no O.E."

"Quit fooling," Parker pleaded. "You ain't got any business doing me this way. It's me, old O.E., I'm back. You ain't afraid of me."

"Who's there?" the same unfeeling voice said.

Parker turned his head as if he expected someone behind him to give him the answer. The sky had lightened slightly and there were two or three streaks of yellow floating above the horizon. Then as he stood there, a tree of light burst over the skyline.

Parker fell back against the door as if he had been pinned there by a lance.

"Who's there?" the voice from inside said and there was a quality about it now that seemed final. The knob rattled and the voice said peremptorily, "Who's there, I ast you?"

Parker bent down and put his mouth near the stuffed keyhole. "Obadiah," he whispered and all at once he felt the light pouring through him, turning his spider web soul into a perfect arabesque of colors, a garden of trees and birds and beasts.

"Obadiah Elihue!" he whispered.

The door opened and he stumbled in. Sarah Ruth loomed there, hands on her hips. She began at once, "That was no hefty blonde woman you was working for and you'll have to pay her every penny on her tractor you busted up. She don't keep insurance on it. She came here and her and me had us a long talk and I . . ."

Trembling, Parker set about lighting the kerosene lamp.

"What's the matter with you, wasting that kerosene this near daylight?" she demanded. "I ain't got to look at you."

A yellow glow enveloped them. Parker put the match down and began to unbutton his shirt.

"And you ain't going to have none of me this near morning," she said.

"Shut your mouth," he said quietly. "Look at this and then I don't want to hear no more out of you." He removed the shirt and turned his back to her.

"Another picture," Sarah Ruth growled. "I might have known you was off after putting some more trash on yourself."

Parker's knees went hollow under him. He wheeled around and cried, "Look at it! Don't just say that! *Look* at it!"

"I done looked," she said.

"Don't you know who it is?" he cried in anguish.

"No, who is it?" Sarah Ruth said. "It ain't anybody I know."

"It's him," Parker said.

"Him who?"

"God!" Parker cried.

"God? God don't look like that!"

"What do you know how he looks?" Parker moaned. "You ain't seen him."

"He don't *look*," Sarah Ruth said. "He's a spirit. No man shall see his face."

"Aw listen," Parker groaned, "this is just a picture of him."

"Idolatry!" Sarah Ruth screamed. "Idolatry! Enflaming yourself with idols under every green tree! I can put up with lies and vanity but I don't want no idolator in this house!" and she grabbed up the broom and began to thrash him across the shoulders with it.

Parker was too stunned to resist. He sat there and let her beat him until she had nearly knocked him senseless and large welts had formed on the face of the tattooed Christ. Then he staggered up and made for the door.

She stamped the broom two or three times on the floor and went to the window and shook it out to get the taint of him off it. Still gripping it, she looked toward the pecan tree and her eyes hardened still more. There he was —who called himself Obadiah Elihue—leaning against the tree, crying like a baby.

John Barth

NIGHT-SEA JOURNEY

"One way or another, no matter which theory of our journey is correct, it's myself I address; to whom I rehearse as to a stranger our history and condition, and will disclose my secret hope though I sink for it.

"Is the journey my invention? Do the night, the sea, exist at all, I ask myself, apart from my experience of them? Do I myself exist, or is this a dream? Sometimes I wonder. And if I am, who am I? The Heritage I supposedly transport? But how can I be both vessel and contents? Such are the questions that beset my intervals of rest.

"My trouble is, I lack conviction. Many accounts of our situation seem plausible to me—where and what we are, why we swim and whither. But implausible ones as well, perhaps especially those, I must admit as possibly correct. Even likely. If at times, in certain humors—striking in unison, say, with my neighbors and chanting with them 'Onward! Upward'—I have supposed that we have after all a common Maker, Whose nature and motives we may not know, but Who engendered us in some mysterious wise and launched us forth toward some end known but to Him —if (for a moodslength only) I have been able to entertain such notions, very popular in certain quarters, it is because our night-sea journey partakes of their absurdity. One might even say: I can believe them *because* they are absurd.

"Has that been said before?

"Another paradox: it appears to be these recesses from swimming that sustain me in the swim. Two measures onward and upward, flailing with the rest, then I float exhausted and dispirited, brood upon the night, the sea, the journey, while the flood bears me a measure back and down: slow progress, but I live, I live, and make my way, aye, past many a drownèd comrade in the end, stronger, worthier than I, victims of their unremitting *joie de nager*. I have seen the best swimmers of my generation go under. Numberless the number of the dead! Thousands drown as I think this thought, millions as I rest before returning to the swim. And scores, hundreds of millions have expired since we surged forth, brave in our innocence, upon our dreadful way. 'Love! Love!' we sang then, a quarter-billion strong, and churned the warm sea white with joy of swimming! Now all are gone down—the buoyant, the sodden, leaders and followers, all gone under, while wretched I swim on. Yet these same reflective intervals that keep me afloat have led me into wonder, doubt, despair—strange emotions for a swimmer!—have led me, even, to suspect . . . that our night-sea journey is without meaning.

"Indeed, if I have yet to join the hosts of the suicides, it is because (fatigue apart) I find it no meaningfuller to drown myself than to go on swimming.

"I know that there are those who seem actually to enjoy the night-sea; who claim to love swimming for its own sake, or sincerely believe that 'reaching the Shore,' 'transmitting the Heritage' (*Whose* Heritage, I'd like to know? And to whom?) is worth the staggering cost. I do not. Swimming itself I find at best not actively unpleasant, more often tiresome, not infrequently a torment. Arguments from function and design don't impress me: granted that we can and do swim, that in a manner of speaking our long tails and streamlined heads are 'meant for' swimming; it by no means follows—for me, at least—that we *should* swim, or otherwise endeavor to 'fulfill our destiny.' Which is to say, Someone Else's destiny, since ours, so far as I can see, is merely to perish, one way or another, soon or late. The heartless zeal of our (departed) leaders, like the blind ambition and good cheer of my own youth, appalls me now; for the death of my comrades I am inconsolable. If the night-sea journey has justification, it is not for us swimmers ever to discover it.

"Oh, to be sure, 'Love!' one heard on every side: 'Love it is that drives and sustains us!' I translate: we don't know *what* drives and sustains us, only that we are most miserably driven and, imperfectly, sustained. *Love* is how we call our ignorance of what whips us. 'To reach the Shore,' then: but what if the Shore exists in the fancies of us swimmers merely, who dream it to account for the dreadful fact that we swim, have always and only swum, and continue swimming without respite (myself excepted) until we die? Supposing even that there *were* a Shore—that, as a cynical companion of mine once imagined, we rise from the drowned to discover all those vulgar superstitions and exalted metaphors to be literal truth: the giant Maker of us all, the Shores of Light beyond our night-sea journey!—whatever would a swimmer do there? The fact is, when we imagine the Shore, what comes to mind is just the opposite of our condition: no more night, no more sea, no more journeying. In short, the blissful estate of the drowned.

" 'Ours not to stop and think; ours but to swim and sink. . . .' Because a moment's thought reveals the pointlessness of swimming. 'No matter,' I've heard some say, even as they gulped their last: 'The night-sea journey may be absurd, but here we swim, will-we nill-we, against the flood, onward and upward, toward a Shore that may not exist and couldn't be reached if it did.' The thoughtful swimmer's choices, then, they say, are two: give over thrashing and go under for good, or embrace the absurdity; affirm in and for itself the night-sea journey; swim on with neither motive nor destination, for the sake of swimming, and compassionate moreover with your fellow swimmer, we being all at sea and equally in the dark. I find neither course acceptable. If not even the hypothetical Shore can justify a sea-full of drownèd comrades, to speak of the swim-in-itself as somehow doing so strikes me as obscene. I continue to swim—but only because blind habit, blind instinct, blind fear of drowning are still more strong than the horror of our journey. And if on occasion I have assisted a fellow-thrasher, joined in the cheers and songs, even passed along to others strokes of genius from the drownèd great, it's that I shrink by temperament from making myself conspicuous. To paddle off in one's own direction, assert one's independent right-of-way, overrun one's fellows without compunction, or dedicate oneself entirely to pleasures and diversions without regard for conscience—I can't finally condemn those who journey in this wise; in half my moods I envy them and despise the weak vitality that keeps me from following their example. But in reasonabler moments I remind myself that it's their very

freedom and self-responsibility I reject, as more dramati-
cally absurd, in our senseless circumstances, than tailing
along in conventional fashion. Suicides, rebels, affirmers of
the paradox—nay-sayers and yea-sayers alike to our fatal
journey—I finally shake my head at them. And splash
sighing past their corpses, one by one, as past a hundred
sorts of others: friends, enemies, brothers; fools, sages,
brutes—and nobodies, million upon million. I envy them
all.

"A poor irony: that I, who find abhorrent and tauto-
logical the doctrine of survival of the fittest (*fitness* meaning, in my experience, nothing more than survival-ability,
a talent whose only demonstration is the fact of survival,
but whose chief ingredients seem to be strength, guile,
callousness), may be the sole remaining swimmer! But
the doctrine is false as well as repellent: Chance drowns
the worthy with the unworthy, bears up the unfit with the
fit by whatever definition, and makes the night-sea journey
essentially *haphazard* as well as murderous and unjustified.

" 'You only swim once.' Why bother, then?

" 'Except ye drown, ye shall not reach the Shore of
Light.' Poppycock.

"One of my late companions—that same cynic with the
curious fancy, among the first to drown—entertained us
with odd conjectures while we waited to begin our journey.
A favorite theory of his was that the Father does exist,
and did indeed make us and the sea we swim—but not
a-purpose or even consciously; He made us, as it were,
despite Himself, as we make waves with every tail-thrash,
and may be unaware of our existence. Another was that
He knows we're here but doesn't care what happens to us,
inasmuch as He creates (voluntarily or not) other seas
and swimmers at more or less regular intervals. In bitterer
moments, such as just before he drowned, my friend even
supposed that our Maker wished us unmade; there was
indeed a Shore, he'd argue, which could save at least
some of us from drowning and toward which it was our
function to struggle—but for reasons unknowable to us
He wanted desperately to prevent our reaching that happy
place and fulfilling our destiny. Our 'Father', in short, was
our adversary and would-be killer! No less outrageous,
and offensive to traditional opinion, were the fellow's

speculations on the nature of our Maker: that He might well be no swimmer Himself at all, but some sort of monstrosity, perhaps even tailless; that He might be stupid, malicious, insensible, perverse, or asleep and dreaming; that the end for which He created and launched us forth, and which we flagellate ourselves to fathom, was perhaps immoral, even obscene. Et cetera, et cetera: there was no end to the chap's conjectures, or the impoliteness of his fancy; I have reason to suspect that his early demise, whether planned by 'our Maker' or not, was expedited by certain fellow-swimmers indignant at his blasphemies.

"In other moods, however (he was as given to moods as I), his theorizing would become half-serious, so it seemed to me, especially upon the subjects of Fate and Immortality, to which our youthful conversations often turned. Then his harangues, if no less fantastical, grew solemn and obscure, and if he was still baiting us, his passion undid the joke. His objection to popular opinions of the hereafter, he would declare, was their claim to general validity. Why need believers hold that *all* the drownèd rise to be judged at journeys' end, and non-believers that drowning is final without exception? In *his* opinion (so he'd vow at least), nearly everyone's fate was permanent death; indeed he took a sour pleasure in supposing that every 'Maker' made thousands of separate seas in His creative lifetime, each populated like ours with millions of swimmers, and that in almost every instance both sea and swimmers were utterly annihilated, whether accidentally or by malevolent design. (Nothing if not pluralistical, he imagined there might be millions and billions of 'Fathers,' perhaps in some 'night-sea' of their own!) However—and here he turned infidels against him with the faithful—he professed to believe that in possibly a single night-sea per thousand, say, one of its quarter-billion swimmers (that is, one swimmer in two hundred fifty billions) achieved a qualified immortality. In some cases the rate might be slightly higher; in others it was vastly lower, for just as there are swimmers of every degree of proficiency, including some who drown before the journey starts, unable to swim at all, and others created drowned, as it were, so he imagined what can only be termed impotent Creators, Makers unable to Make, as well as uncommonly fertile ones and all grades between.

And it pleased him to deny any necessary relation between a Maker's productivity and His other virtues—including, even, the quality of His creatures.

"I could go on (*he* surely did) with his elaboration of these mad notions—such as that swimmers in other night-seas needn't be of our kind; that Makers themselves might belong to different *species*, so to speak; that our particular Maker mightn't Himself be immortal, or that we might be not only His emissaries but His 'immortality,' continuing His life and our own, transmogrified, beyond our individual deaths. Even this modified immortality (meaningless to me) he conceived as relative and contingent, subject to accident or deliberate termination: his pet hypothesis was that Makers and swimmers *each generate the other*—against all odds, their number being so great—and that any given 'immortality-chain' could terminate after any number of cycles, so that what was 'immortal' (still speaking relatively) was only the cyclic process of incarnation, which itself might have a beginning and an end. Alternatively he liked to imagine cycles within cycles, either finite or infinite: for example, the 'night-sea,' as it were, in which Makers 'swam' and created night-seas and swimmers like ourselves, might be the creation of a larger Maker, Himself one of many, Who in turn et cetera. Time itself he regarded as relative to our experience, like magnitude: who knew but what, with each thrash of our tails, minuscule seas and swimmers, whole eternities, came to pass—as ours, perhaps, and our Maker's Maker's, was elapsing between the strokes of some supertail, in a slower order of time?

"Naturally I hooted with the others at this nonsense. We were young then, and had only the dimmest notion of what lay ahead; in our ignorance we imagined night-sea journeying to be a positively heroic enterprise. Its meaning and value we never questioned; to be sure, some must go down by the way, a pity no doubt, but to win a race requires that others lose, and like all my fellows I took for granted that I would be the winner. We milled and swarmed, impatient to be off, never mind where or why, only to try our youth against the realities of night and sea; if we indulged the skeptic at all, it was as a droll, half-contemptible mascot. When he died in the initial slaughter, no one cared.

"And even now I don't subscribe to all his views—but I no longer scoff. The horror of our history has purged me of opinions, as of vanity, confidence, spirit, charity, hope, vitality, everything—except dull dread and a kind of melancholy, stunned persistence. What leads me to recall his fancies is my growing suspicion that I, of all swimmers, may be the sole survivor of this fell journey, tale-bearer of a generation. This suspicion, together with the recent sea-change, suggests to me now that nothing is impossible, not even my late companion's wildest visions, and brings me to a certain desperate resolve, the point of my chronicling.

"Very likely I have lost my senses. The carnage at our setting out; our decimation by whirlpool, poisoned cataract, sea-convulsion; the panic stampedes, mutinies, slaughters, mass suicides; the mounting evidence that none will survive the journey—add to these anguish and fatigue; it were a miracle if sanity stayed afloat. Thus I admit, with the other possibilities, that the present sweetening and calming of the sea, and what seems to be a kind of vasty presence, song, or summons from the near upstream, may be hallucinations of disordered sensibility. . . .

"Perhaps, even, I am drowned already. Surely I was never meant for the rough-and-tumble of the swim; not impossibly I perished at the outset and have only imagined the night-sea journey from some final deep. In any case, I'm no longer young, and it is we spent old swimmers, disabused of every illusion, who are most vulnerable to dreams.

"Sometimes I think I am my drownèd friend.

"Out with it: I've begun to believe, not only that *She* exists, but that She lies not far ahead, and stills the sea, and draws me Herward! Aghast, I recollect his maddest notion: that our destination (which existed, mind, in but one night-sea out of hundreds and thousands) was no Shore, as commonly conceived, but a mysterious being, indescribable except by paradox and vaguest figure: wholly different from us swimmers, yet our complement; the death of us, yet our salvation and resurrection; simultaneously our journey's end, mid-point, and commencement; not membered and thrashing like us, but a motionless or hugely gliding sphere of unimaginable dimension; self-contained, yet dependent absolutely, in some wise, upon the chance (always monstrously improbable) that one of us will survive the night-sea journey and reach . . . Her! *Her,* he called it, or *She,* which is to say, Other-than-a-he. I shake my head; the thing is too preposterous; it is myself I talk to, to keep my reason in this awful darkness. There is no She! There is no You! I rave to myself; it's Death alone that hears and summons. To the drowned, all seas are calm. . . .

"Listen: my friend maintained that in every order of creation there are two sorts of creators, contrary yet complementary, one of which gives rise to seas and swimmers, the other to the Night-which-contains-the-sea and to What-waits-at the-journey's-end: the former, in short, to destiny, the latter to destination (and both profligately, involuntarily, perhaps indifferently or unwittingly). The 'purpose' of the night-sea journey—but not necessarily of the journeyer or of either Maker!—my friend could describe only in abstractions: *consummation, transfiguration, union of contraries, transcension of categories.* When we laughed, he would shrug and admit that he understood the business no better than we, and thought it ridiculous, dreary, possibly obscene. 'But one of you,' he'd add with his wry smile, 'may be the Hero destined to complete the night-sea journey and be one with Her. Chances are, of course, you won't make it.' He himself, he declared, was not even going to try; the whole idea repelled him; if we chose to dismiss it as an ugly fiction, so much the better for us; thrash, splash, and be merry, we were soon enough drowned. But there it was, he could not say how he knew or why he bothered to tell us, any more than he could say what would happen after She and Hero, Shore and Swimmer, 'merged identities' to become something both and neither. He quite agreed with me that if the issue of that magical union had no memory of the night-sea journey, for example, it enjoyed a poor sort of immortality; even poorer if, as he rather imagined, a swimmer-hero plus a She equaled or became merely another Maker of future night-seas and the rest, at such incredible expense of life. This being the case—he was persuaded it was—the merciful thing to do was refuse to participate; the genuine heroes, in his opinion, were the suicides, and the hero of heroes would be the swimmer who, in the very presence of the Other, refused Her proffered 'immortality' and thus put an end to at least one cycle of catastrophes.

"How we mocked him! Our moment came, we hurtled forth, pretending to glory in the adventure, thrashing, singing, cursing, strangling, rationalizing, rescuing, killing, inventing rules and stories and relationships, giving up, struggling on, but dying all, and still in darkness, until only a battered remnant was left to croak 'Onward, upward,' like a bitter echo. Then they too fell silent—victims, I can only presume, of the last frightful wave—and the moment came when I also utterly desolate and spent, thrashed my last and gave myself over to the current, to sink or float as might be, but swim no more. Whereupon, marvelous to tell, in an instant the sea grew still! Then warmly, gently, the great tide turned, began to bear me, as it does now, onward and upward will-I nill-I, like a flood of joy—and I recalled with dismay my dead friend's teaching.

"I am not deceived. This new emotion is Her doing; the desire that possesses me is Her bewitchment. Lucidity passes from me; in a moment I'll cry 'Love!' bury myself in Her side, and be 'transfigured.' Which is to say, I die already; this fellow transported by passion is not I; *I am he who abjures and rejects the night-sea journey!* I. . . .

"I am all love. 'Come!' She whispers, and I have no will.

"You who I may be about to become, whatever You are: with the last twitch of my real self I beg You to listen. It is *not* love that sustains me! No; though Her magic makes me burn to sing the contrary, and though I drown even now for the blasphemy, I will say truth. What has fetched me across this dreadful sea is a single hope, gift of my poor dead comrade: that You may be stronger-willed than I, and that by sheer force of concentration I may transmit to You, along with Your official Heritage, a private legacy of awful recollection and negative resolve. Mad as it may be, my dream is that some unimaginable embodiment of myself (or myself plus Her if that's how it must be) will come to find itself expressing, in however garbled or radical a translation, some reflection of these reflections. If against all odds this comes to pass, may You to whom, through whom I speak, do what I cannot: terminate this aimless, brutal business! Stop Your hearing against Her song! Hate love!

"Still alive, afloat, afire. Farewell then my penultimate hope: that one may be sunk for direst blasphemy on the very shore of the Shore. Can it be (my old friend would smile) that only utterest nay-sayers survive the night? But even that were Sense, and there is no sense, only senseless love, senseless death. Whoever echoes these reflections: be more courageous than their author! An end to night-sea journeys! Make no more! And forswear me when I shall forswear myself, deny myself, plunge into Her who summons, singing . . .

" 'Love! Love! Love!' "

John Updike

LIFEGUARD

Beyond doubt, I am a splendid fellow. In the autumn, winter, and spring, I execute the duties of a student of divinity; in the summer I disguise myself in my skin and become a lifeguard. My slightly narrow and gingerly hirsute but not necessarily unmanly chest becomes brown. My smooth back turns the color of caramel, which, in conjunction with the whipped cream of my white pith helmet, gives me, some of my teenage satellites assure me, a delightfully edible appearance. My legs, which I myself can study, cocked as they are before me while I repose on my elevated wooden throne, are dyed a lustreless maple walnut that accentuates their articulate strength. Correspondingly, the hairs of my body are bleached blond, so that my legs have the pointed elegance of, within the flower, umber anthers dusted with pollen.

For nine months of the year, I pace my pale hands and burning eyes through immense pages of Biblical text barnacled with fudging commentary; through multivolumed apologetics couched in a falsely friendly Victorian voice and bound in subtly abrasive boards of finely ridged, prefaded red; through handbooks of liturgy and histories of dogma; through the bewildering duplicities of Tillich's divine politicking; through the suave table talk of Father D'Arcy, Etienne Gilson, Jacques Maritain, and other such moderns mistakenly put at their ease by the exquisite antique furniture and overstuffed larder of the hospitable St. Thomas; through the terrifying attempts of Kierkegaard, Berdyaev, and Barth to scourge God into being. I sway appalled on the ladder of minus signs by which theologians would surmount the void. I tiptoe like a burglar into the house of naturalism to steal the silver. An acrobat, I swing from wisp to wisp. Newman's iridescent cobwebs crush in my hands. Pascal's blackboard mathematics are

erased by a passing shoulder. The cave drawings, astound-
ingly vital by candlelight, of those aboriginal magicians,
Paul and Augustine, in daylight fade into mere anthropol-
ogy. The diverting productions of literary flirts like Chester-
ton, Eliot, Auden, and Greene—whether they regard
Christianity as a pastel forest designed for a fairyland
romp or a deliciously miasmic pit from which chiaroscuro
can be mined with mechanical buckets—in the end all
infallibly strike, despite the comic variety of gongs and
mallets, the note of the rich young man who on the coast
of Judaea refused in dismay to sell all that he had.

Then, for the remaining quarter of the solar revolution,
I rest my eyes on a sheet of brilliant sand printed with
the runes of naked human bodies. That there is no dis-
crepancy between my studies, that the texts of the flesh
complement those of the mind, is the easy burden of my
sermon.

On the back rest of my lifeguard's chair is painted a cross
—true, a red cross, signifying bandages, splints, spirits of
ammonia, and sunburn unguents. Nevertheless, it comforts me. Each morning, as I mount into my chair, my
athletic and youthfully fuzzy toes expertly gripping the
slats that make a ladder, it is as if I am climbing into an
immense, rigid, loosely fitting vestment.

Again, in each of my roles I sit attentively perched on
the edge of an immensity. That the sea, with its multiform
and mysterious hosts, its savage and senseless rages, no
longer comfortably serves as a divine metaphor indicates
how severely humanism has corrupted the apples of our
creed. We seek God now in flowers and good deeds, and
the immensities of blue that surround the little scabs of
land upon which we draw our lives to their unsatisfactory
conclusions are suffused by science with vacuous horror. I
myself can hardly bear the thought of stars, or begin to
count the mortalities of coral. But from my chair the sea,
slightly distended by my higher perspective, seems a misty
old gentleman stretched at his ease in an immense arm-
chair which has for arms the arms of this bay and for an
antimacassar the freshly laundered sky. Sailboats float
on his surface like idle and unrelated but benevolent
thoughts. The soughing of the surf is the rhythmic lifting
of his ripple-stitched vest as he breathes. Consider. We
enter the sea with a shock; our skin and blood shout in

protest. But, that instant, that leap, past, what do we find? Ecstasy and buoyance. Swimming offers a parable. We struggle and thrash, and drown; we succumb, even in despair, and float, and are saved.

With what timidity, with what a sense of trespass, do I set forward even this obliquely a thought so official! Forgive me. I am not yet ordained; I am too disordered to deal with the main text. My competence is marginal, and I will confine myself to the gloss of flesh with which this particular margin, this one beach, is annotated each day.

Here the cinema of life is run backwards. The old are the first to arrive. They are idle, and have lost the gift of sleep. Each of our bodies is a clock that loses time. Young as I am, I can hear in myself the protein acids ticking; I wake at odd hours and in the shuddering darkness and silence feel my death rushing toward me like an express train. The older we get, and the fewer the mornings left to us, the more deeply dawn stabs us awake. The old ladies wear wide straw hats and, in their hats' shadows, smiles as wide, which they bestow upon each other, upon salty shells they discover in the morning-smooth sand, and even upon me, downy-eyed from my night of dissipation. The gentlemen are often incongruous; withered white legs support brazen barrel chests, absurdly potent, bustling with white froth. How these old roosters preen on their "condition"! With what fatuous expertness they swim in the icy water—always, however, prudently parallel to the shore, at a depth no greater than their height.

Then come the middle-aged, burdened with children and aluminum chairs. The men are scarred with the marks of their vocation—the red forearms of the gasoline-station attendant, the pale X on the back of the overall-wearing mason or carpenter, the clammer's nicked ankles. The hair on their bodies has as many patterns as matted grass. The women are wrinkled but fertile, like the Iraqi rivers that cradled the seeds of our civilization. Their children are odious. From their gaunt faces leer all the vices, the greeds, the grating urgencies of the adult, unsoftened by maturity's reticence and fatigue. Except that here and there, a girl, the eldest daughter, wearing a knit suit striped horizontally with green, purple, and brown, walks slowly, carefully, puzzled by the dawn enveloping her thick smooth body, her waist not yet nipped but her throat elongated.

Finally come the young. The young matrons bring fat and fussing infants who gobble the sand like sugar, who toddle blissfully into the surf and bring me bolt upright on my throne. My whistle tweets. The mothers rouse. Many of these women are pregnant again, and sluggishly lie in their loose suits like cows tranced in a meadow. They gossip politics, and smoke incessantly, and lift their troubled eyes in wonder as a trio of flat-stomached nymphs parades past. These maidens take all our eyes. The vivacious redhead, freckled and white-footed, pushing against her boy and begging to be ducked; the solemn brunette, transporting the vase of herself with held breath; the dimpled blonde in the bib and diapers of her Bikini, the lambent fuzz of her midriff shimmering like a cat's belly. Lust stuns me like the sun.

You are offended that a divinity student lusts? What prigs the unchurched are. Are not our assaults on the supernatural lascivious, a kind of indecency? If only you knew what de Sadian degradations, what frightful psychological spelunking, our gentle transcendentalist professors set us to, as preparation for our work, which is to shine in the darkness.

I feel that my lust makes me glow; I grow cold in my chair, like a torch of ice, as I study beauty. I have studied much of it, wearing all styles of bathing suit and facial expression, and have come to this conclusion: a woman's beauty lies, not in any exaggeration of the specialized zones, nor in any general harmony that could be worked out by means of the *sectio aurea* or a similar aesthetic superstition; but in the arabesque of the spine. The curve by which the back modulates into the buttocks. It is here that grace sits and rides a woman's body.

I watch from my white throne and pity women, deplore the demented judgment that drives them toward the braggart muscularity of the mesomorph and the prosperous complacence of the endomorph when it is we ectomorphs who pack in our scrawny sinews and exacerbated nerves the most intense gift, the most generous shelter, of love. To desire a woman is to desire to save her. Anyone who has endured intercourse that was neither predatory nor hurried knows how through it we descend, with a partner, into the grotesque and delicate shadows that until then have remained locked in the most guarded recess of our soul: into this harbor we bring her. A vague and twisted terrain becomes inhabited; each shadow, touched by the exploration, blooms into a flower of act. As if we are an island upon which a woman, tossed by her laboring vanity and blind self-seeking, is blown, and there finds security, until, an instant before the anticlimax, Nature with a smile thumps down her trump, and the island sinks beneath the sea.

There is great truth in those motion pictures which are slandered as true neither to the Bible nor to life. They are —written though they are by demons and drunks—true to both. We are all Solomons lusting for Sheba's salvation. The God-filled man is filled with a wilderness that cries to be populated. The stony chambers need jewels, furs, tints of cloth and flesh, even though, as in Samson's case, the temple comes tumbling. Women are an alien race of pagans set down among us. Every seduction is a conversion.

Who has loved and not experienced that sense of rescue? It is not true that our biological impulses are tricked out with ribands of chivalry; rather, our chivalric impulses go clanking in encumbering biological armor. Eunuchs love. Children love. I would love.

My chief exercise, as I sit above the crowds, is to lift the whole mass into immortality. It is not a light task; the throng is so huge, and its members so individually unworthy. No *memento mori* is so clinching as a photograph of a vanished crowd. Cheering Roosevelt, celebrating the Armistice, there it is, wearing its ten thousand straw hats and stiff collars, a fearless and wooden-faced bustle of life: it is gone. A crowd dies in the street like a derelict; it leaves no heir, no trace, no name. My own persistence beyond the last rim of time is easy to imagine; indeed, the effort of imagination lies the other way—to conceive of my ceasing. But when I study the vast tangle of humanity that blackens the beach as far as the sand stretches, absurdities crowd in on me. Is it as maiden, matron, or crone that the females will be eternalized? What will they do without children to watch and gossip to exchange? What of the thousand deaths of memory and bodily change we endure—can each be redeemed at a final Adjustments Counter? The sheer numbers involved make the mind scream. The race is no longer a tiny clan of simian aristocrats lording it over an ocean of grass; mankind is a plague racing like fire across the exhausted continents. This immense clot gathered on the beach, a fraction of a fraction—can we not say that this breeding swarm is its own immortality and end the suspense? The beehive in a sense survives; and is each of us not proved to be a hive, a galaxy of cells each of whom is doubtless praying, from its pew in our thumbnail or esophagus, for personal resurrection? Indeed, to the cells themselves cancer may seem a revival of faith. No, in relation to other people oblivion is sensible and sanitary.

This sea of others exasperates and fatigues me most on Sunday mornings. I don't know why people no longer go to church—whether they have lost the ability to sing or the willingness to listen. From eight-thirty onward they crowd in from the parking lots, ants each carrying its crumb of baggage, until by noon, when the remote churches are releasing their gallant and gaily dressed minority, the sea itself is jammed with hollow heads and thrashing arms like a great bobbing backwash of rubbish. A transistor radio somewhere in the sand releases in a thin, apologetic gust the closing peal of a transcribed service. And right here, here at the very height of torpor and confusion, I slump, my eyes slit, and the blurred forms of Protestantism's errant herd seem gathered by the water's edge in impassioned poses of devotion. I seem to be lying dreaming in the infinite rock of space before Creation, and the actual scene I see is a vision of impossibility: a Paradise. For had we existed before the gesture that split the firmament, could we have conceived of our most obvious possession, our most platitudinous blessing, the moment, the single ever-present moment that we perpetually bring to our lips brimful?

So: be joyful. Be Joyful in my commandment. It is the message I read in your jiggle. Stretch your skins like pegged hides curing in the miracle of the sun's moment. Exult in your legs' scissoring, your waist's swivel. Romp; eat the froth; be children. I am here above you; I have given my youth that you may do this. I wait. The tides of time have treacherous undercurrents. You are borne continually toward the horizon. I have prepared myself; my muscles are instilled with everything that must be done.

Someday my alertness will bear fruit; from near the horizon there will arise, delicious, translucent, like a green bell above the water, the call for help, the call, a call, it saddens me to confess, that I have yet to hear.

Philip Roth

ELI, THE FANATIC

Leo Tzuref stepped out from back of a white column to welcome Eli Peck. Eli jumped back, surprised; then they shook hands and Tzuref gestured him into the sagging old mansion. At the door Eli turned, and down the slope of lawn, past the jungle of hedges, beyond the dark, untrampled horse path, he saw the street lights blink on in Woodenton. The stores along Coach House Road tossed up a burst of yellow—it came to Eli as a secret signal from his townsmen: "Tell this Tzuref where we stand, Eli. This is a modern community, Eli, we have our families, we pay taxes . . ." Eli, burdened by the message, gave Tzuref a dumb, weary stare.

"You must work a full day," Tzuref said, steering the attorney and his briefcase into the chilly hall.

Eli's heels made a racket on the cracked marble floor, and he spoke about it. "It's the commuting that's killing," he said, and entered the dim room Tzuref waved open for him. "Three hours a day . . . I came right from the train." He dwindled down into a harp-backed chair. He expected it would be deeper than it was and consequently jarred himself on the sharp bones of his seat. It woke him, this shiver of the behind, to his business. Tzuref, a bald shaggy-browed man who looked as if he'd once been very fat, sat back of an empty desk, halfway hidden, as though he were settled on the floor. Everything around him was empty. There were no books in the bookshelves, no rugs on the floor, no draperies in the big casement windows. As Eli began to speak Tzuref got up and swung a window back on one noisy hinge. "May and it's like August," he said, and with his back to Eli, he revealed the black circle on the back of his head. The crown of his head was missing! He returned through the dimness—the lamps had no bulbs

—and Eli realized all he'd seen was a skullcap. Tzuref struck a match and lit a candle, just as the half-dying shouts of children at play rolled in through the open window. It was as though Tzuref had opened it so Eli could hear them.

"Aah, now," he said. "I received your letter."

Eli poised, waiting for Tzuref to swish open a drawer and remove the letter from his file. Instead the old man leaned forward onto his stomach, worked his hand into his pants pocket, and withdrew what appeared to be a week-old handkerchief. He uncrumpled it; he unfolded it; he ironed it on the desk with the side of his hand. "So," he said.

Eli pointed to the grimy sheet which he'd gone over word-by-word with his partners, Lewis and McDonnell. "I expected an answer," Eli said. "It's a week."

"It was so important, Mr. Peck, I knew you would come."

Some children ran under the open window and their mysterious babble—not mysterious to Tzuref, who smiled —entered the room like a third person. Their noise caught up against Eli's flesh and he was unable to restrain a shudder. He wished he had gone home, showered and eaten dinner, before calling on Tzuref. He was not feeling as professional as usual—the place was too dim, it was too late. But down in Woodenton they would be waiting, his clients and neighbors. He spoke for the Jews of Woodenton, not just himself and his wife.

"You understood?" Eli said.

"It's not hard."

"It's a matter of zoning . . ." and when Tzuref did not answer, but only drummed his fingers on his lips, Eli said, "We didn't make the laws . . ."

"You respect them."

"They protect us . . . the community."

"The law is the law," Tzuref said.

"Exactly!" Eli had the urge to rise and walk about the room.

"And then of course"—Tzuref made a pair of scales in the air with his hands—"The law is not the law. When is the law that is the law not the law?" He jiggled the scales. "And vice versa."

"Simply," Eli said sharply. "You can't have a boarding school in a residential area." He would not allow Tzuref to cloud the issue with issues. "We thought it better to tell you before any action is undertaken."

"But a house in a residential area?"

"Yes. That's what residential means." The DP's English was perhaps not as good as it seemed at first. Tzuref spoke slowly, but till then Eli had mistaken it for craft— or even wisdom. "Residence means home," he added.

"So this is my residence."

"But the children?"

"It is their residence."

"*Seventeen* children?"

"Eighteen," Tzuref said.

"But you *teach* them here."

"The Talmud. That's illegal?"

"That makes it a school."

Tzuref hung the scales again, tipping slowly the balance.

"Look, Mr. Tzuref, in America we call such a place a boarding school."

"Where they teach the Talmud?"

"Where they teach period. You are the headmaster, they are the students."

Tzuref placed his scales on the desk. "Mr. Peck," he said, "I don't believe it . . ." but he did not seem to be referring to anything Eli had said.

"Mr. Tzuref, that is the law. I came to ask what you intend to do."

"What I *must* do?"

"I hope they are the same."

"They are." Tzuref brought his stomach into the desk. "We stay." He smiled. "We are tired. The headmaster is tired. The students are tired."

Eli rose and lifted his briefcase. It felt so heavy packed with the grievances, vengeances, and schemes of his clients. There were days when he carried it like a feather —in Tzuref's office it weighed a ton.

"Goodbye, Mr. Tzuref."

"Sholom," Tzuref said.

Eli opened the door to the office and walked carefully down the dark tomb of a corridor to the door. He stepped out on the porch and, leaning against a pillar, looked down across the lawn to the children at play. Their voices whooped and rose and dropped as they chased each other round the old house. The dusk made the children's game look like a tribal dance. Eli straightened up, started off the porch, and suddenly the dance was ended. A long piercing scream trailed after. It was the first time in his life anyone had run at the sight of him. Keeping his eyes on the lights of Woodenton, he headed down the path.

And then, seated on a bench beneath a tree, Eli saw him. At first it seemed only a deep hollow of blackness— then the figure emerged. Eli recognized him from the description. There he was, wearing the hat, that hat which was the very cause of Eli's mission, the source of Woodenton's upset. The town's lights flashed their message once again: "Get the one with the hat. What a nerve, what a nerve . . ."

Eli started towards the man. Perhaps he was less stubborn than Tzuref, more reasonable. After all, it was the law. But when he was close enough to call out, he didn't. He was stopped by the sight of the black coat that fell down below the man's knees, and the hands which held each other in his lap. By the round-topped, wide-brimmed Talmudic hat, pushed onto the back of his head. And by the beard, which hid his neck and was so soft and thin it fluttered away and back again with each heavy breath he took. He was asleep, his sidelocks curled loose on his cheeks. His face was no older than Eli's.

Eli hurried towards the lights.

The note on the kitchen table unsettled him. Scribblings on bits of paper had made history this past week. This one, however, was unsigned. "Sweetie," it said, "I went to sleep. I had a sort of Oedipal experience with the baby today. Call Ted Heller."

She had left him a cold soggy dinner in the refrigerator. He hated cold soggy dinners, but would take one gladly in place of Miriam's presence. He was ruffled, and she never helped that, not with her infernal analytic powers. He loved her when life was proceeding smoothly—and that was when she loved him. But sometimes Eli found being a lawyer surrounded him like quicksand—he couldn't get his breath. Too often he wished he were pleading for the other side; though if he were on the other side, then he'd wish he were on the side he was. The trouble was that sometimes the law didn't seem to be the answer, *law* didn't seem to have anything to do with what was aggravating everybody. And that, of course, made him feel foolish and unnecessary . . . Though that was not the situation here—the townsmen had a case. But not *exactly*, and if Miriam were awake to see Eli's upset, she would set about explaining his distress to him, understanding him, forgiving him, so as to get things back to Normal, for Normal was where they loved one another. The difficulty with Miriam's efforts was they only upset him more; not only did they explain little to him about himself or his predicament, but they convinced him of *her* weakness. Neither Eli nor Miriam, it turned out, was terribly strong. Twice before he'd faced this fact, and on both occasions had found solace in what his neighbors forgivingly referred to as "a nervous breakdown."

Eli ate his dinner with his briefcase beside him. Halfway through, he gave in to himself, removed Tzuref's notes, and put them on the table, beside Miriam's. From time to time he flipped through the notes, which had been carried into town by the one in the black hat. The first note, the incendiary:

To whom it may concern:
    Please give this gentleman the following: Boys shoes with rubber heels and soles.

5 prs size 6c
3 prs size 5c
3 prs size 5b
2 prs size 4a
3 prs size 4c
1 pr size 7b
1 pr size 7c

Total 18 prs. boys shoes. This gentleman has a check already signed. Please fill in correct amount.
                    L. TZUREF
                    Director, Yeshivah of
                    Woodenton, N.Y.
                    (5/8/48)

"Eli, a regular greenhorn," Ted Heller had said. "He didn't say a word. Just handed me the note and stood there, like in the Bronx the old guys who used to come around selling Hebrew trinkets."

"A Yeshivah!" Artie Berg had said. "Eli, in Woodenton, a Yeshivah! If I want to live in Brownsville, Eli, I'll live in Brownsville."

"Eli," Harry Shaw speaking now, "the old Puddington place. Old man Puddington'll roll over in his grave. Eli, when I left the city, Eli, I didn't plan the city should come to me."

Note number two:

> Dear Grocer:
> Please give this gentleman ten pounds of sugar. Charge it to our account, Yeshivah of Woodenton, NY —which we will now open with you and expect a bill each month. The gentleman will be in to see you once or twice a week.
>
> L. TZUREF, Director
> (5/10/48)
>
> P.S. Do you carry kosher meat?

"He walked right by my window, the greenie," Ted had said, "and he nodded, Eli. He's my *friend* now."

"Eli," Artie Berg had said, "he handed the damn thing to a *clerk* at Stop N' Shop—and in that hat yet!"

"Eli," Harry Shaw again, "it's not funny. Someday, Eli, it's going to be a hundred little kids with little *yamalkahs* chanting their Hebrew lessons on Coach House Road, and then it's not going to strike you funny."

"Eli, what goes on up there—my kids hear strange sounds."

"Eli, this is a modern community."

"Eli, we pay taxes."

"Eli."

"Eli!"

"*Eli!*"

At first it was only another townsman crying in his ear; but when he turned he saw Miriam, standing in the doorway, behind her belly.

"Eli, sweetheart, how was it?"

"He said no."

"Did you see the other one?" she asked.

"Sleeping, under a tree."

"Did you let him know how people feel?"

"He was sleeping."

"Why didn't you wake him up? Eli, this isn't an every-day thing."

"He was tired!"

"Don't shout, please," Miriam said.

" 'Don't shout. I'm pregnant. The baby is heavy.' " Eli found he was getting angry at nothing she'd said yet; it was what she was going to say.

"He's a very heavy baby the doctor says," Miriam told him.

"Then sit *down* and make my dinner." Now he found himself angry about her not being present at the dinner which he'd just been relieved that she wasn't present at. It was as though he had a raw nerve for a tail, that he kept stepping on. At last Miriam herself stepped on it.

"Eli, you're upset. I understand."

"You *don't* understand."

She left the room. From the stairs she called, "I do, sweetheart."

It was a trap! He would grow angry knowing she would be "understanding." She would in turn grow more under-standing seeing his anger. He would in turn grow angrier ... The phone rang.

"Hello," Eli said.

"Eli, Ted. So?"

"So nothing."

"Who is Tzuref? He's an American guy?"

"No. A DP. German."

"And the kids?"

"DP's too. He teaches them."

"What? What subjects?" Ted asked.

"I don't know."

"And the guy with the hat, you saw the guy with the hat?"

"Yes. He was sleeping."

"Eli, he sleeps with the *hat*?"

"He sleeps with the hat."

"Goddam fanatics," Ted said. "This is the twentieth century, Eli. Now it's the guy with the hat. Pretty soon all the little Yeshivah boys'll be spilling down into town."

"Next thing they'll be after our daughters."

"Michele and Debbie wouldn't look at them."

"Then," Eli mumbled, "you've got nothing to worry about, Teddie," and he hung up.

In a moment the phone rang. "Eli? We got cut off. We've got nothing to worry about? You worked it out?"

"I have to see him again tomorrow. We can work something out."

"That's fine, Eli. I'll call Artie and Harry."

Eli hung up.

"I thought you said *nothing* worked out." It was Miriam.

"I did."

"Then why did you tell Ted *something* worked out?"

"It did."

"Eli, maybe you should get a little more therapy."

"That's enough of that, Miriam."

"You can't function as a lawyer by being neurotic. That's no answer."

"You're ingenious, Miriam."

She turned, frowning, and took her heavy baby to bed.

The phone rang.

"Eli, Artie. Ted called. You worked it out? No trouble?"

"Yes."

"When are they going?"

"Leave it to me, will you, Artie? I'm tired. I'm going to sleep."

In bed Eli kissed his wife's belly and laid his head upon it to think. He laid it lightly, for she was that day entering the second week of her ninth month. Still, when she slept, it was a good place to rest, to rise and fall with her breathing and figure things out. "If that guy would take off that crazy hat. I know it, what eats them. If he'd take off that crazy hat everything would be all right."

"What?" Miriam said.

"I'm talking to the baby."

Miriam pushed herself up in bed. "Eli, please, baby, shouldn't you maybe stop in to see Dr. Eckman, just for a little conversation?"

"I'm fine."

"Oh, sweetie!" she said, and put her head back on the pillow.

"You know what your mother brought to this marriage —a sling chair and a goddam New School enthusiasm for Sigmund Freud."

Miriam feigned sleep, he could tell by the breathing.

"I'm telling the kid the truth, aren't I, Miriam? A sling

chair, three months to go on a *New Yorker* subscription, and *An Introduction to Psychoanalysis.* Isn't that right?"

"Eli, must you be aggressive?"

"That's all you worry about, is your insides. You stand in front of the mirror all day and look at yourself being pregnant."

"Pregnant mothers have a relationship with the fetus that fathers can't understand."

"Relationship my ass. What is my liver doing now? What is my small intestine doing now? Is my island of Langerhans on the blink?"

"Don't be jealous of a little fetus, Eli."

"I'm jealous of your island of Langerhans!"

"Eli, I can't argue with you when I know it's not me you're really angry with. Don't you see, sweetie, you're angry with yourself."

"You and Eckman."

"Maybe he could help, Eli."

"Maybe he could help you. You're practically lovers as it is."

"You're being hostile again," Miriam said.

"What do you care—it's only *me* I'm being hostile towards."

"Eli, we're going to have a beautiful baby, and I'm going to have a perfectly simple delivery, and you're going to make a fine father, and there's absolutely no reason to be obsessed with whatever is on your mind. All we have to worry about—" she smiled at him "—is a name."

Eli got out of bed and slid into his slippers. "We'll name the kid Eckman if it's a boy and Eckman if it's a girl."

"Eckman Peck sounds terrible."

"He'll have to live with it," Eli said, and he went down to his study where the latch on his briefcase glinted in the moonlight that came through the window.

He removed the Tzuref notes and read through them all again. It unnerved him to think of all the flashy reasons his wife could come up with for his reading and reread-ing the notes. "Eli, why are you so *preoccupied* with Tzuref?" "Eli, stop getting *involved.* Why do you think you're getting *involved,* Eli?" Sooner or later, everybody's wife finds their weak spot. His goddam luck he had to be neurotic! Why couldn't he have been born with a short leg.

He removed the cover from his typewriter, hating

Miriam for the edge she had. All the time he wrote the letter, he could hear what she would be saying about his not being *able* to let the matter drop. Well, her trouble was that she wasn't *able* to face the matter. But he could hear her answer already: clearly, he was guilty of "a reaction formation." Still, all the fancy phrases didn't fool Eli: all she wanted really was for Eli to send Tzuref and family on their way, so that the community's temper would quiet, and the calm circumstances of their domestic happiness return. All she wanted were order and love in her private world. Was she so wrong? Let the world bat its brains out —in Woodenton there should be peace. He wrote the letter anyway:

Dear Mr. Tzuref:

Our meeting this evening seems to me inconclusive. I don't think there's any reason for us not to be able to come up with some sort of compromise that will satisfy the Jewish community of Woodenton and the Yeshivah and yourself. It seems to me that what most disturbs my neighbors are the visits to town by the gentleman in the black hat, suit, etc. Woodenton is a progressive suburban community whose members, both Jewish and Gentile, are anxious that their families live in comfort and beauty and serenity. This is, after all, the twentieth century, and we do not think it too much to ask that the members of our community dress in a manner appropriate to the time and place.

Woodenton, as you may not know, has long been the home of well-to-do Protestants. It is only since the war that Jews have been able to buy property here, and for Jews and Gentiles to live beside each other in amity. For this adjustment to be made, both Jews and Gentiles alike have had to give up some of their more extreme practices in order not to threaten or offend the other. Certainly such amity is to be desired. Perhaps if such conditions had existed in prewar Europe, the persecution of the Jewish people, of which you and those 18 children have been victims, could not have been carried out with such success—in fact, might not have been carried out at all.

Therefore, Mr. Tzuref, will you accept the following conditions? If you can, we will see fit not to carry out legal action against the Yeshivah for failure to comply with township Zoning ordinances No. 18 and No. 23. The conditions are simply:

1. The religious, educational, and social activities of the Yeshivah of Woodenton will be confined to the Yeshivah grounds.

2. Yeshivah personnel are welcomed in the streets and stores of Woodenton provided they are attired in clothing usually associated with American life in the 20th century.

If these conditions are met, we see no reason why the Yeshivah of Woodenton cannot live peacefully and satisfactorily with the Jews of Woodenton—as the Jews of Woodenton have come to live with the Gentiles of Woodenton. I would appreciate an immediate reply.

Sincerely,
ELI PECK, Attorney

Two days later Eli received his immediate reply:

Mr. Peck:
The suit the gentleman wears is all he's got.

Sincerely,
LEO TZUREF, Headmaster

Once again, as Eli swung around the dark trees and onto the lawn, the children fled. He reached out with his briefcase as if to stop them, but they were gone so fast all he saw moving was a flock of skullcaps.

"Come, come . . ." a voice called from the porch. Tzuref appeared from behind a pillar. Did he *live* behind those pillars? Was he just watching the children at play? Either way, when Eli appeared, Tzuref was ready, with no forewarning.

"Hello," Eli said.

"Sholom."

"I didn't mean to frighten them."

"They're scared, so they run."

"I didn't do anything."

Tzuref shrugged. The little movement seemed to Eli strong as an accusation. What he didn't get at home, he got here.

Inside the house they took their seats. Though it was lighter than a few evenings before, a bulb or two would have helped. Eli had to hold his briefcase towards the window for the last gleamings. He removed Tzuref's letter from a manila folder. Tzuref removed Eli's letter from his pants pocket. Eli removed the carbon of his own letter from another manila folder. Tzuref removed Eli's first letter from his back pocket. Eli removed the carbon from his briefcase. Tzuref raised his palms. ". . . It's all I've got . . ."

Those upraised palms, the mocking tone—another accusation. It was a crime to keep carbons! Everybody had an edge on him—Eli could do no right.

"I offered a compromise, Mr. Tzuref. You refused."

"Refused, Mr. Peck? What is, is."

"The man could get a new suit."

"That's all he's got."

"So you told me," Eli said.

"So I told you, so you know."

"It's not an insurmountable obstacle, Mr. Tzuref. We have stores."

"For that too?"

"On Route 12, a Robert Hall—"

"To take away the one thing a man's got?"

"Not take away, *replace.*"

"But I tell you he has nothing. *Nothing.* You have that word in English? *Nicht? Gornisht?*"

"Yes, Mr. Tzuref, we have the word."

"A mother and a father?" Tzuref said. "No. A wife? No. A baby? A little ten-month-old baby? No! A village full of friends? A synagogue where you knew the feel of every seat under your pants? Where with your eyes closed you could smell the cloth of the Torah?" Tzuref pushed out of his chair, stirring a breeze that swept Eli's letter to the floor. At the window he leaned out, and looked, beyond Woodenton. When he turned he was shaking a finger at Eli. "And a medical experiment they performed on him yet! That leaves nothing, Mr. Peck. Absolutely nothing!"

"I misunderstood."

"No news reached Woodenton?"

"About the suit, Mr. Tzuref. I thought he couldn't afford another."

"He can't."

They were right where they'd begun. "Mr. Tzuref!" Eli

demanded. "*Here?*" He smacked his hand to his billfold.

"Exactly!" Tzuref said, smacking his own breast.

"Then we'll buy him one!" Eli crossed to the window and taking Tzuref by the shoulders, pronounced each word slowly. "We-will-pay-for-it. All right?"

"Pay? What, diamonds!"

Eli raised a hand to his inside pocket, then let it drop. Oh stupid! Tzuref, father to eighteen, had smacked not what lay under his coat, but deeper, under the ribs.

"Oh . . ." Eli said. He moved away along the wall. "The suit is all he's got then."

"You got my letter," Tzuref said.

Eli stayed back in the shadow, and Tzuref turned to his chair. He swished Eli's letter from the floor, and held it up. "You say too much . . . all this reasoning . . . all these conditions . . ."

"What can I do?"

"You have the word 'suffer' in English?"

"We have the word suffer. We have the word law too."

"Stop with the law! You have the word suffer. Then try it. It's a little thing."

"They won't," Eli said.

"But you, Mr. Peck, how about you?"

"I am them, they are me, Mr. Tzuref."

"Aach! You are us, we are you!"

Eli shook and shook his head. In the dark he suddenly felt that Tzuref might put him under a spell. "Mr. Tzuref, a little light?"

Tzuref lit what tallow was left in the holders. Eli was afraid to ask if they couldn't afford electricity. Maybe candles were all they had left.

"Mr. Peck, who made the law, may I ask you that?"

"The people."

"No."

"Yes."

"Before the people."

"No one. Before the people there was no law." Eli didn't care for the conversation, but with only candlelight, he was being lulled into it.

"Wrong," Tzuref said.

"We make the law, Mr. Tzuref. It is our community. These are my neighbors. I am their attorney. They pay me. Without law there is chaos."

"What you call law, I call shame. The heart, Mr. Peck, the heart is law! God!" he announced.

"Look, Mr. Tzuref, I didn't come here to talk metaphysics. People use the law, it's a flexible thing. They protect what they value, their property, their well-being, their happiness—"

"Happiness? They hide their shame. And you, Mr. Peck, you are shameless?"

"We do it," Eli said, wearily, "for our children. This is the twentieth century . . ."

"For the goyim maybe. For me the Fifty-eighth." He pointed at Eli. "That is too old for shame."

Eli felt squashed. Everybody in the world had evil reasons for his actions. Everybody! With reasons so cheap, who buys bulbs. "Enough wisdom, Mr. Tzuref. Please. I'm exhausted."

"Who isn't?" Tzuref said.

He picked Eli's papers from his desk and reached up with them. "What do you intend for us to do?"

"What you must," Eli said. "I made the offer."

"So he must give up his suit?"

"Tzuref, Tzuref, leave me be with that suit! I'm not the only lawyer in the world. I'll drop the case, and you'll get somebody who won't talk compromise. Then you'll have no home, no children, nothing. Only a lousy black suit! Sacrifice what you want. I know what I would do."

To that Tzuref made no answer, but only handed Eli his letters.

"It's not me, Mr. Tzuref, it's them."

"They are you."

"No," Eli intoned, "I am me. They are them. You are you."

"You talk about leaves and branches. I'm dealing with under the dirt."

"Mr. Tzuref, you're driving me crazy with Talmudic wisdom. This is that, that is the other thing. Give me a straight answer."

"Only for straight questions."

"Oh, God!"

Eli returned to his chair and plunged his belongings into his case. "Then, that's all," he said angrily.

Tzuref gave him the shrug.

"Remember, Tzuref, you called this down on yourself."

"*I* did?"

Eli refused to be his victim again. Double-talk proved nothing.

"Goodbye," he said.

But as he opened the door leading to the hall, he heard Tzuref.

"And your wife, how is she?"

"Fine, just fine." Eli kept going.

"And the baby is due when, any day?"

Eli turned. "That's right."

"Well," Tzuref said, rising. "Good luck."

"You know?"

Tzuref pointed out the window—then, with his hands, he drew upon himself a beard, a hat, a long, long coat. When his fingers formed the hem they touched the floor. "He shops two, three times a week, he gets to know them."

"He *talks* to them?"

"He sees them."

"And he can tell which is my wife?"

"They shop at the same stores. He says she is beautiful. She has a kind face. A woman capable of love . . . though who can be sure."

"*He* talks about *us*, to *you?*" demanded Eli.

"You talk about us, to her?"

"Goodbye, Mr. Tzuref."

Tzuref said, "Sholom. And good luck—I know what it is to have children. Sholom," Tzuref whispered, and with the whisper the candles went out. But the instant before, the flames leaped into Tzuref's eyes, and Eli saw it was not luck Tzuref wished him at all.

Outside the door, Eli waited. Down the lawn the children were holding hands and whirling around in a circle. At first he did not move. But he could not hide in the shadows all night. Slowly he began to slip along the front of the house. Under his hands he felt where bricks were out. He moved in the shadows until he reached the side. And then, clutching his briefcase to his chest, he broke across the darkest spots of the lawn. He aimed for a distant glade of woods, and when he reached it he did not stop, but ran through until he was so dizzied that the trees seemed to be running beside him, fleeing not towards Woodenton but away. His lungs were nearly ripping their seams as he burst into the yellow glow of the Gulf station at the edge of town.

"Eli, I had pains today. Where were you?"

"I went to Tzuref."

"Why didn't you call? I was worried."

He tossed his hat past the sofa and onto the floor. "Where are my winter suits?"

"In the hall closet. Eli, it's May."

"I need a strong suit." He left the room, Miriam behind him.

"Eli, talk to me. Sit down. Have dinner. Eli, what are you doing? You're going to get moth balls all over the carpet."

He peered out from the hall closet. Then he peered in again—there was a zipping noise, and suddenly he swept a greenish tweed suit before his wife's eyes.

"Eli, I love you in that suit. But not now. Have something to eat. I made dinner tonight—I'll warm it."

"You've got a box big enough for this suit?"

"I got a Bonwit's box, the other day. Eli, *why?*"

"Miriam, you see me doing something, let me do it."

"You haven't eaten."

"I'm *doing* something." He started up the stairs to the bedroom.

"Eli, would you please tell me what it is you want, and why?"

He turned and looked down at her. "Suppose this time you give me the reasons *before* I tell you what I'm doing. It'll probably work out the same anyway."

"Eli, I want to help."

"It doesn't concern you."

"But I want to help *you*," Miriam said.

"Just be quiet, then."

"But you're upset," she said, and she followed him up the stairs, heavily, breathing for two.

"Eli, what now?"

"A shirt." He yanked open all the drawers of their new teak dresser. He extracted a shirt.

"Eli, batiste? With a tweed suit?" she inquired.

He was at the closet now, on his knees. "Where are my cordovans?"

"Eli, why are you doing this so compulsively? You look like you *have* to do something."

"Oh, Miriam, you're supersubtle."

"Eli, stop this and talk to me. Stop it or I'll call Dr. Eckman."

Eli was kicking off the shoes he was wearing. "Where's the Bonwit box?"

"Eli, do you want me to have the baby right *here!*"

Eli walked over and sat down on the bed. He was draped not only with his own clothing, but also with the greenish tweed suit, the batiste shirt, and under each arm a shoe. He raised his arms and let the shoes drop onto the bed. Then he undid his necktie with one hand and his teeth and added that to the booty.

"Underwear," he said. "He'll need underwear."

"Who!"

He was slipping out of his socks.

Miriam kneeled down and helped him ease his left foot out of the sock. She sat with it on the floor. "Eli, just lie back. Please."

"Plaza 9-3103."

"What?"

"Eckman's number," he said. "It'll save you the trouble."

"Eli—"

"You've got that goddam tender 'You need help' look in your eyes, Miriam, don't tell me you don't."

"I don't."

"I'm not flipping," Eli said.

"I know, Eli."

"Last time I sat in the bottom of the closet and chewed on my bedroom slippers. That's what I did."

"I know."

"And I'm not doing that. This is not a nervous breakdown, Miriam, let's get that straight."

"Okay," Miriam said. She kissed the foot she held. Then, softly, she asked, "What *are* you doing?"

"Getting clothes for the guy in the hat. Don't tell me why, Miriam. Just let me do it."

"That's all?" she asked.

"That's all."

"You're not leaving?"

"No."

"Sometimes I think it gets too much for you, and you'll just leave."

"What gets too much?"

"I don't *know*, Eli. Something gets too much. Whenever everything's peaceful for a long time, and things are nice and pleasant, and we're expecting to be even happier. Like now. It's as if you don't think we *deserve* to be happy."

"Damn it, Miriam! I'm giving this guy a new suit, is that all right? From now on he comes into Woodenton like everybody else, is that all right with you?"

"And Tzuref moves?"

"I don't even know if he'll take the suit, Miriam! Wha do you have to bring up moving!"

"Eli, I didn't bring up moving. Everybody did. Tha what everybody wants. Why make everybody un*happy*. even a law, Eli."

"Don't tell me what's the law."

"All right, sweetie. I'll get the box."

"*I'll* get the box. Where is it?"

"In the basement."

When he came up from the basement, he found all th clothes neatly folded and squared away on the sofa: shir tie, shoes, socks, underwear, belt, and an old gray flann suit. His wife sat on the end of the sofa, looking like an anchored balloon.

"Where's the green suit?" he said.

"Eli, it's your loveliest suit. It's my favorite suit. Whenever I think of you, Eli, it's in that suit."

"Get it out."

"Eli, it's a Brooks Brothers suit. You say yourself how much you love it."

"Get it out."

"But the gray flannel's more practical. For shopping."

"Get it out."

"You go overboard, Eli. That's your trouble. You won't do anything in moderation. That's how people destroy themselves."

"I do *everything* in moderation. That's my trouble. The suit's in the closet again?"

She nodded, and began to fill up with tears. "Why does it have to be *your* suit? Who are you even to decide to give a suit? What about the others?" She was crying openly, and holding her belly. "Eli, I'm going to have a baby. Do we need all *this*?" and she swept the clothes off the sofa to the floor.

At the closet Eli removed the green suit. "It's a J. Press," he said, looking at the lining.

"I hope to hell he's happy with it!" Miriam said, sobbing.

A half hour later the box was packed. The cord he'd found in the kitchen cabinet couldn't keep the outfit from popping through. The trouble was there was too much: the gray suit *and* the green suit, an oxford shirt as well as the batiste. But let him have two suits! Let him have three, four, if only this damn silliness would stop! And a hat—of course! God, he'd almost forgotten the hat. He took the stairs two at a time and in Miriam's closet yanked a hatbox from the top shelf. Scattering hat and tissue paper to the floor, he returned downstairs, where he packed away the hat he'd worn that day. Then he looked at his wife, who lay outstretched on the floor before the fireplace. For the third time in as many minutes she was saying, "Eli, this is the real thing."

"Where?"

"Right under the baby's head, like somebody's squeezing oranges."

Now that he'd stopped to listen he was stupefied. He said, "But you have two more weeks . . ." Somehow he'd really been expecting it was to go on not just another two weeks, but another nine months. This led him to suspect, suddenly, that his wife was feigning pain so as to get his mind off delivering the suit. And just as suddenly he resented himself for having such a thought. God, what had he become! He'd been an unending bastard towards her since this Tzuref business had come up—just when her pregnancy must have been most burdensome. He'd allowed her no access to him, but still, he was sure, for good reasons: she might tempt him out of his confusion with her easy answers. He could be tempted all right, it was why he fought so hard. But now a sweep of love came over him at the thought of her contracting womb, and his child. And yet he would not indicate it to her. Under such splendid marital conditions, who knows but she might extract some promise from him about his concern with the school on the hill.

* * *

Having packed his second bag of the evening, Eli sped his wife to Woodenton Memorial. There she proceeded not to have her baby, but to lie hour after hour through the night having at first oranges, then bowling balls, then basketballs, squeezed back of her pelvis. Eli sat in the waiting room, under the shattering African glare of a dozen rows of fluorescent bulbs, composing a letter to Tzuref.

> Dear Mr. Tzuref:
>
> The clothes in this box are for the gentleman in the hat. In a life of sacrifice what is one more? But in a life of no sacrifices even one is impossible. Do you see what I'm saying, Mr. Tzuref? I am not a Nazi who would drive eighteen children, who are probably frightened at the sight of a firefly, into homelessness. But if you want a home here, you must accept what we have to offer. The world is the world, Mr. Tzuref. As you would say, what is, is. All we say to this man is change your clothes. Enclosed are two suits and two shirts, and everything else he'll need, including a new hat. When he needs new clothes let me know.
>
> We await his appearance in Woodenton, as we await friendly relations with the Yeshivah of Woodenton.

He signed his name and slid the note under a bursting flap and into the box. Then he went to the phone at the end of the room and dialed Ted Heller's number.

"Hello."

"Shirley, it's Eli."

"Eli, we've been calling all night. The lights are on in your place, but nobody answers. We thought it was burglars."

"Miriam's having the baby."

"At home?" Shirley said. "Oh, Eli, what a fun-idea!"

"Shirley, let me speak to Ted."

After the ear-shaking clatter of the phone whacking the floor, Eli heard footsteps, breathing, throat-clearing, then Ted. "A boy or a girl?"

"Nothing yet."

"You've given Shirley the bug, Eli. Now she's going to have *our* next one at home."

"Good."

"That's a terrific way to bring the family together, Eli."

"Look, Ted, I've settled with Tzuref."

"When are they going?"

"They're not exactly going, Teddie. I settled it—you won't even know they're there."

"A guy dressed like 1000 B.C. and I won't know it? What are you thinking about, pal?"

"He's changing his clothes."

"Yeah, to what? Another funeral suit?"

"Tzuref promised me, Ted. Next time he comes to town, he comes dressed like you and me."

"What! Somebody's kidding somebody, Eli."

Eli's voice shot up. "If he says he'll do it, he'll do it!"

"And, Eli," Ted asked, "he said it?"

"He said it." It cost him a sudden headache, this invention.

"And suppose he doesn't change, Eli. Just suppose. I mean that *might* happen, Eli. This might just be some kind of stall or something."

"No," Eli assured him.

The other end was quiet a moment. "Look, Eli," Ted said, finally, "he changes. Okay? All right? But they're still up there, aren't they? *That* doesn't change."

"The point is you won't know it."

Patiently Ted said, "Is this what we asked of you, Eli? When we put our faith and trust in you, is that what we were asking? We weren't concerned that this guy should become a Beau Brummel, Eli, believe me. We just don't think this is the community for them. And, Eli, we isn't me. The Jewish members of the community appointed me, Artie, and Harry to see what could be done. And we appointed you. And what's happened?"

Eli heard himself say, "What happened, happened."

"Eli, you're talking in crossword puzzles."

"My wife's having a baby," Eli explained, defensively.

"I realize that, Eli. But this is a matter of zoning, isn't it? Isn't that what we discovered? You don't abide by the ordinance, you go. I mean I can't raise mountain goats, say, in my backyard—"

"This isn't so simple, Ted. People are involved—"

"People? Eli, we've been through this and through this. We're not just dealing with people—these are religious fanatics is what they are. Dressing like that. What I'd really like to find out is what goes on up there. I'm getting more and more skeptical, Eli, and I'm not afraid to admit it. It smells like a lot of hocus-pocus abracadabra stuff to me. Guys like Harry, you know, they think and they think and they're afraid to admit what they're thinking. I'll tell you. Look, I don't even know about this Sunday school business. Sundays I drive my oldest kid all the way to Scarsdale to learn Bible stories . . . and you know what she comes up with? This Abraham in the Bible was going to kill his own *kid* for a sacrifice. She gets nightmares from it, for God's sake! You call that religion? Today a guy like that they'd lock him up. This is an age of science, Eli. I size people's feet with an X-ray machine, for God's sake. They've disproved all that stuff, Eli, and I refuse to sit by and watch it happening on my own front lawn."

"Nothing's happening on your front lawn, Teddie. You're exaggerating, nobody's sacrificing their kid."

"You're damn right, Eli—I'm not sacrificing mine. You'll see when you have your own what it's like. All the place is, is a hideaway for people who can't face life. It's a matter of *needs*. They have all these superstitions, and why do you think? Because they can't face the world, because they can't take their place in society. That's no environment to bring kids up in, Eli."

"Look, Ted, see it from another angle. We can convert them," Eli said, with half a heart.

"What, make a bunch of Catholics out of them? Look, Eli—pal, there's a good healthy relationship in this town because it's modern Jews and Protestants. That's the point, isn't it, Eli? Let's not kid each other, I'm not Harry. The way things are now are fine—like human beings. There's going to be no pogroms in Woodenton. Right? 'Cause there's no fanatics, no crazy people—" Eli winced, and closed his eyes a second—"just people who respect each other, and leave each other be. Common sense is the ruling thing, Eli. I'm for common sense. Moderation."

"Exactly, exactly, Ted. I agree, but common sense, maybe, says make this guy change his clothes. Then maybe—"

"Common sense says that? Common sense says to me

they go and find a nice place somewhere else, Eli. New York is the biggest city in the world, it's only 30 miles away —why don't they go there?"

"Ted, give them a chance. Introduce them to common sense."

"Eli, you're dealing with *fanatics*. Do they display common sense? Talking a dead language, that makes sense? Making a big thing out of suffering, so you're going oy-oy-oy all your life, that's common sense? Look, Eli, we've been through all this. I don't know if you know—but there's talk that *Life* magazine is sending a guy out to the Yeshivah for a story. With pictures."

"Look, Teddie, you're letting your imagination get inflamed. I don't think *Life*'s interested."

"But I'm interested, Eli. And we thought you were supposed to be."

"I am," Eli said, "I am. Let him just change the clothes, Ted. Let's see what happens."

"They live in the medieval ages, Eli—it's some superstition, some *rule*."

"Let's just *see*," Eli pleaded.

"Eli, every day—"

"One more day," Eli said. "If he doesn't change in one more day. . . ."

"What?"

"Then I get an injunction first thing Monday. That's that."

"Look, Eli—it's not up to me. Let me call Harry—"

"You're the spokesman, Teddie. I'm all wrapped up here with Miriam having a baby. Just give me the day—them the day."

"All right, Eli. I want to be fair. But tomorrow, that's all. Tomorrow's the judgment day, Eli, I'm telling you."

"I hear trumpets," Eli said, and hung up. He was shaking inside—Teddie's voice seemed to have separated his bones at the joints. He was still in the phone booth when the nurse came to tell him that Mrs. Peck would positively not be delivered of a child until the morning. He was to go home and get some rest, he looked like *he* was having the baby. The nurse winked and left.

But Eli did not go home. He carried the Bonwit box out into the street with him and put it in the car. The night was soft and starry, and he began to drive the streets of Woodenton. Square cool windows, apricot-colored, were all one could see beyond the long lawns that fronted the homes of the townsmen. The stars polished the permanent baggage carriers atop the station wagons in the driveways. He drove slowly, up, down, around. Only his tires could be heard taking the gentle curves in the road.

What peace. What incredible peace. Have children ever been so safe in their beds? Parents—Eli wondered—so full in their stomachs? Water so warm in its boilers? Never. Never in Rome, never in Greece. Never even did walled cities have it so good! No wonder then they would keep things just as they were. Here, after all, were peace and safety—what civilization had been working toward for centuries. For all his jerkiness, that was all Ted Heller was asking for, peace and safety. It was what his parents had asked for in the Bronx, and his grandparents in Poland, and theirs in Russia or Austria, or wherever else they'd fled to or from. It was what Miriam was asking for. And now they had it—the world was at last a place for families, even Jewish families. After all these centuries, maybe there just had to be this communal toughness—or numbness—to protect such a blessing. Maybe that was the trouble with the Jews all along—too soft. Sure, to live takes guts . . . Eli was thinking as he drove on beyond the train station, and parked his car at the darkened Gulf station. He stepped out, carrying the box.

At the top of the hill one window trembled with light. What *was* Tzuref doing up there in that office? Killing babies—probably not. But studying a language no one understood? Practicing customs with origins long forgotten? Suffering sufferings already suffered once too often? Teddie was right—why keep it up! However, if a man chose to be stubborn, then he couldn't expect to survive. The world is give-and-take. What sense to sit and brood over a suit. Eli would give him one last chance.

He stopped at the top. No one was around. He walked slowly up the lawn, setting each foot into the grass, listening to the shh shhh shhhh his shoes made as they bent the wetness into the sod. He looked around. Here there was nothing. Nothing! An old decaying house—and a suit.

On the porch he slid behind a pillar. He felt someone was watching him. But only the stars gleamed down. And

at his feet, off and away, Woodenton glowed up. He set
his package on the step of the great front door. Inside the
cover of the box he felt to see if his letter was still there.
When he touched it, he pushed it deeper into the green
suit, which his fingers still remembered from winter. He
should have included some light bulbs. Then he slid back
by the pillar again, and this time there was something on
the lawn. It was the second sight he had of him. He was
facing Woodenton and barely moving across the open
space towards the trees. His right fist was beating his
chest. And then Eli heard a sound rising with each knock
on the chest. What a moan! It could raise hair, stop hearts,
water eyes. And it did all three to Eli, plus more. Some
feeling crept into him for whose deepness he could find no
word. It was strange. He listened—it did not hurt to hear
this moan. But he wondered if it hurt to make it. And so,
with only stars to hear, he tried. And it did hurt. Not the
bumblebee of noise that turned at the back of his throat
and winged out his nostrils. What hurt buzzed down. It
stung and stung inside him, and in turn the moan sharp-
ened. It became a scream, louder, a song, a crazy song
that whined through the pillars and blew out to the grass,
until the strange hatted creature on the lawn turned and
threw his arms wide, and looked in the night like a scare-
crow.

Eli ran, and when he reached the car the pain was only
a bloody scratch across his neck where a branch had
whipped back as he fled the greenie's arms.

The following day his son was born. But not till one in
the afternoon, and by then a great deal had happened.

First, at nine-thirty the phone rang. Eli leaped from the
sofa—where he'd dropped the night before—and picked
it screaming from the cradle. He could practically smell
the hospital as he shouted into the phone, "Hello, yes!"

"Eli, it's Ted. Eli, he *did* it. He just walked by the store.
I was opening the door, Eli, and I turned around and I
swear I thought it was you. But it was him. He still walks
like he did, but the clothes, Eli, the clothes."

"Who?"

"The greenie. He has on man's regular clothes. And the
suit, it's a beauty."

The suit barreled back into Eli's consciousness, pushing all else aside. "What color suit?"

"Green. He's just strolling in the green suit like it's a holiday. Eli . . . is it a Jewish holiday?"

"Where is he now?"

"He's walking straight up Coach House Road, in this damn tweed job. Eli, it worked. You were right."

"We'll see."

"What next?"

"We'll see."

He took off the underwear in which he'd slept and went into the kitchen where he turned the light under the coffee. When it began to perk he held his head over the pot so it would steam loose the knot back of his eyes. It still hadn't when the phone rang.

"Eli, Ted again. Eli, the guy's walking up and down every street in town. Really, he's on a tour or something. Artie called me, Herb called me. Now Shirley calls that he just walked by our house. Eli, go out on the porch you'll see."

Eli went to the window and peered out. He couldn't see past the bend in the road, and there was no one in sight.

"Eli?" He heard Ted from where he dangled over the telephone table. He dropped the phone into the hook, as a few last words floated up to him—"Eliyousawhim . . . ?" He threw on the pants and shirt he'd worn the night before and walked barefoot on to his front lawn. And sure enough, his apparition appeared around the bend: in a brown hat a little too far down on his head, a green suit too far back on the shoulders, an unbuttoned-down button-down shirt, a tie knotted so as to leave a two-inch tail, trousers that cascaded onto his shoes—he was shorter than that black hat had made him seem. And moving the clothes was that walk that was not a walk, the tiny-stepped shlumpy gait. He came round the bend, and for all his strangeness—it clung to his whiskers, signaled itself in his locomotion—he looked as if he belonged. Eccentric, maybe, but he belonged. He made no moan, nor did he invite Eli with wide-flung arms. But he did stop when he saw him. He stopped and put a hand to his hat. When he felt for its top, his hand went up too high. Then it found the level and fiddled with the brim. The fingers fiddled, fumbled, and when they'd finally made their greeting, they traveled down the fellow's face and in an instant seemed to have touched each one of his features. They dabbed the eyes, ran the length of the nose, swept over the hairy lip, until they found their home in the hair that hid a little of his collar. To Eli the fingers said, *I have a face, I have a face at least.* Then his hand came through the beard and when it stopped at his chest it was like a pointer—and the eyes asked a question as tides of water shifted over them. *The face is all right, I can keep it?* Such a look was in those eyes that Eli was still seeing them when he turned his head away. They were the hearts of his jonquils, that only last week had appeared —they were the leaves on his birch, the bulbs in his coach lamp, the droppings on his lawn: those eyes were the eyes in his head. They were his, he had made them. He turned and went into his house and when he peeked out the side of the window, between shade and molding, the green suit was gone.

The phone.

"Eli, Shirley."

"I saw him, Shirley," and he hung up.

He sat frozen for a long time. The sun moved around the windows. The coffee steam smelled up the house. The phone began to ring, stopped, began again. The mailman came, the cleaner, the bakery man, the gardener, the ice cream man, the League of Women Voters lady. A Negro woman spreading some strange gospel calling for the revision of the Food and Drug Act knocked at the front, rapped the windows, and finally scraped a half-dozen pamphlets under the back door. But Eli only sat, without underwear, in last night's suit. He answered to no one.

Given his condition, it was strange that the trip and crash at the back door reached his inner ear. But in an instant he seemed to melt down into the crevices of the chair, then to splash up and out to where the clatter had been. At the door he waited. It was silent, but for a fluttering of damp little leaves on the trees. When he finally opened the door, there was no one there. He'd expected to see green, green, green, big as the doorway, topped by his hat, waiting for him with those eyes. But there was no one out there, except for the Bonwit's box which lay bulging at his feet. No string tied it and the top rode high on the bottom.

The coward! He couldn't do it! He couldn't!

The very glee of that idea pumped fuel to his legs. He tore out across his back lawn, past his new spray of forsythia, to catch a glimpse of the bearded one fleeing naked through yards, over hedges and fences, to the safety of his hermitage. In the distance a pile of pink and white stones—which Harriet Knudson had painted the previous day—tricked him. "Run," he shouted to the rocks, "Run, you . . ." but he caught his error before anyone else did, and though he peered and craned there was no hint anywhere of a man about his own size, with white, white, terribly white skin (how white must be the skin of his body!) in cowardly retreat. He came slowly, curiously, back to the door. And while the trees shimmered in the light wind, he removed the top from the box. The shock at first was the shock of having daylight turned off all at once. Inside the box was an eclipse. But black soon sorted from black, and shortly there was the glassy black of lining, the coarse black of trousers, the dead black of fraying threads, and in the center the mountain of black: the hat. He picked the box from the doorstep and carried it inside. For the first time in his life he *smelled* the color of blackness: a little stale, a little sour, a little old, but nothing that could overwhelm you. Still, he held the package at arm's length and deposited it on the dining room table.

Twenty rooms on a hill and they store their old clothes with me! What am I supposed to do with them? Give them to charity? That's where they came from. He picked up the hat by the edges and looked inside. The crown was smooth as an egg, the brim practically threadbare. There is nothing else to do with a hat in one's hands but put it on, so Eli dropped the thing on his head. He opened the door to the hall closet and looked at himself in the full-length mirror. The hat gave him bags under the eyes. Or perhaps he had not slept well. He pushed the brim lower till a shadow touched his lips. Now the bags under his eyes had inflated to become his face. Before the mirror he unbuttoned his shirt, unzipped his trousers, and then, shedding his clothes, he studied what he was. What a silly disappointment to see yourself naked in a hat. Especially in that hat. He sighed, but could not rid himself of the great weakness that suddenly set on his muscles and joints, beneath the terrible weight of the stranger's strange hat.

He returned to the dining room table and emptied the box of its contents: jacket, trousers, and vest (*it* smelled deeper than blackness). And under it all, sticking between the shoes that looked chopped and bitten, came the first gleam of white. A little fringed serape, a gray piece of semiunderwear, was crumpled at the bottom, its thready border twisted into itself. Eli removed it and let it hang free. What is it? For warmth? To wear beneath underwear in the event of a chest cold? He held it to his nose but it did not smell from Vick's or mustard plaster. It was something special, some Jewish thing. Special food, special language, special prayers, why not special BVD's? So fearful was he that he would be tempted back into wearing his traditional clothes—reasoned Eli—that he had carried and buried in Woodenton everything, including the special underwear. For that was how Eli now understood the box of clothes. The greenie was saying, Here, I give up. I refuse even to be tempted. We surrender. And that was how Eli continued to understand it until he found he'd slipped the white fringy surrender flag over his hat and felt it clinging to his chest. And now, looking at himself in the mirror, he was momentarily uncertain as to who was tempting who into what. Why *did* the greenie leave his clothes? Was it even the greenie? Then who was it? And why? But, Eli, for Christ's sake, in an age of science things don't happen like that. Even the goddam pigs take drugs . . .

Regardless of who was the source of the temptation, what was its end, not to mention its beginning, Eli, some moments later, stood draped in black, with a little white underneath, before the full-length mirror. He had to pull down on the trousers so they would not show the hollow of his ankle. The greenie, didn't he wear socks? Or had he forgotten them? The mystery was solved when Eli mustered enough courage to investigate the trouser pockets. He had expected some damp awful thing to happen to his fingers should he slip them down and out of sight—but when at last he jammed bravely down he came up with a khaki army sock in each hand. As he slipped them over

his toes, he invented a genesis: a G.I.'s present in 1945.
Plus everything else lost between 1938 and 1945, he had
also lost his socks. Not that he had lost the socks, but that
he'd had to stoop to accepting these, made Eli almost cry.
To calm himself he walked out the back door and stood
looking at his lawn.

On the Knudson back lawn, Harriet Knudson was giving
her stones a second coat of pink. She looked up just as Eli
stepped out. Eli shot back in again and pressed himself
against the back door. When he peeked between the cur-
tain all he saw were paint bucket, brush, and rocks scattered on the Knudsons' pink-spattered grass. The phone
rang. Who was it—Harriet Knudson? Eli, there's a Jew at
your door. *That's me.* Nonsense, Eli, I saw him with my
own eyes. *That's me, I saw you too, painting your rocks
pink.* Eli, you're having a nervous breakdown again.
Jimmy, Eli's having a nervous breakdown again. Eli, this
is Jimmy, hear you're having a little breakdown, anything
I can do, boy? Eli, this is Ted, Shirley says you need help.
Eli, this is Artie, you need help. Eli, Harry, you need help
you need help . . . The phone rattled its last and died.

"God helps them who help themselves," intoned Eli, and
once again he stepped out the door. This time he walked
to the center of his lawn and in full sight of the trees, the
grass, the birds, and the sun, revealed that it was he, Eli,
in the costume. But nature had nothing to say to him, and
so stealthily he made his way to the hedge separating his
property from the field beyond and he cut his way through,
losing his hat twice in the underbrush. Then, clamping the
hat to his head, he began to run, the threaded tassels
jumping across his heart. He ran through the weeds and
wild flowers, until on the old road that skirted the town he
slowed up. He was walking when he approached the Gulf
station from the back. He supported himself on a huge
tireless truck rim, and among tubes, rusted engines, dozens of topless oil cans, he rested. With a kind of brainless
cunning, he readied himself for the last mile of his journey.

"How are you, Pop?" It was the garage attendant, rub-
bing his greasy hands on his overalls, and hunting among
the cans.

Eli's stomach lurched and he pulled the big black coat
round his neck.

"Nice day," the attendant said and started around to the front.

"Sholom," Eli whispered and zoomed off towards the hill.

The sun was directly overhead when Eli reached the top. He had come by way of the woods, where it was cooler, but still he was perspiring beneath his new suit. The hat had no sweatband and the cloth clutched his head. The children were playing. The children were always playing, as if it was that alone that Tzuref had to teach them. In their shorts, they revealed such thin legs that beneath one could see the joints swiveling as they ran. Eli waited for them to disappear around a corner before he came into the open. But something would not let him wait—his green suit. It was on the porch, wrapped around the bearded fellow, who was painting the base of a pillar. His arm went up and down, up and down, and the pillar glowed like white fire. The very sight of him popped Eli out of the woods onto the lawn. He did not turn back, though his insides did. He walked up the lawn, but the children played on; tipping the black hat, he mumbled, "Shhh . . . shhhh," and they hardly seemed to notice.

At last he smelled paint.

He waited for the man to turn to him. He only painted. Eli felt suddenly that if he could pull the black hat down over his eyes, over his chest and belly and legs, if he could shut out all light, then a moment later he would be home in bed. But the hat wouldn't go past his forehead. He couldn't kid himself—he was there. No one he could think of had forced him to do this.

The greenie's arm flailed up and down on the pillar. Eli breathed loudly, cleared his throat, but the greenie wouldn't make life easier for him. At last, Eli had to say "Hello."

The arm swished up and down; it stopped—two fingers went out after a brush hair stuck to the pillar.

"Good day," Eli said.

The hair came away; the swishing resumed.

"Sholom," Eli whispered and the fellow turned.

The recognition took some time. He looked at what Eli wore. Up close, Eli looked at what he wore. And then Eli had the strange notion that he was two people. Or that he was one person wearing two suits. The greenie looked to be suffering from a similar confusion. They stared long at one another. Eli's heart shivered, and his brain was momentarily in such a mixed-up condition that his hands went out to button down the collar of his shirt that somebody else was wearing. What a mess! The greenie flung his arms over his face.

"What's the matter . . ." Eli said. The fellow had picked up his bucket and brush and was running away. Eli ran after him.

"I wasn't going to hit . . ." Eli called. "Stop . . ." Eli caught up and grabbed his sleeve. Once again, the greenie's hands flew up to his face. This time, in the violence, white paint spattered both of them.

"I only want to . . ." But in that outfit Eli didn't really know what he wanted. "To talk . . ." he said finally. "For you to look at me. Please, just *look* at me . . ."

The hands stayed put, as paint rolled off the brush onto the cuff of Eli's green suit.

"Please . . . please," Eli said, but he did not know what to do. "Say something, speak *English*," he pleaded.

The fellow pulled back against the wall, back, back, as though some arm would finally reach out and yank him to safety. He refused to uncover his face.

"Look," Eli said, pointing to himself. "It's your suit. I'll take care of it."

No answer—only a little shaking under the hands, which led Eli to speak as gently as he knew how.

"Well . . . we'll moth-proof it. There's a button missing" —Eli pointed—"I'll have it fixed. I'll have a zipper put in . . . Please, please—just look at me . . ." He was talking to himself, and yet how could he stop? Nothing he said made any sense—that alone made his heart swell. Yet somehow babbling on, he might babble something that would make things easier between them. "Look . . ." He reached inside his shirt to pull the frills of underwear into the light. "I'm wearing the special underwear, even . . . Please," he said, *"please, please, please"* he sang, as if it were some sacred word. "Oh, *please* . . ."

Nothing twitched under the tweed suit—and if the eyes watered, or twinkled, or hated, he couldn't tell. It was driving him crazy. He had dressed like a fool, and for what? For this? He reached up and yanked the hands away.

"There!" he said—and in that first instant all he saw of the greenie's face were two white droplets stuck to each cheek.

"Tell me—" Eli clutched his hands down to his sides —"Tell me, what can I do for you, I'll do it . . ."

Stiffly, the greenie stood there, sporting his two white tears.

"Whatever I can do . . . Look, look, what I've done *already*." He grabbed his black hat and shook it in the man's face.

And in exchange, the greenie gave him an answer. He raised one hand to his chest, and then jammed it, finger first, towards the horizon. And with what a pained look! As though the air were full of razors! Eli followed the finger and saw beyond the knuckle, out past the nail, Woodenton.

"What do you want?" Eli said. "I'll bring it!"

Suddenly the greenie made a run for it. But then he stopped, wheeled, and jabbed that finger at the air again. It pointed the same way. Then he was gone.

And then, all alone, Eli had the revelation. He did not question his understanding, the substance or the source. But with a strange, dreamy elation, he started away.

On Coach House Road, they were double-parked. The Mayor's wife pushed a grocery cart full of dog food from Stop N' Shop to her station wagon. The President of the Lions Club, a napkin around his neck, was jamming pennies into the meter in front of the Bit-in-Teeth Restaurant. Ted Heller caught the sun as it glazed off the new Byzantine mosaic entrance to his shoe shop. In pinkened jeans, Mrs. Jimmy Knudson was leaving Halloway's Hardware, a paint bucket in each hand. Roger's Beauty Shoppe had its doors open—women's heads in silver bullets far as the eye could see. Over by the barbershop the pole spun, and Artie Berg's youngest sat on a red horse, having his hair cut; his mother flipped through *Look*, smiling: the greenie had changed his clothes.

And into this street, which seemed paved with chromium, came Eli Peck. It was not enough, he knew, to walk up one side of the street. That was not enough. Instead he walked ten paces up one side, then on an angle, crossed to the other side, where he walked ten more paces, and crossed back. Horns blew, traffic jerked, as Eli made his way up Coach House Road. He spun a moan high up in his nose as he walked. Outside no one could hear him, but he felt it vibrate the cartilage at the bridge of his nose.

Things slowed around him. The sun stopped rippling on spokes and hubcaps. It glowed steadily as everyone put on brakes to look at the man in black. They always paused and gaped, whenever he entered the town. Then in a minute, or two, or three, a light would change, a baby squawk, and the flow continue. Now, though lights changed, no one moved.

"He shaved his beard," Eric the barber said.

"Who?" asked Linda Berg.

"The . . . the guy in the suit. From the place there."

Linda looked out the window.

"It's Uncle Eli," little Kevin Berg said, spitting hair.

"Oh, God," Linda said, "Eli's having a nervous breakdown."

"A nervous breakdown!" Ted Heller said, but not immediately. Immediately he had said "Hoooly . . ."

Shortly, everybody in Coach House Road was aware that Eli Peck, the nervous young attorney with the pretty wife, was having a breakdown. Everybody except Eli Peck. He knew what he did was not insane, though he felt every inch of its strangeness. He felt those black clothes as if they were the skin of his skin—the give and pull as they got used to where he bulged and buckled. And he felt eyes, every eye on Coach House Road. He saw headlights screech to within an inch of him, and stop. He saw mouths: first the bottom jaw slides forward, then the tongue hits the teeth, the lips explode, a little thunder in the throat, and they've said it: Eli Peck Eli Peck Eli Peck Eli Peck. He began to walk slowly, shifting his weight down and forward with each syllable: E-li–Peck–E-li–Peck–E-li–Peck. Heavily he trod, and as his neighbors uttered each syllable of his name, he felt each syllable shaking all his bones. He knew who he was down to his marrow—they were telling him. Eli Peck. He wanted them to say it a thousand times, a million times, he would walk forever in that black suit, as adults whispered of his strangeness and children made "Shame . . . shame" with their fingers.

"It's going to be all right, pal . . ." Ted Heller was motioning to Eli from his doorway. "C'mon, pal, it's going to be all right . . ."

Eli saw him, past the brim of his hat. Ted did not move from his doorway, but leaned forward and spoke with his hand over his mouth. Behind him, three customers peered through the doorway. "Eli, it's Ted, remember Ted . . ."

Eli crossed the street and found he was heading directly towards Harriet Knudson. He lifted his neck so she could see his whole face.

He saw her forehead melt down to her lashes. "Good morning, Mr. Peck."

"Sholom," Eli said, and crossed the street where he saw the President of the Lions.

"Twice before . . ." he heard someone say, and then he crossed again, mounted the curb, and was before the bakery, where a delivery man charged past with a tray of powdered cakes twirling above him. "Pardon me, Father," he said, and scooted into his truck. But he could not move it. Eli Peck had stopped traffic.

He passed the Rivoli Theater, Beekman Cleaners, Harris' Westinghouse, the Unitarian Church, and soon he was passing only trees. At Ireland Road he turned right and started through Woodenton's winding streets. Baby carriages stopped whizzing and creaked—"Isn't that . . ." Gardeners held their clipping. Children stepped from the sidewalk and tried the curb. And Eli greeted no one, but raised his face to all. He wished passionately that he had white tears to show them . . . And not till he reached his own front lawn, saw his house, his shutters, his new jonquils, did he remember his wife. And the child that must have been born to him. And it was then and there he had the awful moment. He could go inside and put on his clothes and go to his wife in the hospital. It was not irrevocable, even the walk wasn't. In Woodenton memories are long but fury short. Apathy works like forgiveness. Besides, when you've flipped, you've flipped—it's Mother Nature.

What gave Eli the awful moment was that he turned away. He knew exactly what he could do but he chose not to. To go inside would be to go halfway. There was more . . . So he turned and walked towards the hospital and all the time he quaked an eighth of an inch beneath his skin to think that perhaps he'd chosen the crazy way. To think that he'd *chosen* to be crazy! But if you chose to be crazy, then you weren't crazy. It's when you didn't choose. No, he wasn't flipping. He had a child to see.

"Name?"

"Peck."

"Fourth floor." He was given a little blue card.

In the elevator everybody stared. Eli watched his black shoes rise four floors.

"Four."

He tipped his hat, but knew he couldn't take it off.

"Peck," he said. He showed the card.

"Congratulations," the nurse said. ". . . the grand-father?"

"The father. Which room?"

She led him to 412. "A joke on the Mrs?" she said, but he slipped in the door without her.

"Miriam?"

"Yes?"

"Eli."

She rolled her white face towards her husband. "Oh, Eli . . . Oh, Eli."

He raised his arms. "What could I do?"

"You have a son. They called all morning."

"I came to see him."

"Like *that!*" she whispered harshly. "Eli, you can't go around like that."

"I have a son. I want to see him."

"Eli, why are you doing this to me!" Red seeped back into her lips. *"He's* not your fault," she explained. "Oh, Eli, sweetheart, why do you feel guilty about everything. Eli, change your clothes. I forgive you."

"Stop forgiving me. Stop understanding me."

"But I love you."

"That's something else."

"But, sweetie, you *don't* have to dress like that. You didn't do anything. You don't have to feel guilty because . . . because everything's all right. Eli, can't you see that?"

"Miriam, enough reasons. Where's my son?"

"Oh, please, Eli, don't flip now. I need you now. Is that why you're flipping—because I need you?"

"In your selfish way, Miriam, you're very generous. I want my son."

"Don't flip now. I'm afraid, now that he's out." She was beginning to whimper. "I don't know if I love him, now that he's out. When I look in the mirror, Eli, he won't be there . . . Eli, Eli, you look like you're going to your own funeral. Please, can't you leave well enough *alone?* Can't we just have a family?"

"No."

In the corridor he asked the nurse to lead him to his son. The nurse walked on one side of him, Ted Heller on the other.

"Eli, do you want some help? I thought you might want some help."

"No."

Ted whispered something to the nurse; then to Eli he whispered, "Should you be walking around like this?"

"Yes."

In his ear Ted said, "You'll . . . you'll frighten the kid . . ."

"There," the nurse said. She pointed to a bassinet in the second row and looked, puzzled, to Ted. "Do I go in?" Eli said.

"No," the nurse said. "She'll roll him over." She rapped on the enclosure full of babies. "Peck," she mouthed to the nurse on the inside.

Ted tapped Eli's arm. "You're not thinking of doing something you'll be sorry for . . . are you, Eli? Eli—I mean you know you're still Eli, don't you?"

In the enclosure, Eli saw a bassinet had been wheeled before the square window.

"Oh, Christ. . . ." Ted said. "You don't have this Bible stuff on the brain—" And suddenly he said, "You wait, pal." He started down the corridor, his heels tapping rapidly.

Eli felt relieved—he leaned forward. In the basket was what he'd come to see. Well, now that he was here, what did he think he was going to say to it? I'm your father, Eli, the Flipper? I am wearing a black hat, suit, and fancy underwear, all borrowed from a friend? How could he admit to this reddened ball—*his* reddened ball—the worst of all: that Eckman would shortly convince him he wanted to take off the whole business. He couldn't admit it! He wouldn't do it!

Past his hat brim, from the corner of his eye, he saw Ted had stopped in a doorway at the end of the corridor.

Two interns stood there smoking, listening to Ted. Eli ignored it.

No, even Eckman wouldn't make him take it off! No! He'd wear it, if he chose to. He'd make the kid wear it! Sure! Cut it down when the time came. A smelly hand-me-down, whether the kid liked it or not!

Only Teddie's heels clacked; the interns wore rubber soles—for they were there, beside him, unexpectedly. Their white suits smelled, but not like Eli's.

"Eli," Ted said, softly, "visiting time's up, pal."

"How are you feeling, Mr. Peck? First child upsets everyone. . . ."

He'd just pay no attention; nevertheless, he began to perspire, thickly, and his hat crown clutched his hair.

"Excuse me—Mr. Peck. . . ." It was a new rich bass voice. "Excuse me, rabbi, but you're wanted . . . in the temple." A hand took his elbow, firmly; then another hand, the other elbow. Where they grabbed, his tendons went taut.

"Okay, rabbi. Okay okay okay okay okay okay. . . ." He listened; it was a very soothing word, that okay. "Okay okay everything's going to be okay." His feet seemed to have left the ground some, as he glided away from the window, the bassinet, the babies. "Okay easy does it everything's all right all right—"

But he rose, suddenly, as though up out of a dream, and flailing his arms, screamed: *"I'm the father!"*

But the window disappeared. In a moment they tore off his jacket—it gave so easily, in one yank. Then a needle slid under his skin. The drug calmed his soul, but did not touch it down where the blackness had reached.

Bernard Malamud

ANGEL LEVINE

Manischevitz, a tailor, in his fifty-first year suffered many reverses and indignities. Previously a man of comfortable means, he overnight lost all he had, when his establishment caught fire and, after a metal container of cleaning fluid exploded, burned to the ground. Although Manischevitz was insured against fire, damage suits by two customers who had been hurt in the flames deprived him of every penny he had collected. At almost the same time, his son, of much promise, was killed in the war, and his daughter, without so much as a word of warning, married a lout and disappeared with him as off the face of the earth. Thereafter Manischevitz was victimized by excruciating backaches and found himself unable to work even as a presser—the only kind of work available to him—for more than an hour or two daily, because beyond that the pain from standing became maddening. His Fanny, a good wife and mother, who had taken in washing and sewing, began before his eyes to waste away. Suffering shortness of breath, she at last became seriously ill and took to her bed. The doctor, a former customer of Manischevitz, who out of pity treated them, at first had difficulty diagnosing her ailment but later put it down as hardening of the arteries at an advanced stage. He took Manischevitz aside, prescribed complete rest for her, and in whispers gave him to know there was little hope.

Throughout his trials Manischevitz had remained somewhat stoic, almost unbelieving that all this had descended upon his head, as if it were happening, let us say, to an acquaintance or some distant relative; it was in sheer quantity of woe incomprehensible. It was also ridiculous, unjust, and because he had always been a religious man, it was in a way an affront to God. Manischevitz believed this in all his suffering. When his burden had grown too crushingly heavy to be borne he prayed in his chair with shut hollow eyes: "My dear God, sweetheart, did I deserve that this should happen to me?" Then recognizing the worthlessness of it, he put aside the complaint and prayed humbly for assistance: "Give Fanny back her health, and to me for myself that I shouldn't feel pain in every step. Help now or tomorrow is too late. This I don't have to tell you." And Manischevitz wept.

Manischevitz's flat, which he had moved into after the disastrous fire, was a meager one, furnished with a few sticks of chairs, a table, and bed, in one of the poorer sections of the city. There were three rooms: a small, poorly-papered living room; an apology for a kitchen, with a wooden icebox; and the comparatively large bedroom where Fanny lay in a sagging secondhand bed, gasping for breath. The bedroom was the warmest room of the house and it was here, after his outburst to God, that Manischevitz, by the light of two small bulbs overhead, sat reading his Jewish newspaper. He was not truly reading, because his thoughts were everywhere; however the print offered a convenient resting place for his eyes, and a word or two, when he permitted himself to comprehend them, had the momentary effect of helping him forget his troubles. After a short while he discovered, to his surprise, that he was actively scanning the news, searching for an item of great interest to him. Exactly what he thought he would read he couldn't say—until he realized, with some astonishment, that he was expecting to discover something about himself. Manischevitz put his paper down and looked up with the distinct impression that someone had entered the apartment, though he could not remember having heard the sound of the door opening. He looked around: the room was very still, Fanny sleeping, for once, quietly. Half-frightened, he watched her until he was satisfied she wasn't dead; then, still disturbed by the thought of an unannounced visitor, he stumbled into the living room and there had the shock of his life, for at the table sat a Negro reading a newspaper he had folded up to fit into one hand.

"What do you want here?" Manischevitz asked in fright.

The Negro put down the paper and glanced up with a gentle expression. "Good evening." He seemed not to be sure of himself, as if he had got into the wrong house. He was a large man, bonily built, with a heavy head covered by a hard derby, which he made no attempt to remove. His eyes seemed sad, but his lips, above which he wore a slight mustache, sought to smile; he was not otherwise prepossessing. The cuffs of his sleeves, Manischevitz noted, were frayed to the lining and the dark suit was badly fitted. He had very large feet. Recovering from his fright, Manischevitz guessed he had left the door open and was being visited by a case worker from the Welfare Department—some came at night—for he had recently applied for relief. Therefore he lowered himself into a chair opposite the Negro, trying, before the man's uncertain smile, to feel comfortable. The former tailor sat stiffly but patiently at the table, waiting for the investigator to take out his pad and pencil and begin asking questions; but before long he became convinced the man intended to do nothing of the sort.

"Who are you?" Manischevitz at last asked uneasily.

"If I may, insofar as one is able to, identify myself, I bear the name of Alexander Levine."

In spite of all his troubles Manischevitz felt a smile growing on his lips. "You said Levine?" he politely inquired.

The Negro nodded. "That is exactly right."

Carrying the jest farther, Manischevitz asked, "You are maybe Jewish?"

"All my life I was, willingly."

The tailor hesitated. He had heard of black Jews but had never met one. It gave an unusual sensation.

Recognizing in afterthought something odd about the tense of Levine's remark, he said doubtfully, "You ain't Jewish anymore?"

Levine at this point removed his hat, revealing a very white part in his black hair, but quickly replaced it. He replied, "I have recently been disincarnated into an angel. As such, I offer you my humble assistance, if to offer is within my province and ability—in the best sense." He lowered his eyes in apology. "Which calls for added explanation: I am what I am granted to be, and at present the completion is in the future."

"What kind of angel is this?" Manischevitz gravely asked.

"A bona fide angel of God, within prescribed limitations," answered Levine, "not to be confused with the members of any particular sect, order, or organization here on earth operating under a similar name."

Manischevitz was thoroughly disturbed. He had been expecting something but not this. What sort of mockery was it—provided Levine was an angel—of a faithful servant who had from childhood lived in the synagogues, always concerned with the word of God?

To test Levine he asked, "Then where are your wings?"

The Negro blushed as well as he was able. Manischevitz understood this from his changed expression. "Under certain circumstances we lose privileges and prerogatives upon returning to earth, no matter for what purpose, or endeavoring to assist whosoever."

"So tell me," Manischevitz said triumphantly, "how did you get here?"

"I was transmitted."

Still troubled, the tailor said, "If you are a Jew, say the blessing for bread."

Levine recited it in sonorous Hebrew.

Although moved by the familiar words Manischevitz still felt doubt that he was dealing with an angel.

"If you are an angel," he demanded somewhat angrily, "give me the proof."

Levine wet his lips. "Frankly, I cannot perform either miracles or near miracles, due to the fact that I am in a condition of probation. How long that will persist or even consist, I admit, depends on the outcome."

Manischevitz racked his brains for some means of causing Levine positively to reveal his true identity, when the Negro spoke again:

"It was given me to understand that both your wife and you require assistance of a salubrious nature?"

The tailor could not rid himself of the feeling that he was the butt of a jokester. Is this what a Jewish angel looks like? he asked himself. This I am not convinced.

He asked a last question. "So if God sends to me an angel, why a black? Why not a white that there are so many of them?"

"It was my turn to go next," Levine explained.

Manischevitz could not be persuaded. "I think you are a faker."

Levine slowly rose. His eyes showed disappointment and

worry. "Mr. Manischevitz," he said tonelessly, "if you
should desire me to be of assistance to you any time in
the near future, or possibly before, I can be found"—he
glanced at his fingernails—"in Harlem."

He was by then gone.

The next day Manischevitz felt some relief from his
backache and was able to work four hours at pressing.
The day after, he put in six hours; and the third day four
again. Fanny sat up a little and asked for some halvah to
suck. But on the fourth day the stabbing, breaking ache
afflicted his back, and Fanny again lay supine, breathing
with blue-lipped difficulty.

Manischevitz was profoundly disappointed at the return
of his active pain and suffering. He had hoped for a longer
interval of easement, long enough to have some thought
other than of himself and his troubles. Day by day, hour
by hour, minute after minute, he lived in pain, pain his
only memory, questioning the necessity of it, inveighing
against it, also, though with affection, against God. Why
so much, Gottenyu? If He wanted to teach His servant a
lesson for some reason, some cause—the nature of His
nature—to teach him, say, for reasons of his weakness, his
pride, perhaps, during his years of prosperity, his frequent
neglect of God—to give him a little lesson, why then any
of the tragedies that had happened to him, any *one* would
have sufficed to chasten him. But *all together*—the loss of
both his children, his means of livelihood, Fanny's health
and his—that was too much to ask one frail-boned man to
endure. Who, after all, was Manischevitz that he had been
given so much to suffer? A tailor. Certainly not a man of
talent. Upon him suffering was largely wasted. It went nowhere, into nothing: into more suffering. His pain did not
earn him bread, nor fill the cracks in the wall, nor lift, in
the middle of the night, the kitchen table; only lay upon
him, sleepless, so sharply oppressively that he could many
times have cried out yet not heard himself through this
thickness of misery.

In this mood he gave no thought to Mr. Alexander
Levine, but at moments when the pain wavered, slightly
diminishing, he sometimes wondered if he had been mistaken to dismiss him. A black Jew and angel to boot—very
hard to believe, but suppose he *had* been sent to succor

him, and he, Manischevitz, was in his blindness too blind to comprehend? It was this thought that put him on the knife-point of agony.

Therefore the tailor, after much self-questioning and continuing doubt, decided he would seek the self-styled angel in Harlem. Of course he had great difficulty, because he had not asked for specific directions, and movement was tedious to him. The subway took him to 116th Street, and from there he wandered in the dark world. It was vast and its lights lit nothing. Everywhere were shadows, often moving. Manischevitz hobbled along with the aid of a cane, and not knowing where to seek in the blackened tenement buildings, looked fruitlessly through store windows. In the stores he saw people and *everybody* was black. It was an amazing thing to observe. When he was too tired, too unhappy to go farther, Manischevitz stopped in front of a tailor's store. Out of familiarity with the appearance of it, with some sadness he entered. The tailor, an old skinny Negro with a mop of woolly gray hair, was sitting cross-legged on his workbench, sewing a pair of full-dress pants that had a razor slit all the way down the seat.

"You'll excuse me, please, gentleman," said Manischevitz, admiring the tailor's deft, thimbled fingerwork, "but you know maybe somebody by the name Alexander Levine?"

The tailor, who Manischevitz thought, seemed a little antagonistic to him, scratched his scalp.

"Cain't say I ever heared dat name."

"Alex-ander Lev-ine," Manischevitz repeated it.

The man shook his head. "Cain't say I heared."

About to depart, Manischevitz remembered to say: "He is an angel, maybe."

"Oh *him*," said the tailor clucking. "He hang out in dat honky tonk down here a ways." He pointed with his skinny finger and returned to the pants.

Manischevitz crossed the street against a red light and was almost run down by a taxi. On the block after the next, the sixth store from the corner was a cabaret, and the name in sparkling lights was Bella's. Ashamed to go in, Manischevitz gazed through the neon-lit window, and when the dancing couples had parted and drifted away, he discovered at a table on the side, towards the rear, Levine.

He was sitting alone, a cigarette butt hanging from the corner of his mouth, playing solitaire with a dirty pack of

cards, and Manischevitz felt a touch of pity for him, for
Levine had deteriorated in appearance. His derby was
dented and had a gray smudge on the side. His ill-fitting
suit was shabbier, as if he had been sleeping in it. His
shoes and trouser cuffs were muddy, and his face was
covered with an impenetrable stubble the color of licorice.
Manischevitz, though deeply disappointed, was about to
enter, when a big-breasted Negress in a purple evening
gown appeared before Levine's table, and with much
laughter through many white teeth, broke into a vigorous
shimmy. Levine looked straight at Manischevitz with a
haunted expression, but the tailor was too paralyzed to
move or acknowledge it. As Bella's gyrations continued,
Levine rose, his eyes lit in excitement. She embraced him
with vigor, both his hands clasped around her big restless buttocks and they tangoed together across the floor,
loudly applauded by the noisy customers. She seemed to
have lifted Levine off his feet and his large shoes hung
limp as they danced. They slid past the windows where
Manischevitz, white-faced, stood staring in. Levine winked
slyly and the tailor left for home.

Fanny lay at death's door. Through shrunken lips she
muttered concerning her childhood, the sorrows of the marriage bed, the loss of her children, yet wept to live. Manischevitz tried not to listen, but even without ears he would
have heard. It was not a gift. The doctor panted up the
stairs, a broad but bland, unshaven man (it was Sunday)
and soon shook his head. A day at most, or two. He left
at once, not without pity, to spare himself Manischevitz's
multiplied sorrow; the man who never stopped hurting.
He would someday get him into a public home.

Manischevitz visited a synagogue and there spoke to
God, but God had absented himself. The tailor searched
his heart and found no hope. When she died he would live
dead. He considered taking his life although he knew he
wouldn't. Yet it was something to consider. Considering,
you existed. He railed against God— Can you love a rock,
a broom, an emptiness? Baring his chest, he smote the
naked bones, cursing himself for having believed.

Asleep in a chair that afternoon, he dreamed of Levine.
He was standing before a faded mirror, preening small

decaying opalescent wings. "This means," mumbled Manischevitz, as he broke out of sleep, "that it is possible he could be an angel." Begging a neighbor lady to look in on Fanny and occasionally wet her lips with a few drops of water, he drew on his thin coat, gripped his walking stick, exchanged some pennies for a subway token, and rode to Harlem. He knew this act was the last desperate one of his woe: to go without belief, seeking a black magician to restore his wife to invalidism. Yet if there was no choice, he did at least what was chosen.

He hobbled to Bella's but the place had changed hands. It was now, as he breathed, a synagogue in a store. In the front, towards him, were several rows of empty wooden benches. In the rear stood the Ark, its portals of rough wood covered with rainbows of sequins; under it a long table on which lay the sacred scroll unrolled, illuminated by the dim light from a bulb on a chain overhead. Around the table, as if frozen to it and the scroll, which they all touched with their fingers, sat four Negroes wearing skullcaps. Now as they read the Holy Word, Manischevitz could, through the plate glass window, hear the singsong chant of their voices. One of them was old, with a gray beard. One was bubble-eyed. One was humpbacked. The fourth was a boy, no older than thirteen. Their heads moved in rhythmic swaying. Touched by this sight from his childhood and youth, Manischevitz entered and stood silent in the rear.

"Neshoma," said bubble eyes, pointing to the word with a stubby finger. "Now what dat mean?"

"That's the word that means soul," said the boy. He wore glasses.

"Let's git on wid de commentary," said the old man.

"Ain't necessary," said the humpback. "Souls is immaterial substance. That's all. The soul is derived in that manner. The immateriality is derived from the substance, and they both, causally an' otherwise, derived from the soul. There can be no higher."

"That's the highest."

"Over de top."

"Wait a minute," said bubble eyes. "I don't see what is dat immaterial substance. How come de one gits hitched up to de odder?" He addressed the humpback.

"Ask me something hard. Because it is substanceless immateriality. It couldn't be closer together, like all the parts of the body under one skin—closer."

"Here now," said the old man.

"All you done is switched de words."

"It's the primum mobile, the substanceless substance from which comes all things that were incepted in the idea—you, me and everything and body else."

"Now how did all dat happen? Make it sound simple."

"It de speerit," said the old man. "On de face of de water moved de speerit. An' dat was good. It say so in de Book. From de speerit ariz de man."

"But now listen here. How come it become substance if it all de time a spirit?"

"God alone done dat."

"Holy! Holy! Praise His Name."

"But has dis spirit got some kind of a shade or color?" asked bubble eyes, deadpan.

"Man of course not. A spirit is a spirit."

"Then how come we is colored?" he said with a triumphant glare.

"Ain't got nothing to do wid dat."

"I still like to know."

"God put the spirit in all things," answered the boy. "He put it in the green leaves and the yellow flowers. He put it with the gold in the fishes and the blue in the sky. That's how come it came to us."

"Amen."

"Praise Lawd and utter loud His speechless name."

"Blow de bugle till it bust the sky."

They fell silent, intent upon the next word. Manischevitz approached them.

"You'll excuse me," he said. "I am looking for Alexander Levine. You know him maybe?"

"That's the angel," said the boy.

"Oh, *him*," snuffed bubble eyes.

"You'll find him at Bella's. It's the establishment right across the street," the humpback said.

Manischevitz said he was sorry that he could not stay, thanked them, and limped across the street. It was already night. The city was dark and he could barely find his way.

But Bella's was bursting with the blues. Through the

window Manischevitz recognized the dancing crowd and among them sought Levine. He was sitting loose-lipped at Bella's side table. They were tippling from an almost empty whiskey fifth. Levine had shed his old clothes, wore a shiny new checkered suit, pearl-gray derby, cigar, and big, two-tone button shoes. To the tailor's dismay, a drunken look had settled upon his formerly dignified face. He leaned toward Bella, tickled her ear lobe with his pinky, while whispering words that sent her into gales of raucous laughter. She fondled his knee.

Manischevitz, girding himself, pushed open the door and was not welcomed.

"This place reserved."

"Beat it, pale puss."

"Exit, Yankel, Semitic trash."

But he moved towards the table where Levine sat, the crowd breaking before him as he hobbled forward.

"Mr. Levine," he spoke in a trembly voice. "Is here Manischevitz."

Levine glared blearily. "Speak yo' piece, son."

Manischevitz shuddered. His back plagued him. Cold tremors tormented his crooked legs. He looked around, everybody was all ears.

"You'll excuse me. I would like to talk to you in a private place."

"Speak, Ah is a private pusson."

Bella laughed piercingly. "Stop it, boy, you killin' me."

Manischevitz, no end disturbed, considered fleeing but Levine addressed him:

"Kindly state the pu'pose of yo' communication with yo's truly."

The tailor wet cracked lips. "You are Jewish. This I am sure."

Levine rose, nostrils flaring. "Anythin' else yo' got to say?"

Manischevitz's tongue lay like stone.

"Speak now or fo'ever hold off."

Tears blinded the tailor's eyes. Was ever man so tried? Should he say he believed a half-drunken Negro to be an angel?

The silence slowly petrified.

Manischevitz was recalling scenes of his youth as a wheel in his mind whirred: believe, do not, yes, no, yes, no.

The pointer pointed to yes, to between yes and no, to no, no it was yes. He sighed. It moved but one had still to make a choice.

"I think you are an angel from God." He said it in a broken voice, thinking, If you said it it was said. If you believed it you must say it. If you believed, you believed.

The hush broke. Everybody talked but the music began and they went on dancing. Bella, grown bored, picked up the cards and dealt herself a hand.

Levine burst into tears. "How you have humiliated me."

Manischevitz apologized.

"Wait'll I freshen up." Levine went to the men's room and returned in his old clothes.

No one said goodbye as they left.

They rode to the flat via subway. As they walked up the stairs Manischevitz pointed with his cane at his door.

"That's all been taken care of," Levine said. "You best go in while I take off."

Disappointed that it was so soon over but torn by curiosity, Manischevitz followed the angel up three flights to the roof. When he got there the door was already padlocked.

Luckily he could see through a small broken window. He heard an odd noise, as though of a whirring of wings, and when he strained for a wider view, could have sworn he saw a dark figure borne aloft on a pair of magnificent black wings.

A feather drifted down. Manischevitz gasped as it turned white, but it was only snowing.

He rushed downstairs. In the flat Fanny wielded a dust mop under the bed and then upon the cobwebs on the wall.

"A wonderful thing, Fanny," Manischevitz said. "Believe me, there are Jews everywhere."

Peter De Vries

From *The Blood of the Lamb*

I was steered into the infirmary by a middle-aged nurse
and put to bed with orders to remain there. I was given a
thermometer, known affectionately here as a "temp stick,"
and a chart on which to record four readings a day (early
morning, noon, late afternoon, and evening) as well as my
pulse on each of these occasions. The nurse left, to return
with receptacles for specimens of more things than need
be named, but one of which, blood, was drawn from a vein
while I gazed negligently at the trees outside my window.
"Your meals will be brought in. The doctor will see you
sometime tomorrow or the next day or the next." And so
on. "Meanwhile, I repeat, stay in bed."

Thus were banished my visions of a sanitarium as a
place where one sat on benches philosophizing in the
sun, in the manner of *The Magic Mountain*, or contracted
imprudent passions in the music room. I raised myself on
one elbow and gazed out the window. Beyond a row of
evergreens stretched a length of flagstone walk on which
presently two codgers materialized conversing wildly, shaking their heads and with that maximum of gesture familiar to me as the pantomime of theological dispute. I
dropped back on the pillow, emitting a long, baleful moan.

Adhering to the ceiling, I now noted, were inspirational
thoughts slanted to the shut-in. They were not the hospital's idea of interior decorating, I learned later, but the
work of a previous inmate whose principle had been that,
to the bedridden, the ceiling bore the same relation that
walls do to those privileged to live perpendicularly;
therefore "wall mottoes" belonged properly overhead where
their contents could be absorbed in prostration. These
truths were pasted to the calcimine. Most were from the
Gospels and St. Paul and therefore possessed literary
merit, but a few appeared to be creations of the muralist's

own, being crudely inked on squares of what seemed to be shirt cardboard. One such effort read: "Flat on your back? Best way to see Heaven." Another: "Maybe this will make you upright in heart."

I rolled over from supine to prone, half expecting to find similar maxims affixed to the floor, for moments of true despair. I thought moodily of home, of the University, of Greta. . . . Rolling up an eye, I took inventory of the bedside table. On a linen tidy were a Bible, the temp stick, and a small clock reading five-fifteen. Enthusiastically, I sat up and poked the thermometer into my mouth. Time for the afternoon reading.

I improved the five minutes I had been instructed to leave the thermometer under my tongue by gazing out at the distant Rockies, seen today for the first time. I tried to guess which might be the celebrated peaks among those mantled with perpetual snow. One seemed to have a cross of white upon its side. The original of the Longfellow poem? "There is a mountain in the distant West that, sun-defying in its deep ravines, displays a cross of snow upon its side. Such is the cross I wear upon my breast these something years . . . something something changeless since the day she died." As I tried to reconstruct the verse, and to analyze the failure of the range to flood my being with aesthetic awe, the door was kicked open by a young nurse with a face like an amiable sparrow who entered with my supper.

"Well!" she said with that humoring air reserved for children and invalids. "Seeing the sights?" She set the tray down on the table and heaved her shoulders with a bright sigh.

"Yes," I mumbled, removing the thermometer. "Now, which is Mount McKinley?"

"That is in Alaska. You mean Pikes Peak." She leaned across the bed and pointed through the window. "There it is—the tallest one."

I jerked her into bed, tore the clothes from her back, and raped her, in spirit. When she had gone I consulted the thermometer, noting that my brow had become beaded with moisture as a result of these exertions. The mercury stood at ninety-eight point six. Normal. Avidly I made my first entry on the chart provided.

After supper, I read a chapter or two of Ecclesiastes,

then listened to a bedside radio equipped with earphones. My temperature at eight o'clock was the same. I fell into a deep sleep, from which I awoke with the certainty that I had been unconscious only an hour or two. The room was still dark, but I sensed some compulsion to look out the window. Above the gloom still overspreading the earth, the snowpeaks were a flaming scarlet in the first rays of the rising sun.

The middle-aged nurse appeared in the course of the morning to say that the doctor would see me at eleven o'clock; meanwhile, I might sit for a few minutes in the easy chair and read the morning *News*, which she had brought me.

I had the end room of this wing in the infirmary, so there was a single window at right angles to the main bay exposure next my bed. The sun was streaming through this window, and swinging the chair around, I sat in its rays stripped to the waist, the chintz curtains parted and the sash up. As I basked in the luscious warmth, the door opened again, following a short rap. An elderly man's face was thrust into the room, wearing an expression of tentative cordiality which quickly froze into a violent frown.

"Are you mad!" he said, rushing into the room and drawing the shade. "Who gave you permission to sit in the sun and with your chest exposed like that?"

"Why, nobody, I . . . It felt so good to—"

"To be alive? Well if you want to stay that way, keep out of the sun until you're given permission. Worst thing in the world for most T.B. patients—can stir up trouble, reopen old lesions."

"I'm sorry. I naturally thought the sun—"

"Common mistake. You don't take it unless it's specifically prescribed. Is that clear? I'll examine you this morning, and then we'll see whether you join the Sunshine Club. I'm Dr. Simpson."

He held out a hand of which the skin was loose as a glove, and which remained extended while we both despaired of my getting my own through my tangled pajama-sleeve in order that I might grasp it. He had a salt-and-pepper suit so natty, linen so fresh, and shoes so polished one read into them instinctively a meticulous and no doubt vain nature. An ironic smile encircled teeth too white to be his own, a smile echoed in deep-set brown eyes capable of all the forms of mockery, one felt, save self-mockery. He asked whether this was my first taste of the West, and hurried off before I could answer, as though the impressions of sight-seers were inherently tedious.

It was a half hour later that I shuffled in pajamas and robe down the corridor to his office, which lay between the infirmary and the ambulatory wing. By that time I had learned that he was an old lunger in his own right, possessed Scotch Presbyterian origins, and preferred making the jokes himself.

He was standing at the desk when I entered his consulting room, his head bent over a cardiogram. Fingering untidy festoons of this, he resembled a stockbroker surprised at the ticker tape. He finished his scrutiny of it before dropping it on the desk with a cryptic smile.

His examination was brief. After an X ray by a woman assistant, he fluoroscoped me and then listened to my chest, instructing me first to cough into my fist and then to repeat "ninety-nine" monotonously as the bell of the stethoscope stalked my ribs. He dropped the stethoscope on the desk and told me I might get back into my pajamas.

"Well, I can hear a little music in there, but I don't think it's playing 'Nearer, My God, to Thee.' Just the very tip of one side has any *râles* whatever. Very little activity. Next to nothing."

"How long—?"

He arrested me with a hand. "Give me a chance to ask you not to ask that question." He made a brief, no doubt set speech, to the effect that the longer he practiced the less confidently he could predict when anybody would go home, if ever; that he had seen people enter these gates with no very noticeable lesions six years ago who were still on hand, while others with craters you could have dropped billiard balls into left in as many months; that added to all the honored ministrations of rest, food, and fresh air was an imponderable which he would simply call mental attitude. He had evidently drunk deep of the newly welling springs of psychosomatic medicine. "I used to think mental attitude half the battle, then seventy-five per cent of the cure; now I'm not sure it isn't more like ninety-five. Or maybe I should say ninety-eight six." The ironic grin conveyed the malicious implication not to be stated: that if one determined the prolongation of a disease, mightn't one

also have willed its acquisition? "I have more people in
here than I can tell you, about whom I wonder what they're
running away from. You will no doubt make a game of
picking them out for yourself."

"I wasn't going to ask when I could go home;" I lied.
"Just when can I go to ambulo?"

"You pick up the slang fast." He waved an indifferent
hand. "Any time. Why don't you give the infirmary another
week, then I think we'll have room for you in the ambulatory wing. There's a man moving out of there back to the
infirmary," he added, with that sardonic gleam in his eye
which was not to be confused with a mischievous twinkle.

As he rose and shook my hand, I could not resist another question.

"Not many go *back* there, do they? I mean Eugene
O'Neill overcame it, and Gide, and didn't Maugham
once—?"

"Ah, yes. We have some of those too, as you'll find
when you hear the typewriters starting up in ambulo." He
looked at me in alarm. "You haven't brought one, have
you?" I assured him he need have no fears on that score.
"Good. Then why don't you come to dinner at the house
soon. Mrs. Simpson and I occasionally have people in on
Thursday evenings, and we're always especially glad to
find someone who won't read us the first act of something.
In fact we collect discoveries—Young Men Who Don't
Write. You're mine, remember. I saw you first."

Thus that circle of kindred spirits for which I had
pined, that urbanity that I had loved long since and lost
a while, was to be found right here where I had least
expected it—in the bosom, however infected, of the church.
What I had thought to take by storm fell into my hands as
simply as fruit from a tree.

On hand when I arrived at the good doctor's house, a
half-timbered Normandy cottage just inside the sanitarium gate, were most of the regulars currently composing the band of Elect whom the Simpsons—themselves
apparently put to it for society in this eventless backwater
—cultivated and maintained for their "Thursdays." They
all looked up from their chairs in speculation, even alarm,
when I entered, a scrawny youth in a tweed coat which
fit him too soon, in a torn pocket of which he clutched a
cold pipe by no means to be lit under the doctor's eye, a

prospect definitely on probation. Mrs. Simpson, a plump, effusive woman the reverse of her husband, propelled me amiably before her for the round of introductions.

First was a portly native of Amsterdam named Carl Horswissel, who wore a Norfolk jacket and a string tie. I had seen him from my window promenading the grounds. He spoke with a thick Dutch accent and was said to be a ruined cocoa importer. The most formidably intellectual of the lot was Leslie Foyle, a Colorado mining heir whose family could well afford the fees exacted of Episcopalians. A clear-cut snob, his air of aloof languor was naturally aided by a pulmonary condition noted officially as "third stage, moderately advanced." The blue nails in which his drooping fingers terminated recalled to mind the old term "phthisic." Next were a voluble couple who were not patients at the sanitarium but neighbors of the Simpsons. Their name was Twitty, and I was surprised to learn they had domestic discord, which they freely aired. In fact, long stretches of these Thursdays were devoted to the ventilation of their problems, on the complexity of which they tended to preen themselves. They had tried to save their marriage by bicycling through the Palatinate, and it was to a travelogue of a spring so spent that much of this evening was given over. For the immediate moment, however, it was I who was subjected to note, rather like a fraternity prospect of whom as yet precious little is known.

"Wanderhope here has so little wrong with him," Dr. Simpson began in his most derisive vein as he poured me a sherry, "that he's practically an impostor. I could hardly detect any *râles* at all. So I'm going to try out a pet theory of mine on him. Short doses of really awful exercise, to see if winding the patient has any curative powers. All this sitting in bed blowing up balloons!"

"Yes, really, Horswissel," Foyle interjected, "don't you realize it's all a mammillary obsession?" Horswissel, without having the faintest idea what had been said, nevertheless wriggled with pleasure at being the butt of so erudite a thrust. I learned later that he had squeaked into the Elect by the skin of his teeth, and that some among them openly considered his inclusion a mistake.

"There must be a better way of exercising the lungs. Maybe deliberately getting the patient out of breath is it," said the doctor, handing me my sherry. "We're breaking fresh ground for you."

"Already?" I bleated humorously.

This was best absorbed by the final member of the group, a chubby youth named Bontekoe who aspired to be its clown. Most of his contributions were puns, following each of which he would raise an arm to ward off an expected blow, at the same time sinking down in his chair in a display of guilt. He was from Detroit, and in his "sophomore" year here. He and Foyle were among those suspected of having abused the Simpsons' hospitality by reading aloud selections from their works. Bontekoe observed now that Dr. Simpson had so many "pet theories" that he ought perhaps to set up shop as a veterinarian, and shrank into the depths of his wingback.

In sharpest possible contrast to my social life with this band of the Elect, by whom I was tolerated at least on approval, was the roommate with whom I was paired in ambulo.

He was a Kansas primitive named Hank Hoos. His hulking six and a half feet suggested an allegorical embodiment of Rustic Manhood to which the sculptor, perhaps due to an untimely death or loss of interest in the subject, had not put the finishing touches. His rough-hewn good looks were crowned by waves of glossy brown hair which he spent hours at the dresser combing, sagging at the knees in order to keep his head in the glass. It was hard to think of Hoos as ailing, and he dealt a damaging blow to Dr. Simpson's theories of self-invalidation since he had obviously only one thing on his mind: to get out of there and resume the womanizing this incarceration had interrupted. He had now done eight months of his "stretch," as he called it, and gave warning that he could endure little more unless his sexual needs were met—criminally if no other means soon presented themselves. Before I had quite unpacked my things he asked me if I had any information as to whether saltpeter or any other antiaphrodisiac was put in the food. When I professed ignorance of this whole matter, he asked me to pledge myself to get to the bottom of it with him. Walking across the room to put a few shirts into a drawer, I murmured some evasive reply, not clear in my mind whether he considered such dietetic resorts desirable or to be opposed under conditions thus delineated as taxing. Outside on the porch where we slept, our beds standing foot to foot, he spent hours relating some of the amorous exploits he intended to revive. Then one night, after bouncing into position under the covers, he suddenly said: "O.K., now let's hear about you. When was the last time you were with a girl?"

This was all too easily recalled, of course. I told him about Greta and her family, withholding names to protect the innocent, as he had certainly not done in the case of his cornland friends.

"Her father was a real estate contractor," I narrated softly in the dark, for only frame partitions separated the porches and I could hear Horswissel breathing alertly twelve inches from my head. His Montaigne had already been heard in its nightly drop to the floor, like a third shoe. "We were so in love," I said, wincing at the clichés by means of which I strove to gear my odyssey to my audience's comprehension, and at the same time divorce myself in spirit from its rather shabby content, "but had a hard time getting together. We felt we had our right to happiness. Then do you know what happened? Her father put up a development with a Model Home in it. We went into that one night. It was completely furnished, hey."

"You went to bed?"

"You know it."

"Tell me everything that happened. Don't leave out a thing."

It was a point he need not have pressed. In my eagerness to oblige, like those club members making "frank" revelations of amorous details not all of which have occurred, I thought I had an insight into the motives and techniques of the so-called "honest realists" of literature —honest to the point of mendacity.

"Her father was fit to be tied," I whispered when I reached the part having to do with our discovery. "He nearly killed me before he was hauled off bodily by two men. His wife stood there screaming bloody murder—a hysterical madwoman. She tried to bash my head in with the vanity stool," I improvised. "But it was worth it. Ah, that hour before we were busted in on," I said, hoping by such untypical descents in speech to invent a character who was "not myself," to whom could be attributed the admittedly sordid lapse of which I was being guilty.

"Tell me everything about it," Hoos said. "What was she like?"

"Now see here."

"What difference does it make? I'll never see her. What kind of breasts did she have?"

Talking about Greta in this fashion was simply out of the question, but feeling I owed Hoos some return for the tales with which he had regaled me—my own share in the game we were after all playing—I rhapsodized in terms applicable to womanly beauty in general, those visions and fantasies by which, indeed, we were scarcely for a day untormented. "Think of lilies," I said, "of lilies in mounds of drifted snow . . ." Hoos flung an arm over his eyes, as though shielding them from some blinding light or intolerable pain. At the same time Horswissel's bed creaked sharply and was still, as the man no doubt got on all fours with his ear to the partition.

I broke off, ashamed of myself. But I had already begun to see myself as Hoos saw himself, a prisoner of inflammations that time and improving health could only intensify. Perhaps T.B. had been a mistake. There must be a better way of evading reality. It was with matters at such a pass that I made the third connection of what I recall as a sort of triangular life during those fall and winter months at the sanitarium.

In the dining room, which was common but segregated, I saw one evening a new face on the women's side. A slender girl with blonde hair gathered into a ponytail sat gazing downward as she waited for the bowls of food to reach her. She listened to the chatter of the women among whose hands they passed down the table, smiling when appropriate, but keeping her eyes fixed on her blank plate. Her hands were folded in her lap, and she had a habit of chewing the insides of her cheeks. I inquired about her from Horswissel, who was on my right. He said she must be the girl just moved over to ambulo from the infirmary, where she had been for a year or more. She had had a pneumothorax, the operation by which gas is pumped into the pleural cavity in order to collapse the lung on one side. She was said to be shy and rather religious. In her pale face were the roses obligingly supplied by the disease to either cheek. Her fair hair prepared me for blue eyes when she turned once toward the men's tables—perhaps sensing she was being watched—but what met mine was a soft fawn's gaze of the most melting brown. Something shot along the surface of my heart like ice cracking on a pond. Her head bowed momentarily lower, lifting the gold tassel of hair off her neck.

I scarcely knew what I ate. I hurried to the main lounge after dinner, arriving just in time to see her walk up the corridor to the women's wing with a rather formidable maiden lady of middle age who was notorious, even with the chaplain, for the hymn sings she organized in her room when other people wanted to read or rest. I loitered on the gravel path outside the women's porches, hearing there presently a swell of feminine voices coming clear and wonderfully sweet through an open window:

> There is a fountain filled with blood
> Drawn from Immanuel's veins,
> And sinners plunged beneath that flood
> Lose all their guilty stains.

I returned to my room feeling melancholy and vaguely troubled. The mood continued all through the following morning, Sunday. I failed to see the girl at breakfast, and made no more progress except to learn that her name was Rena Baker. She turned up at midday dinner, after which she was again swept from my view in a tide of companions making for the women's ward. I did not mind this frustration too much, having by now devised a plan. I went to chapel that afternoon with a will.

The sanitarium chaplain was a charming codger of great sensitivity and learning whose pithy sermons were anything but a bore. Today, however, we drew a substitute, a visiting parson so long-winded that his mid-service invocation carried us well past the point at which old Wenzel would have released us into the summer sunshine. Early in its course I stole a glance over my shoulder at Dr. Simpson. He had the look of a man dozing rather than praying; the familiar smile curled his lips, as though some irony too fine for consciousness were turning on the lathe of slumber. Knowing Rena to be sitting directly behind him, I gave my neck another quarter turn. Her head, under a solemn bonnet, was bowed. It lifted just then, and the eyes opened—and banged shut again.

After the benediction I hurried out as fast as the lagging congregation would permit. From the chapel steps I saw her walking toward the main building, alone. I overtook her on the gravel path.

"How did you like the sermon?"

She brought black-gloved palms together in surprise and laughed—a whispered little laugh that conveyed a feeling of the most intense reserve yet the most curious intimacy. "Well, anybody who talks for forty-five minutes on the value of silent meditation . . ."

I fell in beside her as we discussed the minister's text, which had been the words from First Kings in which Elijah finds God not in the wind nor the earthquake nor the fire, but in the still voice. We agreed we had heard too many sermons on this verse, which was supposedly calculated to disarm prolonged and complex exposition. By now we had reached the sanitarium. Sounds of tea being poured in the main lounge reached us on the doorstep where we lingered.

"Will you have some with me?"

She again joined her palms, stiffening her fingers as though to tighten the fit of her gloves. "Oh," she cried in that rippling whisper of a laugh, "I'm supposed to chase till supper." This was institutional slang for resting—chasing the germs. "I'm here on trial, you know, and I don't want to go back there." She pointed in a loop over my head to the infirmary. "Some other time though, maybe."

"My name is Don Wanderhope. I already know yours."

It was three days later that I found her alone again. She was sitting in the lounge reading some mail, including a religious periodical of which she clutched the crumpled wrapper in one hand. "Oh, it's you again."

"Perseverance of the saints. How about a walk? It's nice and bright."

"Well, a short one. I'll get my coat."

Thus began a relationship which I pursued with a kindled heart and what are known as honorable intentions, but one subject to a tarnish for which I had only myself to blame. I mean its natural misinterpretation by the one-dimensional Hoos.

This lout's gossip of our observed ambles about the grounds and into the surrounding fields at first annoyed, then infuriated me. I entered the men's lounge one evening after seeing Rena home, as it were, to hear the conversation come to a stop so sudden there could be no mistaking its theme. A patient changed the subject with a gusto obvious enough to banish any remaining doubt. This was a recent arrival named Niebuhr, a professor of economics from a Midwestern college, here for his second stay. Niebuhr could rarely be got off his professional ground once he had secured the floor, and would discourse on real wages and gold reserves with a heat that was needless since no one there understood what he was saying enough to take issue with it even were he so minded. But he would harangue away till some impassioned declaration would explode in a fit of coughing, the results of which he would commit to a small *crachoir* carried on the person for that purpose. An economist with conspicuous consumption was all Bontekoe needed to make his day, as he soon let us know, ducking behind an arm to fend off the expected cuffs.

I sensed a certain constraint in Hoos's manner when we went to our room after the bell and set about preparing for bed. He retired without a word. The next evening I hurried out after dinner to keep a tryst with Rena behind the garage, into which we sometimes slipped to sit in the pickup truck and talk in peace, I behind the wheel, she with her head on my shoulder. We must have resembled a pair of young lovers going for a drive, or rather rehearsing for the glad day when they might do so, in a vehicle of a more romantic sort, of course. As I went down the corridor I caught faint footsteps behind me and turned in time to see Hoos dart into the lounge, with a last-second effort at nonchalance that was something to behold. The next time it was he who went out first, to stalk me from God knew what cover, for I was now certain that he was spying on me—or on us. The mystery deepened when he vanished on an evening when I stayed in, and stole back into the room in stocking feet long after Lights Out. Asked where he had been, he was at first evasive, then blurted out, "I'm stir-crazy. I warn you." He flung the words at me accusingly, as though I were in some way responsible for his plight.

The huggermugger reached its climax one night when I had no date but slipped out for the purpose of decoying Hoos into the open in hopes of getting to the bottom of this thing. This much accomplished, as was discernible from the stealthy padding in my wake, I strolled past a clump of firs where, screened from his view, I suddenly doubled back and raced around the sanitarium water tower in a wide arc that fetched me up in arrears of my pursuer. He presented rightly the appearance of a dog who has lost the scent, but my relish of his bafflement was short-lived. No doubt assuming I had vanished for my rendezvous in the garage, he stood looking through its soiled windowpanes, shading his eyes, then went around to the back and listened at the closed door, again resembling a snuffling hound. So he had indeed been spying there. And not alone there, I presently learned.

I went for a tramp about the grounds, to cool down and calm my nerves. As time for the Lights Out bell drew near, I made a last swing around the women's wing, in hopes of catching a glimpse of Rena for a moment outdoors—or even a snatch of evensong—but was arrested instead by a figure of another sort. It was Hoos again, peering surreptitiously over the porch rail into Rena's room.

I slipped into the shadows when he turned his head, instinctively avoiding embarrassment. I was squatting in cover when the bell sounded and, presently, the rooms darkened one by one, suggesting well enough what had rewarded his gaze. I floundered in doubt as to what course to take. I was seething, yet loath to make matters any more deplorable by creating a scene, certainly then and there. Watching a voyeur would appear a specialty admitting of only one refinement, and our little nocturne had that. Hearing a rustle behind me, I turned and saw a pair of bespectacled eyes peering at me through the bushes. It would have been futile for Horswissel and me to pretend we had not recognized one another, and so, parting the breast-high foliage, I swam through greenery to his side. "Shh," I said, leading him away by the arm. "Were you observed?"

"So dot's it. You got a good ting of it, watching de girls," he said, as he permitted himself to be drawn onto the gravel path.

"Oh, this is ridiculous," I said. "For heaven's sake, man, let me handle this. Is that clear? Not a word of it must be breathed."

"No!"

It turned out to be impossible in the confusion to avoid Hoos, who, frightened off by noises, possibly our own, turned and bolted through the landscaping into our arms. The three of us now engaged in furious whispers, rendered more chaotic by Horswissel's lewd misconstruction of my plea for secrecy—his thought being to keep "a good thing of it" among ourselves—as well as by our being illegally abroad, so that we stole to the darkened men's quarters like a trio of desperadoes. Once alone with Hoos in our room, however, I lost no time in expressing my disgust with his conduct.

"Look, I'm no prig, but if you're going to do that sort of thing, I'll thank you to do it at somebody else's window. And keep away from the garage."

"It's all well and good for you to talk," he retorted, "but how do you think I feel, thinking of you doing pushups in the back of that pickup truck?"

"Now look, you bastard. If you've managed to see anything at all, which I doubt, you must know we just sit in the cabin."

"Don't give me that. And why apologize? Who wouldn't want to get out of this clink once in a while and cut himself a piece of cake?"

"If you don't shut your foul mouth, I'll shut it for you!"

"You mean this is the real thing?"

"Oh, you wouldn't understand."

"So you're smitten. Damned if he isn't smitten."

After this wretched colloquy, conducted while stumbling about in the dark undressing, I lay seething in bed for an hour or more. Could I gracefully request a change of roommate? The only double room currently half vacant that I knew of was Horswissel's, transfer to whose company could scarcely be considered an improvement. Despite his former money and pretense at reading the books that had gotten him by the skin of his teeth into the Elect, Horswissel remained for me a Dumb Dutchman whom I wanted to kick in the pork. And on sober reflection the next morning the whole idea of a move seemed ill-advised. Natures as coarse as Hoos's are often equivalently sensitive, and a slight could transform him from a nuisance into an enemy, possibly a very nasty one. It was all very well for Foyle to keep him at a distance by deliberate rudeness, as he said he did, on the ground that vinegar repelled more flies than honey, but his problem was not my problem. There was one ray of hope. Hoos had lately expressed confidence of being "sprung" after his next quarterly examination, a mere month off. Better to rub along till then.

Thoughts of Hoos's welfare, however, even for that matter my own, were banished from my mind by a turn in Rena's.

Her health had been precarious for some time. Now after an encouraging spell of normal temperatures she suddenly shot a fever of a hundred and one. She was seized by coughing fits that left her weak and dizzy, and were marked by increasingly ominous flecks of red. The doctor confined her to bed, which was a woe for me as well as for her. Men were barred from the women's dormitory except for the regular visiting hours, and my calls on her then were almost unfailingly ruined by the presence of other visitors or, what was worse, that of her roommate, Cora Nyhoff.

This woman loved God and hated men in nearly equal measure. She would stick around whenever I came, allegedly to help "cheer Rena up" but in effect to queer my progress with Rena, sensed as a threat to her own domination of the girl, of which I glimpsed an unhealthy side. The two had been paired off as being both "religious," stupidly, since there was no resemblance between Cora's bigotry and Rena's piety. Though Rena never admitted it, I suspected that the older woman had begun to pall. Indeed, I wondered if her continuous abrasive presence wasn't responsible for Rena's reversal. I was about to suggest as much to Dr. Simpson when I learned that she had gone back to the infirmary.

Here I could visit her freely with at least an even chance of not running into Cora when I walked in. Though confined to bed, Rena would sit on it tailorwise, drinking the tea I brought in or fingering the letters, papers, and books with which the counterpane was everlastingly strewn. She never held her teacup by the ear, preferring to warm her hands around the china, always

watching me as she sipped, as though I bore constant reap-
praisal. We talked of poets, composers, the West, last
Sunday's sermon—always last Sunday's sermon, of which
a vital interest in human faith prompted her to be critical,
as distinguished from Cora's dull evangelical chatter about
"blessings." Divine worship was piped in for infirmary
patients to hear from earphones plugged into bedside
sockets.

"He seemed to think," said Rena one Sunday evening of
a seminary student who had preached at vespers on the
injunction not to cast one's pearls before swine, "that
Jesus meant the pearls would only be ignored, but the
text says clearly enough 'lest they turn again and rend
you.' It's a popular mistake, but imagine a divinity student making it!"

"You could remove your earphones. I had to sit there
and take it."

"Are you an atheist?"

"Not a very devout one," I reassured her, smiling from
my chair. "I'm backsliding fast."

"Do you believe in a God?"

"With nothing certain, anything is possible."

"You're slippery as an eel, aren't you? Do you believe
you have a soul?"

"No, but I believe you do."

With a terrier-like interest in everything that caught
her eye or took her fancy, she would change the subject
without a moment's notice. She now glimpsed, through
the window, the figure of a middle-aged patient named
Swigart, the sole Methodist among us, walking along with
a cigar in his mouth. His affliction lay elsewhere than in
his lungs. Rena reported that Swigart, a tobacco addict
fated to have been born into a denomination where nico-
tine was proscribed, was happy for the first time in his life
among the Dutch, who of course smoke like chimneys.
"He's been declared arrested but won't go home," she
laughed. "There's a story that he used to smoke behind
the barn after he was forty, but it's probably too good
to be true." We watched the object of this gossip, puffing
contentedly, disappear in a blue cloud among the frozen
lilacs.

"Do you pray for me?"

"Well, that would mean the one I was addressing had

done this to you to begin with, which I find hard to believe anybody would."

"I don't quite follow you."

"I simply mean that asking Him to cure you—or me, or anybody—implies a personal being who arbitrarily does us this dirt. The prayer then is a plea to have a heart. To knock it off. I find the thought repulsive. I prefer thinking we're the victims of chance to dignifying any such force with the name of Providence."

"We're supposed to deserve it," she said, poking about in a box of cookies which my mother had baked and sent me, and which I had passed along to Rena.

"Not you."

"I'm a sinner."

"Stop giving yourself airs. You're beginning to sound like Cora."

"What would you do if you were God?"

"Put a stop to all this theology."

I came over to the bed and rummaged among the cookies too. Touching her hand, I took it and raised it to my lips.

"If we could only kiss," she said, pressing my fingers to her cheek. Under her silk pajamas I saw a neat, tilted breast, which I longed to touch. I started to sit on the bed, but footsteps in the corridor sent me ignominiously back to my chair. Munching a star-shaped cookie, I sat listening to Cora's voice greeting a nurse outside the door. Dull rage riled my emotion as I watched Rena, averting her eyes, tidy herself and the bed. I not only rose when the smiling visitor entered, but gave her my seat. I left instantly, as always seemed best under these circumstances.

But we had a beautiful afternoon the next week.

At dusk, Rena and I happened both to be gazing out the window when snow began suddenly to fall and the world to turn white under our eyes. Great feathery flakes descended in the windless air, weaving a veil of absolute white. Everything lost its outline. The mountains vanished; trees and houses were swallowed in a featureless void in which we watched mesmerized, not breathing a word. The room darkened slowly, and the monochrome outside took on here and there a golden glow as lights blossomed in every window but this. We hung suspended in a trance, an eternity of leisure. But mystic as the spell might have been said to be, it released desires long held in check. There could have been no errors now. When I drew near she averted her mouth with the gentle, rather rueful, movement with which she had always confined my kisses to her cheek, but my hand now grazed for the first time below her throat. I thought for a moment that encountering her own meant rebuke, till I felt her fingers at work undoing the buttons of her pajama blouse for me. Lying down, she offered up two small breasts as white as the snow. Bent to those, I heard her moan my name on the pillow. Beneath my journeying hand her slim body arched in a convulsion about which there could be no mistake.

"I won't ask whether I'm a virgin any longer after that."

"You know I love you."

"Isn't it wonderful? And we won't say anything about how insane it is."

"Everything else seems insane now. Except this."

"Yes. Oh, my God, here comes the supper cart."

Two days later, when I called, the room was empty. The bed had been stripped. Curtains blew at the open window. I found the superintending nurse at the linen closet at the end of the corridor. I imagined she had watched me emerge, then turned busily back to her work. She did not, at any rate, choose to withdraw her head from among the towels and linen while she answered my questions.

"Where's Rena Baker?"

"Not back from surgery yet."

"Surgery? What for?"

"Some ribs removed."

This was the last resort for patients whom pneumothorax and other measures had failed: collapse of the lung. She had not told me any such thing had been scheduled, or even contemplated. Nor that she had had rheumatic fever as a child and that her heart was not all it might be. I learned it all from Cora Nyhoff, to whom I hurried in the hope of more information than the bare facts related by the nurse.

I could eat no dinner. Rather ironically, the diningroom matron called on me for grace, which I managed like everyone else from a common store of clichés. Then I hurried to the infirmary. Rena was not yet back from surgery. I bundled myself into boots and overcoat and went outside. Rena's room was dark. Through the hospital windows, behind the infirmary, nothing could be seen but an occasional white apparition floating between the gaps in the draperies.

Tightening my scarf, I trooped around the sanitarium grounds with my gloved hands in my pockets. It was brutally cold, the snow hard as iron underfoot. The stars throbbed in the clear air. Jigging in the driveway ruts, I sorted out the constellations as taught me by Rena on our night walks; she was a country girl who had supplied my city-bred ignorance of the heavens, so that I could mark their mythological progress from my porch bed on wakeful nights. Orion, Cassiopeia . . . There were no Christians in that pagan congress. All the voyeurs were inside tonight. Some could be seen at their snug windows, watching. I went inside myself. After half an hour of hovering over a chess game in the lounge, and a few minutes in my room, I got into my clothes again and went out. As I neared the hospital, a courier came out and stumbled across the snow to the doctor's cottage. Dr. Simpson stood a moment in his doorway with the light behind him, nodding, then shaking his head. Then the caller left, and the doctor went back inside, not to reappear. The rooms in the dormitories darkened one by one. I hadn't heard the bell. Too late to make it now anyway. I walked to keep warm, wandering to the doctor's cottage, then back to the hospital. I stood irresolutely at the back door, raised my arm to press the bell, and dropped it again as my courage failed me. I went back toward the cottage, aimlessly. A bird suddenly rose from the brush beside the brook behind me, flew into the trees, and was silent. Another sound drew my gaze toward the gate. Under its arch a black vehicle rolled across the frozen snow, stopped behind the hospital, and a scavenger in a Homburg entered it carrying a wicker basket.

The stars swam in a mist of tears. The Rockies were invisible now, but I knew from memory where the mountain stood with the cross of snow upon its side. There was a cry from an animal down in the brush beside the icy brook, where nature was also keeping itself in balance.

"Thou shalt not kill." This was advertised as the law of someone who had also created a universe in which one thing ate another. Were not believers aware of the holes a single thought tore in their fabric? Perfect love did not quite cast out fear, but rage did grief, or nearly so.

I walked around to the other side, where the wheels grinding in departure could be heard but not seen. She was as dead as the moon, who had warmed me. The little creeks of blood were stilled, the breasts I had kissed as cold as stone.

Dr. Simpson was evidently a watcher too, or someone had reported a delinquent by phone, because his door burst open and footsteps crunched the snow behind me. He had thrown on a coat, and his face above an untidy loop of scarf was demented with anger.

"What the devil are you doing out here?"

"Letting the moon open old lesions."

"Oh, for God's sake! What kind of tenth-rate Rossetti . . . ? Go to bed this instant! I order it! It's an hour past Lights Out. What the devil do you think this is, a country club?"

"I'm sorry, Dr. Simpson."

He came a step closer, scrutinizing me. "What's the matter with you?"

"Rena's dead, isn't she?"

"She slipped away quietly. The doctor in charge of surgery assured me." He hesitated, glaring toward the cottage. "Come inside. We'll both freeze out here."

The living room was empty. He kicked the remains of a fire into life and poured us brandies.

"Her heart gave out. Unexpectedly, because we checked it thoroughly, knowing she had a history of rheumatic fever. You can never tell about the heart—makes a fool of good cardiograms and bad. I have found women's as capricious as the poets say. Ah well, it may be a mercy, because frankly she didn't stand a chance. I doubt whether the collapse would have helped. It might have been a nasty third act."

"I admire the objectivity of science," I said, pacing helplessly about the room. "How they can—I had a brother once . . . Surely you no longer think this is a managed universe?"

"Why do you think you have anything to tell me, young

man? I had a son once, whom I had to watch die of leukemia. He was seven. Stevie. He was such a boy as you see riding dolphins in the fountains in the parks. A dolphin boy. A faun. I watched him bleed to death."

"What did you do then, sing 'Come Thou fount of every blessing, tune my heart to sing Thy praise'?"

"Go on. I am an old man. I have shed my tears. Go ahead."

He went over to the fireplace and kicked the embers again. Then he walked to the window, where he sent a kind of snort between the damask draperies into the black night. He padded back to his chair, into which he flopped once more. I saw that he was wearing house slippers.

"The thing I must say is a little hard on me now is the operatic type we occasionally get here. All this *Liebestod*, and going off into the night and one thing and another. I had a romantic a few years ago who went out for walks bareheaded in the moonlight. I'll be glad to tell you where he is now. Wagner, Chopin . . ." He broke off his improvisation as fruitless, and after an audible swallow of brandy grunted apologetically and said, "Death is the commonest thing in the universe. What was this girl to you?"

"I was in love with her."

He writhed about in his chair, like a man being strapped into it for execution. "Oh, dear."

"I suppose you don't like to hear any more about these attachments than you have to, but they do develop. What are we supposed to do?"

"Where did you go, for heaven's sake?"

"In the garage. The pickup truck."

He sipped his brandy warily, as though on the lookout for emotional ambush everywhere. We faced one another in the wingbacks flanking the revived fire. I gathered that I had at least cleared myself of the charge of romanticism by admitting I was in love. It was realism he was up against. The old irony curled his lips as he said: "Did you kiss her?"

"Of course."

"You may live to regret it. Or then again, you may not," he added with one of his grim little jokes.

I set my brandy down and said: "Dr. Simpson, do you believe in a God?"

He just perceptibly raised his eyes, as if in entreaty to

Heaven to spare him at least this. It took me some years to attain his mood and understand my blunder. He resented such questions as people do who have thought a great deal about them. The superficial and the slipshod have ready answers, but those looking this complex life straight in the eye acquire a wealth of perception so composed of delicately balanced contradictions that they dread, or resent, the call to couch any part of it in a bland generalization. The vanity (if not outrage) of trying to cage this dance of atoms in a single definition may give the weariness of age with the cry of youth for answers the appearance of boredom. Dr. Simpson looked bored as he ground his teeth and gazed away.

"Oh, one man's opinion about these things is as good as another's," he said. "You believe what you must in order to stave off the conviction that it's all a tale told by an idiot. You know, of course, you took a chance with that girl."

"It was worth it," I retorted, bitterly.

I finished my brandy and left the good doctor to his rest. A wind had come out of the north, and I hurried up the path through the cottage wood lot toward the dark hospital grounds, where winter clutched in his tight fist the flowers of May.

James Giles

EASTER SUNDAY

I.

He knew they would ask him again. For the third year in
a row. Ever since he had left Austin that afternoon (catching a last glimpse of the university tower in his rear-view
mirror), he had felt a mounting dread, and even something
like anger. Nearing the end of the four hour drive now, he
desperately tried to concentrate on something else. He
glanced at the clumps of scrub-oak, the stretches of dry
brown grass, and the grazing Herefords along the side of
the highway. Growing up feeding cattle just like those he
saw, he had inherited the cowman's mixed feeling of love
and contempt for the white-faced beasts. They progress
toward their slaughter with no protest, only a great deal
of annoying stupidity—but a man can look at them and
see something he owns and has doctored and fed.

Then his mind was jarred back to the pent-up hostility
from which the countryside had momentarily distracted
him by the first of a trinity of signs:

> The Travis City
> Church of Christ
> Welcomes You

A halfmile, then the First Baptist's identical declaration
(or challenge?) of welcome—then the First Methodist's.
And those "welcomes" inevitably symbolized the problem
with which he was faced. "By God! I won't do it!"

At his parents' home—a deceptively roomy red brick
structure four blocks from "downtown" Travis City (pop.
5,600—all white because "the Bible says the sons of
Ham. . . .")—he parked in back, got out, jerked his suit-

case (black with an orange University sticker) from the
trunk, and walked toward the house. He stopped for a
moment by his mother's garden (tomatoes, peas, etc.),
then hesitantly approached the back door. The screen
slammed, "Joey!" After she hugged him, he and his mother
(she now carrying the suitcase) went into the den. The
den was his father's room (the gleaming horns from the
Longhorn he had once owned above the door leading into
his and his wife's bedroom with one horn supporting his
sweat-stained felt hat, the four deer-heads on the opposite
wall, the heads just above the mounted raccoon's pecker,
the three rifles above the fireplace in the intervening wall).

"Supper'll be ready in 'bout an hour. Do you want to go
downtown and drive around for a while first?"

"No, I'll just rest." He slumped into his father's old
black recliner and propped his feet on the footstool.
Hesitantly at first, then abruptly, he took out a cigarette
and lit it with his UT lighter.

His mother started to protest, then gave up in a defeated
sigh. She asked instead: "How has it really been down
there?"

"Fine."

"Are your professors—do any of them, well . . . have
funny ideas?"

"No mom, they're all right." He knew that his mother
was proud of his going to college (more so than of anything in her life), but he also knew she felt that fear and
awe which the women of her depression-generation who
had not finished the two-room public schools felt for "the
university" (hippies, godlesscommunistprofessors, Charles
Whitman, etc.).

"Have you met any girls there you like?"

"Not really." And he couldn't help thinking of the long-
blond-haired girl from Dallas he had screwed in the back
seat of his parked car by the lake two miles outside Austin. ("I just knew you wouldn't have one," she had said,
handing him the rubber which he at first honest-to-God
didn't recognize. Then, in seemingly-one-motion, jerking
up her skirt and down her panties and then challenging,
"You put it on." Then, with sweating, trembling fingers,
he started to unbutton his fly. "Oh hell, pull your pants
down!" After more fumbling and one broken thumbnail,

he had gotten his Levis down around his knees and finally, in a desperate tug, his shorts too, and goddam it was still soft. "Don't worry, country boy, I'll take care of that" and she did; and then, with an expertise surprising himself, he had done the rest. On the way back to town, after a long silence, she had awkwardly put her arm around him and said in a trembling voice, and my god, it wasn't an act: "I . . . I . . . like you. Do you like me?") But he had answered his mother honestly.

The back screen slammed and his father came in. Not a tall man, wearing a blue Levi jacket, khaki pants, and boots, he stood in front of his son. The superficial harshness of his face, burned red by the Texas sun, was mitigated by soft, gentle blue eyes. "Hello, son."

Joey stood up and shook hands. "Hi, dad."

Then the nervous silence that always fell between them. His father, like his mother, was simultaneously proud of and mystified by Joey. ("He's always readin' books and goin' to church," he would tell his cowmen buddies at the auctions. "I hope 'the university' don't get him all fucked up.") The "books and church" had always kept Mr. Carter from communicating with his son in either of the two ways at which he was expert in talking with his auction-lot buddies—seriously about cattle and the grass and rain or about hunting, or humorously, risquély about sex (the raccoon's pecker) and drinking (which all of them did in enormous quantities on certain significant occasions, such as an unexpected rainfall, a sudden rise in the price of beef). Finally, "How's school?"

"Fine." More nervous silence, interrupted by his mother, "I'll go see about supper." Then pausing at the kitchen door, smiling, "Reverend Dickson called this morning. He wants you to be Christ again."

Joey flushed and started to answer, but didn't. His father only said, "Come on outside, son, let's talk till suppertime."

Outside, leaning against the garden fence, his father spoke after a long silence: "Joey, I know you're a religious boy, but you're a boy, and if, . . . well if . . . sometime, you want some . . . well not nice girls, Joey, and . . . and . . . there's things you can use. . . ."

Joey's face reddened as he gazed across the garden.

II.

In Reverend Dickson's stuffy office with the rows of blue-jacketed religious books (*You wouldn't think there could be so many books saying the same damned thing*), Joey waited. *I should have just not come, said no, not this time.* But he was there, and he was angry with Reverend Dickson, with the town, with himself.

"Joey!" In a voice which was meant to be warm and friendly, but somehow came off terse and condescending, Reverend Dickson greeted him, wearing his usual blue suit (*Do all preachers wear that kind of blue suit?*). The minister was six feet tall with a face which seemed the product of an expert mortician (*How in hell, in Texas for god's sake, can all preachers be so pale?*).

After seating himself directly in front of Joey, Dickson began, "We didn't even consider anyone else, Joey, and. . . ." Mistaking the look of barely contained hostility for surprise, he paused. "Your mother told you, didn't she?"

"Yessir."

Now genuinely puzzled. "Well, what's the matter, son?"

"I don't think I want to this time, sir. I mean, I've done it twice already and. . . ."

"But, son, don't you realize what an honor it is? Why our passion-Sunday is something the entire congregation looks forward to the entire year. God-Is-With-Us-Then, Joey!" The last with his hand on Joey's knee.

"But, Reverend Dickson, it's . . . well . . . embarrassing. I mean to be nearly naked like that in front of all those people."

The reverend leaned back, sighed, and said with sternness, "Joey, I've told you before. In His house on That-Day, no one is thinking like that."

"But maybe someone is . . . and there are the girls. . . ."

"Joey, I must speak firmly. You are enacting the passion of Our Lord on That-Day, and our girls' thoughts and eyes are not aware of your body as your body then. They feel quite a different emotion, I assure you, as you should too, as you always used to. Son, I was afraid of this when you went to Austin. Joey, have you fallen away from the cross?"

"No, sir." Trying not to think of the blond, but somehow wanting to.

With an obviously forced sigh of relief, "I'm glad, Joey. You are, you know, the most devout, sincere boy I've ever converted. On That-Day-When-You-Came-Forth and then when I held you under the water, I felt 'this boy is a Christian!' That's why I've wanted you the last three years to be the Saviour. You know it's necessary that the person who stands up there be 'right' inside as well as outside." (Joey knew that he *was* physically "right," with the build of a high school tailback.)

"I know, sir, but. . . . (But I don't know how to tell him why after seven months in Austin all this doesn't seem honest or important or whatever-the-hell-it-doesn't-seem.) He finally blurted out, without knowing why he did it: "But the splinters!"

"The what?" Miraculously and mercifully at that moment, Yvonne entered.

"Oh, Joey, I didn't know you were here." She seemed to have grown up incredibly since he had last seen her, a year ago. In fact, for the first time that he could remember, he could see the outline of her breasts beneath her soft white dress.

"I'm going to be Mary Magdalene again, Joey."

Joey smiled.

III.

He couldn't sleep that night. The two preceding Easters dominated his mind. The first time, especially, he had felt honored; and "on the cross" during the actual service, he even attained a certain sense of glorious "oneness" with the Saviour. Truly the only thing that had bothered him then was the near nakedness with only a loincloth (stamped MADE IN WACO inside) covering him. But the entire ritual then had seemed sacred and had made him proud. Even when he had entered the church's private room and stripped nude and then slipped on the skimpy loincloth, he had felt the proper awe of the day's symbolism, after an initial moment of shock. And during his "performance" on the artificial "cross" raised high over the heads of the congregation, he had been stirred by Reverend Dickson's sermon warning, pleading against the awful pain and torment of everlasting hell *almost* inevitable in a world which had crucified Christ (a man without sin) and which yearly, daily, hourly grew more attached to the temptations of the world (lust, liquor, movie-going, dancing), but not inevitable, after all, if you would only turn to Christ and away from the world, because Christ would forgive. And high above the congregation (still technically "without sin" himself—not counting masturbation, of course), Joey's lips had formed the silent words, "Yes, I do forgive," and he could really feel pain in the "wounds" in his hands and side and feet, and he had closed his eyes and felt enormous power. Later at home, he still walked in an aura of power-through-capacity-for-mercy and a haze was before his eyes and the horns above the door had somehow reminded him of the "cross" and he had felt an irresistible urge to stand beneath them, arms outspread. . . .

But then last year, the sense of embarrassment and strangeness at the exposure of his body had never completely left him, not even during the sermon. And he felt shame, deep, deep shame; and then he recalled the girl in the little town twenty-five miles away with whom two months before he had lost his technical "oneness with the Saviour" (she had chewed gum during the whole thing), and he felt completely exposed to the upward-gazing flock of farmers and cowmen. (*Not much meat on them ribs*. . . .) And, jerking back from their eyes, he had felt real, not imagined, pain as three splinters from the "cross" jabbed his rump. . . .

Joey sat up in bed and lit a cigarette. Sweat drenched his forehead. He tried desperately to concentrate on something else—Austin, the football games (religious rituals in themselves but ones in which he was safely in the congregation), the taste of beer on the warm fall nights sitting outside at the beergarten, even the excitement of wading into that vast stream of world literature of which he had been almost ignorant before, the blond by the lake. . . .

Then he thought of Yvonne. She really had changed. The fresh, but apparently full breasts, the slender waist, the nice furry voice, the cute little rear which her proper church dress and walk could not disguise. She had been Mary Magdalene the last two years, kneeling beneath him and looking up at him; and it seemed suddenly that he could remember her smiling upward with reverent adoration yes, but maybe with something else. . . .

IV.

His mother woke him the next morning, bringing him the Fort Worth sportspage as always. "Today is your day, son," and she smiled beatifically. She had on her pale pink Easter-Sunday dress. It had once crossed Joey's mind that his mother's tolerance of the mounted raccoon's organ in the den was surprising, but then the den *was* his father's room. Mrs. Carter sat on the side of the bed: "I've always been so pleased, son, that you are a Christian and that Easter means what it should to you." Her face was tired, but really radiant. Like all of the women of her generation in Travis City (with the exception of the waitresses in the cafes), she had found her salvation from living in a male world in her church (the songs, the promise of a land of cool rivers, the story of the truly gentle man whom the world had killed and *his mother*) and in her own maternal responsibilities. And Joey knew that his role in the Easter pageant was a manifestation of both her "rocks of salvation."

At the breakfast table, she still smiled in the otherworldly contentment as she served her two males their bacon, eggs, toast, and coffee. After talking a while about his cattle and about football (*that fumble* against Arkansas which had cost Texas a perfect season and "bygod the national championship"), Mr. Carter said only "we're proud of you, son."

Joey left early for church—he had to "get ready." Entering the private room alone, he sat for a moment, smoked a cigarette he had hidden in his pants' pocket, while glancing nervously around. Then he crushed it out on the bottom of the bench. Finally, he stood up and stripped. Just after he had dropped his shorts to the floor, he heard the door open behind him. He jumped. "Joey," said Reverend Dickson, and he sounded more sanctimonious than ever. Joey expected that the minister would elaborately ignore the boy's nudity. But shockingly the preacher gave him a sharp slap on his left buttock. (*Just like a goddam*

football coach, Joey couldn't help thinking.) He didn't look
at Dickson, but he sensed the reverend's surprise and
mortification at his own action. Finally, "Better slip on the
cloth, son," he managed. Joey did and sat down (the
bench felt cold to his bare flesh). Then, still embarrassed,
the preacher painted the "nail marks" on Joey's hands and
feet and the spear-wound on his side, and placed the plastic crown of thorns on his head. Joey suddenly noticed
that these acts were accompanied by a smile almost identical to that of his mother. Finally, they left the narrow
room and walked into the still empty church auditorium,
Dickson following and making Joey's hip seem to sting all
over again. The boy hurriedly looked out at the rows in
which the congregation of farmers, ranchers, and "small
town merchants" would sit. Rock-hard mahogany, slanting
slightly backward at the top, the pews seemed even more
intimidating than usual, even though today Joey would
not be sitting in one of them. Both walls of the auditorium
were lined wtih imitation stained glass windows (the washing of the feet, the journey with the cross, the manger,
Calvary). When they arrived before the ladder by which
Joey mounted his "cross," he turned suddenly and discovered unmistakably that the preacher's eyes were on his
hips. Now really angry, Joey abruptly turned, ascended the
ladder, and stuck his arms and then his legs through the
leather straps. The Reverend followed and buckled the
support across his waist. Immediately, a splinter jabbed
him in the identical place the preacher had slapped.
"God . . . !" he caught himself just in time. Dickson, however, jumped back at the exclamation and nearly toppled
off the ladder into the front row of seats. Sweating pro-
fusely, he regained his balance and descended the ladder,
just as Yvonne and "the other Mary" (a college sophomore,
short and plump, named Dorothy) and the two Roman
sentries (high school senior football stars—one tackle and
one halfback) came in. Then the choir behind him, but
unable to see objectionably much of him because of the
width of the vertical part of the "cross" (made ten years
ago from a couple of scrub-oak trees on a deacon's ranch).
Joey heard them sit down in the three rows of pews under
the baptismal font (a window revealing a pool of water)
and near a painting of *A Scene from the Holy Land* (one
of a series of Holy Land paintings—all emphasizing the

River Jordan, which always looked amazingly like a stretch of the Red River thirty miles from Travis City, done by an old-maid-backbone-of-the-church who went to the Near East every year and came back with her latest works). Then the congregation began to file in, and Joey abruptly looked down and saw Yvonne and "the other Mary" kneeling just beneath him smiling and the two sentries looking grimly determined (*We need these four yards bad, gang*).

Finally the congregation was seated, and looking out Joey could see his mother and dad in the fifth row—his mother's face fulfilled and serene, his father's Consciously-Aware-of-the-Significance-of-the-Day. Then the organ and choir struck up "That Old Rugged Cross" just as a splinter jabbed his right buttock—he barely managed to swallow the oath.

In a haze for the next few minutes, he stared over the heads of the congregation. Initially, he tried to recapture the glorious "oneness" with the Saviour of his first crucifixion—attempted to forgive the seated congregation, but he just couldn't. *By god, it is their fault, and they are humiliating me!*

Then *buzz, buzz, buzz*—the air vibrating. He didn't see it, but then he felt it crawling slowly, agonizingly just below his navel. Desperately, he tried to free his arms, then to wriggle his abdomen sideways, but the center strap was too tight for that. He leaned back further against the "cross," but the slight motion did not daunt the fly, still continuing its odyssey, now upward toward the center of his chest (*God, you have forsaken me and every damn rule of propriety ever invented*). The itch became intolerable as the insect neared his right nipple. "Jesus was a mother-fuckin' Jew!" He thought he must have screamed it and everyone would have heard it, and he had a brief vision of the entire assemblage advancing toward him in one concerted assertion of the inadequacy of mere symbolized crucifixion. However, the words must not have been loud enough to be heard except by the two Marys, the two sentries, Reverend Dickson, and the fly who fortuitously abandoned his victim at that point.

Heroically undaunted by the words from on high, Reverend Dickson was already well into his sermon before Joey was aware of his voice, progressing from calm to high to shrill: ". . . sins of the flesh, women in short dresses tempting our fine young men to worldly thoughts, movie stars, books with decadent views of sex. . . ." Suddenly Joey felt Yvonne's eyes, and he looked down to see her smiling at him with her eyes focused on the loincloth. Immediately, he felt himself begin to stiffen beneath the cloth and a sharp, but wonderful, pain filled his lower body. He jerked his eyes away, and this time he couldn't help but scream, "Jesus Christ!" But the stiffening continued, remarkably, and he knew the bulge (at least) had to be visible to the two Marys kneeling just beneath him. Hastily, he glanced down at "the other Mary"—she was staring now at the floor, visibly red even from his lofty position. The two sentries now had their Saturday-morning-drugstore-grins on. But when he looked at Yvonne again, she was smiling "bigger than Dallas." Meanwhile, the Reverend Dickson was reaching the climax of his pleas for "decisions for Christ."

v.

The next night before he picked Yvonne up, he stopped at the Mobil station where he bought a pack of rubbers. They made it great parked on a country road five miles from town, and he didn't break a single thumbnail.

A. J. Langguth

From *Jesus Christs*

The following pieces are taken from a collection of visions and revisions of Christ stories. Langguth, in a series of vignettes, retells episodes of the life and teachings of Christ, a Christ who is usually found in the modern garb of a spaceman, salesman, television celebrity, or dozens of other unlikely poses that at once are uproariously funny and bitingly satiric. Unlike Ivan Karamazov who wonders what would happen if Christ were to return to the earth today, Langguth has him return in what usually prove to be futile but darkly comic attempts to fulfill his mission. One reviewer suggested that Langguth's stories are a combination of Heller and Kazantzakis; that they are.

During one triumphal entry into Jerusalem, a fair-skinned man thrust himself in front of the animal that bore Jesus. "Lord!" he called. "Do you remember me?"

"Certainly," Jesus responded warmly. Three years spent campaigning among the people had taught him to be politic.

"I was afraid you might not." The man, about fifty-five years old, bobbed his head gratefully. "You had only been on earth one day when I visited you."

That clue was enough for Jesus. Thirty years before, Melchior had already been old, and Balthasar was far darker than this pale man. "I am happy to see you again, Gaspar." Jesus dismounted to walk a few paces with the descendant of Ham.

"So often I had wondered what became of you," Gaspar said. "You have no idea how pleased I am that your promise at last is being fulfilled."

"Your good wishes are important to me," Jesus replied. "My mother still recalls your visit and the generosity of your gifts."

Gaspar hardly seemed to hear. He had sunk for a

moment in a thought of his own. "You're Earth, aren't you?" he asked abruptly. "I'm sure that's right—Earth?"

"I was born of woman to traverse the earth and bring God's word to man," Jesus allowed, puzzled at the excitement in Gaspar's voice.

"No, I mean your birthday. You were born in the trigon of Earth?"

Jesus wondered if he had fallen in step with a lunatic. "I don't know what you mean," he said coldly.

"Astrology! The true guide to foretelling the future. Surely you are a believer?"

"I believe in the One God."

"But you must believe! It was the conjunction of Jupiter and Saturn in Pisces that produced the star that led us to Judea. You were heralded to the world through astrology."

"I was heralded through centuries of messianic prophecy."

Again Gaspar had withdrawn to his own thoughts. Lengthening his stride to keep up with Jesus, he started to rummage through his robe. "Let me give you proof," he said. "I will cast your horoscope from the stars."

"I foresee my future," Jesus said. "It is nothing I wish to anticipate."

Gaspar had already begun to consult the symbols painted on a parchment scroll. "You are right," he said awesomely. "The coming week holds many perils. It favors quiet evenings at the fireside with your family. New ventures should be postponed. Friends may prove difficult. Above all, keep your natural good humor."

Convinced that Gaspar's idolatry was harmless, Jesus began to tease him. "What can you tell me about next Friday?"

"Friday?" Gaspar studied the brightly colored charts and circles. "Friday is all right. In fact, Friday could turn out to be unusually propitious. If there's a day that should concern you, it's Sunday—one week from today. That's a day with a number of bad portents."

Jesus thought, His predictions are accurate enough. Friday I escape the world and Sunday I am compelled to return. These forecasts are designed for men, and men long ago set a low value on life.

Worried by Jesus' long silence, Gaspar asked, "What do you think of astrology now? It's not blasphemous, is it?"

"It's too accurate to be blasphemous."

"Do you mean that truth is always reverent?" he persisted. But Jesus had boarded his mount again, and Gaspar was caught in the midst of fifty children waving palm leaves.

* * *

Jesus!

Who is it?

It's God, Jesus. Listen to me.

It's not God. It's one of my own voices.

Believe me.

It's a voice I've heard coming from my own heart.

Please.

You've fooled me too often.

Trust me.

I will trust you as my own voice. You have as much right to speak as any of my other voices.

Trust me as God.

No.

This is your last chance.

You've said that before. I might believe you if you didn't always come back.

Good-bye, Jesus.

You didn't fool me.

* * *

Luke had devised a new version of the parable. In it, the prodigal son preferred to starve to death rather than humiliate himself by seeking his father's pardon. Jesus read the story and tore it up.

Then Luke produced an ending in which the prodigal son tried to return home but found that his family had moved to a destination unknown to the neighbors. Jesus tore up what Luke had shown him.

"We need a new ending," Luke pleaded. "In the classrooms they're no longer interested in the original story."

"Then write about a starving beggar who imagines in his delirium that pride had once driven him to leave his father's fine estate. Let his hunger cause him to believe that he has returned to that unreal house and that he has been welcomed with love and banquets."

"Is that the end?"

"At the height of the delirium, let him be visited by a traveler who breaks into his fantasy and convinces him that the house, the father, the fatted calf are all lies, and that he is dying ignored and alone."

"We cannot call it the story of the prodigal son."

"Call it the story of the Samaritan."

"The Good Samaritan?"

"Let your students worry about that."

*   *   *

A warning: If I survive without you and learn to pass the days without straining for your voice, then I will never listen to you afterward. Then if you come to me and say, "It will be again as it has been," I will tell you, "No." I will tell you that I wanted to progress in faith, and you denied that progress to me. If I progress now in doubt, my success may disgust me. But my progress will be undeniable. A warning.

*   *   *

JESUS: Guess what's more debasing than to believe in something that never existed.

SIMON: What?

JESUS: To stop believing in something that never existed.

Jesus thought, If bombs fell tomorrow, I would not be a failure.

JESUS: Guess what's the most romantic idea.

PETER: That men wanted to reform their lives?

JESUS: That's the second most romantic idea.

PETER: What's first?

JESUS: That I wanted them to.

*   *   *

What have I learned?

That what men call goodness is nothing more than a search for pain. That what they call evil is the inflicting of pain.

Two brief lessons, only long enough to threaten my existence.

Rising again, I ask myself, Can I live if they don't eat my flesh? Can I die if they won't drink my blood?

Michael Moorcock

BEHOLD THE MAN

He has no material power as the god-emperors had; he has
only a following of desert people and fishermen. They tell
him he is a god; he believes them. The followers of Alexander said: "He is unconquerable, therefore he is a god."
The followers of this man do not think at all; he was their
act of spontaneous creation. Now he leads them, this madman called Jesus of Nazareth.

And he spoke, saying unto them: Yeah verily I *was* Karl
Glogauer and now I am Jesus the Messiah, the Christ.

And it was so.

I

The time machine was a sphere full of milky fluid in which
the traveler floated, enclosed in a rubber suit, breathing
through a mask attached to a hose leading to the wall of
the machine. The sphere cracked as it landed and the
fluid spilled into the dust and was soaked up. Instinctively,
Glogauer curled himself into a ball as the level of the liquid
fell and he sank to the yielding plastic of the sphere's inner
lining. The instruments, cryptographic, unconventional,
were still and silent. The sphere shifted and rolled as the
last of the liquid dripped from the great gash in its side.

Momentarily, Glogauer's eyes opened and closed, then
his mouth stretched in a kind of yawn and his tongue
fluttered and he uttered a groan that turned into a ulula-
tion.

He heard himself. The Voice of Tongues, he thought.
The language of the unconscious. But he could not guess
what he was saying.

His body became numb and he shivered. His passage
through time had not been easy and even the thick fluid
had not wholly protected him, though it had doubtless

saved his life. Some ribs were certainly broken. Painfully, he straightened his arms and legs and began to crawl over the slippery plastic towards the crack in the machine. He could see harsh sunlight, a sky like shimmering steel. He pulled himself halfway through the crack, closing his eyes as the full strength of the sunlight struck them. He lost consciousness.

Christmas term, 1949. He was nine years old, born two years after his father had reached England from Austria.

The other children were screaming with laughter in the gravel of the playground. The game had begun earnestly enough and somewhat nervously Karl had joined in in the same spirit. Now he was crying.

"Let me *down!* Please, Mervyn, stop it!"

They had tied him with his arms spreadeagled against the wire-netting of the playground fence. It bulged outwards under his weight and one of the posts threatened to come loose. Mervyn Williams, the boy who had proposed the game, began to shake the post so that Karl was swung heavily back and forth on the netting.

"Stop it!"

He saw that his cries only encouraged them and he clenched his teeth, becoming silent.

He slumped, pretending unconsciousness; the school ties they had used as bonds cut into his wrists. He heard the children's voices drop.

"Is he all right?" Molly Turner was whispering.

"He's only kidding." Williams replied uncertainly.

He felt them untying him, their fingers fumbling with the knots. Deliberately, he sagged, then fell to his knees, grazing them on the gravel, and dropped face down to the ground.

Distantly, for he was half-convinced by his own deception, he heard their worried voices.

Williams shook him.

"Wake up, Karl. Stop mucking about."

He stayed where he was, losing his sense of time until he heard Mr. Matson's voice over the general baffle.

"What on earth were you doing, Williams?"

"It was a play, sir, about Jesus. Karl was being Jesus. We tied him to the fence. It was his idea, sir. It was only a game, sir."

Karl's body was stiff, but he managed to stay still, breathing shallowly.

"He's not a strong boy like you, Williams. You should have known better."

"I'm sorry, sir. I'm really sorry." Williams sounded as if he were crying.

Karl felt himself lifted; felt the triumph. . . .

He was being carried along. His head and side were so painful that he felt sick. He had had no chance to discover where exactly the time machine had brought him, but, turning his head now, he could see by the way the man on his right was dressed that he was at least in the Middle East.

He had meant to land in the year 29 A.D. in the wilderness beyond Jerusalem, near Bethlehem. Were they taking him to Jerusalem now?

He was on a stretcher that was apparently made of animal skins; this indicated that he was probably in the past, at any rate. Two men were carrying the stretcher on their shoulders. Others walked on both sides. There was a smell of sweat and animal fat and a musty smell he could not identify. They were walking towards a line of hills in the distance.

He winced as the stretcher lurched and the pain in his side increased. For the second time he passed out.

He work up briefly, hearing voices. They were speaking what was evidently some form of Aramaic. It was night, perhaps, for it seemed very dark. They were no longer moving. There was straw beneath him. He was relieved. He slept.

In those days came John the Baptist preaching in the wilderness of Judaea, And saying, Repent ye: for the kingdom of heaven is at hand. For this is he that was spoken of by the prophet Esaias, saying, The voice of one crying in the wilderness, Prepare ye the way of the Lord, make his paths straight. And the same John had his raiment of camel's hair, and a leathern girdle about his loins; and his meat was locusts and wild honey. Then went out to him Jerusalem, and all Judaea, and all the region round about Jordan, And were baptized of him in Jordan, confessing their sins.

(Matthew 3:1–6)

* * *

They were washing him. He felt the cold water running over his naked body. They had managed to strip off his protective suit. There were now thick layers of cloth against his ribs on the right, and bands of leather bound them to him.

He felt very weak now, and hot, but there was less pain.

He was in a building—or perhaps a cave; it was too gloomy to tell—lying on a heap of straw that was saturated by the water. Above him, two men continued to sluice water down on him from their earthenware pots. They were stern-faced, heavily-bearded men, in cotton robes.

He wondered if he could form a sentence they might understand. His knowledge of written Aramaic was good, but he was not sure of certain pronunciations.

He cleared his throat. "Where—be—this—place?"

They frowned, shaking their heads and lowering their water jars.

"I—seek—a—Nazarene—Jesus. . . ."

"Nazarene. Jesus." One of the men repeated the words, but they did not seem to mean anything to him. He shrugged.

The other, however, only repeated the word Nazarene, speaking it slowly as if it had some special significance for him. He muttered a few words to the other man and went towards the entrance of the room.

Karl Glogauer continued to try to say something the remaining man would understand.

"What—year—doth—the   Roman   Emperor—sit—in Rome?"

It was a confusing question to ask, he realized. He knew Christ had been crucified in the fifteenth year of Tiberius' reign, and that was why he had asked the question. He tried to phrase it better.

"How many—year—doth Tiberius rule?"

"Tiberius?" The man frowned.

Glogauer's ear was adjusting to the accent now and he tried to simulate it better. "Tiberius. The emperor of the Romans. How many years has he ruled?"

"How many?" The man shook his head. "I know not."

At least Glogauer had managed to make himself understood.

"Where is this place?" he asked.

"It is the wilderness beyond Machaerus," the man replied. "Know you not that?"

Machaerus lay to the southeast of Jerusalem, on the other side of the Dead Sea. There was no doubt that he was in the past and that the period was sometime in the reign of Tiberius, for the man had recognized the name easily enough.

His companion was now returning, bringing with him a huge fellow with heavily muscled hairy arms and a great barrel chest. He carried a big staff in one hand. He was dressed in animal skins and was well over six feet tall. His black, curly hair was long and he had a black, bushy beard that covered the upper half of his chest. He moved like an animal and his large, piercing brown eyes looked reflectively at Glogauer.

When he spoke, it was in a deep voice, but too rapidly for Glogauer to follow. It was Glogauer's turn to shake his head.

The big man squatted down beside him. "Who art thou?"

Glogauer paused. He had not planned to be found in this way. He had intended to disguise himself as a traveler from Syria, hoping that the local accents would be different enough to explain his own unfamiliarity with the language. He decided that it was best to stick to this story and hope for the best.

"I am from the north," he said.

"Not from Egypt?" the big man asked. It was as if he had expected Glogauer to be from there. Glogauer decided that if this was what the big man thought, he might just as well agree to it.

"I came out of Egypt two years since," he said.

The big man nodded, apparently satisfied. "So you are a magus from Egypt. That is what we thought. And your name is Jesus, and you are the Nazarene."

"I *seek* Jesus, the Nazarene," Glogauer said.

"Then what is your name?" The man seemed disappointed.

Glogauer could not give his own name. It would sound too strange to them. On impulse he gave his father's first name. "Emmanuel," he said.

The man nodded, again satisfied. "Emmanuel."

Glogauer realized belatedly that the choice of name had

been an unfortunate one in the circumstances, for Emmanuel meant in Hebrew "God with us" and doubtless had a mystic significance for his questioner.

"And what is your name?" he asked.

The man straightened up, looking broodingly down on Glogauer. "You do not know me? You have not heard of John, called the Baptist?"

Glogauer tried to hide his surprise, but evidently John the Baptist saw that his name was familiar. He nodded his shaggy head. "You do know of me, I see. Well, magus, now I must decide, eh?"

"What must you decide?" Glogauer asked nervously.

"If you be the friend of the prophecies or the false one we have been warned against by Adonai. The Romans would deliver me into the hands of mine enemies, the children of Herod."

"Why is that?"

"You must know why, for I speak against the Romans who enslave Judaea, and I speak against the unlawful things that Herod does, and I prophesy the time when all those who are not righteous shall be destroyed and Adonai's kingdom will be restored on Earth as the old prophets said it would be. I say to the people, 'Be ready for that day when ye shall take up the sword to do Adonai's will.' The unrighteous know that they will perish on this day, and they would destroy me."

Despite that intensity of his words, John's tone was matter of fact. There was no hint of insanity or fanaticism in his face or bearing. He sounded most of all like an Anglican vicar reading a sermon whose meaning for him had lost its edge.

The essence of what he said, Karl Glogauer realized, was that he was arousing the people to throw out the Romans and their puppet Herod and establish a more "righteous" regime. The attributing of this plan to "Adonai" (one of the spoken names of Jahweh and meaning The Lord) seemed, as many scholars had guessed in the 20th century, a means of giving the plan extra weight. In a world where politics and religion, even in the west, were inextricably bound together, it was necessary to ascribe a supernatural origin to the plan.

Indeed, Glogauer thought, it was more than likely that

John believed his idea had been inspired by God, for the Greeks on the other side of the Mediterranean had not yet stopped arguing about the origins of inspiration—whether it originated in a man's head or was placed there by the gods. That John accepted him as an Egyptian magician of some kind did not surprise Glogauer particularly, either. The circumstances of his arrival must have seemed extraordinarily miraculous and at the same time acceptable, particularly to a sect like the Essenes who practiced self-mortification and starvation and must be quite used to seeing visions in this hot wilderness. There was no doubt now that these people were the neurotic Essenes, whose ritual washing—baptism—and self-deprivation, coupled with the almost paranoiac mysticism that led them to invent secret languages and the like, was a sure indication of their mentally unbalanced condition. All this occurred to Glogauer the psychiatrist manqué, but Glogauer the man was torn between the poles of extreme rationalism and the desire to be convinced by the mysticism itself.

"I must meditate," John said, turning towards the cave entrance. "I must pray. You will remain here until guidance is sent to me."

He left the cave, striding rapidly away.

Glogauer sank back on the wet straw. He was without doubt in a limestone cave, and the atmosphere in the cave was surprisingly humid. It must be very hot outside. He felt drowsy.

II

Five years in the past. Nearly two thousand in the future. Lying in the hot, sweaty bed with Monica. Once again, another attempt to make normal love had metamorphosed into the performance of minor aberrations which seemed to satisfy her better than anything else.

Their real courtship and fulfillment was yet to come. As usual, it would be verbal. As usual, it would find its climax in argumentative anger.

"I suppose you're going to tell me you're not satisfied again." She accepted the lighted cigarette he handed to her in the darkness.

"I'm all right," he said.

There was silence for a while as they smoked.

Eventually, and in spite of knowing what the result would be if he did so, he found himself talking.

"It's ironic, isn't it?" he began.

He waited for her reply. She would delay for a little while yet.

"What is?" she said at last.

"All this. You spend all day trying to help sexual neurotics to become normal. You spend your nights doing what they do."

"Not to the same extent. You know it's all a matter of degree."

"So you say."

He turned his head and looked at her face in the starlight from the window. She was a gaunt-featured redhead, with the calm, professional seducer's voice of the psychiatric social worker that she was. It was a voice that was soft, reasonable and insincere. Only occasionally, when she became particularly agitated, did her voice begin to indicate her real character. Her features never seemed to be in repose, even when she slept. Her eyes were forever wary, her movements rarely spontaneous. Every inch of her was protected, which was probably why she got so little pleasure from ordinary lovemaking.

"You just can't let yourself go, can you?" he said.

"Oh, shut up, Karl. Have a look at yourself if you're looking for a neurotic mess."

Both were amateur psychiatrists—she a psychiatric social worker, he merely a reader, a dabbler, though he had done a year's study some time ago when he had planned to become a psychiatrist. They used the terminology of psychiatry freely. They felt happier if they could name something.

He rolled away from her, groping for the ashtray on the bedside table, catching a glance of himself in the dressing table mirror. He was a sallow, intense, moody Jewish bookseller, with a head full of images and unresolved obsessions, a body full of emotions. He always lost these arguments with Monica. Verbally, she was the dominant one. This kind of exchange often seemed to him more perverse than their lovemaking, where usually at least his role was masculine. Essentially, he realized, he was pas-

sive, masochistic, indecisive. Even his anger, which came
frequently, was impotent. Monica was ten years older than
he was, ten years more bitter. As an individual, of course,
she had far more dynamism than he had; but as a psychiatric social worker she had had just as many failures. She
plugged on, becoming increasingly cynical on the surface
but still, perhaps, hoping for a few spectacular successes
with patients. They tried to do too much, that was the
trouble, he thought. The priests in the confessional supplied
a panacea; the psychiatrists tried to cure, and most of the
time they failed. But at least they tried, he thought, and
then wondered if that was, after all, a virtue.

"I did look at myself," he said.

Was she sleeping? He turned. Her wary eyes were still
open, looking out of the window.

"I did look at myself," he repeated. "The way Jung did.
'How can I help those persons if I am myself a fugitive
and perhaps also suffer from the *morbus sacer* of a
neurosis?' That's what Jung asked himself. . . ."

"That old sensationalist. That old rationalizer of his
own mysticism. No wonder you never became a psychiatrist."

"I wouldn't have been any good. It was nothing to do
with Jung. . . ."

"Don't take it out on me. . . ."

"You've told me yourself that you feel the same—you
think it's useless. . . ."

"After a hard week's work, I might say that. Give me
another fag."

He opened the packet on the bedside table and put two
cigarettes in his mouth, lighting them and handing one to
her.

Almost abstractedly, he noticed that the tension was
increasing. The argument was, as ever, pointless. But it
was not the argument that was the important thing; it was
simply the expression of the essential relationship. He
wondered if that was in any way important, either.

"You're not telling the truth." He realized that there was
no stopping now that the ritual was in full swing.

"I'm telling the practical truth. I've no compulsion to
give up my work. I've no wish to be a failure. . . ."

"Failure? You're more melodramatic than I am."

"You're too earnest, Karl. You want to get out of your-self a bit."

He sneered. "If I were you, I'd give up my work, Monica. You're no more suited for it than I was."

She shrugged. "You're a petty bastard."

"I'm not jealous of you, if that's what you think. You'll never understand what I'm looking for."

Her laugh was artificial, brittle. "Modern man in search of a soul, eh? Modern man in search of a crutch, I'd say. And you can take that any way you like."

"We're destroying the myths that make the world go round."

"Now you say 'And what are we putting in their place?' You're stale and stupid, Karl. You've never looked ration-ally at anything—including yourself."

"What of it? You say the myth is unimportant."

"The reality that creates it is important."

"Jung knew that the myth can also create the reality."

"Which shows what a muddled old fool he was."

He stretched his legs. In doing so, he touched hers and he recoiled. He scratched his head. She still lay there smoking, but she was smiling now.

"Come on," she said. "Let's have some stuff about Christ."

He said nothing. She handed him the stub of her ciga-rette and he put it in the ashtray. He looked at his watch. It was two o'clock in the morning.

"Why do we do it?" he said.

"Because we must." She put her hand to the back of his head and pulled it towards her breast. "What else can we do?"

We Protestants must sooner or later face this question: Are we to understand the "imitation of Christ" in the sense that we should copy his life and, if I may use the expres-sion, ape his stigmata; or in the deeper sense that we are to live our own proper lives as truly as he lived his in all its implications? It is no easy matter to live a life that is modeled on Christ's, but it is unspeakably harder to live one's own life as truly as Christ lived his. Anyone who did this would . . . be misjudged, derided, tortured and cruci-fied. . . . A neurosis is a dissociation of personality.

(Jung: Modern Man in Search of a Soul)

For a month, John the Baptist was away and Glogauer lived with the Essenes, finding it surprisingly easy, as his ribs mended, to join in their daily life. The Essenes' township consisted of a mixture of single-story houses, built of limestone and clay brick, and the caves that were to be found on both sides of the shallow valley. The Essenes shared their goods in common and this particular sect had wives, though many Essenes led completely monastic lives. The Essenes were also pacifists, refusing to own or to make weapons—yet this sect plainly tolerated the warlike Baptist. Perhaps their hatred of the Romans overcame their principles. Perhaps they were not sure of John's entire intention. Whatever the reason for their toleration, there was little doubt that John the Baptist was virtually their leader.

The life of the Essenes consisted of ritual bathing three times a day, of prayer and of work. The work was not difficult. Sometimes Glogauer guided a plough pulled by two other members of the sect; sometimes he looked after the goats that were allowed to graze on the hillsides. It was a peaceful, ordered life, and even the unhealthy aspects were so much a matter of routine that Glogauer hardly noticed them for anything else after a while.

Tending the goats, he would lie on a hilltop, looking out over the wilderness which was not a desert, but rocky scrubland sufficient to feed animals like goats or sheep. The scrubland was broken by low-lying bushes and a few small trees growing along the banks of the river that doubtless ran into the Dead Sea. It was uneven ground. In outline, it had the appearance of a stormy lake, frozen and turned yellow and brown. Beyond the Dead Sea lay Jerusalem. Obviously Christ had not entered the city for the last time yet. John the Baptist would have to die before that happened.

The Essenes' way of life was comfortable enough, for all its simplicity. They had given him a goatskin loincloth and a staff and, except for the fact that he was watched by day and night, he appeared to be accepted as a kind of lay member of the sect.

Sometimes they questioned him casually about his chariot—the time machine they intended soon to bring in from the desert—and he told them that it had borne him from

Egypt to Syria and then to here. They accepted the miracle calmly. As he had suspected, they were used to miracles.

The Essenes had seen stranger things than his time machine. They had seen men walk on water and angels descend to and from heaven; they had heard the voice of God and His archangels as well as the tempting voice of Satan and his minions. They wrote all these things down in their vellum scrolls. They were merely a record of the supernatural as their other scrolls were records of their daily lives and of the news that traveling members of their sect brought to them.

They lived constantly in the presence of God and spoke to God and were answered by God when they had sufficiently mortified their flesh and starved themselves and chanted their prayers beneath the blazing sun of Judaea.

Karl Glogauer grew his hair long and let his beard come unchecked. He mortified his flesh and starved himself and chanted his prayers beneath the sun, as they did. But he rarely heard God and only once thought he saw an archangel with wings of fire.

In spite of his willingness to experience the Essenes' hallucinations, Glogauer was disappointed, but he was surprised that he felt so well considering all the self-inflicted hardships he had to undergo, and he also felt relaxed in the company of these men and women who were undoubtedly insane. Perhaps it was because their insanity was not so very different from his own that after a while he stopped wondering about it.

John the Baptist returned one evening, striding over the hills followed by twenty or so of his closest disciples. Glogauer saw him as he prepared to drive the goats into their cave for the night. He waited for John to get closer.

The Baptist's face was grim, but his expression softened as he saw Glogauer. He smiled and grasped him by the upper arm in the Roman fashion.

"Well, Emmanuel, you are our friend, as I thought you were. Sent by Adonai to help us accomplish His will. You shall baptize me on the morrow, to show all the people that He is with us."

Glogauer was tired. He had eaten very little and had spent most of the day in the sun, tending the goats. He yawned, finding it hard to reply. However, he was relieved.

John had plainly been in Jerusalem trying to discover if the Romans had sent him as a spy. John now seemed reassured and trusted him.

He was worried, however, by the Baptist's faith in his powers.

"John," he began. "I'm no seer. . . ."

The Baptist's face clouded for a moment, then he laughed awkwardly. "Say nothing. Eat with me tonight. I have wild-honey and locusts."

Glogauer had not yet eaten this food, which was the staple of travelers who did not carry provisions but lived off the food they could find on the journey. Some regarded it as a delicacy.

He tried it later, as he sat in John's house. There were only two rooms in the house. One was for eating in, the other for sleeping in. The honey and locusts was too sweet for his taste, but it was a welcome change from barley or goat-meat.

He sat cross-legged, opposite John the Baptist, who ate with relish. Night had fallen. From outside came low murmurs and the moans and cries of those at prayer.

Glogauer dipped another locust into the bowl of honey that rested between them. "Do you plan to lead the people of Judaea in revolt against the Romans?" he asked.

The Baptist seemed disturbed by the direct question. It was the first of its nature that Glogauer had put to him.

"If it be Adonai's will," he said, not looking up as he leant towards the bowl of honey.

"The Romans know this?"

"I do not know, Emmanuel, but Herod the incestuous has doubtless told them I speak against the unrighteous."

"Yet the Romans do not arrest you."

"Pilate dare not—not since the petition was sent to the Emperor Tiberius."

"Petition?"

"Aye, the one that Herod and the Pharisees signed when Pilate the procurator did place votive shields in the palace at Jerusalem and seek to violate the Temple. Tiberius rebuked Pilate and since then, though he still hates the Jews, the procurator is more careful in his treatment of us."

"Tell me, John, do you know how long Tiberius has ruled in Rome?" He had not had the chance to ask that question again until now.

"Fourteen years."

It was 28 A.D.—something less than a year before the crucifixion would take place, and his time machine was smashed.

Now John the Baptist planned armed rebellion against the occupying Romans, but, if the Gospels were to be believed, would soon be decapitated by Herod. Certainly no large-scale rebellion had taken place at this time. Even those who claimed that the entry of Jesus and his disciples into Jerusalem and the invasion of the Temple were plainly the actions of armed rebels had found no records to suggest that John had led a similar revolt.

Glogauer had come to like the Baptist very much. The man was plainly a hardened revolutionary who had been planning revolt against the Romans for years and had slowly been building up enough followers to make the attempt successful. He reminded Glogauer strongly of the resistance leaders of the Second World War. He had a similar toughness and understanding of the realities of his position. He knew that he would only have one chance to smash the cohorts garrisoned in the country. If the revolt became protracted, Rome would have ample time to send more troops to Jerusalem.

"When do you think Adonai intends to destroy the unrighteous through your agency?" Glogauer said tactfully.

John glanced at him with some amusement. He smiled. "The Passover is a time when the people are restless and resent the strangers most," he said.

"When is the next Passover?"

"Not for many months."

"How can I help you?"

"You are a magus."

"I can work no miracles."

John wiped the honey from his beard. "I cannot believe that, Emmanuel. The manner of your coming was miraculous. The Essenes did not know if you were a devil or a messenger from Adonai."

"I am neither."

"Why do you confuse me, Emmanuel? I know that you

are Adonai's messenger. You are the sign that the Essenes sought. The time is almost ready. The kingdom of heaven shall soon be established on earth. Come with me. Tell the people that you speak with Adonai's voice. Work mighty miracles."

"Your power is waning, is that it?" Glogauer looked sharply at John. "You need me to renew your rebels' hopes?"

"You speak like a Roman, with such lack of subtlety." John got up angrily. Evidently, like the Essenes he lived with, he preferred less direct conversation. There was a practical reason for this, Glogauer realized, in that John and his men feared betrayal all the time. Even the Essenes' records were partially written in cipher, with one innocent-seeming word or phrase meaning something else entirely.

"I am sorry, John. But tell me if I am right." Glogauer spoke softly.

"Are you not a magus, coming in that chariot from nowhere?" The Baptist waved his hands and shrugged his shoulders. "My men saw you! They saw the shining thing take shape in air, crack and let you enter out of it. Is that not magical? The clothing you wore—was that earthly raiment? The talismans within the chariot—did they not speak of powerful magic? The prophet said that a magus would come from Egypt and be called Emmanuel. So it is written in the Book of Micah! Are none of these things true?"

"Most of them. But there are explanations—" He broke off, unable to think of the nearest word to "rational." "I am an ordinary man, like you. I have no power to work miracles! I am just a man!"

John glowered. "You mean you refuse to help us?"

"I'm grateful to you and the Essenes. You saved my life almost certainly. If I can repay that . . ."

John nodded his head deliberately. "You can repay it, Emmanuel."

"How?"

"Be the great magus I need. Let me present you to all those who become impatient and would turn away from Adonai's will. Let me tell them the manner of your coming to us. Then you can say that all is Adonai's will and that they must prepare to accomplish it."

John stared at him intensely.

"Will you, Emmanuel?"

"For your sake, John. And in turn, will you send men to bring my chariot here as soon as possible? I wish to see if it may be mended."

"I will."

Glogauer felt exhilarated. He began to laugh. The Baptist looked at him with slight bewilderment. Then he began to join in.

Glogauer laughed on. History would not mention it, but he, with John the Baptist, would prepare the way for Christ.

Christ was not born yet. Perhaps Glogauer knew it, one year before the crucifixion.

And the Word was made flesh, and dwelt among us (and we beheld his glory, the glory as of the only begotten of the Father), full of grace and truth. John bare witness of him, and cried, saying, This was he of whom I spake, He that cometh after me is preferred before me; for he was before me.

(John 1:14–15)

Even when he had first met Monica they had had long arguments. His father had not then died and left him the money to buy the Occult Bookshop in Great Russell Street, opposite the British Museum. He was doing all sorts of temporary work and his spirits were very low. At that time Monica had seemed a great help, a great guide through the mental darkness engulfing him. They had both lived close to Holland Park and went there for walks almost every Sunday of the summer of 1962. At twenty-two, he was already obsessed with Jung's strange brand of Christian mysticism. She, who despised Jung, had soon begun to denigrate all his ideas. She never really convinced him. But, after a while, she had succeeded in confusing him. It would be another six months before they went to bed together.

It was uncomfortably hot.

They sat in the shade of the cafeteria, watching a distant cricket match. Nearer to them, two girls and a boy sat on the grass, drinking orange squash from plastic cups. One of the girls had a guitar across her lap and she set the cup down and began to play, singing a folksong in a high, gentle voice. Glogauer tried to listen to the words. As a student, he had always liked traditional folk music.

"Christianity is dead." Monica sipped her tea. "Religion is dying. God was killed in 1945."

"There may yet be a resurrection," he said.

"Let us hope not. Religion was the creation of fear. Knowledge destroys fear. Without fear, religion can't survive."

"You think there's no fear about these days?"

"Not the same kind, Karl."

"Haven't you ever considered the *idea* of Christ?" he asked her, changing his tack. "What that means to Christians?"

"The idea of the tractor means as much to a Marxist," she replied.

"But what came first? The idea or the actuality of Christ?"

She shrugged. "The actuality, if it matters. Jesus was a Jewish troublemaker organizing a revolt against the Romans. He was crucified for his pains. That's all we know and all we need to know."

"A great religion couldn't have begun so simply."

"When people need one, they'll make a great religion out of the most unlikely beginnings."

"That's my point, Monica." He gesticulated at her and she drew away slightly. "The *idea* preceded the *actuality* of Christ."

"Oh, Karl, don't go on. The actuality of *Jesus* preceded the idea of *Christ*."

A couple walked past, glancing at them as they argued.

Monica noticed them and fell silent. She got up and he rose as well, but she shook her head. "I'm going home, Karl. You stay here. I'll see you in a few days."

He watched her walk down the wide path towards the park gates.

The next day, when he got home from work, he found a letter. She must have written it after she had left him and posted it the same day.

Dear Karl,

Conversation doesn't seem to have much effect on you, you know. It's as if you listen to the tone of the voice, the rhythm of the words, without ever hearing what is trying to be communicated. You're a bit like a sensitive animal who can't understand what's being said to it, but can tell if the person talking is pleased or angry and so on. That's why I'm writing to you—to try to get my idea across. You respond too emotionally when we're together.

You make the mistake of considering Christianity as something that developed over the course of a few years, from the death of Jesus to the time the Gospels were written. But Christianity wasn't new. Only the name was new. Christianity was merely a stage in the meeting, cross-fertilization metamorphosis of Western logic and Eastern mysticism. Look how the religion itself changed over the centuries, re-interpreting itself to meet changing times. Christianity is just a new name for a conglomeration of old myths and philosophies. All the Gospels do is retell the sun myth and garble some of the ideas from the Greeks and Romans. Even in the second century, Jewish scholars were showing it up for the mish-mash it was! They pointed out the strong similarities between the various sun myths and the Christ myth. The miracles didn't happen—they were invented later, borrowed from here and there.

Remember the old Victorians who used to say that Plato was really a Christian because he anticipated Christian thought? Christian thought! Christianity was a vehicle for ideas in circulation for centuries before Christ. Was Marcus Aurelius a Christian? He was writing in the direct tradition of Western philosophy. That's why Christianity caught on in Europe and not in the East! You should have been a theologian with your bias, not a psychiatrist. The same goes for your friend Jung.

Try to clear your head of all this morbid nonsense and you'll be a lot better at your job.

Yours,
Monica.

He screwed the letter up and threw it away. Later that evening he was tempted to look at it again, but he resisted the temptation.

III

John stood up to his waist in the river. Most of the Essenes stood on the banks watching him. Glogauer looked down at him.

"I cannot, John. It is not for me to do it."

The Baptist muttered, "You must."

Glogauer shivered as he lowered himself into the river beside the Baptist. He felt light-headed. He stood there trembling, unable to move.

His foot slipped on the rocks of the river and John reached out and gripped his arm, steadying him.

In the clear sky, the sun was at zenith, beating down on his unprotected head.

"Emmanuel!" John cried suddenly. "The spirit of Adonai is within you!"

Glogauer still found it hard to speak. He shook his head slightly. It was aching and he could hardly see. Today he was having his first migraine attack since he had come here. He wanted to vomit. John's voice sounded distant.

He swayed in the water.

As he began to fall toward the Baptist, the whole scene around him shimmered. He felt John catch him and heard himself say desperately: "John, baptize *me!*" And then there was water in his mouth and throat and he was coughing.

John's voice was crying something. Whatever the words were, they drew a response from the people on both banks. The roaring in his ears increased, its quality changing. He thrashed in the water, then felt himself lifted to his feet.

The Essenes were swaying in unison, every face lifted upwards towards the glaring sun.

Glogauer began to vomit into the water, stumbling as John's hands gripped his arms painfully and guided him up the bank.

A peculiar, rhythmic humming came from the mouths of the Essenes as they swayed; it rose as they swayed to one side, fell as they swayed to the other.

Glogauer covered his ears as John released him. He was still retching, but it was dry now, and worse than before.

He began to stagger away, barely keeping his balance,

running, with his ears still covered; running over the rocky scrubland; running as the sun throbbed in the sky and its heat pounded at his head; running away.

But John forbade him, saying, I have need to be baptized of thee, and comest thou to me? And Jesus answering said unto him, Suffer it to be so now: for thus it becometh us to fulfill all righteousness. Then he suffered him. And Jesus, when he was baptized, went up straightway out of the water: and, lo, the heavens were opened unto him, and he saw the Spirit of God descending like a dove, and lighting upon him: And lo a voice from heaven, saying, This is my beloved Son, in whom I am well pleased.

(Matthew 3:14–17)

He had been fifteen, doing well at the grammar school. He had read in the newspapers about the Teddy Boy gangs that roamed South London, but the odd youth he had seen in pseudo-Edwardian clothes had seemed harmless and stupid enough.

He had gone to the pictures in Brixton Hill and decided to walk home to Streatham because he had spent most of the bus money on an ice cream. They came out of the cinema at the same time. He hardly noticed them as they followed him down the hill.

Then, quite suddenly, they had surrounded him. Pale, mean-faced boys, most of them a year or two older than he was. He realized that he knew two of them vaguely. They were at the big council school in the same street as the grammar school. They used the same football ground.

"Hello," he said weakly.

"Hello, son," said the oldest Teddy Boy. He was chewing gum, standing with one knee bent, grinning at him. "Where you going, then?"

"Home."

"Heouwm," said the biggest one, imitating his accent. "What are you going to do when you get there?"

"Go to bed." Karl tried to get through the ring, but they wouldn't let him. They pressed him back into a shop doorway. Beyond them, cars droned by on the main road. The street was brightly lit, with street lamps and neon from the shops. Several people passed, but none of them stopped. Karl began to feel panic.

"Got no homework to do, son?" said the boy next to the leader. He was redheaded and freckled and his eyes were a hard gray.

"Want to fight one of us?" another boy asked. It was one of the boys he knew.

"No. I don't fight. Let me go."

"You scared, son?" said the leader, grinning. Ostentatiously, he pulled a streamer of gum from his mouth and then replaced it. He began chewing again.

"No. Why should I want to fight you?"

"You reckon you're better than us, is that it, son?"

"No." He was beginning to tremble. Tears were coming into his eyes. " 'Course not."

" 'Course not, son."

He moved forward again, but they pushed him back into the doorway.

"You're the bloke with the kraut name, ain't you?" said the other boy he knew. "Glow-worm or somethink."

"Glogauer. Let me go."

"Won't your mummy like it if you're back late?"

"More a yid name than a kraut name."

"You a yid, son?"

"He looks like a yid."

"You a yid, son?"

"You a Jewish boy, son?"

"You a yid, son?"

"Shut up!" Karl screamed. He pushed into them. One of them punched him in the stomach. He grunted with pain. Another pushed him and he staggered.

People were still hurrying by on the pavement. They glanced at the group as they went past. One man stopped, but his wife pulled him on. "Just some kids larking about," she said.

"Get his trousers down," one of the boys suggested with a laugh. "That'll prove it."

Karl pushed through them and this time they didn't resist. He began to run down the hill.

"Give him a start," he heard one of the boys say.

He ran on.

They began to follow him, laughing.

They did not catch up with him by the time he turned into the avenue where he lived. He reached the house and ran along the dark passage beside it. He opened the back door. His stepmother was in the kitchen.

"What's the matter with you?" she said.

She was a tall, thin woman, nervous and hysterical. Her dark hair was untidy.

He went past her into the breakfast-room.

"What's the matter, Karl?" she called. Her voice was high-pitched.

"Nothing," he said.

He didn't want a scene.

It was cold when he woke up. The false dawn was gray and he could see nothing but barren country in all directions. He could not remember a great deal about the previous day, except that he had run a long way.

Dew had gathered on his loincloth. He wet his lips and rubbed the skin over his face. As he always did after a migraine attack he felt weak and completely drained. Looking down at his naked body, he noticed how skinny he had become. Life with the Essenes had caused that, of course.

He wondered why he had panicked so much when John had asked him to baptize him. Was it simply honesty— something in him which resisted deceiving the Essenes into thinking he was a prophet of some kind? It was hard to know.

He wrapped the goatskin about his hips and tied it tightly just above his left thigh. He supposed he had better try to get back to the camp and find John and apologize, see if he could make amends.

The time machine was there now, too. They had dragged it there, using only rawhide ropes.

If a good blacksmith could be found, or some other metalworker, there was just a chance that it could be repaired. The journey back would be dangerous.

He wondered if he ought to go back right away, or try to shift to a time nearer to the actual crucifixion. He had not gone back specifically to witness the crucifixion, but to get the mood of Jerusalem during the Feast of the Passover, when Jesus was supposed to have entered the city. Monica had thought Jesus had stormed the city with an armed band. She had said that all the evidence pointed to that. All the evidence of one sort did point to it, but he could not accept the evidence. There was more to it, he was sure. If only he could meet Jesus. John had apparently never heard of him, though he had told Glogauer that there was a prophecy that the Messiah would be a Nazarene. There were many prophecies, and many of them conflicted.

He began to walk back in the general direction of the Essene camp. He could not have come so far. He would soon recognize the hills where they had their caves.

Soon it was very hot and the ground more barren. The air wavered before his eyes. The feeling of exhaustion with which he had awakened increased. His mouth was dry and his legs were weak. He was hungry and there was nothing to eat. There was no sign of the range of hills where the Essenes had their camp.

There was one hill, about two miles away to the south. He decided to make for it. From there he would probably be able to get his bearings, perhaps even see a township where they would give him food.

The sandy soil turned to floating dust around him as his feet disturbed it. A few primitive shrubs clung to the ground and jutting rocks tripped him.

He was bleeding and bruised by the time he began, painfully, to clamber up the hillside.

The journey to the summit (which was much farther away than he had originally judged) was difficult. He would slide on the loose stones of the hillside, falling on his face, bracing his torn hands and feet to stop himself from sliding down to the bottom, clinging to tufts of grass and lichen that grew here and there, embracing larger projections of rock when he could, resting frequently, his mind and body both numb with pain and weariness.

He sweated beneath the sun. The dust stuck to the moisture on his half-naked body, caking him from head to foot. The goatskin was in shreds.

The barren world reeled around him, sky somehow merging with land, yellow rock with white clouds. Nothing seemed still.

He reached the summit and lay there gasping. Everything had become unreal.

He heard Monica's voice, thought he glanced at her for a moment from the corner of his eye.

Don't be melodramatic, Karl. . . .

She had said that many times. His own voice replied now.

I'm born out of my time, Monica. This age of reason has no place for me. It will kill me in the end.

Her voice replied.

Guilt and fear and your own masochism. You could be a brilliant psychiatrist, but you've given in to all your own neuroses so completely. . . .

"Shut up!"

He rolled over on his back. The sun blazed down on his tattered body.

"Shut up!"

The whole Christian syndrome, Karl. You'll become a Catholic convert next I shouldn't doubt. Where's your strength of mind?

"Shut up! Go away, Monica."

Fear shapes your thoughts. You're not searching for a soul or even a meaning for life. You're searching for comforts.

"Leave me alone, Monica!"

His grimy hands covered his ears. His hair and beard were matted with dust. Blood had congealed on the minor wounds that were now on every part of his body. Above, the sun seemed to pound in unison with his heartbeats.

You're going downhill, Karl, don't you realize that? Downhill. Pull yourself together. You're not entirely incapable of rational thought. . . .

"Oh, Monica! Shut up!"

His voice was harsh and cracked. A few ravens circled the sky above him now. He heard them calling back at him in a voice not unlike his own.

God died in 1945. . . .

"It isn't 1945—it's 28 A.D. God is alive!"

How you can bother to wonder about an obvious syncretistic religion like Christianity—Rabbinic Judaism, Stoic ethics, Greek mystery cults, Oriental ritual. . . .

"It doesn't matter!"

Not to you in your present state of mind.

"I need God!"

That's what it boils down to, doesn't it? Okay, Karl, carve your own crutches. Just think what you could have been if you'd have come to terms with yourself. . . .

Glogauer pulled his ruined body to its feet and stood on the summit of the hill and screamed.

The ravens were startled. They wheeled in the sky and flew away.

The sky was darkening now.

Then was Jesus led up of the Spirit into the wilderness to be tempted of the devil. And when he had fasted forty days and forty nights, he was afterward an hungred.

(Matthew 4:1–2)

IV

The madman came stumbling into the town. His feet stirred the dust and made it dance and dogs barked around him as he walked mechanically, his head turned upwards to face the sun, his arms limp at his sides, his lips moving.

To the townspeople, the words they heard were in no familiar language; yet they were uttered with such intensity and conviction that God himself might be using this emaciated, naked creature as his spokesman.

They wondered where the madman had come from.

The white town consisted primarily of double- and single-storied houses of stone and clay-brick, built around a market place that was fronted by an ancient, simple synagogue outside which old men sat and talked, dressed in dark robes. The town was prosperous and clean, thriving on Roman commerce. Only one or two beggars were in the streets and these were well-fed. The streets followed the rise and fall of the hillside on which they were built. They were winding streets, shady and peaceful: country streets. There was a smell of newly-cut timber everywhere in the air, and the sound of carpentry, for the town was chiefly famous for its skilled carpenters. It lay on the edge of the Plain of Jezreel, close to the trade route between Damascus and Egypt, and wagons were always leaving it, laden with the work of the town's craftsmen. The town was called Nazareth.

The madman had found it by asking every traveler he saw where it was. He had passed through other towns—Philadelphia, Gerasa, Pella and Scythopolis, following the Roman roads—asking the same question in his outlandish accent: "Where lies Nazareth?"

Some had given him food on the way. Some had asked for his blessing and he had laid hands on them, speaking in that strange tongue. Some had pelted him with stones and driven him away.

He had crossed the Jordan by the Roman viaduct and continued northwards towards Nazareth.

There had been no difficulty in finding the town, but it had been difficult for him to force himself towards it. He had lost a great deal of blood and had eaten very little on the journey. He would walk until he collapsed and lie there until he could go on, or, as had happened increasingly, until someone found him and had given him a little sour wine or bread to revive him.

Once some Roman legionaries had stopped and with brusque kindness asked him if he had any relatives they could take him to. They had addressed him in pidgin-Aramaic and had been surprised when he replied in a strangely-accented Latin that was purer than the language they spoke themselves.

They asked him if he was a Rabbi or a scholar. He told them he was neither. The officer of the legionaries had offered him some dried meat and wine. The men were part of a patrol that passed this way once a month. They were stocky, brown-faced men, with hard, clean-shaven faces. They were dressed in stained leather kilts and breastplates and sandals, and had iron helmets on their heads, scabbarded short swords at their hips. Even as they stood around him in the evening sunlight they did not seem relaxed. The officer, softer-voiced than his men but otherwise much like them save that he wore a metal breastplate and a long cloak, asked the madman what his name was.

For a moment the madman had paused, his mouth opening and closing, as if he could not remember what he was called.

"Karl," he said at length, doubtfully. It was more a suggestion than a statement.

"Sounds almost like a Roman name," said one of the legionaries.

"Are you a citizen?" the officer asked.

But the madman's mind was wandering, evidently. He looked away from them, muttering to himself.

All at once, he looked back at them and said: "Nazareth?"

"That way." The officer pointed down the road that cut between the hills. "Are you a Jew?"

This seemed to startle the madman. He sprang to his feet and tried to push through the soldiers. They let him through, laughing. He was a harmless madman.

They watched him run down the road.

"One of their prophets, perhaps," said the officer, walking towards his horse. The country was full of them. Every other man you met claimed to be spreading the message of their god. They didn't make much trouble and religion seemed to keep their minds off rebellion. *We should be grateful,* thought the officer.

His men were still laughing.

They began to march down the road in the opposite direction to the one the madman had taken.

Now the madman was in Nazareth and the townspeople looked at him with curiosity and more than a little suspicion as he staggered into the market square. He could be a wandering prophet or he could be possessed by devils. It was often hard to tell. The rabbis would know.

As he passed the knots of people standing by the merchants' stalls, they fell silent until he had gone by. Women pulled their heavy woolen shawls about their well-fed bodies and men tucked in their cotton robes so that he would not touch them. Normally their instinct would have been to have taxed him with his business in the town, but there was an intensity about his gaze, a quickness and vitality about his face, in spite of his emaciated appearance, that made them treat him with some respect and they kept their distance.

When he reached the center of the market place, he stopped and looked around him. He seemed slow to notice the people. He blinked and licked his lips.

A woman passed, eyeing him warily. He spoke to her, his voice soft, the words carefully formed. "Is this Nazareth?"

"It is." She nodded and increased her pace.

A man was crossing the square. He was dressed in a woolen robe of red and brown stripes. There was a red skull cap on his curly, black hair. His face was plump and cheerful. The madman walked across the man's path and stopped him. "I seek a carpenter."

"There are many carpenters in Nazareth. The town is famous for its carpenters. I am a carpenter myself. Can I help you?" The man's voice was good-humored, patronizing.

"Do you know a carpenter called Joseph? A descendant of David. He has a wife called Mary and several children. One is named Jesus."

The cheerful man screwed his face into a mock frown and scratched the back of his neck. "I know more than one Joseph. There is one poor fellow in yonder street." He pointed. "He has a wife called Mary. Try there. You should soon find him. Look for a man who never laughs."

The madman looked in the direction in which the man pointed. As soon as he saw the street, he seemed to forget everything else and strode towards it.

In the narrow street he entered the smell of cut timber was even stronger. He walked ankle-deep in wood-shavings. From every building came the thud of hammers, the scrape of saws. There were planks of all sizes resting against the pale, shaded walls of the houses and there was hardly room to pass between them. Many of the carpenters had their benches just outside their doors. They were carving bowls, operating simple lathes, shaping wood into everything imaginable. They looked up as the madman entered the street and approached one old carpenter in a leather apron who sat at his bench carving a figurine. The man had gray hair and seemed short-sighted. He peered up at the madman.

"What do you want?"

"I seek a carpenter called Joseph. He has a wife— Mary."

The old man gestured with his hand that held the half-completed figurine. "Two houses along on the other side of the street."

The house the madman came to had very few planks leaning against it, and the quality of the timber seemed poorer than the other wood he had seen. The bench near the entrance was warped on one side and the man who sat hunched over it repairing a stool seemed misshapen also. He straightened up as the madman touched his shoulder. His face was lined and pouched with misery. His eyes were tired and his thin beard had premature streaks of gray. He coughed slightly, perhaps in surprise at being disturbed.

"Are you Joseph?" asked the madman.

"I've no money."

"I want nothing—just to ask a few questions."

"I'm Joseph. Why do you want to know?"

"Have you a son?"

"Several, and daughters, too."

"Your wife is called Mary? You are of David's line."

The man waved his hand impatiently. "Yes, for what good either have done me. . . ."

"I wish to meet one of your sons. Jesus. Can you tell me where he is?"

"That good-for-nothing. What has he done now?"

"Where is he?"

Joseph's eyes became more calculating as he stared at the madman. "Are you a seer of some kind? Have you come to cure my son?"

"I am a prophet of sorts. I can foretell the future."

Joseph got up with a sigh. "You can see him. Come." He led the madman through the gateway into the cramped courtyard of the house. It was crowded with pieces of wood, broken furniture and implements, rotting sacks of shavings. They entered the darkened house. In the first room—evidently a kitchen—a woman stood by a large clay stove. She was tall and bulging with fat. Her long, black hair was unbound and greasy, falling over large, lustrous eyes that still had the heat of sensuality. She looked the madman over.

"There's no food for beggars," she grunted. "He eats enough as it is." She gestured with a wooden spoon at a small figure sitting in the shadow of a corner. The figure shifted as she spoke.

"He seeks our Jesus," said Joseph to the woman. "Perhaps he comes to ease our burden."

The woman gave the madman a sidelong look and shrugged. She licked her red lips with a fat tongue. "Jesus!"

The figure in the corner stood up.

"That's him," said the woman with a certain satisfaction.

The madman frowned, shaking his head rapidly. "No."

The figure was misshapen. It had a pronounced hunched back and a cast in its left eye. The face was vacant and foolish. There was a little spittle on the lips. It giggled as its name was repeated. It took a crooked step forward. "Jesus," it said. The word was slurred and thick. "Jesus."

"That's all he can say." The woman sneered. "He's always been like that."

"God's judgment," said Joseph bitterly.

"What is wrong with him?" There was a pathetic, desperate note in the madman's voice.

"He's always been like that." The woman turned back to the stove. "You can have him if you want him. Addled inside and outside. I was carrying him when my parents married me off to that half-man. . . ."

"You shameless—" Joseph stopped as his wife glared at him. He turned to the madman. "What's your business with our son?"

"I wished to talk to him. I . . ."

"He's no oracle—no seer—we used to think he might be. There are still people in Nazareth who come to him to cure them or tell their fortunes, but he only giggles at them and speaks his name over and over again. . . ."

"Are—you sure—there is not—something about him— you have not noticed?"

"Sure!" Mary snorted sardonically. "We need money badly enough. If he had any magical powers, we'd know."

Jesus giggled again and limped away into another room.

"It is impossible," the madman murmured. Could history itself have changed? Could he be in some other dimension of time where Christ had never been?

Joseph appeared to notice the look of agony in the madman's eyes.

"What is it?" he said. "What do you see? You said you foretold the future. Tell us how we will fare?"

"Not *now*," said the prophet, turning away. "Not *now*."

He ran from the house and down the street with its smell of planed oak, cedar and cypress. He ran back to the market place and stopped, looking wildly about him. He saw the synagogue directly ahead of him. He began to walk towards it.

The man he had spoken to earlier was still in the market place, buying cooking pots to give to his daughter as a wedding gift. He nodded towards the strange man as he entered the synagogue. "He's a relative of Joseph the carpenter," he told the man beside him. "A prophet, I shouldn't wonder."

The madman, the prophet, Karl Glogauer, the time-traveler, the neurotic psychiatrist manqué, the searcher for meaning, the masochist, the man with a death-wish and the messiah-complex, the anachronism, made his way into the synagogue gasping for breath. He had seen the man he had sought. He had seen Jesus, the son of Joseph and Mary. He had seen a man he recognized without any doubt as a congenital imbecile.

"All men have a messiah-complex, Karl," Monica had said.

The memories were less complete now. His sense of time and identity was becoming confused.

"There were dozens of messiahs in Galilee at the time. That Jesus should have been the one to carry the myth and the philosophy was a coincidence of history. . . ."

"There must have been more to it than that, Monica."

Every Tuesday in the room above the Occult Bookshop, the Jungian discussion group would meet for purposes of group analysis and therapy. Glogauer had not organized the group, but he had willingly lent his premises to it and had joined it eagerly. It was a great relief to talk with like-minded people once a week. One of his reasons for buying the Occult Bookshop was so that he would meet interesting people like those who attended the Jungian discussion group.

An obsession with Jung brought them together, but everyone had special obsessions of his own. Mrs. Rita Blen charted the courses of flying saucers, though it was not clear if she believed in them or not. Hugh Joyce believed that all Jungian archetypes derived from the original race of Atlantides who had perished millennia before. Alan Cheddar, the youngest of the group, was interested in Indian mysticism, and Sandra Peterson, the organizer, was a great witchcraft specialist. James Headington was interested in time. He was the group's pride; he was Sir James Headington, war-time inventor, very rich and with all sorts of decorations for his contribution to the Allied victory. He had had the reputation of being a great improviser during the war, but after it he had become something of an embarrassment to the War Office. He was a crank, they thought, and what was worse, he aired his crankiness in public.

Every so often, Sir James would tell the other members of the group about his time machine. They humored him. Most of them were liable to exaggerate their own experiences connected with their different interests.

One Tuesday evening, after everyone else had left, Headington told Glogauer that his machine was ready.

"I can't believe it," Glogauer said truthfully.

"You're the first person I've told."

"Why me?"

"I don't know. I like you—and the shop."

"You haven't told the government."

Headington had chuckled. "Why should I? Not until I've tested it fully, anyway. Serves them right for putting me out to pasture."

"You don't know it works?"

"I'm sure it does. Would you like to see it?"

"A time machine." Glogauer smiled weakly.

"Come and see it."

"Why me?"

"I thought you might be interested. I know you don't hold with the orthodox view of science. . . ."

Glogauer felt sorry for him.

"Come and see," said Headington.

He went down to Banbury the next day. The same day he left 1976 and arrived in 28 A.D.

The synagogue was cool and quiet with a subtle scent of incense. The rabbis guided him into the courtyard. They, like the townspeople, did not know what to make of him, but they were sure it was not a devil that possessed him. It was their custom to give shelter to the roaming prophets who were now everywhere in Galilee, though this one was stranger than the rest. His face was immobile and his body was stiff, and there were tears running down his dirty cheeks. They had never seen such agony in a man's eyes before.

"Science can say how, but it never asks why," he had told Monica. "It can't answer."

"Who wants to know?" she'd replied.

"I do."

"Well, you'll never find out, will you?"

"Sit down, my son," said the rabbi. "What do you wish to ask of us?"

"Where is Christ?" he said. "Where is Christ?"

They did not understand the language.

"Is it Greek?" asked one, but another shook his head.

Kyrios: The Lord.

Adonai: The Lord.

Where was the Lord?

He frowned, looking vaguely about him.

"I must rest," he said in their language.

"Where are you from?"

He could not think what to answer.

"Where are you from?" a rabbi repeated.

"*Ha-Olam Hab-bah . . .*" he murmured at length.

They looked at one another. "*Ha-Olam Hab-bah,*" they said.

Ha-Olam Hab-bah; Ha-Olam Haz-zeh: The world to come and the world that is.

"Do you bring us a message?" said one of the rabbis. They were used to prophets, certainly, but none like this one. "A message?"

"I do not know," said the prophet hoarsely. "I must rest. I am hungry."

"Come. We will give you food and a place to sleep."

He could only eat a little of the rich food and the bed with its straw-stuffed mattress was too soft for him. He was not used to it.

He slept badly, shouting as he dreamed, and, outside the room, the rabbis listened, but could understand little of what he said.

Karl Glogauer stayed in the synagogue for several weeks. He would spend most of his time reading in the library, searching through the long scrolls for some answer to his dilemma. The words of the Testaments, in many cases capable of a dozen interpretations, only confused him further. There was nothing to grasp, nothing to tell him what had gone wrong.

The rabbis kept their distance for the most part. They had accepted him as a holy man. They were proud to have him in their synagogue. They were sure that he was one of the special chosen of God and they waited patiently for him to speak to them.

But the prophet said little, muttering only to himself in snatches of their own language and snatches of the incomprehensible language he often used, even when he addressed them directly.

In Nazareth, the townsfolk talked of little else but the mysterious prophet in the synagogue, but the rabbis would not answer their questions. They would tell the people to go about their business, that there were things they were not yet meant to know. In this way, as priests had always done, they avoided questions they could not answer while at the same time appearing to have much more knowledge than they actually possessed.

Then, one sabbath, he appeared in the public part of the synagogue and took his place with the others who had come to worship.

The man who was reading from the scroll on his left stumbled over the words, glancing at the prophet from the corner of his eye.

The prophet sat and listened, his expression remote.

The Chief Rabbi looked uncertainly at him, then signed that the scroll should be passed to the prophet. This was done hesitantly by a boy who placed the scroll into the prophet's hands.

The prophet looked at the words for a long time and then began to read. The prophet read without comprehending at first what he read. It was the book of Esaias.

The Spirit of the Lord is upon me, because he hath anointed me to preach the gospel to the poor; he hath sent me to heal the broken-hearted, to preach deliverance to the captives, and recovering of sight to the blind, to set at liberty them that are bruised, to preach the acceptable year of the Lord. And he closed the book, and gave it again to the minister, and sat down. And the eyes of all of them that were in the synagogue were fastened on him.

(Luke 4:18–20)

V

They followed him now, as he walked away from Nazareth towards the Lake of Galilee. He was dressed in the white linen robe they had given him and though they thought he led them, they, in fact, drove him before them.

"He is our messiah," they said to those that inquired. And there were already rumors of miracles.

When he saw the sick, he pitied them and tried to do what he could because they expected something of him. Many he could do nothing for, but others, obviously in psychosomatic conditions, he could help. They believed in his power more strongly than they believed in their sickness. So he cured them.

When he came to Capernaum, some fifty people followed him into the streets of the city. It was already known that he was in some way associated with John the Baptist, who enjoyed huge prestige in Galilee and had been declared a true prophet by many Pharisees. Yet this man had a power greater, in some ways, than John's. He was not the orator that the Baptist was, but he had worked miracles.

Capernaum was a sprawling town beside the crystal lake of Galilee, its houses separated by large market gardens. Fishing boats were moored at the white quayside, as well as trading ships that plied the lakeside towns. Though the green hills came down from all sides to the lake, Capernaum itself was built on flat ground, sheltered by the hills. It was a quiet town and, like most others in Galilee, had a large population of gentiles. Greek, Roman and Egyptian traders walked its streets and many had made permanent homes there. There was a prosperous middle-class of merchants, artisans and ship-owners, as well as doctors, lawyers and scholars, for Capernaum was on the borders of the provinces of Galilee, Trachonitis and Syria and though a comparatively small town was a useful junction for trade and travel.

The strange, mad prophet in his swirling linen robes, followed by the heterogeneous crowd that was primarily composed of poor folk but also could be seen to contain men of some distinction, swept into Capernaum. The news spread that this man really could foretell the future, that he had already predicted the arrest of John by Herod Antipas and soon after Herod had imprisoned the Baptist at Peraea. He did not make the predictions in general terms, using vague words the way other prophets did. He spoke of things that were to happen in the near future and he spoke of them in detail.

None knew his name. He was simply the prophet from Nazareth, or the Nazarene. Some said he was a relative, perhaps the son, of a carpenter in Nazareth, but this could be because the written words for "son of a carpenter" and "magus" were almost the same and the confusion had come about in that way. There was even a very faint rumor that his name was Jesus. The name had been used once or twice, but when they asked him if that was, indeed, his name, he denied it or else, in his abstracted way, refused to answer at all.

His actual preaching tended to lack the fire of John's. This man spoke gently, rather vaguely, and smiled often. He spoke of God in a strange way, too, and he appeared to be connected, as John was, with the Essenes, for he preached against the accumulation of personal wealth and spoke of mankind as a brotherhood, as they did.

But it was the miracles that they watched for as he was guided to the graceful synagogue of Capernaum. No prophet before him had healed the sick and seemed to understand the troubles that people rarely spoke of. It was his sympathy that they responded to, rather than the words he spoke.

For the first time in his life, Karl Glogauer had forgotten about Karl Glogauer. For the first time in his life he was doing what he had always sought to do as a psychiatrist.

But it was not his life. He was bringing a myth to life— a generation before that myth would be born. He was completing a certain kind of psychic circuit. He was not changing history, but he was giving history more substance.

He could not bear to think that Jesus had been nothing more than a myth. It was in his power to make Jesus a physical reality rather than the creation of a process of mythogenesis.

So he spoke in the synagogues and he spoke of a gentler God than most of them had heard of, and where he could remember them, he told them parables.

And gradually the need to justify what he was doing faded and his sense of identity grew increasingly more tenuous and was replaced by a different sense of identity, where he gave greater and greater substance to the rôle he had chosen. It was an archetypal rôle. It was a rôle to appeal to a disciple of Jung. It was a rôle that went beyond a mere imitation. It was a rôle that he must now play out to the very last grand detail. Karl Glogauer had discovered the reality he had been seeking.

And in the synagogue there was a man, which had a spirit of an unclean devil, and cried out with a loud voice, saying, Let us alone; what have we to do with thee, thou Jesus of Nazareth? art thou come to destroy us? I know thee who thou art; the Holy One of God. And Jesus rebuked him, saying, Hold thy peace, and come out of him. And when the devil had thrown him in the midst, he came out of him, and hurt him not. And they were all amazed, and spake among themselves, saying, What a word is this! for with authority and power he commandeth the unclean spirits, and they come out. And the fame of him went out into every place of the country round about.

(Luke 4:33–37)

"Mass hallucination. Miracles, flying saucers, ghosts, it's all the same," Monica had said.

"Very likely," he had replied. "But *why* did they see them?"

"Because they wanted to."

"Why did they want to?"

"Because they were afraid."

"You think that's all there is to it?"

"Isn't it enough?"

When he left Capernaum for the first time, many more people accompanied him. It had become impractical to stay in the town, for the business of the town had been brought almost to a standstill by the crowds that sought to see him work his simple miracles.

He spoke to them in the spaces beyond the towns. He talked with intelligent, literate men who appeared to have something in common with him. Some of them were the owners of fishing fleets—Simon, James and John among them. Another was a doctor, another a civil servant who had first heard him speak in Capernaum.

"There must be twelve," he said to them one day. "There must be a zodiac."

He was not careful in what he said. Many of his ideas were strange. Many of the things he talked about were unfamiliar to them. Some Pharisees thought he blasphemed.

One day he met a man he recognized as an Essene from the colony near Machaerus.

"John would speak with you," said the Essene.

"Is John not dead yet?" he asked the man.

"He is confined at Peraea. I would think Herod is too frightened to kill him. He lets John walk about within the walls and gardens of the palace, lets him speak with his men, but John fears that Herod will find the courage soon to have him stoned or decapitated. He needs your help."

"How can I help him? He is to die. There is no hope for him."

The Essene looked uncomprehendingly into the mad eyes of the prophet.

"But, master, there is no one else who can help him."

"I have done all that he wished me to do," said the prophet. "I have healed the sick and preached to the poor."

"I did not know he wished this. Now he needs help, master. You could save his life."

The prophet had drawn the Essene away from the crowd.

"His life cannot be saved."

"But if it is not the unrighteous will prosper and the Kingdom of Heaven will not be restored."

"His life cannot be saved."

"Is it God's will?"

"If I am God, then it is God's will."

Hopelessly, the Essene turned and began to walk away from the crowd.

John the Baptist would have to die. Glogauer had no wish to change history, only to strengthen it.

He moved on, with his following, through Galilee. He had selected his twelve educated men, and the rest who followed him were still primarily poor people. To them he offered their only hope of fortune. Many were those who had been ready to follow John against the Romans, but now John was imprisoned. Perhaps this man would lead them in revolt, to loot the riches of Jerusalem and Jericho and Caesarea. Tired and hungry, their eyes glazed by the burning sun, they followed the man in the white robe. They needed to hope and they found reasons for their hope. They saw him work greater miracles.

Once he preached to them from a boat, as was often his custom, and as he walked back to the shore through the shallows, it seemed to them that he walked over the water.

All through Galilee in the autumn they wandered, hearing from everyone the news of John's beheading. Despair at the Baptist's death turned to renewed hope in this new prophet who had known him.

In Caesarea they were driven from the city by Roman guards used to the wildmen with their prophecies who roamed the country.

They were banned from other cities as the prophet's fame grew. Not only the Roman authorities, but the Jewish ones as well seemed unwilling to tolerate the new prophet as they had tolerated John. The political climate was changing.

It became hard to find food. They lived on what they could find, hungering like starved animals.

He taught them how to pretend to eat and take their minds off their hunger.

Karl Glogauer, witch-doctor, psychiatrist, hypnotist, messiah.

Sometimes his conviction in his chosen rôle wavered and those that followed him would be disturbed when he contradicted himself. Often, now, they called him the name they had heard, Jesus the Nazarene. Most of the time he did not stop them from using the name, but at others he became angry and cried a peculiar, guttural name.

"Karl Glogauer! Karl Glogauer!"

And they said, Behold, he speaks with the voice of Adonai.

"Call me not by that name!" he would shout, and they would become disturbed and leave him by himself until his anger had subsided.

When the weather changed and the winter came, they went back to Capernaum, which had become a stronghold of his followers.

In Capernaum he waited the winter through, making prophecies.

Many of these prophecies concerned himself and the fate of those that followed him.

Then charged he his disciples that they should tell no man that he was Jesus the Christ. From that time forth began Jesus to shew unto his disciples, how that he must go unto Jerusalem, and suffer many things of the elders and chief priests and scribes, and be killed, and be raised again the third day.

(Matthew 16:20–21)

They were watching television at her flat. Monica was eating an apple. It was between six and seven on a warm Sunday evening. Monica gestured at the screen with her half-eaten apple.

"Look at that nonsense," she said. "You can't honestly tell me it means anything to you."

The program was a religious one, about a pop-opera in a Hampstead Church. The opera told the story of the crucifixion.

"Pop-groups in the pulpit," she said. "What a come-down."

He didn't reply. The program seemed obscene to him, in an obscure way. He couldn't argue with her.

"God's corpse is really beginning to rot now," she jeered. "Whew! The stink!"

"Turn it off, then," he said quietly.

"What's the pop-group called? The Maggots?"

"Very funny. I'll turn it off, shall I?"

"No. I want to watch. It's funny."

"Oh, turn it off!"

"Imitation of Christ!" she snorted. "It's a bloody carica-ture."

A Negro singer, who was playing Christ and singing flat to a banal accompaniment, began to drone out lifeless lyrics about the brotherhood of man.

"If he sounded like that, no wonder they nailed him up," said Monica.

He reached forward and switched the picture off.

"I was enjoying it." She spoke with mock disappointment. "It was a lovely swan-song."

Later, she said with a trace of affection that worried him, "You old fogey. What a pity. You could have been John Wesley or Calvin or someone. You can't be a messiah these days, not in your terms. There's nobody to listen."

VI

The prophet was living in the house of a man called Simon, though the prophet preferred to call him Peter. Simon was grateful to the prophet because he had cured his wife of a complaint which she had suffered from for some time. It had been a mysterious complaint, but the prophet had cured her almost effortlessly.

There were a great many strangers in Capernaum at that time, many of them coming to see the prophet. Simon warned the prophet that some were known agents of the Romans or the Pharisees. The Pharisees had not, on the whole, been antipathetic towards the prophet, though they distrusted the talk of miracles that they heard. However, the whole political atmosphere was disturbed and the Roman occupation troops, from Pilate, through his officers, down to the troops, were tense, expecting an outbreak but unable to see any tangible signs that one was coming.

Pilate himself hoped for trouble on a large scale. It would prove to Tiberius that the emperor had been too lenient with the Jews over the matter of the votive shields. Pilate would be vindicated and his power over the Jews increased. At present he was on bad terms with all the Tetrarchs of the provinces—particularly the unstable Herod Antipas who had seemed at one time his only supporter. Aside from the political situation, his own domestic situation was upset in that his neurotic wife was having her nightmares again and was demanding far more attention from him than he could afford to give her.

There might be a possibility, he thought, of provoking an incident, but he would have to be careful that Tiberius never learnt of it. This new prophet might provide a focus, but so far the man had done nothing against the laws of either the Jews or the Romans. There was no law that forbade a man to claim he was a messiah, as some said this one had done, and he was hardly inciting the people to revolt—rather the contrary.

Looking through the window of his chamber, with a view of the minarets and spires of Jerusalem, Pilate considered the information his spies had brought him.

Soon after the festival that the Romans called Saturnalia, the prophet and his followers left Capernaum again and began to travel through the country.

There were fewer miracles now that the hot weather had passed, but his prophecies were eagerly asked. He warned them of all the mistakes that would be made in the future, and of all the crimes that would be committed in his name.

Through Galilee he wandered, and through Samaria, following the good Roman roads towards Jerusalem.

The time of the Passover was coming close now.

In Jerusalem, the Roman officials discussed the coming festival. It was always a time of the worst disturbances. There had been riots before during the Feast of the Passover, and doubtless there would be trouble of some kind this year, too.

Pilate spoke to the Pharisees, asking for their cooperation. The Pharisees said they would do what they could, but they could not help it if the people acted foolishly.

Scowling, Pilate dismissed them.

His agents brought him reports from all over the territory. Some of the reports mentioned the new prophet, but said that he was harmless.

Pilate thought privately that he might be harmless now, but if he reached Jerusalem during the Passover, he might not be so harmless.

Two weeks before the Feast of the Passover, the prophet reached the town of Bethany near Jerusalem. Some of his Galilean followers had friends in Bethany and these friends were more than willing to shelter the man they had heard of from other pilgrims on their way to Jerusalem and the Great Temple.

The reason they had come to Bethany was that the prophet had become disturbed at the number of the people following him.

"There are too many," he had said to Simon. "Too many, Peter."

Glogauer's face was haggard now. His eyes were set deeper into their sockets and he said little.

Sometimes he would look around him vaguely, as if unsure where he was.

News came to the house in Bethany that Roman agents had been making inquiries about him. It did not seem to disturb him. On the contrary, he nodded thoughtfully, as if satisfied.

Once he walked with two of his followers across country to look at Jerusalem. The bright yellow walls of the city looked splendid in the afternoon light. The towers and tall buildings, many of them decorated in mosaic reds, blues and yellows, could be seen from several miles away.

The prophet turned back towards Bethany.

"When shall we go into Jerusalem?" one of his followers asked him.

"Not yet," said Glogauer. His shoulders were hunched and he grasped his chest with his arms and hands as if cold.

Two days before the Feast of the Passover in Jerusalem, the prophet took his men towards the Mount of Olives and a suburb of Jerusalem that was built on its side and called Bethphage.

"Get me a donkey," he told them. "A colt. I must fulfill the prophecy now."

"Then all will know you are the Messiah," said Andrew.

"Yes."

Glogauer sighed. He felt afraid again, but this time it was not physical fear. It was the fear of an actor who was about to make his final, most dramatic scene and who was not sure he could do it well.

There was cold sweat on Glogauer's upper lip. He wiped it off.

In the poor light he peered at the men around him. He was still uncertain of some of their names. He was not interested in their names, particularly, only in their number. There were ten here. The other two were looking for the donkey.

They stood on the grassy slope of the Mount of Olives, looking towards Jerusalem and the great Temple which lay below. There was a light, warm breeze blowing.

"Judas?" said Glogauer inquiringly.

There was one called Judas.

"Yes, master," he said. He was tall and good looking, with curly red hair and neurotic intelligent eyes. Glogauer believed he was an epileptic.

Glogauer looked thoughtfully at Judas Iscariot. "I will want you to help me later," he said, "when we have entered Jerusalem."

"How, master?"

"You must take a message to the Romans."

"The Romans?" Iscariot looked troubled. "Why?"

"It must be the Romans. It can't be the Jews—they would use a stake or an axe. I'll tell you more when the time comes."

The sky was dark now, and the stars were out over the Mount of Olives. It had become cold. Glogauer shivered.

> Rejoice greatly O daughter of Zion,
> Shout, O daughter of Jerusalem:
> Behold, thy King cometh unto thee!
> He is just and having salvation;
> Lowly and riding upon an ass,
> And upon a colt, the foal of an ass.
>
> (Zechariah 9:9)

"Osha'na! Osha'na! Osha'na!"

As Glogauer rode the donkey into the city, his followers ran ahead, throwing down palm branches. On both sides of the street were crowds, forewarned by the followers of his coming.

Now the new prophet could be seen to be fulfilling the prophecies of the ancient prophets and many believed that he had come to lead them against the Romans. Even now, possibly, he was on his way to Pilate's house to confront the procurator.

"Osha'na! Osha'na!"

Glogauer looked around distractedly. The back of the donkey, though softened by the coats of his followers, was uncomfortable. He swayed and clung to the beast's mane. He heard the words, but could not make them out clearly.

"Osha'na! Osha'na!"

It sounded like "hosanna" at first, before he realized that they were shouting the Aramaic for "Free us."

"Free us! Free us!"

John had planned to rise in arms against the Romans

this Passover. Many had expected to take part in the rebellion.

They believed that he was taking John's place as a rebel leader.

"No," he muttered at them as he looked around at their expectant faces. "No, I am the messiah. I cannot free you. I can't. . . ."

They did not hear him above their own shouts.

Karl Glogauer entered Christ. Christ entered Jerusalem. The story was approaching its climax.

"*Osha'na!*"

It was not in the story. He could not help them.

Verily, verily, I say unto you, that one of you shall betray me. Then the disciples looked one on another, doubting of whom he spake. Now there was leaning on Jesus' bosom one of his disciples, whom Jesus loved. Simon Peter therefore beckoned to him, that he should ask who it should be of whom he spake. He then lying on Jesus' breast saith unto him, Lord, who is it? Jesus answered, He it is, to whom I shall give a sop, when I have dipped it. And when he had dipped the sop, he gave it to Judas Iscariot, the son of Simon. And after the sop Satan entered into him. Then said Jesus unto him, That thou doest, do quickly.

(John 13:21–27)

Judas Iscariot frowned with some uncertainty as he left the room and went out into the crowded street, making his way towards the governor's palace. Doubtless he was to perform a part in a plan to deceive the Romans and have the people rise up in Jesus' defense, but he thought the scheme foolhardy. The mood amongst the jostling men, women and children in the streets was tense. Many more Roman soldiers than usual patrolled the city.

Pilate was a stout man. His face was self-indulgent and his eyes were hard and shallow. He looked disdainfully at the Jew.

"We do not pay informers whose information is proved to be false," he warned.

"I do not seek money, lord," said Judas, feigning the ingratiating manner that the Romans seemed to expect of the Jews. "I am a loyal subject of the Emperor."

"Who is this rebel?"

"Jesus of Nazareth, lord. He entered the city today . . ."

"I know. I saw him. But I heard he preached of peace and obeying the law."

"To deceive you, lord."

Pilate frowned. It was likely. It smacked of the kind of deceit he had grown to anticipate in these soft-spoken people.

"Have you proof?"

"I am one of his lieutenants, lord. I will testify to his guilt."

Pilate pursed his heavy lips. He could not afford to offend the Pharisees at this moment. They had given him enough trouble. Caiaphas, in particular, would be quick to cry "injustice" if he arrested the man.

"He claims to be the rightful king of the Jews, the descendant of David," said Judas, repeating what his master had told him to say.

"Does he?" Pilate looked thoughtfully out of the window.

"As for the Pharisees, lord . . ."

"What of them?"

"The Pharisees distrust him. They would see him dead. He speaks against them."

Pilate nodded. His eyes were hooded as he considered this information. The Pharisees might hate the madman, but they would be quick to make political capital out of his arrest.

"The Pharisees want him arrested," Judas continued. "The people flock to listen to the prophet and today many of them rioted in the Temple in his name."

"Is this true?"

"It is true, lord." It was true. Some half-a-dozen people had attacked the money-changers in the Temple and tried to rob them. When they had been arrested, they had said they had been carrying out the will of the Nazarene.

"I cannot make the arrest," Pilate said musingly. The situation in Jerusalem was already dangerous, but if they were to arrest this "king," they might find that they precipitated a revolt. Tiberius would blame him, not the Jews. The Pharisees must be won over. They must make the arrest. "Wait here," he said to Judas. "I will send a message to Caiaphas."

And they came to a place which was named Gethsem-
ane: and he saith to his disciples, Sit ye here, while I
shall pray. And he taketh with him Peter and James and
John, and began to be sore amazed, and to be very heavy;
And saith unto them, My soul is exceeding sorrowful unto
death: tarry ye here, and watch.

(Mark 14:32–34)

Glogauer could see the mob approaching now. For the
first time since Nazareth he felt physically weak and exhausted. They were going to kill him. He had to die; he
accepted that, but he was afraid of the pain that was to
come. He sat down on the ground of the hillside, watching
the torches as they came closer.

"The ideal of martyrdom only ever existed in the minds
of a few ascetics," Monica had said. *"Otherwise it was*
morbid masochism, an easy way to forgo ordinary respon-
sibility, a method of keeping repressed people under con-
trol. . . ."

"It isn't as simple as that. . . ."

"It is, Karl."

He could show Monica now. His regret was that she
was unlikely ever to know. He had meant to write everything down and put it into the time machine and hope that
it would be recovered. It was strange. He was not a religious man in the usual sense. He was an agnostic. It was
not conviction that had led him to defend religion against
Monica's cynical contempt for it; it was rather *lack* of conviction in the ideal in which she had set her own faith,
the ideal of science as a solver of all problems. He could
not share her faith and there was nothing else but religion,
though he could not believe in the kind of God of Christianity. The God seen as a mystical force of the mysteries of
Christianity and other great religions had not been personal
enough for him. His rational mind had told him that God
did not exist in any personal form. His unconscious had
told him that faith in science was not enough.

"Science is basically opposed to religion," Monica had
once said harshly. *"No matter how many Jesuits get to-*
gether and rationalize their views of science, the fact re-
mains that religion cannot accept the fundamental atti-

tudes of science and it is implicit to science to attack the fundamental principles of religion. The only area in which there is no difference and need be no war is in the ultimate assumption. One may or may not assume there is a supernatural being called God. But as soon as one begins to defend one's assumption, there must be strife."

"You're talking about organized religion. . . ."

"I'm talking about religion as opposed to a belief. Who needs the ritual of religion when we have the far superior ritual of science to replace it? Religion is a reasonable substitute for knowledge. But there is no longer any need for substitutes, Karl. Science offers a sounder basis on which to formulate systems of thought and ethics. We don't need the carrot of heaven and the big stick of hell any more when science can show the consequences of actions and men can judge easily for themselves whether those actions are right or wrong."

"I can't accept it."

"That's because you're sick. I'm sick, too, but at least I can see the promise of health."

"I can only see the threat of death. . . ."

As they had agreed, Judas kissed him on the cheek and the mixed force of Temple guards and Roman soldiers surrounded him.

To the Romans he said, with some difficulty, "I am the King of the Jews." To the Pharisees' servants he said: "I am the messiah who has come to destroy your masters." Now he was committed and the final ritual was to begin.

VII

It was an untidy trial, an arbitrary mixture of Roman and Jewish law which did not altogether satisfy anyone. The object was accomplished after several conferences between Pontius Pilate and Caiaphas and three attempts to bend and merge their separate legal systems in order to fit the expediencies of the situation. Both needed a scapegoat for their different purposes and so at last the result was achieved and the madman convicted, on the one hand of rebellion against Rome and on the other of heresy.

A peculiar feature of the trial was that the witnesses

were all followers of the man and yet had seemed eager to see him convicted.

The Pharisees agreed that the Roman method of execution would fit the time and the situation best in this case and it was decided to crucify him. The man had prestige, however, so that it would be necessary to use some of the tried Roman methods of humiliation in order to make him into a pathetic and ludicrous figure in the eyes of the pilgrims. Pilate assured the Pharisees that he would see to it, but he made sure that they signed documents that gave their approval to his actions.

And the soldiers led him away into the hall, called Praetorium; and they call together the whole band. And they clothed him with purple, and platted a crown of thorns, and put it about his head, And began to salute him, Hail, King of the Jews! And they smote him on the head with a reed, and did spit upon him, and bowing their knees worshipped him. And when they had mocked him, they took off the purple from him, and put his own clothes on him, and led him out to crucify him.

(Mark 15:16–20)

His brain was clouded now, by pain and by the ritual of humiliation; by his having completely given himself up to his rôle.

He was too weak to bear the heavy wooden cross and he walked behind it as it was dragged towards Golgotha by a Cyrenian whom the Romans had press-ganged for the purpose.

As he staggered through the crowded, silent streets, watched by those who had thought he would lead them against the Roman overlords, his eyes filled with tears so that his sight was blurred and he occasionally staggered off the road and was nudged back onto it by one of the Roman guards.

"You are too emotional, Karl. Why don't you use that brain of yours and pull yourself together? . . ."

He remembered the words, but it was difficult to remember who had said them or who Karl was.

The road that led up the side of the hill was stony and he slipped sometimes, remembering another hill he had climbed long ago. It seemed to him that he had been a child, but the memory merged with others and it was impossible to tell.

He was breathing heavily and with some difficulty. The pain of the thorns in his head was barely felt, but his whole body seemed to throb in unison with his heartbeat. It was like a drum.

It was evening. The sun was setting. He fell on his face, cutting his head on a sharp stone, just as he reached the top of the hill. He fainted.

And they bring him unto the place Golgotha, which is, being interpreted, The place of a skull. And they gave him to drink wine mingled with myrrh: but he received it not.
                         (Mark 15:22–23)

He knocked the cup aside. The soldier shrugged and reached out for one of his arms. Another soldier already held the other arm.

As he recovered consciousness Glogauer began to tremble violently. He felt the pain intensely as the ropes bit into the flesh of his wrists and ankles. He struggled.

He felt something cold placed against his palm. Although it only covered a small area in the center of his hand it seemed very heavy. He heard a sound that also was in rhythm with his heartbeats. He turned his head to look at the hand.

The large iron peg was being driven into his hand by a soldier swinging a mallet as he lay on the cross which was at this moment horizontal on the ground. He watched, wondering why there was no pain. The soldier swung the mallet higher as the peg met the resistance of the wood. Twice he missed the peg and struck Glogauer's fingers.

Glogauer looked to the other side and saw that the second soldier was also hammering in a peg. Evidently he missed the peg a great many times because the fingers of the hand were bloody and crushed.

The first soldier finished hammering in his peg and turned his attention to the feet. Glogauer felt the iron slide through his flesh, heard it hammered home.

Using a pulley, they began to haul the cross into a vertical position. Glogauer noticed that he was alone. There were no others being crucified that day.

He got a clear view of the lights of Jerusalem below him. There was still a little light in the sky but not much. Soon it would be completely dark. There was a small crowd looking on. One of the women reminded him of Monica. He called to her.

"Monica?"

But his voice was cracked and the word was a whisper. The woman did not look up.

He felt his body dragging at the nails which supported it. He thought he felt a twinge of pain in his left hand. He seemed to be bleeding very heavily.

It was odd, he reflected, that it should be him hanging here. He supposed that it was the event he had originally come to witness. There was little doubt, really. Everything had gone perfectly.

The pain in his left hand increased.

He glanced down at the Roman guards who were playing dice at the foot of his cross. They seemed absorbed in their game. He could not see the markings of the dice from this distance.

He sighed. The movement of his chest seemed to throw extra strain on his hands. The pain was quite bad now. He winced and tried somehow to ease himself back against the wood.

The pain began to spread through his body. He gritted his teeth. It was dreadful. He gasped and shouted. He writhed.

There was no longer any light in the sky. Heavy clouds obscured stars and moon.

From below came whispered voices.

"Let me down," he called. "Oh, please let me down!"

The pain filled him. He slumped forward, but nobody released him.

A little while later he raised his head. The movement caused a return of the agony and again he began to writhe on the cross.

"Let me down. Please. Please stop it!"

Every part of his flesh, every muscle and tendon and bone of him, was filled with an almost impossible degree of pain.

He knew he would not survive until the next day as he had thought he might. He had not realized the extent of his pain.

> *And at the ninth hour Jesus cried with a loud voice, saying, Eloi, Eloi, lama sabachthani? which is, being interpreted, My God, my God, why hast thou forsaken me?*
>
> (Mark 15:34)

Glogauer coughed. It was a dry, barely heard sound. The soldiers below the cross heard it because the night was now so quiet.

"It's funny," one said. "Yesterday they were worshiping him. Today they seemed to want us to kill him—even the ones who were closest to him."

"I'll be glad when we get out of this country," said another.

He heard Monica's voice again. "It's weakness and fear, Karl, that's driven you to this. Martyrdom is a conceit. Can't you see that?"

Weakness and fear.

He coughed once more and the pain returned, but it was duller now.

Just before he died he began to talk again, muttering the words until his breath was gone. "It's a lie. It's a lie. It's a lie."

Later, after his body was stolen by the servants of some doctors who believed it to have special properties, there were rumors that he had not died. But the corpse was already rotting in the doctors' dissecting rooms and would soon be destroyed.

Walker Percy

From *Love in the Ruins*

Thomas More, M.D., who sees himself as a new messiah to a sick and dying world in Walker Percy's futuristic novel, has passed out in the sun while on a call in the black district of his typical and old-fashioned Southern city. Victor Charles, a black man, helps him walk up the long hill to Leroy Ledbetter's bar, in the white district. The incident that follows parodies that told in St. John 21:15–17 in which Jesus asks Peter three times if Peter loves him. Walker Percy's irony cuts deeper than his vision of Jim Crow alive and well at the apocalypse; it points to the deep "fault in the soul's terrain" and the need for a new kind of messiah to heal it.

Victor takes me as far as the Little Napoleon. There I make a mistake, a small one with small consequences but a mistake nevertheless, which I'd ordinarily not have made. But it has been a strange day. Hanging on to Victor, I did not let him go until we were inside. I should have either dismissed him outside or held on to him longer. As it was, letting go Victor when the bar was within reach, I let go a second too early, so that Leroy Ledbetter, turning toward me in the same second, did not see me let go but saw Victor just beside me and so registered a violation. Not even that: a borderline violation because Victor was not even at the bar but still a step away. What with his white attendant's clothes and if he had been a step closer to me, it would have been clear that he was attending me in some capacity or other. A step or two in the other direction and he'd have been past the end of the bar and in the loading traffic where Negroes often pass carrying sacks of oysters, Cokes, and such. As it was, he seemed to be standing, if not at the bar, then one step too close and Leroy, turning, saw him in the split second before Victor started to leave, Victor in the act of backing up when Leroy said as his eyes went past him, said not even quite to Victor, "The window's there," nodding toward the service window opening into the alley; even then giving Victor the benefit of the doubt and not even allowing the possibility that Victor was coming to the bar for a drink, but the possibility only that he had come to buy his flat pint of muscatel and for some reason had not known or had forgotten about the service window. In the same second that he speaks, Leroy knows better, for in that second Victor steps back and turns toward me and I can see that Leroy sees that Victor is with me, sees it even before I can say, too late, "Thank you, Victor, for helping me up the hill," and signifies his error by a pass of his rag across the bar, a ritual glance past Victor at the storm cloud above the saloon door, a swinging back of his eyes past Victor and a saying in Victor's direction, "Looks like we going to get it yet," said almost to Victor but not quite because it had not been quite a violation so did not quite warrant a correction thereof. Victor nods, not quite acknowledging because total acknowledgment is not called for, withholding perhaps 20 percent acknowledgment (2 percent too much?). He leaves by the side door.

A near breach, an insignificant incident. A stranger observing the incident would not have been aware that anything had happened at all, much less that in the space of two seconds there had occurred a three-cornered transaction entailing an assignment of zones, a near infraction of zoning, a calling attention to the infraction, a triple simultaneous perception of the mistake, a correction thereof, and an acknowledgment of that—a minor breach with no consequences other than these: an artery beats for a second in Leroy's temple, there is a stiffness about Victor's back as he leaves, and there comes in my throat a metallic taste.

It is not even worth mentioning even though Victor withholds perhaps 2 percent of the acknowledgment that was due and his back is 2 percent stiffer than it might be.

"What's wrong with you, Tom?"

"I'm all right now. It was hot in the Hollow. I got dizzy."

He gives me my toddy. I peel an egg.

"Is that your lunch? No wonder you fainted. And you a doctor."

I look at the mirror. Behind the bar towers a mahogany piece, a miniature cathedral, an altarpiece, an intricate business of shelves for bottles, cupboards, stained-glass windows, and a huge mirror whose silvering is blighted with an advancing pox, clusters of vacuoles, expanding naughts. Most of the customers of the Little Napoleon have long since removed to the lounges of the suburbs, the nifty refrigerated windowless sealed-up Muzaked hideaways, leaving stranded here a small band of regulars and old-timers, some of whom have sat here in the same peaceable gloom open to the same twilight over the same swinging doors that swung their way straight through Prohibition and saw Kingfish Huey P. Long promise to make every man a king on the courthouse lawn across the street. Next door *Gone with the Wind* had its final run at the old Majestic Theater.

The vines are sprouting here in earnest. A huge wistaria with a tree-size trunk holds the Little Napoleon like a rock in a root. The building strains and creaks in its grip.

The storm is closer, the sun gone, and it is darker than dusk. The martins are skimming in from the swamp, sliding down the dark glassy sky like flecks of soot. Soon the bullbats will be thrumming.

Leroy Ledbetter stands by companionably. Like me he is seventh-generation Anglo-Saxon American, but unlike me he is Protestant, countrified, sweet-natured. He's the sort of fellow, don't you know, who if you run in a ditch or have a flat tire shows up to help you.

We were partners and owners of the old Paradise Bowling Lanes until the riot five years ago. In fact, the riot started when Leroy wouldn't let a bushy-haired Bantu couple from Tougaloo College have an alley. I wasn't there at the time. When Leroy told me about it later, an artery beat at his temple and the same metallic taste came in my throat. If I had been there. . . . But on the other hand, was I glad that I had not been there?

"Lucky I had my learner ready," Leroy told me.

"Your learner?" Then I saw his forearm flex and his big fist clench. "You mean you—"

"The only way to learn them is upside the head."

"You mean you—?" The taste in my mouth was like brass.

Where did the terror come from? Not from the violence; violence gives release from terror. Not from Leroy's wrongness, for if he were altogether wrong, an evil man, the matter would be simple and no cause for terror. No, it came from Leroy's goodness, that he is a decent, sweet-natured man who would help you if you needed help, go out of his way and bind up a stranger's wounds. No, the terror comes from the goodness and what lies beneath, some fault in the soul's terrain so deep that all is well on top, evil grins like good, but something shears and tears deep down and the very ground stirs beneath one's feet.

"Ellen was looking for you," Leroy is saying, leaning close but not too close, a good drinking friend. He's fixed himself a toddy. "She's got some patients."

"That's impossible. I don't see patients Saturday afternoon."

"You're a doctor, aren't you?"

Leroy, like Ellen, believes that right is right and in doing right. You're a doctor, so you do what a doctor is supposed to do. Doctors cure sick people.

The terror comes from piteousness, from good gone wrong and not knowing it, from Southern sweetness and cruelty, God why do I stay here? In Louisiana people still stop and help strangers. Better to live in New York where life is simple, every man's your enemy, and you walk with your eyes straight ahead.

Leroy believes that doctors do wonders, transplant hearts, that's the way of it, right? Isn't that what doctors are supposed to do? He knows about my lapsometer, believes it will do what I say it will do—fathom the deep abcess in the soul of Western man—yes, that's what doctors do, so what? Then do it. Doctors see patients. Then see patients.

"Looks like it's going to freshen up," says Leroy. We drink toddies, eat eggs, and watch the martins come skimming home, sliding down the glassy sky.

In the dark mirror there is a dim hollow-eyed Spanish Christ. The pox is spreading on his face. Vacuoles are opening in his chest. It is the new Christ, the spotted Christ, the maculate Christ, the sinful Christ. The old Christ died for our sins and it didn't work, we were not reconciled. The new Christ shall reconcile man with his sins. The new Christ lies drunk in a ditch. Victor Charles and

Leroy Ledbetter pass by and see him. "Victor, do you love me?" "Sho, Doc." "Leroy, do you love me?" "Cut it out, Tom, you know better than to ask that." "Then y'all help me." "O.K., Doc." They laugh and pick up the new Christ, making a fireman's carry, joining four hands. They love the new Christ and so they love each other.

"You all right now?" Leroy asks, watching me eat eggs and drink my toddy.

"I'm fine."

"You better get on over there."

"Yes."

I leave cheerfully, knowing full well that Ellen must be gone, that I shall be free to sit in my doorway, listen to *Don Giovanni*, sip Early Times, and watch the martins come home.

The bestselling analysis of the psychological and spiritual malaise of modern man that has sold over 200,000 copies in hardcover.

"wise, rich, witty and indispensable . . ."
—John Leonard, *The New York Times*

Love and Will

by ROLLO MAY

From his many years' practice of psychotherapy and study of modern culture, Dr. Rollo May writes thoughtfully and sympathetically of the problems of modern man. The heart of our dilemma, according to Dr. May, is our failure to understand the real meaning of love and will, their sources, and their interrelation. In bringing fresh insight and interpretation to these concepts, he shows how we can attain a deeper consciousness.

A DELL BOOK $1.75

Also available in a Delta edition $2.95

Two powerful novels of our times

____ **THE LYNCHERS** *John Edgar Wideman*

In this searing novel of rage and revenge, four black men plan to frame a white policeman for murder and then lynch him—a symbolic revolutionary act that will begin to free the oppressed blacks. With incisive characterization and extraordinary skill, Wideman builds the inexorable logic of the plot and its ultimate failure. "Wideman has a weapon more powerful than any knife or gun. His weapon is art. Eloquence is his arsenal."—*The New York Times* 95¢

____ **THE CALL GIRLS** *Arthur Koestler*

The first novel in 22 years by the author of *Darkness at Noon* is a frightening and funny view of mankind's chance for survival. The "call girls" are scientists, philosophers, and sociologists—male and female—gathered to discuss "Approaches to Survival" at an international symposium of intellectuals which is revealed as a microcosm of the ailing world they are trying to heal. $1.25

LAUREL EDITIONS

Biggest dictionary value
ever offered in paperback!

The Dell paperback edition of

THE AMERICAN HERITAGE DICTIONARY
OF THE ENGLISH LANGUAGE

- Largest number of entries—55,000
- 832 pages—nearly 300 illustrations
  The only paperback dictionary with photographs

These special features make this new, modern dictionary clearly superior to any comparable paperback dictionary:

- More entries and more illustrations than any other paperback dictionary
- The first paperback dictionary with photographs
- Words defined in modern-day language that is clear and precise
- Over one hundred notes on usage with more factual information than any comparable paperback dictionary
- Unique appendix of Indo-European roots
- Authoritative definitions of new words from science and technology
- More than one hundred illustrative quotations from Shakespeare to Salinger, Spenser to Sontag
- Hundreds of geographic and biographical entries
- Pictures of all the Presidents of the United States
- Locator maps for all the countries of the world

A DELL BOOK $1.25

If you cannot obtain copies of this title from your local bookseller, just send the price (plus 25c per copy for handling and postage) to Dell Books, Post Office Box 1000, Pinebrook, N. J. 07058.